3 4143 10106 1784

KT-500-396

THE SACRED SWORD

Scott Mariani grew up in Scotland and now lives in the wilds of Wales. *The Sacred Sword* is the seventh book in *The Sunday Times* bestselling series featuring ex-SAS hero and former theology scholar Ben Hope, translated into over twenty languages worldwide. Scott is also the author of the Vampire Federation series, featuring novels *Uprising* and *The Cross*. For further information please visit: www.scottmariani.com

WITHDRAWN FOR SALE

By the same author

SCOTT MARIANI

The Sacred Sword

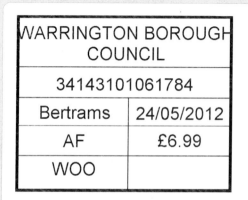

WARRINGTON BOROUGH COUNCIL

34143101061784	
Bertrams	24/05/2012
AF	£6.99
WOO	

AVON

This novel is entirely a work of fiction.
The names, characters and incidents portrayed in it are
the work of the author's imagination. Any resemblance to
actual persons, living or dead, events or localities is
entirely coincidental.

AVON

A division of HarperCollins*Publishers*
77–85 Fulham Palace Road,
London W6 8JB

www.harpercollins.co.uk

A Paperback Original 2012
1

Copyright © Scott Mariani 2012

Scott Mariani asserts the moral right to
be identified as the author of this work

A catalogue record for this book is
available from the British Library

ISBN-13: 978-1-84756-198-5

Set in Minion by Palimpsest Book Production Limited,
Falkirk, Stirlingshire

Printed and bound in Great Britain by
Clays Ltd, St Ives plc

All rights reserved. No part of this publication may be
reproduced, stored in a retrieval system, or transmitted,
in any form or by any means, electronic, mechanical,
photocopying, recording or otherwise, without the prior
permission of the publishers.

MIX
Paper from
responsible sources
FSC™ C007454

FSC™ is a non-profit international organisation established to promote
the responsible management of the world's forests. Products carrying the
FSC label are independently certified to assure consumers that they come
from forests that are managed to meet the social, economic and
ecological needs of present and future generations,
and other controlled sources.

Find out more about HarperCollins and the environment at
www.harpercollins.co.uk/green

Acknowledgements

They say no man is an island . . . and it's true to say that no author is either: so many thanks to my editor Caroline Hogg and all the worthy crew at Avon for their dedication and enthusiasm in helping place this novel into your, the reader's, hands.

To B.D., without whose inspiration
this story would never have been written

Prologue

The Fortress of Masada
Roman Province of Judea, The Holy Land
73 A.D.

'They will soon be upon us,' said the young man called John, turning around from the battlements with fear in his eyes.

His commander, Eleazar ben Yair, made no reply. Leaning out over the craggy, sandy fortress wall he shielded his eyes from the blazing sun and scanned the scene below. Far beneath them, swarming like a gigantic colony of ants around the foot of the mountain as they laboured in the dust and the choking desert heat, the teeming masses of the Roman Tenth Legion were close to finishing the construction of the enormous stone siege ramp.

Eleazar knew in his heart that John was right. The siege would soon be over. Within a matter of hours, there'd be nothing to do except watch helplessly as column after column of soldiers marched up the ramp and stormed the battlements, the sun glinting off their armour and massed spear heads. Nothing to do but wait for the slaughter to begin.

Had they really thought that a rag-tag handful of

defenders, many of them women and young children, could hold out indefinitely against the crushing might of Rome? Had they really believed that the fortress of Masada would prove impregnable?

Eleazar himself had seen what his sworn enemies were capable of. Three years earlier, he'd been one of the few Jewish rebels who'd managed to escape from the carnage that the Roman army had inflicted on his home city of Jerusalem, razing it to the ground and claiming a million innocent lives in retaliation against the Jews who dared to defy Caesar's rule. The army now encamped around the mountaintop fortress of Masada, commanded by Lucius Flavius Silva, the Governor of Judea himself, had been sent to destroy the final pocket of resistance. Silva's forces had built an impassable siege wall that stretched for seven miles around the base of the mountain, ensuring that no rebel could escape and nobody could come to their aid. Along the wall's perimeter stood the Romans' siege towers and giant catapults. They were terrifying, but nothing struck fear into the rebels' hearts like the assault ramp and the promise of what was to come.

'Nobody can resist such an army,' John quavered. 'The Romans will rape our women, slaughter our children in front of us and make slaves of us all.'

Eleazar closed his eyes in sadness. He already knew what had to be done. Over nine hundred people. As their leader, he had no choice but to make the fateful decision himself. He turned away from the battlements to face the young man. 'I would rather die a free man than submit to that,' he said softly.

'Then what shall we do?'

'We shall deliver our souls to God,' Eleazar replied. 'All of us. The Romans will find none alive.'

But before addressing the grim task that lay before him, he had to ensure that one special duty was taken care of.

He reached down to his belt and drew out the glittering sword that he'd carried with him from Jerusalem. Reverently clutching the bronze hilt with both hands, he raised the blade to his mouth and kissed the cool steel.

'The sword must be hidden,' he said. 'Whatever happens, it cannot fall into the hands of the Romans.'

They prayed.

And then the final plans were begun.

Chapter One

Near Millau, Midi-Pyrénées, Southern France
December 2nd
The present day

It was as Father Fabrice Lalique was driving home through the dark, misty night that he saw the car behind him again.

Up until then, the fifty-three-year-old priest had been reflecting on the hours he'd just spent with his parishioners Pierre and Madeleine Robichon in the nearby village of Briande, trying to quell the latest bitter dispute between the couple. It was his duty to minister to the social and family problems of his diocese; and God knew that the turbulent Robichons had more than their fair share of those. He'd eventually left them settled and in peace, hands clasped across the kitchen table, but the reconciliation had had to be painfully, exhaustingly coaxed out of them and he'd been at it far longer than intended.

The Volkswagen Passat's dashboard clock read almost eleven. A heavy blanket of fog hung over the whole Tarn valley, and as Father Lalique headed back along the deserted country roads away from Millau he had to blink and strain to see where he was going. He couldn't wait to get back to the warm, cosy little rural retreat on the edge of the village of Saint-Christophe where he'd lived alone these many years, pour himself a much-needed glass of Armagnac and go to bed. A nip of brandy might help him forget his own problems, and the worry that had been haunting him for the last several days.

Fabrice sighed. It was probably just a figment of his imagination. Maybe the responsibility of his job was getting to him at last. Perhaps Doctor Bachelard's advice about early retirement was worth taking after all – when an overtired brain began cooking up ideas that you were being followed and watched, it could be a sign that it was time to take things a bit easier.

'That's all it is,' he thought to himself, taking a hand off the wheel to rub his chin. 'Foolish to imagine otherw—'

The sudden dazzle of headlights behind him seemed to fill the interior of the Volkswagen. The priest's heart skipped a beat and then began to thump wildly as all the anxiety came instantly flooding back. He narrowed his eyes at the rear-view mirror, trying to make out the shape of the lights.

Was it the Mercedes again? The same Mercedes he'd been sure was tailing him yesterday on his way home from the church in Saint-Affrique? And the day before, and last Tuesday as well . . . ? He stared so long into the mirror that he almost missed the bend ahead and had to swerve to avoid the verge.

'Damn this fog,' he muttered. But he'd been driving these roads for over a third of a century and knew every inch of them. He'd soon see if he was being followed. Any second now . . . wait for it . . . *yes*, there it was. He swung the car hard right as the junction came up and accelerated as hard as he dared down the narrow lane that would take him the long way round towards Saint-Christophe.

6

He glanced back at the rear-view mirror. Nothing. He felt the heart palpitations begin to subside. *There. See? You're an idiot.*

Then the lights reappeared in his mirror and his mouth went dry. He hung another sharp right, then a left, taking him deeper into the web of country lanes. The lights stayed right there in his mirror.

Terrified to go any faster, Fabrice clenched the steering wheel tightly and willed the night to clear. The trees loomed out of the mist. Man and boy he'd roamed in these woods, but now they seemed filled with a sinister life of their own, as if closing in on him, reaching out to grab him in their claws.

He fumbled for his phone and dialled a familiar number. No reply. At the prompt to leave a message, he spoke urgently and breathlessly, his English faltering in his panic: 'Simeon – it's me, Fabrice. The thing I told you about; I am sure it is happening again. Just now, tonight. I think someone is after me. Please call me as soon as you can.'

The lights were still there, closer now, white and dazzling through the fog. Now what? Fabrice thought of calling Bernard, the local chief of police – he had his home number on his phone. But Bernard would be deep into a bottle by this time of night, if not passed out in front of the TV.

Then Fabrice thought of his old friend Jacques Rabier, whose farm was just a kilometre away beyond the woods. Groaning in panic, he hit the gas. A heart-stopping series of blind crests and hairpin bends later, he slewed the car through Jacques' familiar rickety gate and went bumping wildly up the long track towards the farmhouse.

The place was in darkness, shutters closed. Fabrice killed

the engine and stumbled across the yard to thump on the front door. 'Jacques?' he called out.

No reply. A dog barked in the distance. And then Fabrice heard something else. The soft rumble of tyres coming up the track, and the sound of an engine that wasn't the clatter of Jacques Rabier's old Peugeot 504 pickup truck. As the lights appeared through the trees, Fabrice tore himself away from the farmhouse and lumbered awkwardly across the yard towards the big wooden barn where, once upon a time, he and Jacques had played as kids. He pushed open the tall door and ducked inside just in time to avoid being seen in the car headlights that swept across the yard. Their blinding glare shone through the slats, partly illuminating the inside of the barn, the farm machinery covered in tarpaulins, the stack of straw bales against the far wall.

Fabrice didn't have to search hard for a place to hide. As boys, he and Jacques had used the storage space under the barn floor as their secret den, gang headquarters, pirate ship cabin; in their teens they'd once or twice brought Michelle and Valérie from the village there, to smoke illicit cigarettes and innocently fool around.

As Fabrice stumbled towards the trapdoor, his guts tightened momentarily with the fear that Jacques might have boarded it up or left a piece of machinery across the top of it – but no, here it was, just as he remembered it, lightly buried under dust and straw. His trembling fingers found the edge of the trapdoor lid and lifted it with a creak.

It was a tighter squeeze than it had been in his youth. As he was forcing his bulky shoulders through the hole, he felt a sharp painful tug as something cut into the back of his neck. The little silver crucifix he wore around his neck had got snagged on a piece of rough wood and the slim chain had snapped. But there was no time to start hunting around for it. Fabrice hastily lowered the trapdoor above his head and clambered clumsily down the ladder into the hidden pitch-dark space below. He could barely breathe for terror.

This was crazy. He was a respected church official, not some criminal on the run. He had nothing to hide. His conscience was as immaculate as his professional record and he had no reason whatsoever to flee from anyone – yet some overwhelming primal instinct, so strong he could almost taste it between his gritted teeth, told him he was in appalling danger.

The barn door opened. Footsteps sounded overhead. Three men, it sounded like: they spread out and paced the length of the barn, the darting beams of their torches visible through the cracks in the floorboards as they searched the place briskly and methodically.

Who *were* these men? What did they want? Fabrice swallowed back his panic, terrified to breathe, convinced that they must be able to hear the hammer-beat of his heart. He inched his way deeper into the shadows, away from the torchlight.

Something moved against his arm and he almost cried out in shock. A rat: he brushed the filthy thing away and it slithered up a beam and through a gap in the floorboards overhead, claws scratching on the wood as it scuttled away. The torchlight suddenly swung towards the sound. Fabrice's heart stopped as the light lingered over the trapdoor, catching the drifting dust particles in the air.

The footsteps came closer. 'Just a rat,' said a voice, and he realised the men were speaking English. 'He's not here. Let's go.'

Fabrice let out a silent, trembling sigh of relief as the footsteps headed back towards the entrance to the barn. They were leaving. Once their car was gone, he'd wait a few minutes before climbing out of here. Should he go back to the car? Get away on foot and alert the police? Wait for Jacques to come home?

The sudden ringing of his phone shattered his thoughts and tore through the silence. He plunged his hand into his pocket and pulled it out with horror, the damn thing screeching like a siren as his trembling fingers groped for the button to turn it off. The phone's screen showed the name of the caller: Simeon Arundel.

The shrill ringtone shut off, but it was too late. The footsteps were pounding the floorboards overhead as the men came running back inside the barn. Torchlight shining directly down through the cracks; the trapdoor lid lifting; a dazzling beam right in his face.

Father Fabrice Lalique wasn't a fighting man. Never in his adult life had he had to defend himself physically, and his resistance against three strong and determined attackers was as feeble as his cries of 'Who are you? What do you want with me?' as they dragged him through the barn and outside to the waiting Mercedes. His phone was taken from him. Powerful hands bundled him inside the car's open boot and slammed the lid shut.

Seconds later, Fabrice was being jolted around in his confined space as the Mercedes took off down the bumpy farm track. He beat against the bare metal lid, screamed until his throat was raw – then, completely spent, he gave in to the numbness of despair and curled up in the darkness, barely conscious of the movement of the car or the passage of time.

It was only when the boot lid opened and he looked up

to see the faces of the men gazing down impassively at him that he realised the journey was over. The men hauled him out of the boot. He felt the night air clammy on his brow, solid concrete under his feet. The Mercedes was pulled over at the side of a broad, empty motorway. Through the fog that drifted like smoke across the road, Fabrice saw that his own Volkswagen was parked a few yards behind it.

Fabrice searched the faces of his captors for any trace of expression, of humanity, and saw none. 'Who are you?' he croaked, fighting for breath. 'What's happening to me?'

Fabrice quickly saw which of the men was in charge. His face was lean, the eyes quick and cold. His receding hair was cropped to the same length as the dark stubble on his jaw. As two of the others held Fabrice tightly by the arms, the leader slipped his hand inside his plain black jacket and produced a pistol. Without saying a word, he waved the gun towards the side of the road. The thugs holding Fabrice's arms began to frog-march him in that direction. He blinked and shook his head in bewilderment as the edge of the road came nearer step by step; beyond it nothing but swirling mist.

Then he saw the steel barrier and he knew where he was.

'Oh no,' he said. 'No no no . . .'

The Millau Viaduct. The highest bridge in the world, carrying a long stretch of the A75 autoroute three hundred metres above the Tarn Valley.

And he was headed right for the edge.

Fabrice struggled desperately, but there was no resisting the force driving him towards the plunging abyss.

'Why?' he asked, but all that came out was an animal moan of terror.

A sudden gust of wind parted the mist and he caught a momentary glimpse of the drop into the darkness below, the supporting columns of the bridge like colossal towers, higher than cathedral spires. Fabrice's breath was coming in gasps. He couldn't speak. Managing to tear an arm free, he gripped the cold metal of the barrier and clung on. The leader of the men said nothing, reached across and unpeeled Fabrice's clawed fingers with such brutal force that he broke two of them.

Fabrice didn't even feel the pain. He was way past pain.

The men shoved him over the edge. Father Fabrice Lalique went tumbling down and down, cartwheeling in empty space, his scream fading into the night. The mist had swallowed him up long before he hit the distant ground below.

As the men turned away and started walking back to the Mercedes, the one in charge took out his phone. 'It's done,' was all he needed to say. He climbed into the driver's seat. His colleague who'd followed in Lalique's car left it where it was with the door open and the key in the ignition, and got in the back of the Mercedes.

At the same moment, their associates inside the priest's house were already downloading the material, several hundred megabytes' worth of extremely illicit photographic images, onto his personal computer. Their anonymous source would never be found, and neither would any trace of the intruders' presence in his home.

And soon after the Mercedes' taillights had vanished into the mist, leaving the Volkswagen Passat standing alone on the empty viaduct, the last words of Father Fabrice Lalique had been composed and emailed to every contact in his address book:

My Dear Friends

By the time you read this message, I will be dead. I ask you not to mourn for me, as I am unworthy of your grief.

The shame of my sins is a burden I can no longer bear. May God have mercy on me for the terrible things I have done.

Chapter Two

Two weeks later

Storm clouds scudded darkly overhead as another great rolling wave crashed against the bow of the SeaFrance cross-channel ferry *Rodin*, sending a plume of white foam and spray lashing across her deck. Most of the nine hundred or so passengers braving the gale warnings to cross over to England that freezing December afternoon were huddled in the luxury of the superferry's bars and lounge areas.

Just one man stood on the outer deck. He leaned against the railing, the collar of his scuffed leather jacket turned up, the wind in his thick blond hair, his body moving easily to the heave and sway of the ship. His eyes were narrowed to blue slits against the salt spray as he gazed northwards, just able to make out the shape of the Cliffs of Dover through the murk. He took a draw on his cigarette, and the wisp of smoke was snatched away by a violent gust.

His name was Ben Hope. Half English, half Irish, just turned forty years of age but still as fit as he'd ever been. In his time he'd been a soldier, before leaving the British Special Forces to plunge deep into the shady world of the international kidnap and ransom business.

Working freelance as what he called a 'crisis response

14

consultant', using methods and skills that conventional law enforcement operatives either weren't allowed or weren't trained to employ, Ben had delivered more than a few innocent victims safely back into the arms of their loved ones. More than a few kidnappers had been efficiently dispatched in order for that to happen.

These days, home was a tranquil corner of rural Normandy, a place called Le Val. It had been a working farm for most of its history – now it was a specialised tactical training centre where military and police agencies, hostage rescue specialists, kidnap and ransom negotiators and insurance execs from all across the world flocked to learn from Ben and his team. The world was still a troubled enough place to ensure they were seldom short of clients.

It sometimes happened that Ben had to take a business trip to Britain, but this wasn't one of those times. With Le Val closed for Christmas, he had more personal matters to attend to – both of which, in their different ways, were the reason for his deeply pensive state as he stood there on the deck.

Tomorrow evening he was due to attend the inaugural opening of the new concert venue at Langton Hall, the Oxfordshire music academy created by Leigh Llewellyn. She'd been one of the world's most celebrated and talented opera stars. She'd also been Ben's first love – and much later, and for far too short a time, his wife.

Her death was a wound that he knew would never really heal. How it had happened was something he refused to think about, though the nightmare still haunted him some nights. The man who'd taken Leigh from him had been called Jack Glass. He had outlived her by only a few minutes.

As a trustee of the Leigh Llewellyn Foundation, Ben had been invited to cut the inaugural ribbon to open the grand new concert hall, make a speech and present a prize to the most promising young opera singer training at the school. He wasn't exactly an accomplished public speaker. In his time with the SAS he'd conducted a thousand low-key operational briefings with small teams of men; as a tactical training instructor he was used to giving lectures in the familiar environment of Le Val's little classroom – but the thought of standing up on a stage and addressing a large audience made him nervous. He was as prepared for it as he could be. It was the least he could do for Leigh's memory.

The second reason he was travelling to England made him even more nervous. He'd agonised a long time before deciding to make the stop-off in London on his way to Oxfordshire. London was where Brooke lived: Dr Brooke Marcel, formerly visiting lecturer in hostage psychology at Le Val, as well as something a lot more. The way things had gone between them since the terrible argument in September, Ben didn't know how Brooke would react to his surprise visit. All he knew was how badly he'd missed her these last few months.

When the ferry docked at Dover, Ben headed down to the car deck. While the other passengers climbed into their shiny new Vauxhalls and Nissans and Daewoos, he creaked open the door of the battered and ancient ex-military Series II Land Rover that the guys he worked with referred to as 'Le Crock', slung his bag on the worn-out passenger seat and drove out into the late afternoon drizzle.

Le Crock wasn't the kind of vehicle you could spur along in too much of a hurry – and as he headed for London, Ben wondered if that might have been his unconscious motive for taking the old Landy: he wasn't in any particular hurry to reach his destination. Twice he was seriously tempted to give it a miss, bypass London altogether and head northwest straight for Oxfordshire. The second time that thought occurred to him he very nearly gave in to the temptation – but by then he was already entering the outskirts of the city and Brooke's place in Richmond was just a few more miles away.

'Fuck it,' he said to himself, 'I'm here now. Let's see it through.'

Chapter Three

The rain was threatening to turn to sleet by the time Ben pulled up across the street from the large red-brick Victorian house where Brooke lived. He killed the engine, and for a few seconds his thoughts turned to the whisky flask in his bag that he'd topped up with fifteen-year-old Islay malt before setting out from France. Instead he reached for his crumpled pack of Gauloises and his Zippo lighter. Anything to delay the moment where he'd have to walk up to the door of Brooke's flat on the ground floor.

As he sat and smoked and watched the rainwater streaming down the window, he wondered again whether turning up like this unannounced was the right thing to do. And he thought back again to the events of three months ago that had left his personal life in such a mess.

Life had never turned out as quiet as he'd have liked it, but the previous September had been an eventful time even for him. It wasn't every month that you got wrongly accused of murder, dragged into an intrigue involving Russian mobsters and harried across most of Europe by an army of police commanded by a particularly determined, ambitious female SOCA agent named Darcey Kane.

But narrowly avoiding being tortured to death, crushed in a car wreck, getting incarcerated in an Italian prison or pulverised by a Russian attack helicopter hadn't been the worst things that had happened to Ben that month. None of them had remotely compared to the shock of seeing Brooke in the arms of another man.

Injured and on the run, Ben had been heading for Brooke's secluded holiday place in the Portuguese countryside, thinking it would be empty and he could lie low there for a while and recuperate. He'd been wrong. Approaching the cottage in darkness, he'd been surprised to see a light in the downstairs window, and peeked through the shutters. The sight he'd witnessed had made him recoil. Brooke and the unknown man had been sitting by candlelight, drinking wine, both obviously fresh from the shower. There was only one possible conclusion to draw.

Ben had slipped away unseen. From Portugal he'd beaten a hazardous path to Italy, from there to Monaco, then Georgia and back to Rome. Along the way, he and Darcey Kane had joined forces to defeat the gangsters who were trying to kill them, and unmask a conspiracy at the heart of British Intelligence. One of the toughest parts of the job had been escaping the amorous clutches of the – he had to admit it – extremely attractive and alluring raven-haired Darcey. When it was all over and they'd ended up at a loose end together in Rome, she'd made it very clear to him that her idea of a weekend in the eternal city wasn't about visiting the Sistine Chapel and the Colosseum. 'I won't give up, you know' had been Darcey's disappointed parting words to him as he headed back home to France. 'I always get my man in the end.'

The first thing Ben had done on his return to Le Val had been to check the diary for Brooke's next lecture. He'd made sure he wasn't around when she arrived, and as a pretext to stay away for the two days of her visit he'd made up a story about needing to drive to Nantes to check out a new security system for the armoury room, and from there to Paris to see a prospective client. In reality, he was lying low in a hotel just a few miles away in Valognes. He was all too aware of how weak and pathetic he was acting, but he couldn't help it. He'd sooner have faced a charging bull than get into a confrontation with Brooke.

Jeff Dekker, the former SBS commando who was Ben's right-hand man at Le Val, had finally cracked under the strain of having to cover for him all the time, and called him on his mobile. 'Jesus, Ben. What the hell is going on with you two? She's upset and confused. First she comes back from holiday to find out that her boyfriend's been arrested and chased all around Europe by the cops, now you're avoiding her like she's got leprosy. You can't go on like this, mate.'

'I don't want to talk about it.'

Brooke's flight home from nearby Cherbourg back to London had been booked for 7.15 on the evening of her second day. Just after eight, feeling quite miserable and shamefaced, Ben had come skulking back to Le Val and headed for the farmhouse kitchen to pour himself a glass of wine. He'd been so preoccupied that he'd failed to sense anyone else's presence in the room.

'Were you just going to sneak around behind my back?' Her voice sounded taut with emotion.

Ben almost dropped his glass. He whirled around.

Brooke got up from the chair in the corner where she'd been waiting for him. Her face was flushed almost as red as the auburn of her hair, and there was a glint of fury in her green eyes. 'Aren't you even going to tell me who she is, then?'

'Who?' Ben managed, totally confused.

Brooke snorted. 'Who? Do you think I'm stupid? I've *talked* to her, Ben. She called here. You were off sneaking around trying to avoid me, so I happened to pick up the phone.'

'I don't know what you're talking about.'

'Really? "Lovely time together in Rome? Must do it again sometime?" Not ringing any bells?'

Ben stared blankly for a moment, then it hit him. 'You mean Darcey Kane?' The instant it came out, he knew how feeble it sounded.

Brooke's eyes had misted over and a tear rolled down her cheek. 'Of all the guys in the world, Ben Hope, I *never* would have thought you would do this to me. And you didn't even have the guts to tell me to my face.'

'Stop right there. This is insane.'

'What were you doing in Rome?'

'You know what I was doing in Rome. Trying to stay out of jail. You saw the news, didn't you?'

'I know you had a terrible time, and I'm sorry,' Brooke snapped. 'I mean, what were you doing *with her?*'

'Nothing. Absolutely nothing.'

'Then what's she talking about?'

'It's a long story.'

'I'll bet.'

'I can't believe you're accusing me of this,' Ben said, and then added, 'You, of all people.'

Now he was in trouble. He regretted it instantly.

Brooke glared at him. 'What's *that* supposed to mean?'

He was committed. Point of no return. 'You know perfectly well. I saw you and your fancy-man in Portugal.'

'My *what?*' Brooke exploded.

'You heard me.'

'You went to my place?'

21

'I needed somewhere to go. I didn't think you'd be there. I saw you through the window. The two of you looked very cosy together. Don't insult me by denying it.'

'Ben! That was Marshall – my brother-in-law!'

Ben reeled. 'You're having an affair with your brother-in-law? The banker?'

'Bloody hell, what do you take me for? Of course not!'

'Then what were the two of you doing there together?'

'All right. He followed me to Portugal,' Brooke sighed. 'He thinks . . .' – she corrected herself – '*thought* he was in love with me. He'd been stalking me for weeks. I went to the cottage to get away from him. He turned up and I told him once and for all that he'd better clean up his act.'

Ben was speechless for a few moments as he digested her words. He'd replayed the scene so many times inside his head; now he struggled to revisualise it in a whole new way. 'But he was wearing a bathrobe,' he protested.

'There'd been a storm,' she countered angrily. 'He was soaking wet so I got him to take a shower. I'd just had one myself when he turned up.'

'The candles . . . the wine . . .'

'You know it doesn't take much of a storm to take out the power there. And the wine was for our nerves. He was in a real state. So was I. What you saw was me trying to reason with him gently. I'm a psychologist. It's what I do.'

Ben stared at her. He had to admit what she was saying was possible. But suddenly a new thought was dawning on him. 'So this prick Marshall was stalking you all that time and you didn't even think to tell me?'

'Oh, that would have been just great. Then you'd have gone and kicked the shit out of him, and then what? A right mess we'd all have been in. And my sister would've found out. Phoebe's emotionally fragile. It would have destroyed her. I had to deal with it myself.'

'Is that how you see me? Some kind of violent bastard who can only deal with problems by kicking the shit out of people?'

'No, sometimes you shoot them too.'

'How could you not have trusted me?' he yelled.

Brooke gave a scornful laugh. 'Like you trusted me? How could you think I was cheating on you? All the times I told you I loved you – did you think I was *lying?*'

The argument had raged on for a long time, both of them equally carried away by their sense of outrage, neither of them willing to relent. By the time Ben had sensed it was going too far, tried to back down and apologise, a lot of hurtful things had been said and the damage had been done.

In the end, Brooke had stormed off in a white-hot rage. The last he'd seen of her was the taxicab disappearing up the track from the farmhouse.

Two days later a letter had arrived in the post, coldly and formally addressed to Major Benedict Hope, Managing Director, Le Val Tactical Training Centre. Just three terse lines to say she was resigning from her post with immediate effect and wouldn't be back.

When Ben had tried contacting her to persuade her to change her mind, he'd found her phone numbers changed and his emails bouncing back. His letters were returned unopened.

And so now, three months later, here he was outside her ground-floor flat, seriously questioning the wisdom of being here. Unbuckling the straps of his bag, he took out the present he'd bought for her, carefully wrapped in Christmas gift paper with little Rudolf the Red-nosed Reindeers all over it. It had taken him three attempts to get it right. But at least he was pretty sure she'd like the present inside. Brooke was half French on her father's side, and a big movie fan, so he'd bought her a collection of Eric Rohmer films. He couldn't recall having ever seen one himself.

Feeling like a man stepping up to the gallows, he got out of the Land Rover, crossed the street, went in the little gate that led through Brooke's flower garden and rang her doorbell.

No response. He tried again. Still nothing. The package was too big to shove through the letterbox. He didn't think that a mangled DVD box set would please her much. He'd have to post it to her.

With a strange mixture of bitter disappointment and extreme relief, Ben turned away. As he was about to start heading back towards the Land Rover, a tall, good-looking Asian man came strolling down the street and walked through the gate. He was wearing a heavy parka, carrying a shopping bag. Seeing Ben on the steps, he stopped and smiled. 'Hi,' he said warmly. 'You must be Ben, right?'

Ben eyed the stranger uncertainly.

'I've seen your photo,' said the man. 'Brooke had it on her desk.'

Ben noticed his use of the past tense.

'I'm Amal,' the man said, and as if he'd read Ben's thoughts he added quickly, 'Brooke's neighbour. I have the flat above.'

'You're the writer,' Ben said, remembering. Brooke had sometimes mentioned the aspiring playwright upstairs who somehow managed to pay the extortionate rent despite having no apparent form of income.

'*Trying* to be a writer,' Amal grinned.

'Do you know where Brooke is?' Ben asked him.

Amal's grin turned into a grimace. 'She's not here, I'm afraid. Gone to Vienna with her friend Sam.'

24

Sam, Ben thought. *Right.*

He paused a few beats. 'I had a present for her,' he said, looking down at the package in his hand.

'I can take that, if you want. I'll make sure she gets it.'

'I'd appreciate that.'

Amal glanced up at the sky. The sleet was coming down more heavily, haloed in the amber streetlight. 'You want to come inside for a coffee? It's bloody freezing out here.'

Ben shook his head. 'I'd better get going.' As he was walking out of the gate, Amal called back, 'Ben?'

Ben turned.

'Sam is short for Samantha,' Amal said with a significant look. 'Just in case you didn't . . . still, you know what I mean.'

Ben nodded. 'Thanks for letting me know. Happy Christmas, Amal.'

'You too. Take care, all right?'

Chapter Four

Ben was awake long before sunrise the next day, got out of bed and pumped out five quick sets of twenty press-ups on the carpet of his little room in the farmhouse bed and breakfast. He showered and watched the dawn crack over the rural Oxfordshire skyline with a mug of strong black coffee in his hand. He hadn't slept well, his mind constantly turning over, switching back and forth from one thing to another and keeping him in a state of tension that only his long-established self-discipline prevented him from soothing with a gulp from his whisky flask.

Some time later, he shrugged on his leather jacket and went downstairs to be met by the smell of bacon, sausages and fried eggs cooked up by the proprietor, Mrs Bold, who looked as though she'd gobbled down a few too many of her own full English breakfasts. Ben politely declined her insistent offer of a coronary on a plate and stepped out into the crisp, cold morning air. Yesterday's dark clouds and sleet had given way to a clear sky. Pale sunshine filtered through the bare branches of the oaks and beeches and glittered on the frosty lawn.

He swung himself into the cab of the Land Rover. The engine spluttered on starting, and for a moment or two he thought, 'Oh-oh'; then it fired up with an anaemic-sounding rasp and he went crunching over the gravel of the long drive.

The cemetery was just a few fields away from Langton Hall, in the grounds of a sixteenth-century church ringed by a mossy dry-stone wall. Ben knelt by the grave and delicately brushed away a few dead leaves. The inscription on the granite headstone was simple and plain, as she'd have wanted it to be. Just her name; the year of her birth; that of her death.

She was just thirty-two.

Ben was alone in the graveyard. He said a few words, felt his throat tighten up and then sat silently for a long time with his head bowed. He laid a single white rose on the grave. Then he stood up and walked slowly back to the car.

*

In the end, the speech went better than he'd expected. Ben hadn't worn a tuxedo since his trip to Egypt some years earlier, and the collar felt stiff around his neck, but he'd felt composed and his initial nerves at seeing the large crowd filling every seat of Langton Hall's new auditorium had settled the moment he'd stepped up to the podium and launched into his opening line. The things he said about Leigh were from the heart; judging by the length of the applause he received at the end, they must have touched those of many of the audience too.

Relieved that his moment in the limelight was over, Ben had shaken a few hands, knocked back a glass of champagne and then taken his seat for the opening act of the opera. He was glad the trustees had voted for *The Barber of Seville* over something too tragedy-laden and depressing. Too many opera composers seemed to him to revel in making their characters come to sticky ends, but the Rossini was light-weight and rousing, with jolly arias guaranteed to leave the audience humming their tunes afterwards. Ben felt Leigh would have approved of the choice, as well as of the polished performances of the singers.

He'd never been much of an opera fan himself, though, and it wasn't too long before he started getting lost in the twists and turns of the romantic intrigue between Count Almaviva and the beautiful Rosina. The last scene of Act One, with the appearance of the drunken soldier, perplexed him: who was this guy, and what did he want? Was he actually the Count in disguise, and how could this Dr Bartolo fellow be taken in by this obvious ploy to seduce his daughter? Or was she his daughter? Oh, what the hell. Ben was restless and frustrated by the end of the act, and when the applause began he made a bee-line for the bar.

He was getting started on a measure of scotch when he felt a touch on his shoulder and turned round to see a man and a woman standing there, both dressed for the opera, both smiling broadly at him. For a moment he didn't recognise them – then he realised he was looking at two faces he hadn't seen for twenty years.

'Simeon? Michaela?'

'Fine speech, Benedict.' Simeon Arundel was around Ben's height, sporty and trim at just a shade under six feet. His dark hair was as thick and glossy as it had been back in student days, and he'd aged remarkably well except for the tired, rather drawn look to his face.

Michaela wore her fair hair a little shorter now, and might have gained a few pounds, but the brilliance of her smile took Ben straight back to his youth; a faraway time that often seemed to him like another life, when they'd all been students together at Christ Church, Oxford. Like Ben, Simeon had been a Theologian, only a couple of years older and just beginning his postgraduate studies. Michaela Ward had been in the year below Ben, reading Philosophy, Politics and Economics, or PPE as it was termed at Oxford.

'What a wonderful surprise to meet like this,' Simeon said. 'We had no idea you'd be here. Then suddenly there you are on the stage. I said to Michaela, "Lord, that's Benedict Hope!"'

'It's just Ben these days,' Ben said with a smile.

'It's fantastic to see you again, Ben,' said Michaela. 'You haven't changed a bit.'

'I hope I've changed in some ways,' Ben said. He could see something that definitely had: the identical gold wedding rings that Simeon and Michaela were wearing. 'I should have known you two would have ended up getting married,' he said.

'Just a little while after you . . . after you left the college,' Michaela said. She seemed about to say more, then held it back. The circumstances of Ben's leaving college weren't a topic for small talk.

'I suppose I should offer my belated congratulations, then,' Ben said.

They laughed, and then Simeon's expression suddenly grew serious. 'I'm so sorry to hear about your wife. I had no idea.'

Ben nodded. 'Thanks,' he muttered.

'Are you enjoying the opera?' Michaela asked him, changing the subject.

'Honestly? I'd sooner be at a jazz gig.'

'Please don't tell me you live around here,' she said. 'It would be awful to think we'd been near neighbours all this time without ever realising it.'

'No, I live in Normandy these days. I run a business there. What about you two?' he added, always quick to deflect the

29

inevitable questions about the kind of work that went on at Le Val.

'We have the vicarage at Little Denton,' Simeon said. 'It's just a few miles from here.'

'Simeon has the vicarage,' Michaela said. 'I'm merely the vicar's wife.'

'So you went the whole hog,' Ben said to Simeon. 'I always thought you would.'

'I've never been able to think of anything else I could do with myself except serve God in whatever small way I could offer,' Simeon said.

'He's being modest,' Michaela whispered behind her hand. 'He's quite the superstar.'

'But tell us, Ben,' Simeon said, blushing a little, 'Where are you staying?' When Ben told him the name of the bed and breakfast, he shook his head vehemently. 'Not that Mrs Bold? She's a terrible old battleaxe, God forgive me for saying it. And she overcharges.'

'You must come and stay with us, Ben,' Michaela said.

'It's a very kind offer, but—'

'We absolutely insist,' said Simeon. 'It'll be tremendous fun to chew the fat about old times. And you'll meet Jude.'

'Jude?'

'Our son,' Michaela said. 'Only . . .' She rolled her eyes up at Simeon. 'Darling, I think Jude has other plans for the holidays.'

Simeon frowned slightly. 'Never mind. So what do you say, Ben? We'd love to have you. Stay a day or two – stay for the whole of Christmas, why don't you? If you're still as fond of good wine and scotch as you used to be, I have some real treats in store.'

Ben hesitated, considering. It wasn't as if he had anything else to do for the next few days. Nothing was scheduled at

Le Val until January, and apart from the security guys and the guard dogs, the place would be deserted until Jeff and the team returned from their vacation. He'd have liked to spend time with his sister Ruth in Switzerland, but now that she'd become a high-flying company director she was attending conferences and summits all over the world – currently on a mission to greenify the Far East.

'All right,' he said. 'You persuaded me. I'll pick up my gear from Mrs Bold's and come over sometime tomorrow.'

'Nonsense, man,' Simeon said. 'You must come over tonight. We're always up late anyway, so there'll be plenty of time after the show.'

'Speaking of which . . .' Michaela said, glancing at her watch. The bell had sounded while they were talking, announcing the start of Act Two.

It was pushing midnight by the time Ben turned up at the village of Little Denton. Following the directions Simeon had given him, he turned off by the village pub, wound his way along a twisty lane running parallel to the Thames, and finally found the vicarage nestled behind a high stone wall and surrounded by trees. An owl hooted unseen as he stepped down from the Land Rover in the gravel driveway. The moon was out and shining down on the ivied facade of the old house. A dog barked from inside; Simeon's voice called out 'Quiet, Scruffy!'

The front door opened and the Reverend Arundel appeared in the entrance, looking less formal in jeans and a loose cardigan. He gripped Ben's arm warmly. 'Delighted you're here. Really I am.' He peered past Ben's shoulder at the Land Rover and his eyebrows shot up. 'Heavens, that's seen some action, hasn't it? Series IIa? Must be a '73 vintage at least.'

'Sixty-nine,' Ben said. 'Actually, it's playing up a bit. Think a valve needs seeing to.'

'Good grief, it's the same age as I am. Even more ancient than the old Lotus.'

'You still have that!' Ben had fond memories of the many times the two of them had gone speeding round the Oxfordshire country pubs in Simeon's 1972 Lotus Elan, in their quest to sample every real ale known to mankind. Back in those days, even at Oxford, it had seemed extremely exotic for a student to own a car, especially a bright red 2+2 sports that had been the envy of even the wealthier young gentlemen and given Simeon quite a dashing reputation among the girls.

'I'd never sell her,' Simeon said. 'It's till death us do part, I'm afraid.'

Michaela appeared in the open doorway, gripping onto the collar of a shaggy black-and-white mongrel that was scrabbling to get out and greet the visitor. Ben looked at the mutt and could see how he'd got his name.

'Any chance you boys could tear yourselves away from your old bangers?' Michaela said. 'You're letting the cold in.'

'She drives a *Mazda*,' Simeon whispered to Ben with a conspiratorial wink.

'Is that all the luggage you have, Ben?' Michaela said. 'You certainly travel light.'

The inside of the vicarage was comfortable and warm, with the lived-in, ever-so-slightly frayed patina of a period house that had seen very little modernising. A log fire was crackling in the hearth, and a colourfully decorated Christmas tree stood in one corner opposite a baby grand piano covered in framed photos. Ben stopped to look at one that showed a tousle-haired and somewhat wild-looking young man of about twenty, posing on a beach somewhere hot and palmy. He was wearing a wetsuit and grinning from ear to ear as if completely in his element, clutching a surfboard under his arm.

'This must be Jude?' Ben said.

'That's our boy,' Simeon replied. 'The good looks come from his mother's side.'

'He seems to like the water.'

'You can say that again. He's studying marine biology at Portsmouth University. You can't keep him out of the sea. In fact, he's just spent two weeks cage diving with great white sharks in New Zealand. Completely mad, but he won't be stopped once he's set on something.' Simeon sighed. 'At least he still has all his arms and legs, as far as I know. That's the main thing. Let me get you a drink, Ben. Single malt, no ice?'

'You remembered,' Ben said.

As Simeon busied himself fetching glasses and a bottle from a cabinet at the far end of the room, Michaela emerged from the kitchen carrying a tray of mince pies. Setting the tray down on a table, she smiled at Ben and shot a sideways glance at her husband. 'I'm so pleased you're here,' she whispered. 'It'll cheer him up no end. He's been very down and upset the last few days.'

Simeon was too busy pottering about pouring drinks and putting on a CD of Gregorian chants to hear what she was saying. Lowering her voice further, Michaela added, 'We recently had the most awful news about one of his colleagues . . . well, more of a close acquaintance, in the south of France.'

Ben winced sympathetically. 'Illness?'

'*Suicide.*' Michaela only mouthed the unmentionable word, drawing a straight finger like a knife across her throat for emphasis.

Now Ben understood why Simeon looked so uncharacteristically gaunt. Before he could muster a reply, the vicar was returning from the drinks cabinet holding two generously filled whisky glasses. He pressed one into Ben's hand and clinked his own against it.

'Here's to old friends,' said Simeon Arundel. 'Welcome to our home, Ben.'

Chapter Five

The snow was spiralling down out of the night sky and lying thickly on the private road that led to Wesley Holland's sprawling country residence, the Whitworth Mansion, two miles from the shores of Lake Ontario. Anyone who followed the sixty-seven-year-old billionaire philanthropist's exploits in the media might have been surprised to see him driving alone in a seven-year-old Chrysler, but the fact was that despite his almost uncountable wealth, Wesley Holland was a man of relatively modest tastes. Even in his youth, when he'd inherited his gigantic fortune from his father, he'd had relatively little truck with the conventional trappings of wealth; just as he had little to do with the modern world, of which he disapproved more with each passing year.

Yet every man has his weaknesses, and Wesley Holland's weakness for over five decades, despite his pacifist tendencies and abhorrence of cruelty, had been his all-consuming passion for antique instruments of war, weaponry and armour. If it hadn't been for the vast, unique collection his riches had allowed him to accumulate, he'd have had no need whatsoever for such an enormous house. He sometimes thought he'd be perfectly content living in a one-bedroom apartment. It was just him, after all, apart from the live-in staff and Moses, his old tortoiseshell cat.

Wesley parked the car in front of the mansion and stepped out to be greeted by two of his staff. His longtime personal assistant, Coleman Nash, sheltered him from the falling snow with an umbrella while the other, Hubert Clemm, who had served as Wesley's butler for over twenty-five years, began unloading the luggage from the back of the Chrysler. Moses had had the good sense to stay indoors.

'Careful with that one, Hubert,' Wesley said, watching closely as Clemm unloaded the custom-made black fibreglass case from the car. Theoretically, it was indestructible, but he worried nonetheless. Anyone would, considering what was inside. The oblong box, just under four feet long and secured with steel locks, looked for all the world like the kind of case a serious classical guitarist would use to protect a cherished instrument in transit.

Except that Wesley Holland had never picked up a guitar in his life.

'Did you have a good trip, Mr Holland?' Coleman asked, leading his employer towards the house.

'Thank you, Coleman. Actually, it could have gone better.' Wesley was still feeling quite downcast from this latest encounter with yet another bunch of so-called experts unable to get their cynical, closed little minds around the incredible truth that was right there in front of them. This time it had been the history eggheads at the University of Buffalo. Wesley sometimes feared he was beginning to run out of options – though nothing could completely extinguish the excitement of knowing what he'd found. It was the genuine article and he shouldn't give a damn what the academics thought. They'd wake up one day. He really believed that.

'How have things been here?' he asked Coleman. The billionaire trusted his assistant completely. Coleman watched over the mansion and grounds like a pit bull and even kept a monstrous .700 Nitro Express double-barrelled rifle in his room, 'just in case'. Wesley had often chided him about 'that damned elephant gun'.

'Uneventful,' Coleman told him as they walked into the hallway. Suits of medieval armour flanked the stairs. Originals, not reproductions – the same went for the displays of ancient weaponry that glittered against the panelling. 'I've left the mail on your desk as usual,' Coleman went on. 'The curator of the Wallace Collection in London called three times while you were away.'

'Was it about the Cromwell pieces?'

'He didn't say. I told him you'd contact him when you got back.'

'I'll do that. Oh, Hubert, you can take all the bags upstairs except the black case. Leave that one in the salon. I'll put it away myself.'

'Yes, Mr Holland.'

'By the way,' Coleman said, 'Abigail prepared your favourite veal escalopes for dinner tonight.'

'With cream?' Wesley felt his mouth water. He'd been through innumerable cooks before he'd found Abigail. The woman was a gem. Nothing would cheer him up like a fine meal. He needed it. Quite aside from the disappointment in Buffalo, the revelations about Fabrice Lalique were still hanging over him like a pall. Wesley had been as shocked as anyone to learn of the priest's paedophilia.

He left the black case with its precious cargo on the rug in the salon where Hubert had laid it carefully down, and trotted upstairs to his study, nimble and light on his feet for a man of his vintage. The study walls were lined with rich green velvet and displayed just a fractional part of his gleaming collection of ancient weaponry. He pointed a remote control at the sound system and the room filled with his favourite Soler sonata for harpsichord. The desk on which Coleman had neatly piled the mail had once belonged to General Robert E. Lee. There was no trace of a computer in the study, or, for that matter, anywhere in the house. The telephone was the only concession Wesley Holland allowed to be made to modern telecommunications technology under his roof, despite Coleman's constant bitching about the disadvantages of having no internet connection or email access. As far as Wesley was concerned, if you wanted to write to someone, it ought to be the proper way: by hand, on paper, mailed in an envelope. He sealed his own hand-written letters with red wax. Okay, so he was a dinosaur. The dinosaurs had ruled the earth far longer than mankind ever would.

He spent a few minutes browsing through his mail – nothing especially interesting or pressing there – then looked at his watch. London would still be fast asleep at this time. Brian Cameron at the Wallace Collection had almost certainly been calling about the English Civil War-period armour pieces that the museum had been begging for months to have on loan. Holland wasn't sure he could bring himself to part with them. His collections were his passion. He might phone the Englishman back in the morning, or he might let him stew a while before he made his decision.

One thing that wouldn't wait was veal escalopes in cream sauce.

Wesley shut the study and made his way back downstairs. His stomach rumbled in anticipation of his late dinner as he crossed the marble-floored hallway towards the kitchen. He liked to eat his meals at the simple table there, rather than have Hubert go to the trouble of preparing the vaulted dining hall. As Wesley polished off the delicious meal, feeding tiny titbits to Moses under the table, Abigail would be pottering about the kitchen making his dessert. He enjoyed her company: more than he could have said for any of his four wives, each one more grasping and mercenary than her predecessor. Wesley had been fifty-seven when he'd divorced the last of them and sworn that was an end to it.

The kitchen door seemed to be jammed by some obstruction. 'Abi?' No reply. Wesley pushed harder and it opened a few inches. He could smell burning from inside. 'Abi?' he repeated.

At Wesley's last medical check-up, his doctor had told him he had the heart of a forty-five-year-old. But it gave a terrifying leap and almost stopped beating permanently at the sight in the kitchen. He cried out in horror.

Moses the cat was lapping nonchalantly at a thick blood trail that gleamed under the lights. It led from near the cooking range to the door, where Abigail had managed to drag herself before she died. She'd been shot twice in the chest with a large-calibre weapon. She was still clutching the spatula that she'd been using to stir the cream sauce, now simmered to a black mess on the stove, the extractor fans sucking away the smoke.

'Coleman!' Wesley shouted in panic. 'Coleman!' He darted back across the hallway and into the main salon.

Hubert Clemm's body lay twisted in the middle of the vast Persian rug with his arms outflung and his face turned towards the door. There was a large bullet hole in his forehead, a spray of blood up the upholstery of the couch behind him.

'Coleman!' Wesley screamed.

He heard a sound behind him and whipped round. Before

39

he could react, he was being propelled backwards into the salon and the muzzles of two silenced pistols were looming large in his face. He fell heavily into an armchair and stared helplessly up at the pair of gunmen standing over him. One of them was tall, well over six feet. The long brown coat he wore was made of heavy, full-grained tan leather, like horsehide. The other was wearing a quilted jacket. Both had on black ski masks that hid their faces.

Robbers. Wesley's heart pounded horribly. He could see Hubert's corpse out of the corner of his eye, and it was more than he could bear. 'I keep over a million dollars in cash in a safe upstairs,' he gasped. 'And jewels. I'll open it for you myself. Take what you want and go. Please, just go.'

The masked men exchanged glances. The prospect of making off with a million-plus in cash was appealing, but their orders had been strict and precise. 'The sword,' the big one in the leather coat said tersely. 'Let's have it.' He talked with an English accent. A Londoner, maybe.

Wesley balked. His brain churned faster than it had ever churned before. 'I don't know what sword you mean!' he protested. But he did know, very well. If he and his associates were right about it – and almost three years of tireless efforts had persuaded him beyond a doubt that they were – it was a treasure of incalculable value. What he couldn't understand was how these men could possibly be aware of its very existence. Virtually nobody was, outside of the group. Who could have given away the sworn secret? Hillel Zada? Surely not him. He didn't know enough.

The worst thing for Wesley was that the sword was so nearby. He tried desperately hard not to let his eyes flick across to the black fibreglass container, just a few yards away across the room. 'That's it there,' he said, instead pointing through the open door at the giant two-handed Landsknecht weapon that dominated the display in the hallway. From tip to pommel it stood taller than a tall man, and it was almost four centuries old.

Much too big. Much too new. Totally wrong. A wild bluff, based on the fact that these thugs could hardly be expert enough to know one sword from another. 'Take it,' he said. 'It's worth a fortune.' That part was quite true.

The gunmen gave the monster blade a cursory over-the-shoulder glance. The one in the brown leather coat shook his head. 'Don't fuck with us.' The one in the quilted jacket pressed his gun muzzle hard into Wesley's cheekbone. 'You'd better start talking, old man.' Another Brit. Who were these men?

'Drop your weapons and turn around slowly,' said a calm, steady voice from the doorway, and Wesley's heart soared.

Coleman Nash had the massive twin bores of the elephant gun trained steadily on the robbers.

The two men froze. The pressure of the pistol muzzle against Wesley's cheekbone slackened. Coleman had them cold.

Except for one problem. Coleman had never pointed a gun at a living being before, still less pulled the trigger. These men did it for a living. Amateurs hesitated. Professionals never did.

It all happened too fast for Wesley to follow. The report of the first pistol was a muffled '*dooophh*', followed almost instantly by another, simultaneously with the brain-numbing explosion of the elephant gun as it blasted a moon crater out of the far wall.

Coleman's legs wobbled and then buckled and he went down on his knees. Blood on his lips.

Wesley yelled. Another pistol shot. Then another.

Wesley saw the bullets strike and knew there was nothing he could do to help poor Coleman. He jumped up from the armchair, grabbed the black fibreglass case and bolted like a rabbit for the side exit. The big man in the leather coat turned to stop him, but dived for cover behind the couch as the stricken Coleman let loose with the second barrel. The .700 Nitro Express blew a great ragged hole through the backrest of a hundred-thousand-dollar antique couch.

In the next moment, Coleman was cut down by a volley of bullets. He died before the rifle had dropped from his hands.

By then, Wesley had made it out of the exit and was sprinting in a grief-stricken panic down the passage, carrying his precious case. He heard the door burst open behind him and the footsteps pounding as the gunmen gave chase. The terror pressed him on faster. He hammered up a flight of steps, down another passage, and reached the door.

The panic room had been built several years earlier, in case of just such a contingency. Wesley had let Coleman take care of the arrangements, then signed the cheque and promptly forgotten all about it. Which made it all the more miraculous that the password for the voice-recognition vault door should come back to him now.

'Barbarossa!'

The six forged steel deadlocks opened with a clunk. Wesley rushed inside and the armoured door shut behind him, locking itself automatically.

Safe. More importantly, the sword was too. Wesley leaned against the wall and breathed hard, able to hear the muffled voices of his pursuers cursing on the other side. For the first time in his life, he thanked God for modern technology. If he'd had to fumble for a key, they'd have got him. Would they have killed him outright, or tortured him until they'd found the sword in its case?

Wesley staggered numbly over to the control console and peered at the bank of monitors showing digital hi-definition images of every part of the house. He could see the two bodies on the main living room floor: Coleman's near the entrance, Hubert's on the rug. Abigail's in the kitchen. The blood looked garishly bright.

Wesley tasted bile in his mouth at the sight and turned away, following the gunmen's progress from screen to screen as they dashed furiously from one room to the next. They must have known that the clock was ticking now, but clearly believed they still had a chance of locating their quarry somewhere within the Whitworth Mansion.

They wouldn't hang around too long, if they had any sense. Wesley picked up the phone and dialled 911. He spoke urgently but clearly to the police operator, and was assured that officers were on their way. Then, swallowing back his grief, he moved on to the even more important call he had to make.

*

Halfway across the world, Simeon Arundel picked up on the second ring that dragged him up out of a deep sleep.

'Simeon?' said the familiar voice.

'Wesley, it's three o'clock in the morning here,' Simeon muttered, rubbing his face. It had been a late night, and his head was a little fuzzy from all the whisky they'd drunk. Their visitor's capacity for alcohol seemed to be undiminished with the years. Michaela was fast asleep, the curve under the blanket rising and falling gently in the bed next to him.

'Listen to me,' the American's voice hissed in his ear. 'Something's happened.'

Struggling to clear his head and afraid of waking Michaela, Simeon sat up and swung his legs out of the bed. 'Hold on, Wesley.' In the darkness of the bedroom he padded over to the ensuite bathroom, closed himself quietly inside and turned on the light. 'All right. What's happened?'

'They're after the sword.'

'What? Who?'

'The armed men who broke into my house tonight. Or whoever paid them to come here to steal it.'

Simeon sat down heavily on the edge of the bath, his mind swimming with horror. 'Oh, Lord. Are you all right?'

'I'm safe. The cops are on their way as we speak.' Wesley's voice quavered with emotion. 'They shot Coleman, Simeon.' A sorrowful pause. 'He's dead.'

'Dead!?'

'So are Hubert and Abigail.'

Simeon's heart began to beat even faster. He could feel it thudding violently at the base of his throat. He suddenly felt as if he might need to lurch the two steps across to the toilet and throw up.

Then the suspicions Fabrice had expressed to him just before his death had been true. Someone really was taking an unhealthy interest in the research they'd all tried so hard to keep secret. Someone really was after them.

Someone who was prepared to murder to get what they wanted.

Simeon swallowed back the urge to gag. 'Is it safe?'

'It's right here next to me,' Wesley said, patting the case.

'Didn't I tell you, Wesley? Didn't I tell you something

strange was happening – that I was sure I'd been followed – about the man I saw in the church a couple of weeks ago?' Simeon visualised the scene clearly in his mind as he spoke. The stranger had materialised as if out of the blue while he'd been helping put up the Christmas decorations at one of his churches in a rural part of Oxfordshire. When Simeon had gone to welcome him, the man had slipped away as suddenly as he'd appeared. 'And didn't I tell you that Fabrice would never have killed himself like that? Or done those appalling things?'

They'd been through this over and over, ever since receiving the news of their colleague's death and his shocking circular email. 'I don't know whether Fabrice did those things or not,' Wesley said impatiently. 'Or why he'd have confessed to them if he hadn't. And I don't know if he threw himself off that damn bridge or not. Neither do you. All we can be sure of is that you and I are both in danger and it has to do with this sword. That's the reality we're facing right now.'

'Who *are* these people? How do they know about us?'

'Did you talk to anybody? Anybody at all? They even seem to know what it looks like.'

'Nobody,' Simeon blurted. 'I swear.'

'You're absolutely positive about that?'

'Wesley, I would never . . .'

'Good. Keep it that way. Listen, I can't stay on this line. The cops will be here any minute. When I've dealt with them I'm going to call my lawyer and arrange some private security for you and your family over there, okay?'

'There's no need for that. I'll be making my own arrangements.'

'Can you get armed bodyguards in England?'

'I don't think so, not unless you're the Prime Minister or

something. But I have an old friend with a lot of experience of that kind of thing.'

'He'd better know his business,' Wesley said. 'This is serious.'

'What about you?'

'Me? I'm going to Martha's. Got to get the sword some-where safe. It's more important than any of us. You said that yourself, remember?'

Simeon nodded. He was still reeling. 'Yes. Yes, it is.'

'I'll call you from the road. You watch your back, hear me?'

Chapter Six

Sometime before sunrise, Ben flipped himself out of the comfortable bed in the Arundels' guest annexe, stretched and warmed his muscles and dropped down to the floor to knock out fifty press-ups without a break. He followed those up with fifty sit-ups, and was about to go straight into another set of press-ups when he heard the unmistakable throaty engine note of the Lotus from outside. He rubbed condensation off the window pane and peered out to see Simeon's taillights exiting the vicarage gates. It seemed the vicar was off to an early start this morning.

The thoughts that had been swirling around Ben's mind before he'd finally drifted off to sleep the night before were still lingering. The life that Simeon and Michaela had created for themselves here in this serene heart of rural England had made a strong impression on him, and he couldn't stop thinking about how a life like that might have been possible for him, once, too. There'd been a time, many years ago, when he couldn't have imagined his future any other way.

As he'd done so often in the past, Ben tried to imagine himself in the role of a clergyman. The ivy-clad vicarage, the dog collar, the whole works. Ben Hope, pastor and shepherd of the weak, beacon of virtue and temperance.

The fantasy had always been there, but it was a self-image

he'd never found it easy to believe in with all his heart. If he was a Christian himself, he was an extremely lapsed one – and it had been that way for much too long. Compared to the blazing supernova of Simeon's faith, Ben's was a guttering candle. He seldom prayed with anything approaching conviction, even more seldom picked up a Bible. The old leather-bound King James Version he'd hung onto for years had ended up being tossed out of the window of a moving car on a road in rural Montana; it had been a long time before Ben had come round to regretting his rash action.

And yet faith, of some kind, was something that had never quite left Ben – although whenever he tried to ponder on its nature, as he did now, he was left with only the vaguest, cloudiest impression of the strange yearning he felt somewhere deep inside, at the core of his being. Some indefinable sense that one day, maybe, he could find peace within himself. That one day, a guiding hand would appear out of the darkness to steer him on the right path.

Ben closed his eyes, and for a brief moment he had a vision of himself, a different Ben Hope altogether, living this serene, idyllic life, with Brooke by his side.

The vision made him flinch and open his eyes again. He cursed himself for allowing such a hopelessly absurd and romantic notion to enter his head. Brooke as a vicar's wife – it was nuts. She was as different from Michaela as Ben was from Simeon. She'd have laughed in his face at the very idea of it.

Brooke would probably never want to see him again anyway.

'You're a fool, Ben Hope,' he said out loud. He chased away the darkness in his mind with more rapid-fire press-ups, eighty of them without a rest, so that his muscles screamed and his T-shirt clung damply to his skin.

After a cool shower, he dressed and stepped outside into the frosty dawn and crossed the yard to where the Land Rover was parked. 'Let's see if we can't figure you out,' he muttered, raising the battered matt-green bonnet lid and preparing to get his hands dirty.

He'd been there quite some time before he heard the footsteps on the gravel and looked up to see Michaela approaching, a mug of something hot and steaming in her hand.

'Brought you coffee,' she said, setting the mug down on the Landy's wing. 'You're covered in grime.' She reached over to Ben's face, touched his cheek, looked at her blackened fingertips and grimaced. 'Yuck. Any joy?'

'Jeff was right,' Ben said. 'I shouldn't have come in Le Crock.'

Michaela had the decency not to rub salt into Ben's wounds by mentioning old bangers again. 'Can you fix it?' she asked, peering over his shoulder into the rusty engine compartment.

'Not without a spare part or two,' Ben said.

'Worry about it later. Come inside and I'll make you the best scrambled eggs you've ever had in your life.'

'Coffee's fine for me,' he protested.

'I insist. You're officially on holiday, after all. And it's all beautiful fresh local produce. The eggs are just a day old, courtesy of our neighbours, the Dorans. You can't possibly refuse.'

Ben relented. Scrubbed clean and tucking into a plate of what were indeed the most delicious scrambled eggs he'd ever tasted – just a smidgen of organic butter, just a pinch of sea salt, a little fresh-ground pepper – he said, 'Simeon was off early this morning.'

'He had to drive into Oxford for a radio interview,'

Michaela said, sipping her tea. The eggs were all for Ben. Trying to diet, she'd said.

'You weren't kidding about him being a celebrity.'

'Man on a mission. Fighting a one-man war against the decline of the Church.'

'Is it declining that much?' Ben asked.

'You're a little out of the loop, aren't you?'

'Just a little,' Ben admitted. But he'd seen the signs, in France as well as in England. The chains and padlocks on the church gates. The silent bell towers. Buildings falling into decay, with grids over the windows to stop the vandals smashing the stained glass, whose beauty few people seemed to appreciate any more.

'Simeon's determined to bring youth and vigour back to the Christian faith. That's how he puts it. Heaven knows, it needs someone with his dynamism to give it a shot in the arm, or else it's just going to crumble away to nothing before too long, the whole institution and its churches to boot. When Simeon's father passed away three years ago he left him almost four hundred thousand pounds. Simeon donated every penny of it towards church restoration projects. But as he says, churches are worth nothing without the people inside them. So he fights, and he fights, and he never stops. Twelve hours is a relaxing day for him. When he isn't in church, it's one radio interview after another, as well as the odd television appearance. His blog. His podcasts. Anything he can do to raise the profile of Christianity for a modern audience, he throws himself into it with a passion you wouldn't believe.'

'He's a hard-working guy,' Ben said through a mouthful of egg.

'You have no idea, Ben. Gone are the days when a vicar only had his own cosy little corner to tend to. The C of E is so strapped for cash, old vicars being pensioned off all over the place and a shortage of new recruits, that Simeon now has three churches to look after, and he's constantly zapping about from one to the other. Some of his colleagues have even more, but none of them has managed to boost attendance the way he has. He's amazing. How he still finds the time to research his book is beyond me.'

'What's he writing about?' Ben asked as he helped to clear up the breakfast dishes.

'I only know the title,' Michaela said, piling plates in the cupboard. 'And then only because Simeon accidentally left the draft title page lying on his desk one day. He's calling it *The Sacred Sword*.'

'Interesting,' Ben said.

'And more than a little mysterious,' Michaela added wryly. 'He never stopped prattling on about his first two books while he was working on them. I could almost have written them myself, he told me so much. But this one . . . let's just say he's being extremely secretive. He's taken to locking his study door when he's not around. Even bought a safe to keep his notes in. And that time he accidentally left the printout lying around, he burned it afterwards. I don't think he's printed off a page of it since.'

'Maybe he thinks he's onto a hot bestseller,' Ben said.

'It's not just the book. He spends hours on the phone to people all over the world, then refuses to tell me what it was about. Even when he went to America to meet some "expert" he wouldn't tell me why, or who the man was, not even his name. I think it was him who phoned last night, in the wee small hours. I didn't bother asking Simeon about it this morning, although he seemed very preoccupied and I can only assume it was to do with the phone call. Oh, I don't know. Maybe he'll tell me one day, when he's ready to.'

Michaela went quiet and looked pensive for a while as they finished clearing up. She glanced out of the window and forced a smile. 'Shame to be stuck indoors when it's a lovely day outside. Would you like to go for a walk?'

Ben said he would love to. They stepped out into the crisp sunny winter's morning and walked down the long, sloping garden with Scruffy running rings around them, a stick in his mouth. Ben was wearing a pair of Simeon's wellingtons that crunched on the frosty grass.

'Isn't the air wonderful?' Michaela said. 'Maybe we're in for a nice, cold, dry spell, after all the rain we've had. I'm praying for a white Christmas.'

'That would be nice,' Ben said, a little insincerely. Snow mainly just meant a big clearing headache for him.

A gate at the bottom of the garden led to a little patch of woods. Crows cawed in the cold air. The sunlight sparkled on the fast-flowing river through the gaps in the trees.

Ben pointed at the dog, who was running on ahead of them with a world of rabbits to flush out and chase. 'I like him.'

Michaela seemed pleased. 'He's a real character, isn't he? Turned up here out of the blue, about a year ago. No telling where he came from or who his former owners were. We took him in. I think he's about three or four. I love him to bits.'

Michaela threw the stick for the dog a few times, and Ben watched her, noticing the way that her look of contentment had faded to a frown as they walked on.

'You know, I'm really worried about Simeon,' she said suddenly. 'He's got so much on his mind, and sometimes I'm afraid he's going to burn himself out or make himself ill. He works far too hard, and what with all the quarrelling between him and Jude, not to mention this awful business with Fabrice Lalique . . .'

'The man who committed suicide?'

She nodded. 'He was a Catholic priest. Simeon met him a couple of years ago in France while visiting a church restoration project, and they became friends.' She shook her head. 'I still can't believe it. What a shock. And the worst of it are the revelations that came afterwards.'

'Revelations?'

'A day or two after his death, his home was raided by police, acting on a tip-off. They seized his computer and found . . . how can I put it?' Michaela paused uncomfortably. 'Certain material. Very unpleasant and explicit material. Pictures of children. You can guess what kind of pictures I'm talking about.'

'I can guess,' Ben said, with a stab of revulsion.

'It was the reason he killed himself,' Michaela said. 'Out of guilt, or shame, or perhaps just because he knew what would happen if he was caught. Before he did it, he sent an email to everyone he knew, confessing his sins and asking for forgiveness. Then he threw himself off the highest bridge in France.'

'That'll certainly do it,' Ben said, without the least trace of pity in his voice.

Michaela turned towards him, shading her eyes from the low sun with her hand. 'Do you think it's possible to forgive someone for something so horrible, even if they've repented? I struggle with that, I have to admit.'

Ben paused. He thought of paedophiles he'd blown away at point-blank range with a shotgun. Come to think of it, he'd never stopped to ask them if they'd repented. With a sawn-off pointed at them, they probably would have dropped to their knees and started chanting the Lord's Prayer if they'd thought it could help. It probably wouldn't have.

'Did you know this Lalique well?' he asked her.

'Never met him. Simeon was in touch with him a lot over the last year or so, something to do with the book, I think. I don't really know.' She tried to smile. 'Let's not talk about this any more. It's so good to see you again, Ben. Isn't it strange, the two of us walking along together, after all these years?'

'It's certainly been a long time,' he said.

'We were so young then, weren't we?'

'Nineteen.'

She chuckled. 'You were wild then.'

Memories of college days flashed through Ben's mind. Most of them were unwanted: hazy and unpleasant recollections of drinking and recklessness. Picking, then winning fights with town toughs in pubs. Throwing a TV from a window. Skipping classes, generally acting crazy. A lot of things he'd done that he'd rather forget.

'That was a difficult time,' he said.

'You never talked about your troubles.'

He still didn't talk about them now. 'I'm sorry if I hurt you,' he said.

'I really loved you,' she answered after a beat, glancing at him. 'But I knew you didn't feel the same way about me. How long did we last together? Seven weeks? Six? If that?'

'You ended up with a much better man.'

Michaela made no reply. They walked on a while through the trees, dead leaves crunching underfoot, the dog racing on ahead of them. 'I remember the first time I took you to meet my parents,' Michaela said after a few moments' silence.

'The one and only time,' Ben said, casting his mind far back to a hot summer's afternoon in Surrey. 'The posh garden party.'

Michaela chuckled. 'They still talk about it. You completely scandalised everyone. You must have drunk a gallon of whisky that day. And that was even before you'd started arguing politics with my father.'

Ben rolled his eyes, wishing she'd stop it. 'Please.'

'As for my cousin Eddie, I think you traumatised him for life.'

Ben hadn't forgotten that one either. The instant dislike he'd taken to Eddie had been shared by Michaela's Pekingese, Hamlet. Nobody but Ben had seen Eddie slip Hamlet a sly kick to the head when he thought no-one was watching. Moments later, Eddie had been taking an unplanned nose-dive, fully clothed, into the deep end of the swimming pool in front of eighty guests. The real fun began when it tran-spired that Eddie couldn't swim. Four more guests had suffered a dunking before Eddie could be rescued. At that point, the party had been more or less ruined.

'You dumped me soon afterwards,' Ben said.

'I was awful to you.'

'No, you were right. I was bad medicine. I'm sure your family approved of Simeon slightly more than they did me.'

'Mum and Dad positively idolise him. But we don't see so much of them now that they've moved to Antigua. Couldn't stand the British weather any more.' She started laughing.

'What's funny?'

'I just remembered another time. That night in Oxford when you took on that gang of bikers up Cowley Road? Lord, there must have been eight of them. I can still recall how they scattered in all directions.'

Ben remembered. It had been more like ten. He and Michaela had been walking past when one of them had made a lewd comment about her. 'Are you done tormenting me?' he said.

They walked up a grassy slope to higher ground, where the winding country road to Little Denton was visible through the line of naked beech trees that skirted the meadow.

'So after Oxford you just upped and joined the army?' Michaela asked.

'Pretty much,' Ben said. 'Thirteen years' service.'

'Has there been anyone . . . since Leigh?'

'Yes,' he ventured. 'There is someone. Or was. I don't have much talent in that department. Perhaps it's fate or something.'

'Don't be silly,' she said. Touched his arm. 'You're a better man than you realise, Ben Hope. You always were.'

'Sometimes I've thought that I went off in completely the wrong direction,' Ben confessed. 'When I look at Simeon, and the life the two of you have here . . .'

'You'd have been great in the church. Once you'd settled down a bit.'

'There's the rub,' he laughed.

'It's never too late.'

'I already tried once, a while back. To go back and finish my studies.'

'Really?'

'It didn't work out,' he said. He didn't want to say any more, and decided to change the subject radically. 'It's a shame I won't get to meet your son Jude.'

Michaela shrugged. 'Some other time, I'm sure you will.'

'Was it a very serious quarrel? Between him and Simeon?'

'I suppose it's just typical family stuff,' she said. 'Jude would rebel against his own shadow. Always full of his own ideas about what he wants to do with his life. It'll all come right in the end, I'm sure. Oh, I think I hear the car.'

Ben had heard it too, and spotted the sleek crimson shape of the Lotus darting along beyond the trees in the distance, returning home.

'Let's walk up to the house and meet him,' Michaela said.

Back at the vicarage, Ben thought that Simeon looked even more grim and strained than the night before, although he was obviously struggling hard not to show it as he sipped his coffee and gave Ben the rundown on that morning's radio interview on the topic 'Is there still room for Jesus in the Facebook Age?'

'My secret admirer popped up again during the phone-in at the end,' Simeon said to Michaela. 'As charming as ever. Called me a filthy cockroach and said I'd rot with all the others.'

'I can't understand why they allow that kind of thing on air,' Michaela sniffed. '"Filthy cockroach". That's disgusting.'

'Do you get a lot of that?' Ben asked.

'Oh, I have many enemies,' Simeon told him. He was smiling, but Ben thought he could see something behind the smile, an edge of seriousness.

Michaela was obviously keen to change the subject. 'Ben's car still isn't working properly,' she said, topping up their coffees. 'Darling, do you think Bertie would have a look at it?' She turned to Ben and explained, 'He's the local mechanic, in Greater Denton, just a few minutes' drive away.'

'Marvellous idea,' Simeon said. 'Bertie will have the old girl right as rain in no time. Sorted out the carbs on the Lotus. And he's cheap as chips.'

'Why don't you call him now?' Michaela said. 'If he's fixed it by this evening, we can pick it up on the way.'

'On the way where?' Simeon asked.

'I thought we could have dinner at the Old Windmill tonight, as we have a special guest.'

'There's no need . . .' Ben began.

'Sounds like a fine plan to me,' Simeon said. 'I'll phone Bertie now.'

Chapter Seven

Simeon led the way in the Lotus and Ben followed in the ailing, badly misfiring Land Rover. Simeon had to keep slowing down to let him catch up as they wound their way along the twisty country lanes towards Greater Denton.

Bertie the mechanic, whose garage was a converted stable block on the edge of the village, was one of those work-hardened little guys who looked as if they'd been twisted and hammered together out of wire and leather. Ben got the impression that the grizzled old mechanic would have done anything for Simeon. No sooner had Ben described Le Crock's symptoms, than Bertie grabbed a toolbox and plunged his head and shoulders under the scarred green bonnet lid, apparently set on not re-emerging until he'd cured the problem, if it took him all day and night.

Simeon seemed edgy as he drove fast back towards Little Denton. Rocketing up the long, straight hill a mile before the village, the car almost took off over the crest and went plummeting down the straight and hard into the set of S-bends at the bottom before roaring over the little stone humpbacked bridge, barely wide enough for one and a half cars, that arched across the swollen, fast-moving river.

Ben could tell his old friend was building up to saying something but having difficulty framing his words. Simeon wet his lips and spoke hesitantly over the engine noise. 'Ben, there's something I wanted to . . . Oh, never mind.'

'What?'

Simeon let out a long breath. 'The fact is, it wasn't completely coincidental. Our turning up at the concert, I mean. In fact, opera's not my favourite thing at all.' He paused. 'The point is, Ben, I knew you'd be there. I saw your name in the paper and I deliberately came to see you, for a reason that I haven't discussed with Michaela. She doesn't know anything about this, and I'd like to keep it that way.'

'I understand,' Ben said, and waited for more.

'I've often wondered what you were up to all this time,' Simeon said. 'It seemed like you'd vanished without a trace. Now and again Michaela and I tried to look you up, to no avail. Then a few months ago, I found you on the internet and saw what it is you do now. You help people.'

'What I do is very specific,' Ben said. 'Le Val is a tactical training facility.'

'For bodyguards? That sort of thing?'

'That sort of thing,' Ben said. 'Not exactly.'

'So, when people have a problem – when they're under threat, or when they feel they might be in danger, there are ways they can protect themselves. Aren't there? And that's the kind of line you're in? Providing advice, or services of a sort . . . you can tell I don't know a lot about this stuff.'

'Get to the point, Simeon. What are you trying to say?'

They were coming into Little Denton. Simeon sighed. 'I need help, Ben. At least, I think I do. I'm not sure what's happening, but I'm frightened. Not so much for myself, but for Michaela and Jude. If anything happened to them—'

'Why don't you tell me what's wrong?' Ben said.

'I hardly know where to begin,' Simeon replied. 'I've been working on something, an important project. Well, actually, it's more than just important. It's huge. It's terrifyingly huge.' Simeon shook his head, as if bewildered by just how huge it was.

'To do with your book?' Ben asked.

Simeon glanced at him in surprise.

'Michaela told me you were working on a new one,' Ben said. 'And that you've been keeping a lot to yourself. She's worried about you.'

Simeon hesitated, then nodded. 'Yes, it's very much the subject of the book. I've been working on this day and night for . . . or should I say, *we've* been working on it. It's not just me that's involved.'

The vicarage gates were coming up on the right. Simeon turned in and rasped the Lotus over the gravel. He pulled up, killed the engine and turned to Ben. 'Something awful happened recently,' he said anxiously. 'Something absolutely dreadful, and completely baffling. I mean, when you know someone so well, or at least think you know them, and then you hear they've done something that's just so totally, so *horrifyingly* out of character that you just can't . . .'

Ben understood that Simeon was talking about the priest who'd killed himself. 'Go on.'

Simeon's jaw tightened. 'Two weeks ago . . .' he started. But Michaela's voice from the house interrupted him, and they both turned to see her trotting down the front steps and across the gravel with the landline phone in her hand. 'Yes, in fact he's just got back this moment. I'll pass him to you, archdeacon.'

'Hell and buggery,' Simeon groaned under his breath, and climbed out of the car to take the phone. To Ben he said, 'We'll talk later.' Then, pressing the phone to his ear, 'Dr Grant! What a pleasure to hear from you.'

Michaela took Ben's arm. 'Come on. He'll be on the phone

for ever with that one. Come inside. I have something for you.'

'What is it?'

'It's a surprise.'

Inside the warmth of the living room, she signalled to him to wait, then trotted upstairs and returned a moment later holding a small gift-wrapped package tied up with a ribbon. 'Merry Christmas, Ben.'

'You shouldn't have,' he said, taking the package, embarrassed that he hadn't anything to offer the Arundels in return. 'Am I allowed to open it?'

'No!' Michaela said quickly, reaching out abruptly to stop him tearing open the wrapping – then relaxed and smiled. 'Not now. You have to promise me that you won't peek until you're back in France. Then you can open it and think of us.'

'I promise,' Ben said, wondering what it was. Through the Christmas paper it felt like a small hardback book, not much bigger than a diary.

'Solemnly? You won't be tempted?'

'Get me a Bible,' Ben said. 'I'll swear on it. Or maybe it is a Bible?'

'No,' Michaela said softly. 'It isn't a Bible.' Her expression was a strange blend of relief and apprehension. She was quiet for a few moments, then said something about needing to check something upstairs, and disappeared.

Simeon was still on the phone to the archdeacon. Left to his own devices Ben went to the annexe to put Michaela's present away safely in his bag, then wandered outside to the woodshed to gather some logs for the living room fire, which he'd noticed was getting low. The firewood was neatly stacked along the shed wall near the door, a heavy log-splitting axe and a small hatchet resting against the chopping block. He hefted a piece of well-seasoned oak onto the block, grabbed the axe, and with a downward swing cracked the log neatly in two. He set the split pieces aside and grabbed another log. His breath billowed in clouds as he worked.

He felt something nudge his leg, and turned to see what it was. 'Hey there, Scruffy,' he said as the dog nuzzled against him, and stroked the coarse fur of his head. The dog wasn't the prettiest of creatures – the bull neck and alligator snout of a Staffordshire mixed up with the wiry, untameable coat of a Border Terrier – but there was a look of calm intelligence in those wide-set eyes. Criminal or saint: Ben wasn't too sure which he was.

'You like being a vicar's dog?' Ben said.

Scruffy cocked his head and looked at him curiously, then went off to settle on the floor a few yards away and gnaw contentedly at a piece of wood. If only life could be that simple for humans, Ben thought.

Going on chopping, Ben heard Simeon's voice from inside the vicarage, calling up the stairs to Michaela that he had to rush out to attend to a church matter. Moments later, the Lotus was roaring off into the distance.

Ben added two more split logs to his growing pile and wondered how it could be that Simeon Arundel – this vicar whom everyone seemed to admire and respect, living this cosy life out here in the tranquillity of the English country-side, writing books on religion and running his churches – was talking about being in danger. It seemed so incongruous and bizarre. The way Ben saw it, Simeon was the last person on earth anyone would want to harm.

He suddenly had the feeling he was being watched. He glanced up from the chopping block and through the open door of the barn, just in time to spot Michaela backing away from an upstairs window of the vicarage. In the split second their eyes met, Ben could see the odd look on her face.

Why had she been watching him? He kept seeing her strange expression in his mind as he tossed the split logs into a sack and headed outside. With the dog trotting behind him he lugged the logs inside the house to stack beside the living room fireplace.

As the fire revived, Ben sat with the dog and watched the flames, wondering what secrets were being harboured behind the idyllic face of Arundel family life. Something was going on, and he had the feeling it somehow involved him.

'It's all a bit of a puzzle, isn't it, Scruff?' he said softly, turning to the dog.

Scruffy licked Ben's hand. Whatever he knew about it, he was keeping to himself.

Chapter Eight

The road was long and dark as Wesley Holland threaded his way slowly eastwards across New York State to the beat of his windscreen wipers and the steady flurry of snowflakes in his headlights. The snow had thickened so badly shortly after Oneida in Madison County that he'd thought his route might become impassable – but the snow patrols were fighting to keep the roads open in what was turning out to be one of the toughest winters in years.

He kept driving doggedly on, stopping for gas about an hour beyond Schenectady, at the snowy feet of the Appalachian Mountains. He was still suffering from shock, grief-stricken and freezing and exhausted. It was over five hundred miles to his destination; in this weather it seemed like five thousand. No way for a billionaire to be travelling.

Yet there was no way Wesley Holland was stepping on a plane, either. Even if the conditions had been more clement, the fact that all three of his private jets and all eight of his helicopters were registered to him made it far too easy for whoever was after the sword to track his movements. And after a near crash coming into Taipei in 1996, he'd vowed never to set foot on a commercial airliner again. No, by road was the only way. Nobody could track him or find him out here. Nobody in the world except for Simeon Arundel knew about Martha's. The sword would be safe there.

In the meantime, there it was, locked in its case behind him on the back seat of the car. One of the most important artefacts in history. Perhaps *the* most important.

Wesley Holland wasn't a religious animal. Try as he might, he found it impossible to share the fervent spiritual passion that drove men like Simeon Arundel. There were times when it irked him, but more often he found himself actually envying it, feeling excluded and annoyed at himself for being incapable of fully experiencing something that seemed to be able to offer such fulfilment to people who opened themselves to it. He still remembered the light in Simeon's eyes, and those of Fabrice Lalique, that day in France when he'd first told them about his amazing historical find. But even an agnostic like Wesley couldn't escape the skin-tingling excitement of such a monumental discovery.

The three had met during the repair of a badly deteriorating medieval church near Millau, which Wesley had been funding entirely out of his own pocket. The contractors he'd hired for the job were an up-and-coming Parisian firm reputed to be the best in the business; Wesley had been there to check out their work. So had a young English minister named Simeon Arundel, recently come into some funds of his own and intent on learning all he could about church restoration. Also keeping a watchful eye on the long-needed project had been the local priest in Millau, Fabrice Lalique.

An American, an Englishman and a Frenchman. It could have been the opening of a joke, but instead it became the start of a friendship. One night over dinner and a very expensive bottle of wine provided by Wesley, he'd decided he trusted the pair of clergymen enough to tell them the secret he'd been yearning to share with someone who could truly understand it, appreciate it, and most of all, keep quiet about it. Their initial reaction on hearing of his discovery had been one of stunned disbelief, just as his had been at first. But when he'd shown them the evidence, their scepticism had turned to fascination, then to wonderment and awe.

Simeon had been speechless at the way his life had just changed.

'But we ought to tell people about this,' Fabrice had argued.

'Be patient,' Wesley had urged him. 'The time will come.'

Wesley still believed it would, even after nearly three years of maddening dealings with experts who wouldn't pull their heads out of their asses and realise what they were being shown. For the first time, though, his excitement was now tempered with doubts. People were dying. Was it all worth it?

Yes, it was, he decided as he drove. If Fabrice had died protecting the secret, and if Coleman and the others had died because of it, then Wesley was damn well going to make sure these thugs, whoever they were, didn't get their hands on it. Once he arrived at his destination, he was going to hire an army of the toughest bodyguards money could buy.

Let the sons of bitches come find him then. Let them try.

The red of dawn was burning through the snowclouds by the time Wesley realised he couldn't go on any more without a rest. If he didn't stop awhile, he was going to drift off at the wheel and crash the car. His tense shoulders sagged with relief when he saw the motel sign a few miles on that said 'VACANCY'S'. 'Thank God,' he mumbled.

Wesley pulled into the car park between the shabby, snow-covered wooden buildings. The only other car in sight was an ancient Ford Explorer with jacked-up suspension. He climbed stiffly out of the Chrysler, grabbed the case from the back seat and dragged his heels through the snow over to the dirty glass doors that led into the gloomy reception area.

At the far end of the lobby was a corner desk, and behind that was an unshaven guy in a John Deere baseball cap who stared at Wesley's American Express Platinum card as if it was the only one he'd ever see, then shrugged and shoved it in the card machine. 'Room twelve,' he said, sliding a key across the counter.

Wesley staggered to Room 12 with his only item of luggage. As he might have expected, the place was a shithole, but at that moment he'd gladly have lain down to rest inside a sewer pipe. He locked his door, laid the case down, made straight for the bed and collapsed on it without even taking off his coat or shoes. Within seconds of his face touching the stained pillow, his utter exhaustion carried him off to sleep.

When Wesley awoke he was shivering with cold and feeling clammy from sleeping in his clothes. His back ached from the worn-out mattress and the car key in his pocket felt like it had dug a hole in his leg. Panic gripped him. The case! He twisted round to see.

Still there. He could breathe again.

His fifty thousand-dollar gold watch told him he'd been asleep for a little over four hours. That was all the sleep he needed nowadays, at his age. He'd drink a cup or two of hot coffee to revive and warm him, then hit the road again. With any luck he'd make it all the way to Martha's with just one more stop for gas.

The price of the motel room didn't appear to include any coffee-making facilities. Wesley trudged outside into the cold, taking the case with him and locking his door behind him. More snow had fallen overnight, a two-inch blanket of it lying over the roof and bonnet of his car. The Ford Explorer was gone; in its place a little Honda. There were no other cars in the place. Popular joint, he thought to himself as he headed along the covered walkway towards the reception lobby to find out if they had such things as coffee in these parts.

The unshaven guy had clocked off his shift and been replaced by a crab-faced young woman who was sitting hunched over a magazine at the desk, gazing at fashion pictures of girls eighty pounds lighter than her and listening to scratchy rock music on a tiny electronic device manufactured by one of Wesley's companies. At her fat elbow was a Honda ignition key attached to a pink plastic fob that said 'Kat'. When Wesley enquired about getting a coffee, she gaped at him for a moment as if he'd asked for champagne and oysters, then motioned laconically through a doorway on the far side of the reception lobby and informed him that there was a coffee machine down the hall.

Wesley had trouble first finding the coffee machine, then more trouble getting it to work. After several attempts and a few thumps he persuaded it to accept the loose change he fed into it, and finally the machine sputtered something dark and steaming into the Styrofoam cup he offered to it. He managed to overfill his cup, and had to carry it carefully to avoid spilling any over his thousand-dollar handmade shoes.

On his way back through the reception lobby, coffee scalding one hand, the case weighing down the other, he threw a glance at Kat behind the desk a few yards away. She hadn't moved a millimetre and looked as if she'd been ladled into her chair, a big round flaccid lump of flesh. 'Hey, thanks,' he called across to her, with a touch of sarcasm. She didn't look up from her magazine.

'Great service in this place,' he said. Still no response. He shook his head and awkwardly tugged open the glass door with the hand holding the coffee, wincing as more of it sploshed out onto his fingers. Billionaires shouldn't have such problems.

As he approached his room, Wesley suddenly stopped. The door was lying six inches open.

Hold on. Didn't I just lock that?

Maybe someone had come in to clean the room, he thought. It sure needed it. Wesley peered in through the gap in the door and saw a movement inside. It was a man, and he didn't look like a cleaner. He was a big man wearing a coat of heavy tan leather.

Wesley froze.

The man in the leather coat had his back to the door. Wesley heard him say something indistinct to another man in the room with him. Then he turned a few inches to his left, and Wesley could see the unemotional expression on his face, and the boxy black automatic pistol in his hand with a long cylindrical silencer.

Wesley drew back from the door, stifling a gasp. With what felt like a heart attack coming on he retreated back along the covered walkway towards the reception lobby. The men only had to glance through the open door of his room and they'd spot him.

By some miracle, they didn't. Wesley vowed to start believing in God. He burst through the glass doors into the reception lobby.

Kat was still sitting at the desk, slumped over her magazine. 'Call the police,' he rasped at her. 'There are—' The words died in his mouth. He recoiled in horror.

Kat remained immobile. The only movement from her was the steady drip-drip from the bright pool of blood that had now spread across the desk, soaking the magazine in front of her and splashing to the floor.

The coffee cup slipped out of Wesley's hand and exploded across his shoes. 'Oh, my God.' He had to get out of here. Grasping the handle of the case in a death grip, he dug his car key out of his pocket, scurried back to the doors and peered through the grimy glass into the yard. The snow-covered Chrysler sat halfway between the reception and the door of his room. He could see no other vehicle apart from Kat's Honda. The killers must have left theirs somewhere around the back.

Would he make it to his car and get it started up before the men spotted him? They'd hear the sound of the engine, but maybe he'd manage to drive away before they could stop him.

They had guns. Their bullets could punch through steel and glass as he drove off.

But he had to get away. He pressed his free hand to the door. *Here goes.*

He was just about to push it open when the man in the tan leather coat suddenly emerged from Room 12 and started striding quickly and purposefully across the snowy car park towards the reception lobby. He had the gun at his side.

Wesley backed away from the doors. He didn't think the man could see him through the dirty glass, but he'd be here any moment.

Wesley ran back towards the reception desk, just managing

to avoid the pool of blood. The other side of the desk was a door marked PRIVATE. Kat's arm was draped across the folding hatch. Wanting to throw up at the touch of her dead flesh, he nudged her arm aside and then pressed through the hatch and burst through the door, closing it behind him with jittery haste before the man in the brown coat stepped into the lobby.

He found himself in a poky office. Its cobwebbed sash window overlooked a backyard littered with snow-covered garbage bags and pieces of broken furniture. Beyond a ramshackle fence he could see the highway snaking away into the distance. He threw open the window, clambered up on a chair and shoved the case through the gap before scrambling through after it. He landed painfully on the snowy concrete the other side, snatched the case up and kept moving as fast as he could. His heart was in his mouth as he staggered through the backyard to the fence, fully expecting the muffled clap of a silenced pistol behind him and a bullet burning a hole in his flesh.

But no bullet came. Wesley managed to drag himself and the case over the fence and belted across the snow towards the highway. Twice he slipped and fell as he scrambled over the piles of dirty slush at the side of the road, glancing in terror over his shoulder. His breath was coming in wheezing gasps now as he stumbled on. For the first time since the invention of the mobile telephone, he wished he had one so that he could call for help.

He couldn't run much further. Any second now, the killers would cotton on to his escape. They'd get in their vehicle and come after him. Bundle him in at gunpoint, and it would all be over.

The deep bellow of air horns blasted his terror away. He whirled around at the edge of the road and saw the massive grille of an eighteen-wheeler truck looming over him as it slowed down with a sharp hiss from its airbrakes. Wesley threw down the case, waved his arms frantically and stuck out his thumb. 'Help me,' he wheezed. 'Help.'

The driver beamed a gap-toothed grin down at him from the cab.

'You lookin' for a ride, old timer? Then climb aboard.'

Chapter Nine

By the time Simeon was back from his church business, darkness had fallen and it was nearly time to set off for the evening meal at the Old Windmill. The three of them were in the vicarage's hallway, on the verge of heading outside to the Lotus, when the phone rang.

'It had better not be the bloody archdeacon again,' Simeon said, picking up. 'Oh, it's you, Bertie . . . really? Gosh, that didn't take you long . . . Yes, he'll be delighted. We can come and pick it up right away.'

They definitely didn't make them like Bertie any more. Ben couldn't believe the difference in the Land Rover as he followed the Lotus's taillights along the three miles of winding roads from the garage to the restaurant. The old mechanic had retuned Le Crock's radio to a local station. Ben half-listened as he drove; then the entrance of the Old Windmill appeared through the trees and Ben parked beside the Lotus in the floodlit car park.

The place was aptly named. The ancient stone windmill itself stood silhouetted against the starry sky, while the restaurant was a modern building with large windows over-looking the surrounding woodland. Ben's hosts led him inside, into the bar area where a smiling waitress greeted them with 'Hello, Vicar; hello, Mrs Arundel,' and led them through a doorless archway into the busy restaurant area. The place was decked out in colourful Christmas lights and glittery decorations, with an enormous tree in one corner. The dozen or so tables were cosily laid with rustic chequered tablecloths. Bing Crosby's version of *Hark, the Herald Angels Sing* was playing over the speakers on the walls.

'Good thing I booked in advance,' Michaela said over the buzz of chatter. 'Think we must have got the last table.'

'Damn,' Simeon muttered suddenly, patting his pockets. 'I think I left my mobile in my other trousers.'

'Well, I don't think you'll be needing it tonight, darling,' Michaela said, with a discreet roll of the eyes to Ben, as if to say, 'See what I mean?'

As the three of them crossed the restaurant, there was a chorus of 'Hello, Vicar' from a group of middle-aged women clustered around a heavily drinks-laden table in the corner near the archway. Simeon waved back at them. 'The ladies' badminton club,' he whispered to Ben.

'My husband is a big hit with them,' Michaela said. 'Especially with Petra Norrington.'

'Oh, come on.'

'It's true. She adores and venerates you. Thinks you're gorgeous. Look at her eyeing you from behind her wineglass. Like a peroxide spider.'

'Nonsense,' Simeon said.

They took their seats at the table. Ben had his back to the archway and the bar area beyond it. To his right, a broad expanse of window overlooked the car park and the woods in the background.

The waitress took their orders for drinks. Michaela wanted white wine, Ben asked for a medium glass of house red. 'No wine for me,' Simeon said. 'I'm afraid I might have a migraine coming on if I touch alcohol tonight.'

'Again?' Michaela frowned.

They ordered dinner – roast duck for Ben, on Simeon's recommendation. Michaela went for poached salmon steak. Service was efficient, and the food was excellent. As they ate, occasional peals of laughter erupted from the ladies' badminton club table behind Ben. Simeon sipped his mineral water and looked pensive while Michaela reaffirmed her complete conviction that they were in for a white Christmas.

Ben wondered what it was Simeon had wanted to tell him earlier. He was sure he'd get to hear it later, back at the vicarage that evening over a glass of whisky or two.

They'd finished their main courses and were into their desserts (plum duff for Simeon, sticky toffee pudding for Michaela, while Ben opted for some cheese and crackers to go with the last of his wine) when out of the corner of his eye Ben noticed a dark BMW come rolling in across the car park, its headlights sweeping the windows. The BMW parked across from the Lotus and Le Crock. The driver's door opened. A tall figure of a man climbed out and made his way towards the building and into the bar area. By then, Ben had already forgotten about him, and went on listening to Simeon talking about the planned new satellite TV series that he'd been offered the job of hosting.

'He's being too modest again,' Michaela said. 'It's quite a big thing. The television company are investing millions in it and it's such an honour that they picked Simeon to present it.' She reached across the table and clasped his hand.

'As long as it helps to spread the word, that's all I care about,' Simeon said. 'I'm not interested in the money. Every penny of it'll go the same way as the money my father left me, helping to restore old churches. So many of them are being left to rot these days.'

'Until they get turned into McDonalds drive-throughs,'

Michaela snorted. 'Sign of the times. You know I had to scour the whole of Oxford just to find a set of Nativity Christmas stamps? All I could find anywhere were jolly snowmen and reindeer and cards saying "Happy Holidays". It's the rise of the militant atheists, I'm telling you. They want to secularise the whole world.'

'Well, maybe we can help to turn the tide,' Simeon said. 'The television series will be a big step forward, that's for sure.'

'When do you start filming?' Ben asked.

'Middle of February. The producers are still wrangling over a name for it.'

'I think *Christianity Today* sounds pat,' Michaela said. 'What do you think?' she asked Ben.

Before Ben could offer any suggestion, he was distracted by a camera flash that lit up the room. One of the badminton club ladies, the skinny-looking woman with the leathery fake tan and pearls who'd been ogling Simeon earlier, had stood up to take snaps of the party group. 'Smile!' she called out over the din.

'Oh, no,' Michaela muttered as the woman swayed up to them, camera in hand. 'Here she comes. Hi, Petra.'

Petra Norrington's eyes sparkled as she approached the table and sidled up to Simeon. Ben saw Michaela's face darken.

'That's a beautiful dress, Michaela,' Petra said, her glance still lingering more on Simeon, before shooting discreetly across at Ben. Ben looked away and smiled to himself.

'Thank you,' Michaela said, just a little coolly. She introduced Ben as an old friend. Petra's eyes sparkled some more.

'And where's that handsome young devil of a son of yours? Coming home for Christmas?'

'He's in Cornwall, with his friend Robbie,' Michaela said.

'Oh,' Petra said, with a look of disdain. '*That* place.'

Simeon looked at Michaela and cocked an eyebrow. 'I thought he was coming straight home from New Zealand.'

'I told you he had other plans, darling,' Michaela reminded him patiently.

'Cornwall? Back to that derelict old farm? What's he want to go there for?'

'Don't exaggerate,' Michaela said. 'It's just a bit run down, and he enjoys being there with his friends.'

Simeon gave a disapproving grunt.

'Can I take a pic of you all?' Petra broke in, brandishing her camera like a gun. 'It's for the club's Christmas album.'

'If you absolutely must,' Michaela said coolly.

Ben wasn't too fond of having his picture taken.

'Say cheese!' Petra's camera flashed. She looked at her watch, pulled a face and excused herself, explaining that she had to get home for some reason to do with someone called Billy. There was a brief round of goodbyes and 'nice to meet you' and 'have a wonderful Christmas if we don't see each other before', and then Petra blew kisses at the badminton ladies and breezed out of the restaurant towards her top-of-the-range Volvo estate.

'I suppose we should be thinking about getting home ourselves,' Simeon said, and called for the bill.

'It's on me,' Ben said, taking out his wallet.

'Absolutely not.'

'It's the least I can do to repay your hospitality.'

They were still arguing about it when they heard a loud crunching impact from outside.

'Whoops,' Michaela said, peering out of the window. 'I think Petra has just pranged her car. Serves the silly bitch right.'

'*Michaela*,' Simeon hissed at her.

Ben looked. The rear of the Volvo estate was hard up against the front end of the dark blue BMW. Bits of broken glass littered on the ground shone under the floodlights.

As Ben watched, Petra clambered out of her Volvo, clapped a hand over her mouth at the sight of the damage, and disappeared back inside. He heard her voice coming from the bar area: 'Excuse me, is that your BMW outside? I'm so sorry. I think I've just reversed into it.'

A man's voice muttered, 'It's OK. It's nothing.'

'I've broken your left headlight,' Petra's voice said, high-pitched with stress. 'My fault. So stupid of me. I was in a hurry and I just didn't . . . but if we could exchange details, I'll write to my insurers first thing tom—'

'Forget it,' the man interrupted. His voice sounded hard and flat.

'I'm sorry?'

'You heard me. Forget it.' He sounded angrier this time.

'I still need to inform them—' Petra protested.

'Are you deaf, woman? I said forget it.'

Meanwhile, the waitress had brought the bill over and Ben was laying cash down on the little saucer in her hand and telling her to keep the change. A shocked hush had fallen over the badminton ladies' table at the argument between the unseen man in the bar and Petra Norrington, who was now skulking back to her Volvo.

'Wonder what *that* was all about,' Michaela said. 'He sounded like a right nasty piece of work.'

Simeon wished the badminton ladies good night as they left. By the time the three of them were walking back to their cars, the Volvo had gone.

So had the damaged BMW.

Chapter Ten

'See you back at the vicarage,' Simeon called as he climbed behind the wheel of the Lotus. Shutting the door he gave Ben a meaningful look, as if to say, 'We'll be able to talk more then'.

Ben fired up Le Crock and shivered in the blast of air from its ineffective heater. Snowclouds had drawn a veil across the stars, and frost twinkled on the grass verges in the beams of their headlights as Ben followed Simeon out of the car park. If the temperature dropped another half a degree, the roads would start to get slick with ice.

However sweetly the Land Rover might be running now that Bertie had worked his wonders on it, it was never going to be a racing car. Ben didn't have much chance of keeping up with the Lotus, especially with the spirited way Simeon drove it, the low-slung taillights dipping out of sight around every bend and continually forcing Ben to accelerate to close the distance between them. Powering up the long incline on the approach to Little Denton, the Land Rover lost momentum and its revs began to get bogged down. Ben changed down a gear, then another, and gently cursed Simeon for his impetuous behaviour.

Up ahead, the Lotus sped exuberantly over the top of the rise and vanished from view. Ben smiled to himself at his friend's antics. Even despite whatever it was that was so clearly and deeply troubling Simeon, he was able to enjoy life. Ben envied that quality in his old friend.

Ben was nearing the top of the hill when a halo of white light appeared on the horizon ahead of him and then burst into a dazzling flash that made him blink and avert his eyes. In the same instant, the shape of a big saloon car came speeding over the crest of the hill in the opposite direction, its engine note high and strained as if the driver had his foot pinned aggressively to the floor. The car was just barely under control, all four wheels leaving the road as it sped over the top of the rise and went plummeting down the slope Ben had just driven up.

Ben was blinded for a second. He blinked away the sunspots, peering hard through the Land Rover's windscreen to regain his bearings on the road. In the quarter-second before he'd had to look away from the dazzling headlights, he'd registered something unusual about the speeding car: one of the twin lamps on the saloon car's left side wasn't working – three blinding lights where there should have been four. But in the next moment the car was already roaring off, its taillights receding fast in his rear-view mirror.

'Idiot,' Ben murmured. He cleared the top of the rise and the Land Rover began to pick up speed on the downward incline. He hadn't expected to see any sign of the Lotus up ahead, and wasn't surprised by the sight of the empty road. Simeon had obviously cleared the S-bends at the bottom of the hill and was probably almost into the outskirts of the village by now.

Not wanting to throw an ageing Land Rover into the bends with quite so much aplomb, Ben took the corners gently and slowed for the little stone bridge over the river.

Then he saw the black skidmarks that criss-crossed the road like rubber snakes.

And the gaping hole where the side of the little stone bridge should have been.

Ben slammed on the brakes and the Land Rover slewed to a halt at the entrance to the bridge. His heart was hammering, his instincts telling him the worst as he leaped down out of the car and sprinted towards the jagged gap in the stonework.

A strangled cry burst out of him as he looked down at the fast-moving water below.

The frosty riverbank was littered with broken stone and wreckage. The tail end of the Lotus was sticking up out of the river, the rapid current washing over the roof. The car's headlights were still on, casting a glow under the surface of the water. Ben could see nothing of its two occupants.

The silence was stark and terrible, like a shroud that muted the whole atmosphere around him. Ben had known it many times before. It was the stillness that accompanied the presence of death.

He tore off his leather jacket, kicked off his shoes and dived without hesitation off the side of the wrecked bridge. The shock of the icy-cold water was stunning, heart-stopping, and the powerful current threatened to carry him away downstream. Pressure roared in his ears as he kicked out and swam for all he was worth towards the submerged vehicle. The Lotus' wedge-shaped nose was buried in rocks and dirt, completely destroyed by the impact. Where the crumpled bonnet joined the bodywork of the car, the windscreen was an opaque mass of fissures. Ben could only just make out the shapes of Simeon and Michaela, behind the glass, still strapped into their seats. He could see no sign of movement from inside. Bubbles streamed from his mouth as he called their names.

Then the Lotus' lights dimmed and went dark as the water fused the battery terminals. The depths of the river were plunged into darkness. Ben fought a surge of panic that gripped him and made his heart race. He groped his way blindly around the side of the car and yanked at the driver's side door handle. It wouldn't budge. Either it was locked, or the pressure inside the car still hadn't equalised. Which meant there was still a pocket of air in the cabin. Ben knew that it could take up to a couple of minutes for a submerged car to fill up completely. There might still be hope for them inside, but seconds were like minutes. Ben could feel the pressure in his lungs mounting fast and his heartbeat escalating with every passing moment as oxygen starvation crept up on him.

Clambering astride the crumpled bonnet he punched at the cracked windscreen. Punched again. He felt no pain, only dimly registered the injury. The weakened glass sagged inwards and gave way in an explosion of air bubbles. Ben shoved both hands through the broken screen and, bracing himself against the bonnet and roof and yanking with all his strength, ripped the whole thing away. His vision was getting accustomed to the murk now, and he could make out the forms of Simeon and Michaela inside the car.

How long had they been under now? Ninety seconds? Two minutes?

His movements clumsy against the strong current, he threw the shattered windscreen away and plunged inside the Lotus.

Ben had seen enough death in his life to recognise it instantly in Michaela. With only the Lotus' old-fashioned seatbelts for restraint and no airbag to cushion her body, she'd been thrown forward under impact and collided hard against the dashboard. A murky brown cloud swirled around her head where the skull was crushed in.

Simeon was struggling weakly. His eyes flickered open and seemed to catch sight of Ben. The steering wheel had prevented him from flying forwards. It had almost certainly staved in his ribs, but he was still alive. Ben searched furiously for the seatbelt catch. His chest was bursting. His movements were becoming frantic. *Don't panic. Panic means none of you leaves this river alive.*

Ben's fumbling hands found the seatbelt catch and suddenly it was free. He tore it aside and grabbed Simeon by both arms. Bubbles burst out of Ben's mouth with the effort of hauling his friend over the dashboard and out through the glassless window. With Simeon's arm around his neck he pushed hard with both legs against the bonnet of the Lotus, trying to propel himself and the dead weight of his semi-conscious friend upwards towards the surface. He saw lights on the water a few feet from his head. The surface was just there, so close, so out of reach. His strength was failing.

Two and a half minutes under. Maybe three. He was going to drown.

Don't panic.

Where the strength came from for that final desperate lunge for the surface, Ben would never know. A wheezing gasp erupted from his lungs as his head broke the surface. He dimly heard a yell from across the water. Lights and movement on the bridge. People on the bank. He couldn't understand what they were saying. He paddled hard, keeping a tight hold on Simeon and his head above the surface.

Then, suddenly, there was soft mud under his feet. Reeds prickled his hands and face. With a roar of effort he heaved

Simeon's limp body up onto the bank, where two of the passersby who'd scrambled down from the bridge were waiting with shouts of encouragement. They seized Simeon's arms and hauled him clear of the water. Ben scrambled up the muddy bank and crouched over his friend, turning him over and letting the river water drain from his lungs. He yelled his name. The two passersby stood back in grim silence.

Simeon's eyes were shut. His face was white in the lights from the bridge, his wet hair plastered across his brow. Blood trickled from the corners of his mouth and down his cheeks into the mud. More lights were appearing in the distance, a flashing and swirling of blue on the horizon, accompanied by a building chorus of sirens.

Simeon's pulse was fading. It was barely there at all. Ben knelt helplessly over him, feeling the terrible concavity of his chest where the ribs were crushed inwards and knowing that the emergency chest compressions of cardiopulmonary resuscitation would probably kill him.

Simeon's eyes opened. For a brief moment, they stared right into Ben's. His lips pursed and opened, as if he were trying to say something. His hand twitched, then moved upwards to weakly grasp Ben's arm.

'Jude . . .' Simeon's voice was a dying whisper. His eyes seemed to be imploring Ben.

Then they closed again.

'Simeon!' Ben felt for the pulse once more. This time he could feel nothing at all. He wanted to shake him, slap him, beat him back to life. 'Simeon!'

The first ambulance had screeched to a halt at the bridge, bathing the scene in a blue swirl, its siren drowning out the shocked murmur of conversation among the growing crowd of bystanders. Paramedics burst out of the ambulance doors and came sprinting down the frosty slope to the river bank with their emergency equipment. Ben moved aside as they clapped the defibrillator to Simeon's crushed chest and applied the first electric shock in a desperate attempt to revive him. Simeon's spine arched upwards in an involuntary spasm, as if he was trying to get up. But Ben knew the time for that had come and gone.

'No pulse,' one of the paramedics said.

They tried another shock. Simeon's body arched on the ground, then fell limp again. His face looked like a piece of mud-streaked porcelain, eyes staring upwards.

'No pulse.'

'He's gone, I'm afraid,' said another. 'Nothing more we can do.'

A gentle snowfall had begun to spiral down from the dark sky, turning blue in the flashing lights. Ben stared as snow-flakes settled on the body of his friend. He turned and gazed at the sunken car, thinking of Michaela inside. He said a silent goodbye to them both.

Another ambulance had arrived at the mouth of the bridge, together with a police emergency response vehicle. The officers were herding the bystanders away to clear the area. The place was alive with voices and crackling radios. A woman was led away, crying, someone's arm around her shoulders.

Events followed as if in a dream. Emergency crews surrounded the crashed Lotus, struggling to extricate Michaela's body. By now it was clear to everyone involved that the ambulances would be taking away two corpses that night. There was no longer any need for hurry.

Several minutes passed before Ben even became conscious of the crippling cold and the pain in his torn hands. The paramedics checked him for signs of hypothermia: slurred speech, disorientation, unsteadiness. His wet hair dripping onto the thermal blanket they'd wrapped around him, he sat in the open back of the third ambulance and watched the scene unfold as if from a million miles away. He numbly answered the questions the cops came to ask him before he could be carted off to hospital. Name, address, occupation, relationship to the deceased. He told them what he'd seen. Described the car that had passed him from the direction of the bridge, told them how one of its headlights had appeared to be damaged.

The cops asked him if he'd seen any collision take place between the two vehicles. Ben told them he hadn't.

But as he spoke, he was visualising the scenario in his mind: the two cars meeting on the narrow road before the bridge. The saloon swerving to avoid the speeding Lotus and catching its headlight on the stone wall at the side of the road. The Lotus swerving the other way and spinning out of control. The driver of the saloon panicking and hitting the gas to escape from the scene. Or maybe not even noticing what happened next.

Or maybe it had all happened differently. Ben thought about the positioning of the skidmarks on the road before the bridge. He thought about how a car could have lain there in wait as the distinctive shape of the Lotus came down the hill. How the driver could have waited until just the right moment before lurching out deliberately into Simeon's path and forcing him to swerve and crash.

Ben thought back to the restaurant car park. The BMW. The broken headlight. The behaviour of the car's owner. Like he hadn't wanted to know. Like he hadn't wanted attention drawn to him.

But Ben mentioned none of that to the cops.

Through the mist of his thoughts, he heard one of the officers asking about next of kin. Ben remembered what

Michaela had said about her parents moving to Antigua. He knew nothing about Simeon's. 'They have a son,' he said. He couldn't bring himself to use the past tense. 'Jude Arundel. He's in Cornwall with friends.'

'We'll need to contact him,' the officer said.

'I don't think he'll be that easy to contact,' Ben said. He told them he'd be responsible for informing Jude.

After the police had left him alone, Ben watched the paramedic teams wrapping up their kit. He'd no intention of seeing the inside of a hospital that night. He'd seen enough of them already. As the ambulances carrying Simeon and Michaela left in tandem, he slipped away unnoticed and walked to where the police had moved his Land Rover. The snow was falling more steadily now, dusting everything powdery white.

He climbed into the vehicle and headed back alone towards the vicarage. He had nowhere else to go.

Chapter Eleven

The warm, welcoming glow from the vicarage's windows shone out into the night as Ben climbed out of the Land Rover and trudged towards the house in his wet clothes. He paused to peer in through the window at the empty living room. The lit-up Christmas tree that he could imagine Simeon and Michaela decorating together, which someone else would be taking down. The comfortable furniture they'd never see or use again.

He felt sick as the reality sank in a little deeper.

The dog barked from inside. Ben dug in his pocket and took out the annexe key. Attached to it on a ring was the tarnished brass Yale key for the front door of the vicarage. Feeling strangely like an intruder, he opened the door. The dog was sitting in the hallway, looking at him.

'Hey, Scruffy,' Ben said softly. The dog cocked his head, appearing perplexed that his master and mistress weren't with him. Ben went over to him and scratched his ears. 'They're not coming back, pal. I'm sorry.'

The dog lolled his pink tongue and began to pant.

'All right, you come with me,' Ben said. Squelching in his wet shoes he made his way down the passage to the connecting door that led through into the annexe. Everything seemed so still and empty.

Shuddering with cold, he stripped off his wet things in the annexe's bathroom and stepped under a hot shower. He stayed there a long time, hoping that the scalding jet of water would blast away the nightmare and that when he came out everything would be back to normal.

It didn't happen. He mechanically towelled himself dry and changed into a pair of grey jogging pants and a worn old rugby top from his bag. Finding his whisky flask nestling among the spare clothing, he unscrewed the cap and gulped down a stinging mouthful, then another. That didn't make any difference either. He padded barefoot into the annexe's little living room, flipped off all the lights and lay on the sofa with his eyes shut, trying to let his mind go blank. But there was no escape from the images that kept flashing up inside his mind as he lay there. He couldn't stop seeing Simeon's face in those last moments. The pallor of his skin, the desperation in his eyes. And Michaela, sitting there lifeless inside the sunken car. The horrific crush wounds on her face and brow.

One minute he'd been having dinner with his friends. The next, they were gone, just like that, like blowing out a candle. Tomorrow would see the start of the whole terrible aftermath. Tonight, there was nothing but that sickening emptiness, as if the world had been scraped hollow with a blunt knife.

Ben groped for the flask in the darkness and swallowed down the rest of the whisky. One gulp after another. The visions began to recede. He drifted into a world of vague and restless dreams that seemed to go on forever and were filled with the cries of people in pain. He couldn't help them, no matter how desperately he tried . . . there was nothing he could do . . .

Ben's body tensed and he jerked upright on the sofa, momentarily confused by the unfamiliar sound that had torn through the membrane of his sleep. The luminous green hands of his diver's watch told him it was quarter to one in the morning. He sat up, listening hard.

A few feet away across the darkened room, the dog let out another long, low snarl, and Ben realised what had woken him. He was about to lie down again when he heard something else.

A dull thud, coming from the other side of the wall. The sounds of movement inside the vicarage.

Ben jumped up from the sofa, suddenly wide awake and alert. His first thought was that Jude Arundel must have returned from Cornwall. He went to turn on the light, already preparing mentally for the task of breaking the news to the kid that both his parents were dead.

But Ben's hand stopped short of the light switch when he heard more sounds from inside the vicarage: a muted splintering crash that was unmistakably the sound of a door being forced, followed a moment later by the grinding thump of something hitting a wall.

Scruffy let out another rumbling growl from deep in his throat.

Ben reached out to him in the darkness and laid a hand on his head. 'Quiet, boy. Let me listen.' Creeping across the room towards the connecting door, Ben pressed his ear to it and thought he heard a man's voice.

'Wait,' he whispered back to the dog. There was no time to put on his shoes. Without a sound, he opened the door and stepped through into the passage beyond.

Another thump, louder this time now that he was closer. It was coming from somewhere on the ground floor.

Silently, stealthily, Ben moved towards the sound.

Chapter Twelve

Few men were schooled in the secret of silence. To be able to move unheard, unnoticed yet quickly through any terrain, blending in with the surroundings at all times, was an art that had to be learned and honed through dedicated training and practice – and Ben Hope had been a master of it for many years. Not many of his peers in the SAS had been able to match him.

The art began with knowing where to place your feet. The vicarage's old oak floorboards were broad and thick, but age and use had warped the wood so that it was almost impossible to walk over them without a creak. Ben kept to the edges, feeling with his bare toes as he went for any seam or joint that might shift with his weight. His breathing was slow and shallow, his heartbeat controlled and his mind as still as that of a predatory animal. When stalking a determined and trained enemy, even the scent of your fear could give you away.

Creeping through the darkness, he glanced around him for anything he could use as defence against the intruders. Improvised weapons weren't too abundant in the home of a country vicar. His gaze landed on a foot-high wooden statuette on a side table. He picked it up without a sound. It felt solid in his hand, like a short club.

Another dull thud from up ahead. A grinding of steel against steel, followed by a clanging crash.

As Ben had been expecting to happen any second, the dog let loose with a furious tirade of barking from inside the annexe, muffled behind the thick wall. Ben decided it wasn't such a bad thing: the intruders would be aware that the nearest neighbour was far enough away not to be alerted by the noise. And the knowledge that the dog was contained in another part of the house would make them feel safe. Exactly how Ben wanted them to feel.

Up ahead, the shadowy corridor terminated in a T-junction. To the left, all was darkness. Around the corner to the right, a glow of light shone from an unseen doorway.

Ben stepped closer to the corner. From the source of the dim light he heard a man's voice mutter something he didn't catch. He stopped, blotting out the muted sound of Scruffy's barking and listening hard. Was it the same voice he'd heard a moment ago? Impossible to tell, or to guess how many intruders there might be.

He advanced as far as the corner, back to the wall, ready with his club. He was within sight of the doorway now. It was a couple of inches ajar, and in the light that streamed out of it, he could see the outline of the splintered frame where the door had been forced open. Careful not to let his shadow play on the opposite wall, he stepped up to the door and peered around its edge into the room behind it.

Simeon's study. The walls were lined with bookshelves. A simple computer desk stood in the middle of the room, with a flat-screen monitor and wireless keyboard. In the far corner of the study was a steel safe, like a short gun cabinet, bolted to the wall. The metallic crash Ben had just heard was the sound of it being jemmied open.

The man who'd broken into the safe was crouching beside

it with his back to the doorway. He was wearing a black combat jacket. A black cotton ski mask was pulled down over his face. There was a pistol in a military-style holster at his right hip. As Ben watched, the man grabbed a brown A4-sized envelope from the safe. He stuffed it into the duffel bag at his feet, then reached back inside the safe and came out with a small black laptop, which he bagged as well.

Just one man. Yet Ben had heard him talking. To himself, maybe, or on the phone. Unless . . .

Ben suddenly felt something hard prod him between the shoulder blades. He half-turned and found himself staring into a fat black O nearly three quarters of an inch wide. The muzzle of a pump-action twelve-bore.

'Lose the ornament,' said the man with the shotgun. His face was hidden in the shadows. The accent was East London. The tone was calm.

Ben's fingers loosened and the wooden statuette dropped to the floor.

'Nice one,' the man with the shotgun said. He advanced into the light. The eyes watching Ben through the slits in the ski mask were the colour of steel, hard and cold. He had the buttstock of the short-barrelled shotgun pulled in tight to his shoulder. That meant several things to Ben. The guy was bracing himself against the recoil, because he had no problem with pulling the trigger if he had to. It meant he was familiar with the weapon and had used it before. It also meant the shotgun's five-capacity tube magazine was probably filled with hard-kicking solid slug loads that would take Ben's head clean off his shoulders and paint the wall behind him with his brains.

All of which added up to the fact that these guys were no ordinary house-breakers, no run-of-the-mill opportunist crooks. They were professionals. And if the man with the shotgun was good enough to creep up on Ben like this, it meant he was very good indeed. Someone trained, like him, in the art of silence.

Or maybe Ben was just getting slow.

Ben retreated. The man's eyes didn't leave his. The muzzle of the shotgun was rock steady.

The other side of the wall, the dog was going wild.

'Why are you here?' Ben asked.

'That's it. There's fuck all else in the safe,' the man with the duffel bag said to his companion. He stood up and slung the strap over his shoulder, then left the study, brushing past Ben. The man with the shotgun waved the weapon ever so slightly towards the open doorway. 'You. Get your arse in there,' he told Ben.

Ben took a step backwards into the room. He saw the gunman's gloved finger flick half an inch back from the trigger and depress the small round button set into the rear of the trigger guard. Safety off.

Ben got the picture. The guy wasn't intending to leave any witnesses behind. Not the kind who still had their heads attached.

Nothing to lose, then.

Ben retreated another slow step, raising his arms either side of his head. The guy advanced. Ben watched the muzzle of the gun. A rapid step forward, and Ben's hands flashed towards the weapon. He gripped the cold steel of the barrel and jerked it simultaneously sideways and towards him. As the gun was torn half out of his grip, the man instinctively squeezed the trigger and the gun went off like a bomb just a few inches from Ben's right ear.

Now the pump-action was a lot less dangerous until it could be re-cocked. Ben had no intention of letting that happen. Still gripping the barrel he pushed it violently back towards the gunman, driving the butt end into the guy's face. It caught him on the mouth. With a yell of pain and a spurt of blood he fell back and let go of the gun. Ben clubbed him over the head with the forend.

The whole disarming move had taken less than two seconds. *Maybe I'm not getting that slow*, Ben thought.

The man with the duffel bag froze for an instant, then took off down the passage. Ben spun the shotgun around in his hands and worked the pump as he leaped over the slumped body and out of the study doorway.

The escaping intruder was just rounding the corner. Ben could have shot him, but the blast would have blown the guy in half and Ben wanted him alive. Slinging the gun around his shoulder, he sprinted after him. The man crashed past the side table off which Ben had lifted the statuette earlier, and sent it spinning into Ben's path. Ben vaulted over it, saw that he was catching up, and launched himself at the man with a flying rugby-tackle. Pinned by the ankles, the man sprawled heavily to the floor and let out a grunt of pain. Ben clambered after him. His left hand closed on the strap of the duffel bag as his right fist shot out to land a crippling hammer-punch to the man's testicles.

The punch didn't make contact. Ben didn't see the heavy boot coming for his face until it was too late. The kick slammed into his cheekbone with a huge amount of force behind it, and sent him crashing back against the wall, still tightly clutching the duffel bag by its strap.

The intruder went for his pistol.

Ben went for the shotgun.

The guy thought better of it. He abandoned the bag and ran for the front door. Wrenched it open and burst out into the night.

Scruffy was barking dementedly from the other side of

the wall. Ben struggled to his feet, dazed from the kick. He ran out of the open front door and saw the intruder heading around the side of the vicarage, making for the path that led through the back garden and down to the meadow.

Seconds into the chase, Ben knew he was at a major disadvantage. The intruder wasn't necessarily the faster runner, but he didn't have to sprint barefoot over the hard, cold ground carrying a cumbersome duffel bag and a shotgun. Ben had only just made it to the edge of the meadow when he realised that his quarry had disappeared into the darkness. Moments later, he heard the roar of an engine from beyond the trees, and a car took off at high speed down the road.

Chapter Thirteen

Ben hobbled back to the vicarage on his cut and bruised bare soles. No lights had come on in the neighbouring houses dimly visible through the trees. The blast of a shotgun, muffled within thick stone walls, wasn't much more than a dull 'pop' from a few hundred yards away, not enough to raise the alarm even in a sleepy little village like Little Denton.

It was rather more than that from a few inches away, though. Ben knew he'd have to wait a day or two for the high-pitched whine in his right ear to subside and his full hearing to return. Back inside the vicarage, he strode back to the study. Now to revive his masked friend and get some truth out of him.

But as he walked through the doorway into the room, he stopped dead and stared at the empty patch of floor where the fallen intruder had been lying unconscious just moments ago.

The man was gone.

Ben had hit him pretty hard. Evidently not hard enough, though.

Turning on the lights in the corridor, Ben saw the thin trail of blood spots that led through the house. He followed them all the way to the back door. It was swinging open and bore faint marks from where the intruders had broken in earlier. A clean job, efficient and professional.

And too conveniently timed for the burglary attempt to have been a coincidence. There was no doubt left in Ben's mind now: the car crash had been no accident. Someone had wanted the Arundels out of the way, and it had something to do with the contents of Simeon's safe.

Ben looked closely at the shotgun. It was a Mossberg pump-action with a folding stock and a barrel not much more than a foot long, making it a seriously prohibited weapon in Britain and most other countries of the world. It still had four rounds in the magazine plus another five in a shell holder attached to the butt. The ammunition was solid slug, as he'd suspected. But that wasn't what interested him most.

While the majority of weapons of its kind in circulation among the criminal underworld tended to have been made for civilian use originally, before their crooked new owners adapted them for purpose by sawing the barrels, this one was different. The matt finish and MOD serial numbers and proof marks told him this one clearly had started life as a military weapon. Guns like this didn't generally fall into just anyone's hands, and combined with the way the man holding it had shown such skill in sneaking up on him, it confirmed his impression that he was dealing with a former soldier. And a good one, too. Not many guys could have upped and run from the blow Ben had dealt him.

Ben wondered whether he should call the cops, then decided against it. They'd muddy the ground like a herd of cattle and ask too many questions. In any case, he was disinclined to hand them over the shotgun – knowing the British police, it would be treated as though it were a live nuclear warhead, and he as a terror suspect.

No, it was better to keep this incident to himself and follow up whatever leads he could, on his own.

Ben let the dog out of the annexe. Sniffing everywhere and growling to himself, Scruffy followed him as he carried the thieves' duffel bag through to the kitchen. Ben laid the bag on the old oak kitchen table and pulled up a chair. The numbing sense of grief was losing its bite now, replaced by a mixture of burning rage and adrenaline that made his hands shake as he emptied the bag's contents onto the table.

There was nothing inside but the brown envelope and the small black Toshiba laptop that Ben had seen the thief take from Simeon's safe. He laid the computer aside for the moment and picked up the envelope.

It didn't contain a lot. He found an air ticket to Jerusalem dating back to eighteen months earlier, a hotel bill printed in Hebrew and a collection of glossy photo prints that had presumably been taken while on the same trip to Israel. Most were typical tourist snaps: the Jerusalem skyline at night; the Wailing Wall; a variety of churches and mosques and synagogues; the desert, palm trees, a camel, some sandy ruins.

Ben went through them one by one until he arrived at a group shot of Simeon posing with three other men against a backdrop of the same ancient ruins. They appeared to be on friendly terms, all smiling. Simeon's arm was around the broad shoulders of the man on the left, who was obviously Israeli, burly and grizzled, around sixty. To the right of Simeon stood a smaller man, perhaps European, with white hair and trim beard, in good shape but quite old, closer to seventy than sixty. The man on the far right of the group was about fifteen years younger, with curly salt-and-pepper hair, a round jovial face and the belly of a *bon viveur*.

Ben was unable to tell much from the photos, but he might have more luck with whatever was on the computer.

He flipped open the laptop's lid, turned the machine on and quickly discovered that it was virtually empty apart from a single Word document file titled TSS.

Whatever it was, it must have been important enough to Simeon to warrant keeping it in a safe. Ben clicked to open the document, and a new window opened on the screen.

The computer was asking for a passcode. Ben had just hit a brick wall.

TSS. It didn't look like an initial – more like an acronym for something. But what? Then, after a few more moments' reflection, he remembered what Michaela had told him that morning, and it hit him.

TSS. *The Sacred Sword.* The Word document was the unfinished manuscript of Simeon's book. It could have told Ben a great deal – but he didn't rate his chances of breaking Simeon's security code. Knowing him, it would be some incredibly obscure Bible reference or an unguessable piece of Latin. It was a non-starter. Ben checked the document's properties, but it was like trying to see into a locked room from outside. The only data he could access were the document's size, half a megabyte or so, and the date and time it had last been saved: 15.04 on December 14th.

Ben swore to himself and reluctantly closed the laptop down. Remembering the PC in the study, he decided to see if he might find anything out from Simeon's email.

There was no password to hurdle this time. Sitting at Simeon's desk, Ben scrolled through hundreds of messages, mostly concerning everyday church matters. Some were from the TV production company, others from an outfit called Blackwood Entertainment Management who seemed to have been in the middle of negotiating an agency deal to represent Simeon in his newfound role as television celebrity.

After flicking through a few more emails, Ben felt a pang

of shame and began to sense that he was prying uselessly into Simeon's affairs. He was on the verge of giving up when another of the messages caught his eye.

It was from the man Michaela had talked about on their walk through the woods. Father Fabrice Lalique, the priest whose recent suicide had so upset Simeon. Ben opened the message. It was dated a couple of weeks earlier and read:

> *My Dear Friends*
> *By the time you read this message, I will be dead. I ask you not to mourn for me, as I am unworthy of your grief.*
> *The shame of my sins is a burden I can no longer bear. May God have mercy on me for the terrible things I have done.*

Let his soul rot in hell for all I care, Ben thought. He clicked out of the emails and went online to run a Google search on the name Fabrice Lalique. It didn't take long to dig up a whole collection of French news reports about the priest's suicide and the discovery, shortly after his death, of large amounts of obscene material on the personal computer at his home in Saint-Christophe, near Millau in the Midi-Pyrénées area of southern France.

Revelations about paedophilia had a way of wiping out anything positive that might have been said of a man's past life or career; not surprisingly, the news reports were full of disgust, even hatred. There were various quotes from members of his diocese, all of them expressing their shock at the appalling discovery and very little in the way of sympathy for the dead man. Some online commentators had dubbed Lalique the Paedo Priest. Ben came across forums and websites where the scandal had sparked a furious debate, with pressure groups demanding that governments step in immediately to end the secret culture of perversion and abuse within the Catholic Church or, better still, tear the whole rotten edifice down once and for all.

Most of the online articles had published the same image of Lalique, pictured at some official event wearing his priest's garb. Ben immediately recognised him as the jolly-faced, full-bellied man who'd been standing on the right of the group shot in Simeon's photo. Other images online showed the scene under the Millau viaduct where officials had scooped up what little remained intact of Lalique's body after the enormous fall from the bridge. As suicides went, it had been highly efficient.

Ben shut down the PC, left the study and made his way through to the living room, trying to make sense of it all and knowing he was a long way from succeeding. As he looked around him for inspiration, one of the books in the antique bookcase suddenly caught his eye. He opened the glass door and slipped the old Bible off the shelf. It was a beautifully leather-bound edition, and one that he hadn't seen since his first year at Oxford. Carefully turning the cover, he saw his own faded handwriting. 'To my friend Simeon, from Benedict Hope.'

Ben was touched that Simeon had kept the birthday gift all these years, and saddened. He flicked through the pages of the book he'd once known virtually by heart. He still remembered great chunks of it, though a lot had faded from his memory. Maybe I should read it again, he thought. Simeon wouldn't have minded if he borrowed it.

Ben set the Bible down on a table and was about to close the bookcase when he noticed the collection of videotapes and DVDs on the top shelf. Some were movies, some were documentaries, some were religion-themed programmes taped from TV, with handwritten labels stuck to their spines. The one that especially caught Ben's eye was a home-recorded videotape labelled SIMEON VS THE ENEMY. He remembered Simeon's words from the day before: '*I have many enemies*'. It had been hard to tell to what extent he'd been joking when he said it.

The Arundels' TV rested discreetly on a stand in the corner, with a DVD player and VCR nestling below it. Ben took the tape down from the bookcase and inserted it into the machine.

Chapter Fourteen

According to the date scrawled on the videotape's label with a marker pen, Simeon had recorded the TV programme a little over a year ago. It was one of those highbrow panel discussion shows that tended to be aired late at night, called *The Monday Debate*. The presenter was some tweedy type whose face looked vaguely familiar to Ben from one of the rare past occasions when he'd ever turned on a TV. Since moving to France he'd never bothered with it at all.

'Tonight on The Monday Debate,' the presenter announced, 'we ask the question that is becoming more topical every year: Is religion harmful, and would we be better off without it?'

Poised behind twin lecture rostrums like two rivals in a political standoff were Simeon, on the right, wearing his white dog collar but otherwise casually attired, and a man on the left whom Ben had never seen before. He was somewhat older than Simeon, somewhere in his mid-to-late forties, with thick swept-back hair that could have been dyed to hide the grey. He was less casually turned out than his opponent, wearing an expensive-looking and immaculately pressed light grey suit, and gave the impression of a man who took himself extremely seriously. His eyes were darting and intense. The presenter introduced him as Penrose Lucas,

Professor of Sociology and Anthropology at Durham and author of the recent *Sunday Times* number one bestseller *God? What God?*

Clear enough what side he was on, then, Ben thought. He'd never heard of this Lucas guy. From the brief resumé the presenter gave of the man, it seemed that the sudden runaway success of *God? What God?* had propelled him out of academic obscurity and into the realms of minor celebrity, as something of a figurehead for the growing pro-atheist lobby.

As the debate opened, Penrose Lucas went straight in like a greyhound leaving the gate. Pointedly refusing to refer to his opponent as the Reverend Arundel and insisting on *Mr*, he began a rapid-fire tirade about the centuries of slaughter and persecution and senseless warfare carried out in the name of religion.

It was hardly a new argument, but it was one that many Christians found difficult to refute, and Professor Lucas clearly intended to milk it to its full crushing advantage. He was eloquent and passionate, his case compelling. Religious belief was the most devastating of all the follies ever dreamed up by humanity. Without its destructive influence, mankind would be able to co-exist in a blissful state of utter peace. A new age would emerge in the wake of its long-awaited banishment to the dustbin of history, like young green shoots growing up in abundance on a fire-blighted landscape. An age of reason. An age of secularism. An age of scientific enlightenment.

Having rapidly reduced two millennia of Christian tradition to rubble and its followers to gullible imbeciles, Penrose generously ceded the floor to Simeon. Ben watched his friend on the screen as the cameras zoomed in, and felt his throat tighten with sadness.

'The dogma of Christianity gets worn away before the advances of science,' was Simeon's opening line. The presenter seemed taken aback by his statement, and Penrose Lucas' eyebrows shot up in delight, as if even he hadn't expected to win the debate so quickly. 'Yes! Exactly!' he interrupted, nodding, eyes gleaming. 'Then Mr Arundel concedes the point that—'

'I wasn't conceding anything,' Simeon said calmly. 'I was quoting from a well-known figure from history. One who knew something about war, I might add. I'm sure my learned friend, with his deep knowledge of history among his many other accomplishments, must be aware of who spoke these words that he so enthusiastically seems to embrace?'

Seemingly, Penrose Lucas wasn't aware of anything, except that he'd possibly just walked into a horrible trap. He flushed scarlet under the studio lights.

'That quote comes from Adolf Hitler,' Simeon said. 'An ardent atheist who, if Nazi Germany had won World War II, planned to eradicate Christianity within his empire just as he planned to eradicate the Jews. But I'm sure my learned friend wouldn't try to argue that the war was fought over matters of faith?'

Lucas wisely chose not to expand on the point. Having got his opponent on the ropes, Simeon didn't let go and began plucking more examples at random from history: Vietnam, a conflict fought over ideologies far removed from religion; the American Civil War, ostensibly fought over the issue of slavery, not faith. And on, and on, though Simeon was being careful not to lose his audience in a welter of information. Each new point seemed to hammer Penrose Lucas down a little further behind his rostrum and turn his face a little redder. Just a few minutes into the debate, and his studied composure was already coming apart at the seams.

'In fact,' Simeon challenged him with a winning grin, 'can the Professor name a single major conflict of the last three centuries that was even remotely connected with Christian ideology?'

'It doesn't matter,' Penrose yelled. 'Anyone who believes in the very notion of a god is suffering from a serious mental delusion. These people need treatment.'

'Speaking as a qualified psychiatrist as well?' Simeon asked, still smiling. 'With all due respect, I hope your knowledge in that field is better than your understanding of history.'

The debate turned away from the issue of warfare and raged on, though all the raging was done on Penrose Lucas' side and Simeon preserved his cool impeccably. Ben watched another few minutes, smiling to himself at the way Simeon was able to run rings around his opponent.

By the time he stopped the video playback, the rolling script at the bottom of the screen was already giving the results of the TV phone-in. The vote was running 76% in favour of Simeon.

'If Professor Lucas' book is as well-argued as his effort in this debate,' said one of the scrolling quotes emailed and texted in from viewers, 'I won't be buying it'. Others said much the same thing.

It was highly entertaining stuff, but Ben wasn't in the mood for entertainment. He turned off the TV. Suddenly the room was quiet and still and dark. Simeon was gone again, for the second time that night.

Chapter Fifteen

Professor Penrose Lucas stepped out onto the balcony of the clifftop villa and gazed out from the rocky coast of Capri across the still, dark waters of the Gulf of Naples. His migraine was throbbing, and he was still quaking from the nightmare that had racked him for what seemed like hours before he'd eventually managed to tear himself away from it, sitting bolt upright in bed with a gasp, drenched in sweat.

Even now, his father's roar continued to reverberate in his ears.

'*Hell rip and roast you for a bastard, boy!*' Whack.

Penrose shuddered. He could still smell the dreaded leather belt that the old man had kept coiled ready for use in a jar of vinegar, the filthy sick sadist. Penrose wouldn't ever forget the sting of that belt on his skin. The lashing crack of the leather. The sound of his own screaming, still sharp in his memory after thirty years.

'*Remember me, boy. Those who are tainted shall drink the wine of the wrath of God, and they shall be tormented in the presence of the holy angels!*' Whack. Whack.

Penrose watched the white crests of the waves in the darkness until his father's voice receded to nothing and his migraine began to ease.

How he had detested that man, with a burning force of hatred whose violence had never abated, from his earliest youth to the time he'd left home, to the day of the old man's death eleven years ago. Standing there at the graveside surrounded by those forlorn, snivelling mourners who'd lacked the wits to see through the tyrant's veneer of charm, Penrose hadn't been able to restrain himself from cackling out loud as he'd watched the coffin descend into the ground. His only regret had been that the Reverend Gerald Collingsworth Lucas, Deacon for the Diocese of Winchester, had now been released from the agony of the cancer that had been eating him away, one wretched cell at a time, for over a decade.

By the time of his father's long-awaited, infinitely relished passing, Penrose's academic career had been well on track. A sparkling talent, he'd been set from early on to become one of the youngest university professors of his generation. He'd never married, never formed any serious relationships with women and had few friends, devoted instead to his work and to the first glimmers of what had eventually evolved into his first book. When he hadn't been buried in the rapidly expanding manuscript of *God? What God?* he'd been nailed to his desk writing hosts of long, impassioned online articles about the evils and corruption of organised religion, most especially those of Christianity.

After the completed book manuscript, all one hundred and eighty thousand incendiary words of it, had unexpectedly sparked off a bidding war between major British publishers and Penrose had found himself suddenly in possession of a six-figure advance that he didn't really need, he'd immediately begun putting the money to good use. Thus had begun the second stage of his war against the church and his father's memory.

Penrose secretly paid seventeen thousand pounds to a firm called Hardstaff & Baldwin Ltd, a shabby little private investigation outfit in Darlington, to dig up as much dirt as they could on members of the clergy, of any Christian denomination, across the north-east of England. Within three months, H&B's diligent sleuthing had managed to produce video footage of a well-respected pastor in Leeds, one Reverend Tobias Bateman, sneaking away from his wife at night for regular visits to the notorious Water Lane red light district in Holbeck, where he was reported to enjoy being tied up and beaten by a lady wearing only a shiny leather mask.

Penrose swiftly closed in for the kill. The ensuing media furore led to the defrocking, disgracing and divorce of the good Reverend Bateman. The source of the information remained a secret, naturally. Penrose's money had been well spent, and he had a lot more to burn now that his book was selling like hot cakes. Having tasted blood, he now enlarged his operation to include the whole of England, an initiative that cost him the remainder of his publishing advance and then some more. To his horror, his investigators turned up nothing for months. No church sex romps, no internet poker-addicted bishops or lesbian nuns, not a shred of scandal or intemperance to be found anywhere. Penrose began to realise he was going to have to become more creative.

It wasn't long afterwards that he hit paydirt, in the form of a highly esteemed and well-known psychotherapist called Dr Nora Gibbs, shrink and hypnotist to sports personalities and television celebs. Purely by chance, one of Penrose's growing network of investigators stumbled across an old legal case and happened to report it back to his employer. It appeared that two decades earlier, when Nora Gibbs had been Nora Jamieson and a student at Sussex University, she'd been arrested in possession of amphetamines, cocaine and a quantity of magic mushrooms, which she'd been distributing to her fellow students – one of whom ended up hospitalised as a result. It had been a minor scandal at the time, but nobody had ever before dug up the connection with the famous Dr Gibbs.

Two days after Penrose's tip-off, the celebrity shrink received an anonymous letter giving her very specific and clear instructions on how to avoid revelations about her past being leaked to the national media. Some time later, a very well-known male TV presenter, who'd been receiving hypnotherapy treatment from Dr Gibbs for stress and depression, suddenly recovered deeply repressed and hith-erto undreamed-of memories of serious sexual abuse at the hands of the nuns and priests at the Catholic boarding school he'd attended in his youth. The TV presenter, shaken and angry but eternally grateful to his shrink for having made him aware of his forgotten past, went public with his allegations. Despite the lack of a single shred of evidence, the ensuing storm was enough to bring about the closure of the school. A retired priest called Father O'Rourke narrowly avoided being lynched by a mob that gathered outside his home, and died soon afterwards of heart failure.

It was Penrose 2, God 0. He would lie awake at night, savouring the ingenious brilliance of his coup and fanta-sising about what he could achieve if he had more money to spend. With a big enough budget, he could bring the whole rotten thing down. Squash all of the cockroaches flat. By now he was hard at work researching his second book, *Murdering for God*, a scabrous condemnation of every war atrocity and act of violence ever perpetrated in the name

112

of Christianity. Meanwhile, he'd launched his brand-new website along with its own popular discussion forum that attracted enlightened thinkers and militant atheists from all over the world.

He was rolling.

It had been one rainy early October day, heading back to his car after a hard afternoon's lecturing of a group of second-year anthropology students, that the Hand of Fate had reached out to Penrose Lucas in a very unexpected manner. And his life had changed.

The stranger was loitering near a sleek black Mercedes that Penrose had never seen in the University staff car park before. The Mercedes looked brand new. The number plate was private. The man was about forty, greying above the ears, lean and sharp-featured. He was wearing a dark suit and a camel coat that was worth Penrose's monthly salary. His shoes gleamed on the wet tarmac. As Penrose approached his car, the man stepped away from the Mercedes and walked up to him. 'Professor?'

Penrose stopped. The man was smiling and looking him right in the eye.

'Yes?'

'My name is Rex O'Neill,' the man said. 'I represent The Trimble Group.' He reached into the pocket of the camel coat and came out with a business card. Penrose took it. The card was shiny and black, completely blank except for the organisation's name embossed in gold across the front. No number or address.

'The Trimble Group? What's this about?'

O'Neill smiled. 'Don't bother trying to look us up, Professor Lucas. You won't find us. But we've been watching you, and have taken a special interest in your work.'

'My work?'

'I'm not talking about your academic career,' O'Neill said with a twinkle. 'Let's just say that your . . . *extracurricular activities* have been closely monitored by the people I work for. You're a very clever fellow, aren't you?'

Penrose's legs weakened and his guts twisted. 'What are you talking about? Am I in trouble?' He was convinced that this was some kind of reprisal against him. Someone had been spying on his spies. Now the Church of England had sent hired thugs out to ice him. He was ready to bolt like a scalded cat.

'Relax, professor. Quite the contrary.' O'Neill reached into his pocket, and instead of pulling out a gun he produced a crisp white letter-sized envelope, which he handed to the terrified Penrose. 'Go on, open it.'

Penrose hesitated, swallowed hard and then tore open the envelope. Inside was an unsigned cheque. It was made out to him. The name at the bottom was The Trimble Group. The amount was one hundred thousand pounds. Penrose gaped at it.

O'Neill chuckled at the look on his face. 'That's just a very small taster. My employers have a proposal to make to you. If you're interested in hearing it, meet me in the bar of the King's Lodge Hotel at midday tomorrow. I'll take you to meet them. They've come up from London specially to make your acquaintance.'

'I don't understand. Who are your employers?'

'One step at a time, professor. If once you hear the proposal you're not interested in proceeding any further, there'll be no hard feelings. The cheque will be signed and the money's yours. But if you agree to come on board . . . well, let's just say the rewards will be considerable for someone of your qualities. My employers believe you're just the man for us. In fact, the only man for us.'

Penrose stared again at the cheque. This was no practical joke. It was real. Had to be. 'Come on board what?' he said. 'Just the man for what?'

O'Neill only smiled. 'See you tomorrow, Professor Lucas,' he said, and walked away towards the black Mercedes.

Chapter Sixteen

After he'd finished watching the video recording, Ben sadly poured himself a measure of Glenmorangie from the Arundels' drinks cabinet. So much for Simeon's enemies, he thought as he took a long sip. The ladies of the Little Denton Women's Institute probably posed more threat than some pumped-up egomaniac of a professor.

Ben had that feeling again that he was being watched. He looked down to see the dog peering curiously up at him with one ear cocked.

'I know what you're thinking, Scruffy,' he said out loud. 'What now? Good question.' The answer was clear. Ben gazed across the room at the picture of Jude Arundel that sat on the piano. He had to find him and tell him what had happened.

The Arundels' well-thumbed address book lay on the coffee table. Ben flipped through it and saw it was crammed with numbers, as if Simeon had listed half his parishioners in there. Under J he found a mobile number for Jude. He dialled the number on his phone, holding his breath and searching for the right words to say. How did you tell a complete stranger in the middle of the night that their family had been wiped out?

After two rings, Ben was put through to voicemail. He

left a brief message, not wanting to say too much and asking for Jude to call him back whenever he could. He sighed again and slumped into an armchair. Time passed. His mind whirled until mental exhaustion forced him to close his eyes and his chin sank towards his chest.

The landline phone jangled from across the room, startling him. He raced over to it and snatched up the receiver. 'Is that Jude?'

There was a pause on the crackly line, followed by a man's voice.

'Simeon? It's Wes.'

His accent was American, and he sounded agitated. Before Ben could say anything, he went on: 'Listen, I didn't reach Martha's yet. I'm calling from the road. They're onto me. I . . . damn it, this line's terrible. Hello? Can you hear me?'

'Simeon's not here,' Ben said.

'Who is this?' the voice asked sharply.

'I'm a friend,' Ben said.

There was a silence. Ben could sense the man's deep suspicion. 'Listen. Don't hang up. Let me help you. Who are "they"? What's going on?'

Click. The caller had hung up.

'Shit,' Ben said.

Moments later, he heard another ringtone coming from elsewhere in the house, muffled and only just audible. He ran out of the room, paused in the hallway and realised it was coming from upstairs. He followed the sound, taking the stairs two at a time. The ringtone was coming from behind one of the four glossy white-painted doors off the galleried first-floor landing.

Just as Ben opened the door, the phone stopped ringing. He stepped inside, and saw that it was Simeon and Michaela's bedroom. He was filled with sadness all over again at the sight of the unslept-in bed and the scent of Michaela's perfume that hung in the air.

Where had the ringtone been coming from? Ben suddenly recalled that just after they'd arrived at the Old Windmill, Simeon had complained about having left his mobile in his other trousers. Ben quickly spotted the folded-up pair draped over the back of a chair near the wardrobe. Sure enough, Simeon's BlackBerry was in the right hip pocket. Turning it on, Ben found there were two messages in the voicemail inbox.

The more recent of the two messages had finished recording only moments before, by whoever had just called. Ben listened, and recognised the American accent of the man he'd spoken to minutes earlier. He sounded even more anxious and agitated.

'Simeon? Wes. What's going on? I just called your home and some guy answered saying you're not there. I need to know you're okay. Listen, these people tried again a few hours ago. It was just luck I got away. They want the sword real bad, whoever they are. Soon as I get to Martha's and make sure it's safe there, I'll call you back. Take care, buddy – and I mean take care.'

Ben tried calling back on the BlackBerry, but got no reply. He replayed the message twice, then saved it. It seemed certain to him that the sword the American had mentioned was the same one Simeon's book was about. The 'sacred sword' wasn't just a research topic, then, but a real, actual item that was still obviously in the possession of this Wes.

Was it a historic relic of some kind? A ceremonial artefact? What special significance did it have that was making it the target of such dangerous people?

'It's huge,' Simeon had said to Ben in the car. 'It's terrifyingly huge.'

Just one thing was clear. Whatever the sword was, Simeon and his colleagues had somehow managed to get in way out of their depth.

Ben moved on to the next message in the BlackBerry's inbox. It was one that Simeon had listened to and saved, recorded late on the evening of December 2nd. Ben frowned to himself when he heard who it was from.

'Simeon – it's me, Fabrice. The thing I told you about; I am sure it is happening again. Just now, tonight. I think someone is after me. Please call me as soon as you can.'

Ben sat on the edge of the bed and held Simeon's phone tightly in his fist.

What he'd just heard was not the last message of a guilt-tormented man about to throw himself off a bridge.

Chapter Seventeen

After calling Simeon's mobile and leaving his message, Wesley Holland left the public phone booth and carried his case to the nearby diner, shivering in the late-night cold.

Wesley had been truly sorry to part company with Maynard, the gap-toothed truck driver from Vermont who'd saved his skin by showing up miraculously outside the motel several hundred miles back. Maynard had a drop-off to make further up the road, after which his route would take him northwards into New Hampshire and way off course for Wesley. The little roadside diner had seemed a good enough place to get off. So here he was, stuck in the middle of the night on the edge of some backwater town whose name he didn't know, without transport and still an awfully long way from his destination.

Walking into the warmth and the smell of food and coffee, Wesley found the diner almost deserted. A wolfish-looking guy in a denim jacket and a dirty red-and-white baseball cap was slumped half asleep in one corner near the door. A desultory waitress was clattering cutlery behind the counter. A TV blared from a bracket on the wall. Despite the alluring aroma of frying bacon that hung in the air, Wesley couldn't face the thought of eating. He sat in a booth by the window and pushed the case under the table by his feet. Rubbing a hole in the condensation on the glass, he peered nervously out into the darkness. The lights of a car skimmed by on the highway. He watched it, half expecting it to veer into the diner parking lot and skid to a halt, the man in the tan leather coat and his associates spilling out of it with their guns blazing.

But the car kept going. Wesley let out a long breath.

During the hours in Maynard's truck, he'd racked his brains trying to figure out how the hell his pursuers had managed to find him at the motel, and after much deliberation he'd arrived at the only possible conclusion.

He'd used his AmEx card to pay for the room. A connection had been made. Someone had had access to that information and used it to pinpoint his location instantly. The man in the brown coat and his gang must have been on standby, just waiting for their orders to come and get him.

The thought troubled Wesley immensely, because it meant that these people weren't just anybody. Who had the power and reach to track a person via their credit card payments? He'd always believed only government agencies could do that – FBI, CIA, those kinds of folks. Just who in God's name was after him? Once again, he wondered whether this sword was really worth all this. But it was too late regretting it now. He just had to keep moving and pray they didn't catch up with him again.

Pretending to read the laminated menu card on the table in front of him, Wesley cast a paranoid glance at the solitary guy in the corner booth near the door. He didn't look like an agent, dressed like that. But then, he wouldn't. Wesley kept watching him. The guy yawned, took a slug of coffee, then took off his baseball cap and scratched at his greasy hair. He laid the cap down on the table and lowered his head onto his arms, appearing to go to sleep.

Wesley decided he might not be an undercover agent after all.

After a few more minutes of clattering plates, the waitress eventually threaded her way through the empty tables to take Wesley's order, throwing a disapproving look at the sleeping man in the corner. 'What can I do for you, honey?' she said with a tired smile as she took out a pad.

'Just coffee,' Wesley said. 'Oh, miss,' he added as she was about to turn away. 'Would you mind telling me where I am?'

The waitress balked momentarily at the odd question, then told him a name he'd never even heard of before. From her smile, he guessed not too many of the customers called her 'miss'. 'You know where I could get a ride out of here?' he said.

'Where you heading, honey?' she asked him.

'East, towards Boston.'

'Buses come by here every few hours,' she said, motioning at the dark window. 'Station's over that way. Guess you might try there. Say—' She narrowed her eyes and peered at Wesley curiously. 'You sure you haven't been in here before?'

'I don't think so,' he said blankly. 'I'm not from around here.'

'You sure look familiar.'

With a flash of panic, Wesley suddenly heard someone say his name from across the other side of the diner. He was about to make a dash for it when he realised it was coming from the TV. He cut short a gasp. His face was plastered over the screen! With merciful speed, the picture cut to an image of the Whitworth mansion surrounded by police cars and ambulances. He caught a snatch of the newscaster's commentary: '*Attorneys representing the billionaire philanthropist, whose whereabouts are still unknown, are refusing to comment at this time . . .*'

'A lot of people tell me that,' he said to the waitress, forcing a grin. 'Guess I just have that kind of face.' And how many times had that face of his appeared on air over the last few hours? he thought. This was no good at all. Someone was bound to recognise him.

When his coffee came, he gulped down as much of it as he could, then left the diner in a hurry. The guy in the corner near the door was still slumped on his table, snoring, his baseball cap at his elbow. It was frayed and grimy, with a label that said 'Hoyt Archery'. Wesley glanced back towards the counter, then furtively grabbed the cap and scurried away into the cold night.

The temperature outside seemed to have dropped several more degrees. Wesley jammed the cap on his head, pulled the peak down low over his face and glanced around him. Wherever the bus station might be, it was nowhere in sight. A smattering of traffic was passing by in both directions. He thought about trying to hitch another ride.

Another possible option was the used car lot the other side of a mesh fence. He had just about enough cash on him to get something from there, if he hung around here freezing his ass off till morning. But he worried about the paperwork he'd have to fill in to buy a car. Could his seemingly omniscient pursuers trace him from that, too? Moreover, spending most of his cash would leave him short of ready money, now that his credit card was apparently unusable. If the AmEx could give him away so easily, then an ATM cash withdrawal surely would too. Until he reached the safety of Martha's, every step of the way there was a risk that they'd find him.

They. *They.* It sounded crazy.

But it wasn't crazy. He remembered the old saying: *It's not paranoia if they're really after you.*

'Simeon, my friend, we're in deep shit,' he muttered to himself.

A bus roared by, dimly lit up inside and carrying a smattering of passengers. Wesley watched it go, then pulled the cap down even further to hide his face and set off up the road, case in hand, looking for the nearby station.

Chapter Eighteen

The day after that first meeting with the mysterious Rex O'Neill, Penrose had made sure he was available to make the rendezvous in the bar of the King's Lodge Hotel in Durham, to be taken to meet the man's even more mysterious employers.

The October rain had cleared to make way for a sunny autumnal day. Penrose had arrived at the hotel ten minutes early, clutching the unsigned hundred-thousand-pound cheque in his pocket. O'Neill was already waiting for him. He greeted Penrose with a nod and led him to a car. This time, the gleaming black Mercedes – not the same one, Penrose observed – had a driver. The car sped out of the city to an ultra-exclusive country club that Penrose had heard of but never been to. The clubhouse was a magnificent stately home overlooking the golf course.

O'Neill stayed in the car. Severely baffled and intimidated, Penrose was led inside the opulent clubhouse by two very large fellows in dark suits, who silently escorted him to a conference room. There, seated around a long table, five very serious men were waiting for Penrose.

That had been his first encounter with the senior members of the obscure organisation calling itself the Trimble Group. They were all much older than Penrose, mostly well into their sixties. They had been extremely welcoming and full of praise for his excellent, important book. He'd been offered drinks, which he politely refused as he never touched alcohol. Then, over a long and lavish lunch that Penrose was too nervous to do more than peck at, they'd outlined their proposal to him.

As Penrose now discovered, he had been unanimously picked from a very short list of potential candidates. The group's brief was simple, and it required someone with particular qualities. Motivation was key; as was intelligence, as was secrecy.

As the meeting went on, Penrose had to pinch himself under the table to make sure he wasn't dreaming. He was bursting with questions, but so excited he could barely voice them. What he was hearing seemed utterly incredible. It seemed even more incredible when they revealed to him the size of the budget allocated to the operation they wanted him – him! – to personally lead and oversee. Penrose had to grip the edge of the table to stop himself from keeling over.

There would be an initial injection of twelve million pounds. The account had in fact already been opened and the funds put on standby, just waiting for his signature on the contract, whereupon the wire transfer would take place instantly, enabling him to access the money however he liked, in cash if desired. The twelve million was, he was assured, just a fraction of what was to come if the operation proved successful.

The deal terms were breathtakingly straightforward. Penrose would have a free hand to run the operation as he saw fit, with Rex O'Neill assigned to him as his assistant, liaising with the Trimble Group and acting as a general aide and campaign manager.

Penrose's busy academic schedule might be a concern, they warned. Penrose hastily assured them that it wasn't. He was already mentally drafting his letter of resignation to Durham University. He'd happily relocate to wherever they wanted, he told them. They laughed. 'You can run your show from wherever you like,' one of them said, and the others didn't contradict him. Travel would be no problem. Penrose would have a fleet of cars at his disposal, as well as aircraft, including a Learjet allocated exclusively to him and on permanent standby to fly wherever he pleased.

One other thing, they reminded him gravely. He must never tell a living soul about this meeting or the nature of what had been discussed. To reveal anything of the Trimble Group, he was informed, would cause irreversible complications. This could not be stressed enough. All eyes were on him as the point was pressed home.

Penrose understood and accepted everything. He couldn't sign on the line fast enough.

When he left the meeting, Penrose's head was spinning so badly he could barely walk back to the Mercedes.

Yet it was all true: over the next few days everything happened exactly as the Trimble Group had said it would. Inside of a week, Penrose had quit his job, sold his flat, and was moving to his new headquarters. He chose the beautiful island of Capri, off Italy's Sorrentine Peninsula, once the abode of Roman emperors. With the newfound millions at his disposal he purchased himself the five-acre estate, complete with magnificent clifftop villa and assorted staff quarters, that was to double as his home and operational headquarters.

Nobody tried to stop him. This was really happening. It seemed that he could do whatever he wanted.

Penrose set about his new purpose in life with a ferocious

energy that amazed even him. The Trimble Group could not have picked a better man for the job. Penrose Lucas had arrived, and he was damned if he wouldn't show them what he was made of. Ten years, he thought. Give me ten years and I'll become the most important man in history.

He'd known exactly where to begin his quest, with a score he'd been itching to settle for quite some time. He issued orders to O'Neill, which were duly passed down the line and carried out with extreme efficiency by his wonderful new friends. Within less than twenty-four hours, the first phone tap was in place and Penrose was ready to start digging up whatever dirt he could find on the Reverend Simeon Arundel.

But when they first began to listen in on the vicar's secretive conversations with his overseas associates, Penrose realised what he'd accidentally stumbled upon. It was momentous. Earth-shattering. It had to be stopped.

His time had truly come.

Chapter Nineteen

With the sunrise, Ben tried three more times to contact Jude Arundel on his mobile, and three times was put through to the same voicemail service. The first two calls, he left another message asking him to call back, stressing how important it was. The third time, frustrated, he gave up and went back to trying to figure out the pieces of the puzzle.

He put together what he knew so far: Simeon Arundel and Fabrice Lalique had been working together on the sacred sword project, whatever that was. So much was clear, and it explained why they'd been in close contact for a prolonged period of time and appeared to have travelled to Israel together eighteen months ago. It also seemed that a third man had been involved in the project, an American called Wes, who was very probably the 'expert' whom Simeon had been to visit in the States. Expert at what?

Three men. Three colleagues. One was running scared after 'something' had happened. Another was dead in a suicide that no longer seemed to quite add up. Another had been killed in a car crash involving a mysterious third party and a few too many suspicious circumstances, after which his home had been broken into by heavily armed thieves with a very clear and serious purpose.

Ben thought back to the group photo that had been taken

in Israel. If Wes was one of the men in the picture, he was either the burly olive-skinned man on the left or the fit-looking man in his sixties, standing between Simeon and Fabrice Lalique. Ben reckoned on the latter. Then who was the fourth man in the picture? He looked as though he might be Israeli, and was obviously connected to this as well.

And now a fifth player had apparently just entered the game: Martha. Wes had said he was going to her place to make sure the sword was safe, so she was obviously helping them to hide it. There was no woman in the photo, so maybe she wasn't part of the core group. Or maybe Martha had been the one who took the picture.

Ben paced up and down the length of the living room for a long time, churning over the clues and all too aware that they so far amounted to very little. But he had more things to worry about. The news of Simeon and Michaela's deaths would spread fast. The rest of the family would have been informed by now, and soon the whole grim aftermath would roll into action.

If only he could find Jude.

Ben knew the number by heart now. He tried one more time – still no reply. But now another option occurred to him. He flipped through the Arundels' address book to the letter N, scanned down the list of names and found the number he was looking for.

After four rings, a woman's voice replied, 'Petra Norrington.'

Ben had only wanted to know that she was at home. He hung up the phone. Looking her up in the local telephone directory, he found her address listed. She lived close by in Greater Denton.

'We're going for a drive, Scruff,' he said, and led the dog out to the Land Rover. Scruffy urinated on the rear wheel and jumped in.

As Ben headed under the leaden sky towards Greater Denton, the local radio news came on.

'*Church parishes across west Oxfordshire are in mourning today following the tragic deaths of the Reverend Simeon Arundel and his wife Michaela in a road accident. The Reverend Arundel was a popular figure within the church community. The fatal incident took place on the B4429 outside the village of Little Denton. Official cause of death is to be verified pending the Coroner's report. A church spokesman . . .*'

Ben turned it off.

Petra Norrington lived in a large and expensive-looking thatched cottage at the edge of the village. A Siamese cat hissed at Ben from the front step and slunk away into the frosty bushes. Answering the door, Petra looked Ben disdainfully up and down for a moment before recognition showed on her face. She was wearing the same string of pearls she'd had on the night before, and her hair was hairsprayed into a peroxide blond helmet that looked as if it could withstand a tornado. 'Oh – we met last night at the restaurant, didn't we? You're Mr, er . . .'

'Hope. Please call me Ben. May I come in?'

'I can't believe he's dead,' Petra said as she led Ben inside the spacious cottage and into a chintzy sitting room. 'It's so awful. I've just got off the phone with the ladies' badminton club secretary. Everyone's just devastated.' She sighed and shook her head sadly – though not too sadly. Her Siamese being run over might have upset her more.

'They both are, Mrs Norrington,' Ben said.

Petra nodded hesitantly, and Ben got the impression that she was considerably less concerned about Michaela's death than about Simeon's.

'How can I help you, Mr Hope? Ben?'

'I came to ask you if you knew how I could find Jude,'

Ben said. 'You seemed to know about the place in Cornwall where he hangs out with his friend Robbie.'

Petra nodded, a flicker of disapproval showing. 'That Robbie. His parents' holiday place, apparently. It's out in the middle of the moors. Somewhere not far from Bodmin, I think. I don't know exactly where.'

'I see,' Ben said, feeling his heart sink.

'But Sophie would be able to tell you.'

'Sophie?'

'My daughter.' Petra arched a carefully plucked eyebrow. 'She and Jude went out together – only for a short time, mind you. He took her to the farm once, for a weekend. From what she told me, it's a dreadful place. A whole gang of them hang out there, drinking themselves stupid and God knows what else. I can't imagine what that boy—'

'Is Sophie here?' Ben cut in.

'She's spending Christmas with her father. He lives in Spain.'

'Could I have his number?'

Petra shook her head emphatically. 'Dominic and I haven't spoken for over five years.'

'What about Sophie's mobile number?'

She frowned.

'It's very important,' he said. 'Jude needs to be contacted.'

Petra nodded and went over to a little writing desk in the corner, where her phone lay next to a glasses case, a pile of mail and the small camera Ben remembered she'd been waving around in the restaurant the night before. Petra took her time putting on her glasses, then picked up the phone and pressed a speed-dial key. After a moment she said in a sugary tone: 'Sophie, darling, it's Mummy. Could you call me when you've got a moment? Byeee.'

Ben looked at her. 'That didn't exactly convey a sense of urgency.'

Petra returned his look icily. 'As if he'll be concerned about his parents, anyway,' she muttered. 'That young man is only interested in himself.'

Ben was about to reply, then thought better of it and changed the subject. 'There's something else I need from you,' he said. 'The registration number of the BMW you backed into last night in the Old Windmill car park.'

Petra blinked. 'Whatever for?'

'I haven't got time to explain. I'd appreciate your help.'

'Er . . . are you from the police, Mr Hope? Because if not, I frankly don't see—'

She was interrupted by the doorbell. A UPS delivery van had pulled up in the street outside.

'My Harrods Christmas hamper! At last!' Petra gasped, and rushed out of the room to answer the door. She made a big fuss of signing for the parcel. The delivery man had to lug it inside the hallway for her, amid her cries of 'Oh, be careful! You'll scratch the parquet!'

Meanwhile, Ben was looking up Sophie Norrington's number from the phone and scribbling it on the back of his hand with a biro from the writing desk. Sifting quickly through the pile of mail on top of the desk, he found a sealed, unstamped envelope addressed to a motor insurance company and slipped it into his pocket.

Petra had almost finished harrying the delivery driver in the hallway. Ben looked at the little camera lying on the desk. His mind raced back to replay the scene from the restaurant. When Petra Norrington had jumped up from the noisy ladies' badminton club party table to photograph them all, snapping away left and right, she'd had her back more or less to Ben, which meant she'd been facing roughly in the direction of the archway leading through to the bar area.

The same bar area where the owner of the BMW had

been sitting quietly, unnoticed until the incident with the headlight. Was it possible that he might have been captured by chance in one of her shots?

The guy might not be connected to the crash at all. Maybe he was just some surly bastard who'd been miles away when the Lotus had gone over the bridge. Maybe this was a blind alley. Maybe not.

Ben didn't have long to decide. Petra had shut the front door and was heading back towards the sitting room. He flipped open the side port of the camera, slid out its memory card and pocketed that too.

'Anyway, Mr Hope,' she announced archly as she walked back into the room. 'I'm afraid my private affairs are none of your business.'

Ben gave her his warmest smile. 'You're quite right, Mrs Norrington. I'll be on my way. Thanks for your help, and Merry Christmas to you.'

Chapter Twenty

The meeting had been set in late November, after several weeks of furtive phone calls to a hard-found and extremely cagey contact in London who went by the name of Mick. Palms had been greased, generously and diplomatically, in return for which Penrose Lucas had eventually been given a non-negotiable time and place, as well as a serious warning that he should come alone and prepared. Prepared meant 'bring money'.

Penrose had flown to London in the Lear and hurriedly made his way to his appointment, carrying a briefcase. The location had been a crowded pub in the East End. The man he'd come to see had been sitting at a window alcove table in the corner, nursing a pint of lager and a frown. He was a Londoner, in his mid-to-late thirties, tall and lean, and under his tight-fitting jumper was the hardened physique of a man who worked out seriously and ran ten miles a day. His receding hairline was razored to a stubble and his piercing grey eyes didn't once flinch away from Penrose from the moment he sat down. His voice was soft, yet managed to be infinitely menacing at the same time. The man's name was Steve Cutter, and he was the head of a firm called Cutter Security.

Penrose hadn't come all this way to talk about fitting

alarm systems and fancy locks to his new villa in Capri. Cutter was a private military contractor.

The fact was that Penrose could have approached any one of a hundred suit-and-tie corporate PMC outfits in expensive offices throughout London, but he'd chosen to wade through murkier waters in order to secure the services of someone better suited to his purposes. As far as reputations went, Cutter's outfit was somewhere near the lower end of the spectrum, though not because they weren't proficient at what they did. The elusive Mick had told Penrose enough about Cutter's recent involvements to know that he was exactly the kind of hard-bitten professional mercenary he wanted to engage.

Penrose had been terrified of Cutter at first, and even more terrified of the two scowling and deeply intimidating associates who'd appeared from nowhere, each carrying a pint of beer, and sat down either side of him at the table. It was clear that he was no longer dealing with the likes of the deadbeats from Hardstaff & Baldwin in Darlington.

'This gentleman here is Mr Grinnall,' Cutter said, motioning to his murderous-looking colleague on Penrose's right, the one in the tan leather coat. 'And this is Mr Mills' – pointing at the other, who was tattooed all the way up to his jawline, all the way down to his wrists and probably everywhere else as well. 'Now I gather you have some business to discuss, so let's get started.'

Speaking low so that nobody else could hear him over the noise of the jukebox and the chatter that filled the crowded pub, Penrose had outlined his requirements. They were twofold. First, he wanted personal protection. A suitably armed team on guard, twenty-four hours a day, at his villa in Capri. Second, and most importantly, he needed men of certain skills and experience to help carry out a set of tasks. The job would involve international travel, Penrose explained. All expenses paid, naturally. It would also involve a degree of criminal activity and violence, and the execution of a complex plan which had to be carried out exactly to order.

If any of that worried Cutter, he didn't show it. He studied the photographs and list of names Penrose had slid between the beer mats and pint glasses on the table. 'Who are these men?' he asked tersely. Grinnall and Mills had yet to utter a word. Their faces were blank. Their thick arms lay crossed over their chests, as though waiting to reach out and snap Penrose's neck like a celery stick at the slightest signal from their boss.

'They're people who have something I want,' Penrose said.

'These two are fucking priests.'

'Strictly speaking, only that one is,' Penrose had said, pointing at the picture of Fabrice Lalique. 'The other is a Church of England vicar.' You had to know your enemy.

'And what about this old fart here?'

'He's an American. A very rich American.'

'Rich as in bodyguards with fucking Uzis?'

'He shouldn't be too hard to get to. I'll leave that part to you.'

Cutter had carefully scrutinised the three targets. 'What are we talking about here? Money? Drugs?'

'Neither.'

'Then what? Something they took from you?' Cutter fired questions like bullets.

'Not exactly. Let's just say I don't want these people to have it in their possession.'

'Cut the bullshit. What is it?'

They'll have to know sooner or later, Penrose had thought. 'All right. It's a sword.'

Grinnall and Mills had looked tickled. Cutter hadn't. 'A sword.'

'That's right.'

'You can buy all the fucking swords you want off the internet, mate.'

'Not this one.'

'So what's so special about it?'

'Not your concern.'

'What does it look like?'

Penrose had had to admit his ignorance on that score. 'I've never seen it,' he said irritably. What he had done, however, was hire a very expensive and discreet expert consultant to draft up a computer-generated impression of its possible appearance, based on its historical period and provenance. He showed the colour print to Cutter.

'If you've never seen it, how can you be so sure these blokes have it?'

'Surveillance. Wiretaps. The usual,' Penrose had replied with brilliantly feigned nonchalance. He felt a rush of empowerment at the words. In truth, he had no idea how the phone taps were done. That was Rex O'Neill's department, together with the nameless background figures feeding back the information from some invisible source. All Penrose had done was point them in the right direction, and the rest happened by magic.

'Fair enough. So we're looking at three men in three different countries. Only one of them can have it. Which, the Yank or one of the priests?'

'Either him or him,' Penrose had replied, pointing at the pictures of Arundel and the American. From the tapped phone conversations he was certain the Frenchman was playing second fiddle to the others. 'But we start with him,' he'd added, pointing at the photo of Lalique. 'He goes first. It's all in the plan.'

138

For several silent minutes, Cutter examined the plan of action Penrose had brought to show him. It was like no other job he and his boys had ever been hired for before. His face remained completely impassive as he took in the details, but Penrose knew that nobody could fail to be impressed with the thoroughness of his preparation.

There was no mention anywhere of Penrose's deeper reasons for wanting things carried out the way he did. It was a simple set of instructions. The rest was above Cutter's pay grade.

And pay grades were the next item to discuss. 'This is going to cost you a great deal of money,' Cutter said when he'd surveyed the plan.

'Money's the easy part,' Penrose had said. It was a line he'd taken from a movie. He'd nudged the briefcase towards Cutter under the table. Now he was feeling like a real gangster. The power was rushing to his head and making him feel giddy.

Cutter had opened the case. Not a flicker of expression as his grey eyes scanned the contents. He shut the lid, laid the case beside him on the seat, and thirty grand had changed hands just like that. 'Call it a retainer,' Cutter said.

No complaints from Penrose. 'Mick says you work for six hundred a day.'

'Six-fifty. In cash. For each man.'

Penrose hadn't tried to haggle over the cost. 'I'll need at least a dozen men, all personally vouched for by you. I assume you can provide the necessary hardware.'

'For that price we come fully tooled up. Transportation is your responsibility.'

'Not an issue. You'll have the use of a long-range private jet, as well as any vehicles you require.'

'That sounds acceptable. What about accommodation?'

'Luxurious. I don't think you'll be disappointed. Or in the additional, ah, benefits that will be available.' Penrose had already given some thought to the benefits. He wanted his personal army to be loyally devoted to him. 'If things work out, I'll be in a position to offer you a longer-term contract. This job is just the beginning.'

A flicker of reaction in Cutter's eyes. Even he couldn't stay completely deadpan in the face of a deal like this.

'One more thing. This has to be in motion as soon as possible. Would your outfit be available to start immediately?'

'I think we just became available,' Cutter had said.

Chapter Twenty-One

On the drive back from Petra Norrington's place to the vicarage, Ben pulled into a lay-by, fished out his phone and punched in the number of Sophie Norrington's mobile. When she didn't pick up, he left her a brief message, stressing the need for her to call him back.

The next number he dialled got an instant response. He should have known Darcey Kane's phone would never be switched off. It wasn't in her character.

'Hello, Commander Kane,' he said.

'Ben Hope,' she chuckled, purring with pleasure. 'I knew you'd finally cave in to temptation and call me.'

'It's been the struggle of my life,' he said.

'You're only human.'

'So how are things, Darcey? Have they thrown you out of SOCA yet?' As he spoke, he ripped open the envelope he'd taken from Petra Norrington's desk and pulled out the letter she'd written to the motor insurance company. He nodded to himself. It had all the details he needed.

'I'm right here at my desk,' Darcey said. 'Thinking of you.'

'I can just picture you sitting there.'

She laughed. 'Like what you see?'

'The shoulder holster really matches the colour of your eyes.'

'You flatterer. Still hanging about in the arse end of nowhere?'

'Actually, I'm in the UK. Right now I'm sitting in a lay-by somewhere in Oxfordshire. Calling to ask if you could maybe do me a favour.'

'Interesting. You mean like cancelling all my prior engagements to make way for dinner tonight? My place, eight o'clock?'

'London's a little out of my way at the minute, Darcey. I mean more like running a vehicle registration check for me.'

'I knew it was too good to be true. What a complete and utter fuckhead you are.'

For the first time since the crash, Ben was able to smile. 'You always were the queen of the sweet-talkers.'

'You do realise that asking a senior SOCA agent to run a registration check is like deploying the SAS to get a stuck kitten out of a tree?'

'How about as a friend, then?'

'Not to mention it's illegal. Are you trying to get a girl into trouble?'

'I wouldn't dream of it.'

'That's what I'm afraid of.' She paused. 'All right. But I'll make you pay dearly.'

'I wouldn't expect any less from you,' he said. 'Ready to take down this number? We're looking at a blue BMW 740 saloon.' He read out the registration from the insurance letter.

'Copy that.' Darcey read it back to him.

'How fast can you turn it around for me, Darce?'

'I have some bad guys to go after first.'

'That shouldn't take you long.'

'What's this about, anyway?'

'Don't worry about it.'

142

'Who else is going to worry about you, Hope? Give me an hour or so. I'll see what I can do.'

Back at the vicarage, Ben slipped the camera memory card into Simeon's laptop, clicked open the file and watched as thumbnail images of all eighty-seven of Petra Norrington's photographs filled the screen. He scanned quickly down until he came to the shots she'd taken inside the restaurant. Most of them were useless to him, showing only the walls and decor as background – but the very last image he examined had been taken at the right angle to give a clear view through into the bar area.

And there he was, the BMW owner, sitting alone on a stool with a soft drink in front of him.

Ben zoomed in to take a closer look. It was a good-quality image, sharp enough to make out the man's features in detail. He was in his thirties, dark-haired, with a long, lean face and a scar over one eye. Though it was hard to judge from the angle of the shot, he seemed to be sitting facing directly towards the table where Ben had been dining with the Arundels.

That in itself proved nothing, but scrutinising the guy's features and the sharp expression in his eyes as he gazed fixedly at a point off-camera, Ben was certain that he'd deliberately positioned himself to be able to watch Simeon and Michaela. Which strongly suggested he'd also followed them to the Old Windmill.

Ben ran back through the chain of events. The stranger arrives in his BMW, plants himself in the bar and starts paying unusual attention to the threesome in the restaurant. Next, Petra Norrington leaves and gets in her car, reverses it into the front of the BMW, damaging a headlight. There's a dispute that the stranger is very keen to play down. Shortly afterwards, he slips away, so that by the time the Arundels and their guest have paid for the meal and are setting off for home, the BMW has already gone. Minutes later, a large saloon car with a damaged headlight is seen racing away from the scene of the fatal crash.

Ben couldn't ignore his gut instinct: that the guy in the picture was the same man who had forced Simeon and Michaela's car off the road and caused their deaths. He might even have been one of the two who'd broken inside the vicarage later that night. If not, he was their accomplice.

The real question was, who were they all working for?

Ben used the laser printer in Simeon's study to run off a copy of the zoomed-in portion of the photo, which he folded and slipped into the inside pocket of his jacket. He tried Jude's number one more time. 'Come on, answer the bloody thing,' he muttered as it rang. No reply.

There was only one thing for it. He needed to get to Cornwall, and quickly. He scooped Michaela's Mazda keys from the little stand in the entrance hall, went outside into the cold and walked along the ornamental flagstone path around the side of the vicarage to the double garage. A plastic remote attached to the Mazda key fob activated the doors. They whirred open, revealing the sleek shape of the MX-5 Roadster.

Ben nodded to himself. It wasn't a Maserati but it would carry him the two hundred or so miles to the southwestern-most tip of England faster than Le Crock could ever dream of.

He went back inside and started gathering up his things. Simeon's laptop was going to have to come along. Even if the information inside was inaccessible to him, there was no way he could leave it here at the house in case the raiders decided to come back for it. Deciding that the shotgun was coming too, he folded up the stock and stuffed the shortened weapon into his bag. The dog eyed him suspiciously from a few feet away.

'I suppose you want to come along as well,' Ben said. 'Where else are you going to go?'

He was heading outside with the bag over his shoulder and the dog at his heels when his mobile rang. It was Darcey Kane.

'How are your bad guys?' Ben asked her.

'Shitting in their pants,' she replied. 'How are yours?'

'What makes you think I'm after any?'

'Hmm. I have a feeling you're up to something.'

'I don't know where you'd get a notion like that. Did you manage to trace that number for me?'

'Of course. But you won't be pleased. The registration's a fake. No record of it exists.'

'You double-checked?'

'Quadruple. You know me.'

'Damn,' he muttered under his breath. But now he knew for sure.

'Come on, Hope. Spill it. You're definitely up to something, aren't you?'

'Absolutely not,' Ben said, leaning inside the car to stash his illegal cargo behind the driver's seat. It would be five years in prison, minimum, if any cop saw what was inside the bag.

'Then you're free for dinner tonight. How about Italian instead? It'll be just like Rome.'

'Maybe some other time, Darcey. Thanks for the info.'

'Bastard.'

Chapter Twenty-Two

According to Rex O'Neill's information, the Lear had touched down at the airfield in Naples forty-two minutes ago. The single-engined Cessna, one of the selection of light aircraft provided by the Trimble Group for them to shuttle men and material between Capri and the mainland, should be arriving shortly. Two cars sat parked at the side of the private airstrip, a Mercedes limousine and a high-performance Audi, both black. Penrose Lucas insisted on black for his whole fleet of vehicles, and the Trimble Group were happy to indulge him.

Inside the Mercedes, soundproof glass screened the driver off from the elongated passenger compartment in which sat Penrose and Rex O'Neill. Penrose stretched out his legs. He didn't just sit on the plush limo seat, he lounged on it, sprawled across it. The more contact he made with the cool, soft leather, the more kingly and omnipotent it made him feel.

He'd been buzzing with nervous anticipation all morning since seeing the online news report confirming what he'd known in advance was going to happen: the untimely and tragic demise of the Reverend Simeon Arundel and his beloved wife the previous evening in England. The news had almost completely allayed the extreme displeasure that had spoiled Penrose's day yesterday, knowing that Wesley Holland had somehow managed to slip through the fingers of the team sent out to America to get him. Never mind. Holland's escape was a temporary hitch. It wasn't the end of the world.

And at this moment Penrose was in an even more forgiving mood as he anticipated with relish the arrival of his team from England. He couldn't wait to see the items retrieved from the target's home.

First Lalique; Penrose was especially pleased with the way that had gone. Then Arundel. All in all, the plan was moving along beautifully. Before long they'd have Holland too, and all three of them would be out of the way. Penrose would finally get his hands on this damned troublesome sword and would have the pleasure of personally seeing it melted down, eradicated before the world even took notice of it. Then he'd be able to forge ahead with his greater plans. The Trimble Group would not be disappointed.

Rex O'Neill was perched on the edge of the seat opposite, silent and tight-lipped as he observed his nominal boss and ruminated over his unspoken misgivings about the man. O'Neill had been opposed from the start to the way the Lalique situation had been handled, and he was increasingly unhappy about the direction things were taking. Lucas was moving far too fast. O'Neill could say nothing. He had his orders, and his job to do.

There were other worries, too. As part of O'Neill's role as intermediary between Lucas and the Trimble Group, it had been reported to him that morning that the phone surveillance team had intercepted a long distance phone call from Wesley Holland to the landline at the Little Denton vicarage during the early hours. Somebody had answered the phone there, meaning that the vicarage had not, as they'd previously thought, been empty last night. Somebody was staying there – but who?

'And how is Megan?' Penrose asked suddenly, with an unpleasant little smile. It was unusual for him to make any kind of small talk, and even more unusual for him to express interest in his assistant's home life. O'Neill put it down to his uncharacteristically happy state of mind this morning.

'She's fine, thank you. A little nervous as the weeks go by. It's our first, so . . .' O'Neill shrugged.

Penrose felt slightly disgusted, but covered it well. 'When is the child due?'

'Not for another three and a half months.'

'You must be looking forward to it,' Penrose said.

'We both are, very much.' O'Neill smiled, visualising his wife's face and wondering what she was doing right now. He so wished he could be with her at home in London. It was still hard to believe that such a beautiful and smart young woman could have seen anything in a man like him, fifteen years her senior and obsessively glued to a job he could tell her so little about. The eleven months of their marriage had been the happiest of his life. He was determined to spend more time with her, but knew that his long-overdue leave wouldn't be granted him for a good while yet.

His thoughts were interrupted by the buzz of the Cessna coming in to land. 'They're here,' he said to Penrose, who sprawled up out of his seat with a jerk, threw open the car door and clambered eagerly out.

The Cessna came down over the trees. It touched down with a yelp of tyres and taxied to a halt a few metres from the waiting vehicles. Beaming, Penrose marched across the runway to meet its occupants. The hatch opened and Steve Cutter emerged, followed by Dave Mills.

Penrose's face fell when he saw the state of them. Cutter

148

had a thick wad of dressing taped to his forehead and an ugly split and swollen lip. Mills's cheek was bruised and scuffed from jaw to eye and he was moving stiffly. Neither displayed the body language of men returning victorious from a successful operation. Cutter's expression confirmed it.

Penrose's happiness evaporated instantly. A drumming pulse started up in his left temple that he knew would quickly grow into a painful migraine. 'What happened?' he blurted in the short moments of numb surprise before the fury took him.

'We didn't get the gear,' Cutter said miserably.

'So I gathered,' Penrose growled. The first pang of the headache made his left eye twitch. 'Where are all the others?' The plan had been specific. Two men to raid the vicarage, the rest of them to stand guard nearby.

'Still in position,' Cutter said.

The Cessna pilot was turning the aircraft round for takeoff, and the rising engine note lanced through Penrose's head. 'We'll talk back at the villa,' he barked, then turned on his heel and marched back to his limousine, white-faced with anger, as Cutter and Mills climbed painfully into the Audi.

'*One man?*' Penrose screamed when Cutter had explained what had happened at the Little Denton vicarage. The two mercenaries were standing by the desk, looking sullen. Rex O'Neill was by the window, hands clasped behind his back and remaining silent. Penrose paced dementedly. The migraine was in full force now and the painkillers weren't working. He needed something stronger.

'Just what I said,' Cutter repeated. 'One man.'

Penrose stopped pacing and glowered at him. 'So it wasn't the A-Team who stopped you carrying out your job,' he bellowed, waving his arms. 'It wasn't the U.S. bloody Marines.'

'No.'

'How could you possibly screw this up? What was he doing there?'

'He just appeared. Like he was staying in the place.'

'A visitor?'

'We were told the house would be empty,' Cutter said.

O'Neill listened quietly in the background. Whoever had foiled the robbery had also been there to take the phone call from Wesley Holland some time later. Who was this person?

Penrose's shouts dropped to a hoarse rasp as he went on harrying Steve Cutter. 'Maybe I'm the only one around here who can see straight. Maybe it's time for a little refresher session. Remind me. Are you and I in business together?'

Cutter sighed. 'Yes.'

'And in this business relationship, what role would you say I play?'

'You're the boss,' Cutter said.

'Meaning what?'

'You're in charge. You tell us what to do.'

'That's right!' Penrose shouted. 'I'm in charge. Why? Because I'm the one with the ideas. I'm the one who's worked out this whole plan. This very, very *important* plan. And I'm the one with all the money.'

Cutter made no reply.

But Penrose was far from finished. 'Now, remind me: who exactly in this business relationship are you?'

Cutter shifted from foot to foot, starting to get restless. He needed to remind himself of the perks of this job. More cash than he and his team had ever pulled in before. The poshest quarters they'd ever been put up in, by far. All the whisky and beer and wine they could guzzle, and all the whores from the mainland they could sate themselves with. If it hadn't been for those minor benefits, he'd have smashed this little upstart's

150

teeth down his throat right where he stood. 'The guy you hired,' he said tersely.

'And why did I do that, and pay you all this money?'

'Because my team are the best,' Cutter said, looking him in the eye.

'The best in the business,' Penrose yelled. 'Your very words. So what am I to think when my cherry-picked elite team fail not once, but twice in a row to get me what I want? First you tell me that your cretin Grinnall let Holland get away—'

'Terry Grinnall will find him,' Cutter said.

'And now, when all you had to do was walk into an unoccupied house in some sleepy village and pick up a few simple items, you come back empty-handed and all beaten up, telling me you screwed up because of—' he searched for the right words '—because of some *vicarage guest*? What did he do, throw a prayer book at you?'

Cutter shook his head. 'He wasn't an ordinary vicarage guest. Somebody skilled. Somebody trained.'

'But you just told me *you* were the best!' Penrose screeched. 'What the hell was stopping you going back there after him and finishing him?'

'My orders were to carry out a quick, clean job, not create a war zone,' Cutter said.

'What I *want*,' Penrose exploded, 'is every last one of my enemies stamped out and crushed. Do you understand?'

Rex O'Neill felt like saying something, but he held back and kept his mouth shut.

Cutter gave a shrug. 'Sure.'

Penrose stormed across to his desk, ripped open a drawer and took out a large pistol. Cutter, Mills and Rex O'Neill all stared at the gun. Penrose walked back over to Cutter, gnashing his teeth, and pointed the weapon at his chest. He loved the cool steel of the pistol in his hand. So many years he'd longed for a real gun. Now he could have all the real guns he wanted. This one was a Coonan .357 Magnum automatic. Rare and beautiful, smooth stainless steel with gleaming walnut grips and an eight-shot capacity. He played with it constantly. 'No. I mean, do you really, really understand?' he screamed. 'Because if not I'll put a bullet in you right now and hire someone who can do a better job of this for me. In fact,' he added, 'perhaps I ought to just shoot you anyway, as a punishment. Shall I? Shall I?' He raised the pistol to Cutter's face.

Cutter gazed calmly into the man's eyes. He could easily rip the gun out of Penrose's hand, and the arm out of the socket with it. *You are crazy*, he thought. 'I understand,' he said quietly.

Penrose glowered at him, breathing hard. A vein was popping in his forehead. His carefully coiffured hair was sprawling in all directions. After twenty long, silent seconds, he lowered the gun. 'Pleased to hear it. I want this man dead, whoever he is. I don't care if you have to raze half of England to the ground to get him. I just want you to get him. Nobody is going to stop me. Nobody!'

O'Neill had kept his mouth shut until now, but couldn't hold back any longer. 'If I could remind you, Mr Lucas, my employers have been quite clear that they want this kept as quiet as possible. I thought that was understood.'

Penrose balked in horror at his words, then turned on him. 'Your employers also recruited me to run this operation, yes? Me, not you. That was also understood.'

A number of possible replies occurred to O'Neill. Most of them centred on the theme of 'Yes, but the Trimble Group never realised they were taking on a raving bloody maniac'. But considering the circumstances and the Coonan .357 that was still clutched tightly in Penrose's fist, he wisely chose not to voice them. Shortly afterwards, he left the room and returned to his own office within the villa complex while Cutter and Mills were dismissed back to their quarters to lick their wounds and await further instructions.

Penrose Lucas spent quite a few minutes pacing and seething alone. He pulled out a large holdall from under the desk, unzipped it and lifted out the stacks of banknotes he kept in there. Counting the money sometimes soothed him – but not this time, and as the migraine just kept worsening he was compelled to retreat to the bedroom to lie down.

After an hour in the blacked-out room with a mask over his face and five codeine tablets washing through his bloodstream, he emerged and turned on his computer, intent on finding out all he could about Simeon Arundel's mysterious and peculiarly talented guest.

Thanks to Rex O'Neill and the team behind the scenes whose names and faces Penrose neither knew nor wanted to know, he had unlimited access to police reports and a host of other data, some of it official, some of it not, concerning his victims before and after their deaths. He'd scanned through them already, but as he perused the files again now he paid much more attention to detail.

'Ben Hope,' he said out loud. The name came up twice. Once as the witness at the scene of the fatal car crash, and again as a speaker at the musical event, a concert at the Leigh Llewellyn Foundation, which Simeon Arundel and his wife had attended – shadowed, unknown to them, by Dave Mills.

What was a man like this doing hanging around a supposedly empty vicarage in the middle of the night, and getting in the way of his carefully laid plans? Penrose had always been a keen researcher, and nothing motivated him like utter hatred. Digging a little deeper, he quickly unearthed the connection between this Ben Hope and the deceased opera star Leigh Llewellyn. The old news item announcing their marriage was still viewable online and provided Penrose with his new enemy's full name and title: Major Benedict Hope, British Army, retired.

From there it was just a short skip to Hope's business website. He ran something called a tactical training facility in northern France. Penrose had little idea of what a tactical training facility was, but he understood enough to know what it suggested about the kind of skills this Hope possessed. He opened the page titled 'About the Team' and read, then re-read, the two short paragraphs describing Hope's background. The man's military experience was extensive, that much was patently obvious, but the information seemed carefully pruned, as though much of his past history couldn't be revealed. Even to someone with Penrose's limited understanding of military matters, that in itself was revealing enough. As for the connection between Hope and Arundel, that remained a mystery.

Wasn't bloody O'Neill meant to take care of this kind of stuff?

Penrose summoned Cutter back to his office. Minutes later the mercenary was standing at the desk, looking no less battered and sour than he had earlier, and every bit as wary. He soon understood that his boss's psychopathic rage had settled down to a mere simmering fury, and the gun would remain in the desk this time. Cutter relaxed a little.

His eyes flicked across to the holdall and the bundles of cash that were visible through the open zipper. That looked like one hell of a lot of money in there. Cutter noticed two more holdalls just like it on an armchair at the back of the room. He remembered what the boss had said that night back in London. *Money's the easy part.*

'Is this the man you encountered in Arundel's home?' Penrose demanded, showing him the picture on the website.

'That's him,' Cutter said instantly, with a flash of pain and humiliation.

'You were a soldier. Can you tell more about who he is?'

Cutter studied the webpage. 'Not your regular ex-squaddie. This guy's been in deep.'

'The question is, can we deal with him?'

'We can deal with him. We were just unlucky. He had the element of surprise, that's all.'

Penrose nodded thoughtfully. 'Did you say the rest of the team were still in position?'

'Vince Napier's just waiting for my call.'

'Then make it,' Penrose commanded.

155

Chapter Twenty-Three

Ben headed west on the motorway with the dog perched on the passenger seat beside him. After three hours of fast driving he left the M5 at Exeter to cut across the bleak, rugged landscape of Dartmoor National Park. He still didn't know exactly where he was going. As he drove, he called Jude four, five, six more times. Still no response. Evidently, not all of the younger generation were surgically attached to their mobile phones.

The weather was closing in as the afternoon wore on. Dark rolling clouds scudded menacingly over the craggy landscape, and a freezing mist was descending. The roads were getting narrower now, and almost deserted. This was one of England's last real wildernesses, and the place he was looking for could be just about anywhere. The sense of frustration was slowly rising as he neared Bodmin.

Suddenly feeling the buzz of the phone in his pocket, he made a grab to answer it. 'Jude, is that you?' He'd left him so many messages that he felt he knew the kid.

'This is Sophie Norrington,' said a clipped-sounding female voice.

There was hardly any mobile signal up here, and Ben was worried about getting cut off. He thanked her for calling back, explaining again that he was a friend of the Arundel family.

'Mum told me what's happened. It's awful. Poor Jude!'

'He doesn't know yet,' Ben said. 'I'm travelling to the farm in Cornwall to tell him.'

'That dump,' Sophie sniffed. Like mother, like daughter.

'Your mother told me you'd been there,' Ben said. 'Can you give me directions?'

'It's really isolated. I think the nearest village was called War ... War-something. Warleg. Warlego.' Sophie's voice kept breaking up, and he had to strain to make out her words. He pulled the car over to the side of the road, flipped on the inside light and began scouring the map he'd bought at the last fuel stop. 'There's a place here called Warleggan.'

'That's it.'

'What about the name of the farm itself?' he asked quickly, anxious that he was going to lose the phone signal at any moment.

Sophie thought for a moment. 'It was something suitably grim and lugubrious-sounding like "Bleak Mountain". No, that's not it. Black Rock. Black Rock Farm. Ask any of the locals. They'll tell you how to find it, but you might get some funny looks.' She paused, then said in a softer tone, 'Will you tell Jude I asked after him?'

'I'll do that,' Ben said. He was about to thank her when he realised the phone signal had died on him.

As they'd been speaking, Ben had been looking in the rear-view mirror at the lights of the car behind. Near as he could tell, it was a Range Rover Sport, dark blue or black. It had been there with him for a few miles, holding steady at the same pace as the Mazda. Now it was pulled in at the side of the road a hundred or so yards behind, as if waiting for him to drive on so it could follow. In the dimming light Ben could make out nothing of its occupants. The mist swirled like gunsmoke in the beams of its headlights.

157

Scruffy growled.

'I was thinking the same,' Ben said. He watched the Range Rover a moment longer, then put the Mazda back into gear and pulled away sharply with a rasp of tyres.

Close up ahead was a narrow lane cutting away perpendicular to the road. He waited until the last moment and then threw the Mazda into it, skidding on the loose surface and accelerating away hard.

The Range Rover didn't follow. *I must be imagining things*, Ben thought to himself, and as more miles passed and dusk fell to night, he became convinced of it. The only other light that appeared in his rear-view mirror was that of a solitary motorcyclist who followed him for a while along the winding moor roads and lanes, then shot past in a blast of twin exhausts on the approach to the tiny, remote village of Warleggan. Ben caught a glimpse of the pillion passenger holding on tightly to the grab-rails on the bike's tail; then it was gone in the mist.

As Ben drove through the village he saw the lights of a pub and pulled up outside, climbed out of the car and went in. The place was filled with locals, warm and noisy with chatter. He got the usual sideways glances from a few of the locals taking notice of a stranger as he walked up to the bar, perched on a stool and bought a double of malt scotch. As he sipped it, the barman, a thick-chested man who resembled an old-time sailor with his beard and gold earring, asked him cheerfully if he was on holiday.

'Not exactly,' Ben said. 'I'm looking for Black Rock Farm.'

'It's all hippies up there,' the barman muttered after a pause, his cheerful demeanour instantly evaporated. In just a couple of words, the welcome stranger had morphed into a drug dealer, or worse. 'Got business there, have you, sir?' the barman asked, eyeing Ben sternly as he reached out for a glass to polish.

'Of a kind,' Ben said, meeting his eye but keeping the smile on his face. 'And I'd be grateful for directions, if you know how to get there.'

Outside in the misty street, the leather-clad rider sat astride his motorcycle and blipped the throttle. He had his visor up and was leaning across the bike's fuel tank to speak quietly to the driver of the gleaming black Range Rover Sport that had pulled up beside him and rolled down its window. The driver's face was long and lean. The hem of his beanie hat covered the scar over his eye.

There were five other men inside the car, and they were all gazing in the direction of the pub and the Mazda Roadster parked outside it. So was the bike's pillion passenger, his face hidden behind his helmet's opaque visor.

The scruffy-looking mongrel inside the Mazda had jumped up on the passenger seat and had his nose pressed to the window, staring intently back at the watchers. The dog bared his fangs and let out a long, low snarl.

A few more words passed between the driver and the motorcyclist; then the motorcyclist nodded, lowered his visor, nudged his bike into gear and rode off. The Range Rover purred slowly on past the pub. The driver reached for a mobile phone.

The car rolled to a halt fifty yards up the street. Its lights went out. Waiting.

*

After the interminable journey aboard the cramped, over-heated hellhole of the Greyhound coach, Wesley Holland had reached Boston's South Station intercity bus terminal. Now that he was a seasoned expert in covert travel, he'd paid cash for another bus ride that had taken him and his valuable cargo southwards to the town of Falmouth, Cape Cod. Stepping off the bus in the picturesque village of Woods Hole on the edge of Falmouth, he sucked in a deep lungful of the cold, salty sea air and his heart leaped in jubilation.

He'd made it. Nearly there now, just a six-mile ferry trip left to go. As he hurried towards the port he could see no sign anywhere of his pursuers and was utterly certain that he'd managed to throw them off. The next ferry wasn't for a few hours. Wesley made himself comfortable in a cosy hotel lounge nearby and sipped a glass of warming cognac, gazing out of the window at the steely ocean and thinking of the safe haven that awaited him just a few short miles over the horizon.

He'd be there soon.

Chapter Twenty-Four

The few directions Ben had managed to get out of the barman were just about adequate to find Black Rock Farm. The mist thickened to a blanket of fog as he followed the narrow, twisting road higher and higher. He was pretty sure that on a clear day, you could see for many miles across the rolling moorland. Not tonight.

The dilapidated gate left him in no doubt that he was in the right place. Whoever had hand-carved the name in the wood had done so a long time ago, perhaps back in the days when its owners had cared more about the state of the place. The jagged white-painted scrawl underneath that said PRIVATE PROPERTY – PISS OFF was much more recent and a lot more telling.

Ben stepped out of the car to open the gate, drove through the entrance and started making his way down the long bumpy track. Le Crock would have been better suited to the potholes and ruts; the low-slung Mazda grounded out with a nasty grinding scrape two or three times as he approached the dimly lit buildings.

Rolling up into the frosty yard, Ben glanced around him and could immediately picture the kind of open-toed-sandalled, pot-smoking middle-class hippies who would keep a farm like this as an occasional holiday place and let their son and his mates run riot in it whenever they wanted. If there was a line somewhere between decadent Bohemian chic and out-and-out neglect, Black Rock Farm had crossed it a long time ago. Sophie Norrington hadn't been far wide of the mark when she'd called it 'grim and lugubrious'. Simeon's description 'derelict' hadn't been wildly off, either.

Ben parked the Mazda outside the crumbling low wall that ringed the old stone farmhouse. 'You stay here,' he told the dog. As he climbed out of the car he heard the thump-thump-thump of music in the distance, a riffy rock guitar over bass and drums. He turned to see that it was coming from the looming dark shape of a barn across the far side of the yard. Shards of light glowed out here and there from the gaps in the walls. Ben followed the sound, his footsteps crunching on the deep frost. Through the mist he could see a few cheap cars, the kinds of cars students drove, parked in the shadows. If it had been California there'd have been a couple of bad-boy Harleys, too. But this wasn't California.

As Ben walked up to the barn he could hear that the music was being played live – so much was obvious from the fact that the musicians either weren't very good, or were just too drunk or stoned to hit the right notes or keep a steady beat. He found the door and pushed it open. Warmth, light, noise and the smell of booze and smoke hit him as he stepped inside.

The floor of the barn was compacted earth. The walls were rusty corrugated iron sheets held together in places with baling twine. The halogen lamps that hung from wires draped over the beams were probably a massive fire risk, but not so much as the ancient-looking wood-burner that someone had dragged in and set up on bricks in a corner.

A lot of the heat inside the barn wasn't coming from the blazing logs, but from the thirty or so bodies dancing to the music, young men and women, none of them far out of their teens. Most of them appeared pretty inebriated, almost as far gone as the musicians up on the makeshift stage that was littered with wires, bottles, and amplifiers cranked up to maximum volume. The lead guitarist was using an empty beer bottle as a glass slide to screech out some truly hideous dissonant notes over the lumbering rhythm that his mates onstage were hammering out from the bass and drums. A military firing range would have done a more harmonious job of damaging the eardrums.

Ben shook his head at the spectacle, and hoped to God he'd never managed to look this ridiculous at their age.

Few people seemed to notice his presence. Sitting in a row on a collapsed sofa to one side of the barn were a young girl who was either asleep or maybe in a coma, a spotty gingery youth on whose shoulder her head was resting, and another young guy who seemed about to throw up. Ben reckoned that the spotty gingery one was the best option to speak to. 'I'm looking for Jude Arundel,' he shouted over the noise, bending low to be heard.

The kid's face was blank for a few seconds, then he motioned in the direction of a side door. 'They're in the house,' he slurred. 'Want some of this?' he added, holding up a crumpled joint.

Ben ignored the offer. Glad to escape the noise, he left the barn and cut across towards the farmhouse. Little chimes suspended above the front door tinkled in the cold breeze. He was about to knock, then instead tried the door and found it was open.

Ben stepped inside the hallway and smelled the sickly smell of damp mixed with incense; patchouli or sandalwood. A yin-yang symbol the size of a cartwheel was painted on one wall, opposite a peeling Led Zeppelin poster. From the slightly better-tended state of the place, Ben figured that Robbie's parents probably got around to visiting their holiday home every year or two.

From up the staircase came the sound of a toilet flushing, and moments later a spiky-haired young guy of about Jude Arundel's age appeared. He stopped midway down the stairs, and gaped at Ben with wide eyes.

'Who're you?'

'Are you Robbie?' Ben said.

'I'm Mark,' the young guy said, adding, 'I'm in the band.'

'Where's Jude Arundel?'

'Who's asking?' Mark said, puffing out his chest.

Ben just stared at him. After a couple of seconds Mark lowered his eyes, bravado melting away quickly, and pointed towards a room down the hall from the front door. 'In there. Playing cards with Robbie.'

The reek of booze was strong as Ben slipped into the dimly candle-lit room, apparently unnoticed by the half-dozen young guys who were sitting in varying stages of drunkenness around a worn table. At some point in its progress, the card game they were playing had mutated into a drinking competition whose purpose seemed to be a chal-lenge to whoever could stomach the unholy mixture of Guinness, cheap red wine and vodka one of them was pouring into a grubby pint glass. The contest had already claimed its first victim, who was slumped semi-conscious across the table.

Ben instantly knew which of them was Robbie from the name emblazoned across the front of his red sweatshirt. He was maybe twenty-one, twenty-two, overweight and trying five years too early to grow a beard.

Sitting next to Robbie at the table, leaning his athletic frame back in his chair and laughing at something his friend had just said, was the young man whose picture Ben had seen at the vicarage. Jude looked just as he had in the photo, except that his unruly mop of hair was bleached blonder by the New Zealand sunshine and the wetsuit had been exchanged for a fleece jacket. Still laughing, he went to pick up the pint glass containing the lethal concoction his friend had just poured.

Ben didn't want to have to break news like this to someone half blotto. Stepping brusquely into the candlelight, he reached out and stopped Jude's hand before it could get to the glass.

'Oy!' Jude said, looking up at Ben in surprise and anger. His eyes were only a little glazed over from the drink, which made him by far the soberest person at the table. 'Who the fuck are you?' he demanded.

Robbie swayed up out of his seat. 'What're you doing in my place, man?'

'Sit down, Robbie,' Ben said.

Robbie sat down.

'Jude, my name's Ben Hope. I've been leaving messages for you all day. Didn't you get them?'

'I don't know you. How did you find me?' Jude blustered. Even the drunkest of his friends were beginning to take notice of what was going on.

'Never mind how I found you. We need to talk.' Ben glanced around at the others and shot a warning look at Robbie. 'In private. Can we step outside?'

'What did you say your name was?'

'Ben.'

'These are my friends, *Ben*. Whatever you've got to say to me, you can say it to all of us.'

'I don't think so,' Ben said.

'Really.'

'Listen to me. I'm a friend of your family and this is much more important than you realise.'

'Oh, I get it,' Jude interrupted him. 'You've come to take me home? Did *he* send you?'

Robbie let out a belch, then leered wolfishly at Jude. 'The reverend wants his baby boy home for Christmas.'

'Fuck you, Robbie,' Jude said. 'Who was too chicken to get in the water with the great whites?' He made another grab for the drink, amid a chorus of laughter from the others at the table.

Ben stopped his hand again, a little more firmly this time. The laughter died away abruptly.

Jude flushed. 'You do that to me once more,' he warned Ben.

'You can come outside with me the easy way, right now,' Ben said softly, 'or I can drag you out by the hair. Either way, I'm going to tell you what I came here to tell you.'

'Go fuck yourself,' Jude said. 'I'm not interested. And you can tell my father to stick his Christmas tree up his . . .'

Before he could finish the sentence, Jude was out of his seat and travelling through the air over the top of the table. His feet barely touched the floor as Ben manhandled him through the door and out into the hallway.

'Let go of him!' Robbie yelled, making a feeble grab for Ben's arm.

'You stand down, boy,' Ben commanded him, with the full force of a British Army major's authority. Robbie instantly backed off, deflating like a punctured ball.

Jude put up a spirited resistance as Ben dragged him outside, struggling wildly and trying to lash out with his fists. Ben blocked three pretty good punches before he lost patience with the kid and trapped his wrist in an Aikido lock that very quickly subdued his fighting spirit.

'Aaagghh! That hurts! Please!'

'Have I got your attention now?' Ben asked, keeping the pressure on the wrist.

'Yes!'

'Promise to behave?'

'Yes!'

Ben let go. Jude tore away from him, nursing his hand and about to make some furious retort when the sight of the Mazda parked across the yard stopped him dead. 'What're you doing with my mum's car?' he asked in a hollow voice.

Ben guided him towards the car. The music in the barn had stopped, and a silence thicker than the mist hung over the farm. 'Listen, Jude. There's something you need to know.'

Inside the car, the dog barked at the sight of Jude and started scrabbling at the window.

'Why is Scruffy here?' Jude said.

Ben opened the passenger door. 'Get in.'

'Not before you tell me what this is about.'

'Get in the car, Jude.'

Jude looked at Ben, realisation dawning on his face that this was serious. Without another word, he climbed into the passenger seat. The dog clambered all over him and licked his face. Jude cuddled him affectionately, as if he knew something bad was coming and he had to cling to someone for support.

Ben quietly shut the passenger door, walked around to the driver's side and got in beside Jude.

'I came here to tell you some news,' he said.

And told him.

Chapter Twenty-Five

As Ben talked about the crash, the colour left Jude's face and his jaw hardened. He closed his eyes. Finally he whispered, 'May I get out of the car, please?'

Ben nodded, waiting to see how the young guy was going to respond. He'd had to break bad news before. It was never nice, but it was always different. Sometimes the reaction was complete shock, physical illness, collapse. Other times it was denial – sometimes furious and aggressive denial. Shooting the messenger brought some kind of relief. Ben could understand that. He'd been through it himself, more than once in his life.

Jude hurled open the Mazda's passenger door and staggered out. He paced in a circle on the frosty grass. Let out several gasping breaths, his face contorted in pain. Turning back towards the car he yelled hoarsely at Ben, 'How the fuck do you *know* this? Tell me! How come you're telling me this?'

'Because I was there when it happened,' Ben said quietly. 'I'm sorry.'

Jude shook his head wildly. 'No, no. No. It can't fucking be.' He ripped open the zipper of his fleece jacket pocket, took out a phone and started stabbing at it.

Ben knew what number he was calling. 'There's nobody

at home, Jude.' He watched as the young man stood there with the phone clamped to his ear, shoulders bent, waiting for an answer, willing with all his might for this to be just some cruel, crazy joke being played on him. After a few moments Jude gave up, then an afterthought hit him and he thumbed more buttons on his phone. His eyes brightened momentarily. 'No, no. Wait. I've got messages.'

'They're all from me,' Ben said.

Jude waved at him to shut up. Listening intently to each message in turn, his face grew steadily more and more pallid, as if hope was a colour that was slowly draining out of him with every passing moment.

The hand clutching the phone fell limp at his side. He leaned against the stone wall. His shoulders sagged. Then he bent over and was violently sick.

Ben got out of the car and walked over to where Jude was doubled up by the wall, gasping and gagging. Ben laid a hand on his shoulder. 'I'm sorry.'

'It's not possible,' Jude croaked through his tears. 'I'm never going to see them again. It's just not possible.'

'They're in a better place now,' Ben said.

Jude spun around to face him, red-eyed. 'You believe all that shit about heaven, do you?'

Ben said nothing. He didn't know whether he believed it or not. He said no more, and let the young man be for a few minutes. Leaning against the side of the Mazda he lit a cigarette, watched the smoke whip away on the cold wind and wondered how the hell he should break the rest of the news. Telling Jude that the crash had been no accident was going to be even tougher than just telling him his parents had died.

'I'm stranded here,' Jude said after a while. 'We came in Robbie's car. He's too pissed to drive. Will you take me back?'

'I came to fetch you,' Ben said. 'Get your things.'

'My things don't matter,' Jude said.

'Yes, they do,' Ben said. 'Go and get them.'

'I have to tell Robbie what's happened.'

'Tell him, but be quick.'

Jude slunk back to the farmhouse with his head low, wiping his eyes as he went. Ben felt guilty, as he'd known he would. He'd spend the next month questioning whether he'd broken the news in the right way. Maybe there was no right way. He smoked the rest of his cigarette as he let Scruffy run around the yard. The dog hunted about, cocking his leg over everything in sight.

A few minutes later Jude returned from the farmhouse carrying a rucksack. His eyes were redder than before. Without a word, he stuffed the rucksack in the boot and climbed into the passenger seat. Scruffy bounded in at his feet.

'I'm ready,' Jude whispered. 'Let's go.'

Ben bumped the Mazda back down the track to the road. Jude was silent for a long time as they drove though the darkness. The mist was settling more thickly than ever across the moors now, and visibility was down to about twenty yards. Ben focused carefully on the winding road as he drove. The heater roared on full blast, filling the car with hot stale air.

Beside him, Jude fidgeted about for a while, then felt for the seat adjustment and started reclining his backrest. 'I need to sleep,' he said. 'Wake me when we get to Oxfordshire.'

'We're not going there,' Ben said, and steeled himself for what was coming.

Jude sat up in his seat. 'What are you talking about? Where are we going?'

'I can't take you back home, Jude.'

'I don't understand. You said you'd come to fetch me.'

'That's right. But I didn't say where to.'

Jude's brow furrowed. 'Hold on a minute—'

'Listen, I haven't told you everything.'

'So tell me.'

'This isn't easy for me either,' Ben said.

'What?'

Ben glanced away from the road and looked him in the eye. 'Your parents' death wasn't an accident, Jude.'

'But you just told me they died in a crash,' Jude replied, aghast.

'They did. But somebody else caused it. Deliberately.'

'You're saying they were *murdered*?' Jude burst out. 'But why?'

'Because of your dad's work.'

'He was murdered because he was a vicar?'

'No, something else he and some other people were working on. Some kind of secret project that got them into trouble with some bad people. People who obviously mean harm to your family.'

'What secret project?' Jude yelled. 'What bad people? He was a *vicar*! This is total bullshit! What are you, some kind of fucking nutter?'

'I wish I was,' Ben said evenly. 'I wish none of this were true. But whether you believe me or not, your dad would have wanted me to keep you safe. He knew he was in trouble, and he asked for my help.'

'Why?' Jude demanded.

'Because helping people is what I do,' Ben said. 'And that's why, until I figure out what's happening and who these people are, we're not going back.'

'I have to go back! I have to see them.'

'No, Jude.'

171

'What about the funeral?'

'I'm sorry,' Ben said.

Jude's eyes glistened in the darkness of the car. 'You're saying I can't go to my own parents' *funeral*?'

'You can't bring them back, whatever you do.'

'Fuck you.'

'Thanks.'

'So where is it you think you're taking me?'

'To France,' Ben said. 'I have a place in Normandy. You'll be safe there.'

Jude glowered at him with the deepest suspicion. After a moment of silence he muttered, 'They never once mentioned anybody called Ben.'

'We knew each other a long time ago, before you were born. We were all at college together.'

Jude kept glowering at him. 'And I'm supposed to accept that, without any evidence, and let you take me off to some place in France, just like that? No way. And besides,' he added, 'I can't go anywhere because I don't have my passport with me.'

'So you swam all the way back from New Zealand, did you?' Ben asked him. In a softer tone he said, 'Listen, Jude. This'll go a lot easier if you let me help you, all right?'

'I don't need your help. I need to get back home. Stop the car.'

Ben said nothing. He kept on driving.

'Didn't you hear me?' Jude yelled. 'I said stop the fucking car. Now!'

When Ben still didn't reply, Jude made a grab for the steering wheel. Ben slapped his hand away and shoved him back in his seat. The dog started barking wildly. Jude lashed out. His fist connected with Ben's jaw.

It was a solid punch, and for a moment, Ben reeled. Jude

lunged at the steering wheel again, and Ben didn't react in time to stop him yanking the Mazda violently off course. The wheels ploughed into the slush and mud at the side of the road and lost traction. The car went into a slide that Ben only just managed to control before they went spinning off the road and smashed into a dry stone wall. The Mazda slithered to a halt in the ditch and the engine stalled.

'Well done,' Ben said, rubbing his jaw where Jude had punched him. 'That was really mature.'

Jude didn't speak. Before Ben could stop him, he shoved open his door and leaped out of the car.

'Jude!' Ben shouted.

But Jude was off, racing away into the darkness. The dog sprang out of the car and went belting after him, barking excitedly as if this were some fun new game the two-leggeds were playing for his benefit.

Ben swore furiously and flung open the driver's door. 'Jude!' he yelled. 'Jude!' His voice sounded flat, muffled by the impenetrable mist.

'Fuck it,' he muttered. There was nothing for it but to go after him. Ben broke into a sprint. The mossy, rocky terrain sloped steeply upwards from the road. Jude was already lost in the smoky fog, and Ben was terrified of losing track of him. He ran faster. As an icy gust parted the mist for a moment, he caught sight of him up ahead, darting over the craggy landscape like a man demented. Ben called his name again. Jude didn't look back, and then he was lost in another swirl of mist.

Ben kept running, scrambling up a rough sheep track that carried him steeply upward, stones and dirt sliding underfoot. Had Jude come this way? Ben paused, listening – then heard the dog bark from somewhere beneath him and to the left, and realised that Jude had taken a different path.

Ben peered down the slope and spotted him twenty yards away, just visible through the mist. Jude had skidded to a halt, his progress blocked by thick brambles and a mound of enormous moss-covered rocks that must have come down in a landslide centuries earlier.

Jude hadn't seen Ben standing above him. He hesitated, glanced back, then seemed to decide that he had to clamber over the rocks, as though convinced that there was a perfect escape route or a handy getaway car waiting for him on the other side.

Ben raced down the slope, and before Jude managed to scramble more than a few feet up the rocks, he'd grabbed him tightly by the arms and hauled him down to the ground. 'Where the hell do you think you're running off to?'

Jude wriggled violently in Ben's grip, showering him with foul curses as he tried to throw him off. Ben held him down tightly. 'You're determined to make this difficult for both of us, aren't you?'

'Let me go. You're a fucking weirdo.'

'And you're a stubborn little bastard.'

That was when the first shot cracked off the rock just a few inches from Ben's head.

Chapter Twenty-Six

Flying stone chips stung Ben's face. Almost simultaneously, he heard the muted bark of the gunshot in the distance.

Even as Ben instinctively flattened himself on the cold, wet moss, dragging Jude down with him, he was calculating the position of the shooter. Whoever he was, he was upwind and on higher ground. The hard impact of the bullet told Ben it had been fired from a high-velocity rifle. The muffled report told him the weapon was fitted with a sound moderator and firing subsonic ammunition. Slow and comparatively low-powered but still capable of filleting a man like a fish from half a mile away. This was no place to be.

'Maybe you should have stayed in the car,' Ben said, dragging Jude roughly across the ground to the shelter of a large boulder five feet from the rock pile.

'Oh my God, what's happening?' Jude squawked, face-down in the dirt.

'So do you believe me now?' Ben asked. 'Or do you think I've set this little shooting gallery up on purpose to trick you?'

Jude stared at him in terror. 'Is that a *gun* firing at us?'

'Certainly appears so,' Ben murmured as he peered cautiously over the top of the boulder. A gust of wind brushed his face and the curtain of mist eddied and parted for a moment. Just as he was expecting it, a second shot rang out, and this time Ben saw the muzzle flash pierce the darkness before he ducked down again and the bullet smacked off the boulder uncomfortably close by.

'He's perched on a ridge up there,' Ben said to Jude. 'Back towards the road, about two hundred yards at ten o'clock. Has to be using infra-red night sights.' More military hardware. It was a great time to be completely unarmed. Even if Ben hadn't left the shotgun in the car, it would have been next to useless against a sniper.

'It's someone out hunting,' Jude said, wide-eyed. 'They think we're a deer or something. If we jump out and wave our arms . . .'

'You'll have them blown off,' Ben said. 'He knows what he's shooting at. And it doesn't have antlers.' He counted two seconds, three, long enough for the sniper to work his bolt and line up his next shot.

A crater burst open in the dirt just inches away and the bullet wailed off the rocks behind them. The shooter had moved position, trying to flank them and drive them out from behind cover.

'Scruffy!' Jude called out. The dog was going crazy, barking frenetically at the darkness. Ben reached out and grabbed his collar and thrust him into Jude's arms. 'Hold on to him. Keep behind the rock.'

'Who's firing at us?' Jude quavered, clutching the wriggling terrier in a death grip and pressing himself as tightly as he could behind the boulder.

'That's what bothers me,' Ben said. 'Right now I can only see one of them. But I'm betting he's not alone. They must have followed us from near the farm, driving without lights.' He cursed himself for having been too preoccupied with Jude to notice they'd had company.

'What do they want with us?'

'Well, if they don't just shoot us dead here, they'll probably march us back to the car at gunpoint. Then they'll most likely want to punt us off a cliff or crash us through a nice big stone wall. Maybe they'll burn the wreck once we're dead.'

'I shouldn't have asked,' Jude hissed. 'Are you *kidding me or what*? Oh!' He curled up into a ball as another shot exploded against the underside of the boulder.

Ben gauged the angle and shoved Jude a few inches to the left. 'The media will say I was drunk or on drugs,' he said. 'They'll have a witness from the local pub saying I was looking for directions to Robbie's place. And we all know what goes on there.'

Jude gaped at him, bits of wet grass and dirt stuck to his face. 'How do you know all this stuff?'

'Because that's how these people operate,' Ben said. The wind had dropped for a moment, and the mist was hanging immobile in the air like the sails of a ship lying in a dead calm. The shooter wouldn't be able to see much in his sights until the breeze stirred it again.

That didn't seem to put him off. The fifth bullet tore a chunk the size of a fist off the rocks just a foot and a half away from where he was crouching. Jude flinched. And Ben saw his moment. He quickly peeled off his leather jacket, dumped it on the ground by the boulder and arranged it so that a few inches protruded from behind the rock. In the ghostly image of an infra-red scope it would look like a man's elbow sticking out as he crouched down for cover.

'What are you doing?'

'Wait here.'

'You can't leave me here alone!' Jude burst out.

'Do as I say, and don't move.'

Ben ran out from behind the boulder, keeping low, moving

fast and quiet as a snake over the rough terrain. In the ten yards of open ground he crossed before a stony mound offered reasonable cover, there were no more shots. The silence was uncanny. He moved on, working his way from rock to hollow, gradually skirting around the side of the shooter's position and praying that the mist would keep him hidden.

As he kept moving, he was thinking. You didn't deploy a sniper against your target unless getting up close and personal posed too much of a risk. The enemy were taking no chances, and his guess was that they'd worked out who he was by now. Somebody had been doing their homework. Somebody smart and ruthless. Ben was desperately worried that he'd left Jude alone and unprotected back there. And he was worried because he knew that this shooter wasn't working alone. His associates were out there in the mist.

Ben had covered nearly two hundred yards when a fresh gust of cold wind ruffled his hair and the mist drifted aside like a cloud to reveal the moor and the starry sky above. He could see the boulder behind him and the ridge a little further ahead.

The seventh rifle shot sounded much closer. The white muzzle flash briefly lit up a stony outcrop no more than seventy-five yards away. Ben heard the bullet whip through the air and strike against the boulder. The shooter hadn't seen him, but now Ben knew exactly where he was.

Ben moved closer, coming round in a curve to approach the man from behind. His heart beat hard as he saw the black-clad figure among the rocks, lying prone in the classic sniper position, one leg straight out behind him, one crooked, both elbows on the ground. The rifle was a bolt action, mounted on a bipod, with a long fat silencer attached to the barrel. Ben recognised the night vision scope as a piece of

Russian military hardware. Expensive. Exclusive. Available only to those with the right connections.

Ben didn't breathe as he closed in the last few yards. He felt no emotion, no pity. Pity would get you killed. Like remorse, it could wait until later.

The sniper was about to fire again when Ben landed on him from behind and pressed his knee hard into his spine, clapped one hand over his mouth and the other under his chin and jerked his head back violently, twisting it hard left and then right. The man's struggles lasted no more than a couple of seconds before his neck broke.

Ben let go of the man's head and it smacked down lifelessly against the rocks. Taking the rifle from the dead sniper's arms, he rolled the corpse away with his foot, then raised the rifle to his shoulder and scanned the landscape through the scope. As the mist cleared rapidly, the night vision image brought everything vividly to life. He swivelled the rifle back towards the road. And recognised with a shock the black car that had pulled up behind the Mazda.

It was the Range Rover that had followed him earlier.

Two men were standing on guard nearby, both clad from head to toe in black, both wearing night vision goggles over ski masks. The goggles explained how the Range Rover's driver had been able to follow him in the dark without lights. One of the guards was clutching Ben's bag, the other the shotgun they'd taken from it. Not good.

One sniper, two guards. Three men. No way, Ben thought to himself. They'd have sent more than three men.

He pointed the rifle back towards the boulder where he'd left Jude, and now saw that he'd made a bad mistake. The sniper hadn't meant to kill him and Jude, only to pin them down as the rest of the group moved in to take them alive. Two more men in black were working their way quickly through the rocks towards Jude's hiding place. They wore the same night goggles as their colleagues by the car. The one on the left was clutching a pistol with a long silencer. The one on the right was carrying a submachine gun.

They certainly weren't taking any chances. Ben had been right about that, too.

In the green-hued image of the scope, Jude's anxious face peered out from behind the boulder, searching for Ben. He had no idea that the two men were just yards away and about to close in on him.

But neither the two men stalking up on Jude nor their associates down on the roadside guarding the car had any idea that their sniper friend was now lying among the rocks with his neck snapped. Things were a little more even now.

Chapter Twenty-Seven

Ben pressed the rifle butt in tight against his shoulder, lined the scope crosshairs up on the man on the left and squeezed the trigger. The rifle bucked in his arms and he saw his target crumple to the ground like a puppet whose strings had been cut. Green blood splashed the rocks.

If the two guarding the car had heard the report, they'd assume it was the sniper doing his job. Ben quickly worked the rifle bolt and picked up the second man in his sights. Not quickly enough – before he could get off the next round, the man took off across the rocky hillside. Ben followed his running target ten, fifteen yards, then squeezed off another shot. The man ducked as the bullet passed close by his head, and kept running, clutching his submachine gun to his side. By the time Ben had the sights lined up again, the man had flitted away into shadows so dense that not even the infrared could make him out.

Then he was gone. Still armed and dangerous, still out there. Ben looped the rifle's tactical sling around his shoulder, scrambled down from the ridge and ran back to rejoin Jude.

'Where did you get that thing?' Jude asked in astonishment, gaping at the rifle. He obviously hadn't noticed the corpse lying just a few yards away.

'From the sniper up there,' Ben said.

'You mean you just took it?'

'Something like that.'

'Who *are* you?'

'We don't have time for a conversation,' Ben said. 'Grab the dog and let's go.'

They ran back towards the car, Ben cradling the rifle, Jude clutching Scruffy to his chest. At the top of the slope overlooking the road, Ben caught Jude's arm and pulled him to a halt.

'Shit,' Jude breathed as he saw the Range Rover and the two men standing by the Mazda.

'Turn away,' Ben said.

'What?'

'Don't look.'

Jude understood and turned away. Ben dropped to one knee, levelled the rifle and fired. Slid the bolt smoothly back and forth and fired again. 'Now move,' he said to Jude. The rifle's magazine was empty. He let the weapon drop as they ran down the slope towards the car.

'Are they *dead*?' Jude gasped when he saw the two bodies lying in the road.

'You want to take their pulses?' Ben said. 'Then get in the car and stay there this time.' Jude obeyed numbly as Ben retrieved the things the men had taken from the Mazda. One corpse had the shotgun slung over his shoulder. The other had Ben's bag, with Simeon's laptop still inside. Ben quickly tossed the bag and the sniper rifle into the back of the car. He racked the pump of the shotgun and aimed it at the radiator of the Range Rover. There was still at least one guy out there on the moor, but an ounce of solid lead through the engine block ought to prevent anybody following them.

182

Before Ben could squeeze the trigger, a ripping burst of machine gun fire tore up the road at his feet. He threw himself back behind the Mazda, yelling at Jude to keep his head down. He blasted three shotgun slugs up the hillside, more to cover himself as he retreated to the driver's door than to hit anything. And he hadn't hit anything, because in the next instant another sustained burst of gunfire from the hillside punched a line of 9mm holes through the body-work of the Mazda and shattered the back window. Jude let out a yell from inside the car.

'Are you hit?' Ben shouted.

'No! Get us out of here!'

Ben clambered in behind the wheel, dumping the hot, smoking shotgun in Jude's lap. He twisted the key. The Mazda's starter motor turned over but didn't fire.

Bullets raked the side of the car and shattered the side mirror. The dog was howling in Jude's arms. Ben threw a glance back and saw two men racing down the hillside towards the Range Rover. He twisted the key again.

This time, the Mazda rasped into life. Ben revved it into the red, popped the clutch and the spinning wheels threw up a tide of mud as the car slewed out of the ditch and went skidding away down the road. But something was wrong. The handling was way off, the car pulling badly to the right. Ben realised that both right side tyres were shredded. He put his foot down and wrestled with the steering wheel.

In moments, the two men had reached the Range Rover and were giving chase, headlights dazzling now that they had nothing more to hide. Ben threw the Mazda hard into the bends, but the car was in danger of sliding right off the road on its flat tyres if he drove too fast, and the Range Rover began steadily overhauling them. Its passenger was leaning right out of his window, the wind tearing at his clothes as he let off several three-round automatic bursts from his weapon. Ben felt a bullet punch through the head restraint of his seat, an inch from his ear. The Mazda's windscreen suddenly became a white mass of fissures. Without hesitating or taking his foot off the gas, he grabbed the shotgun from Jude's lap and swung it one-handed at the windscreen, punching a hole that he could see through to drive. The inside of the Mazda became a howling tornado of freezing cold wind. Narrowing his eyes against the icy blast, he lobbed the weapon back into Jude's hands. 'Shoot!'

'I can't!' Jude yelled back.

'Point it, hold on tight and pull the damn trigger,' Ben shouted at him as he struggled to keep the car on the road through a hairpin bend. There was a loud crunching scrape as the back of the Mazda broke out of line and hit the barrier at the side of the road. Ben couldn't see beyond the barrier. At this moment, he didn't even want to know what was beyond it.

Terrified, Jude twisted round and poked the shotgun through the gap between the front seats. The car filled with a deafening blast and a white-orange flash as the gun went off like a bomb. Ben saw the Range Rover swerve in his rear-view mirror, then come on again. 'Keep firing,' he yelled at Jude.

But now the Range Rover came roaring right up behind them at full throttle and rammed into the rear of the Mazda with brutal force. The shotgun spun out of Jude's hands as the impact sent him sprawling half over the seat. The Mazda careened all over the road, and Ben couldn't hold it any more. There was a jarring crash as its front end smashed through the roadside barrier. For a second, the vehicle bucked crazily as it hammered over a stretch of bumpy grass. Too late to do anything about it, Ben realised they were heading straight for a sheer drop.

Then the Mazda's nose dipped violently downwards, and they were falling over the edge.

Chapter Twenty-Eight

For a heartstopping moment as the car tipped over, Ben thought they were about to sail right off the edge of a precipice – but then the front wheels touched solid ground with a jarring thump and they were racing down a near-vertical slope, crashing over rocks and ruts. The Range Rover cleared the edge of the drop and came roaring after them, its four-wheel drive and elevated ride height enabling it to negotiate the extreme slope with greater control. More strobing white muzzle flashes burst from the passenger window. Bullets punched into the Mazda. The dashboard blew apart in front of Ben. Sparks began to fizz from mangled wiring.

'Do something!' Jude screamed.

There was nothing Ben could do, except pray that the bullet-torn car wouldn't start to tumble end-over-end, destroying itself and battering them to death inside. But even as the worst seemed inevitable, the slope suddenly began to level out. Open moorland was ahead of them, a few isolated copses of wind-ravaged trees flashing by in the headlights. Down here on lower ground, the going was much less rocky and much more marshy. Ben kept his foot to the floor and the engine revved into the red as the wheels spun in the mud. The front of the car threw up a constant fountain of brown spray that spattered the broken windscreen and half-blinded Ben as he kept doggedly surging ahead at over sixty miles an hour.

They were driving into a real marsh now, thick with clumps of reeds and ancient, rotted tree stumps that stuck up out of the mud like gravestones. Ben only just managed to prevent the bucking Mazda from crashing straight into one.

More gunfire exploded from the Range Rover. Bullets ripped through the Ben's window and door. A red-hot sear of pain made him glance down and see the blood on his forearm where a round had grazed him, splitting the flesh.

A few more seconds of this and they were dead.

But then, suddenly, their pursuers seemed to be falling back. Ben twisted his head round to look out of the shattered rear window, and saw that the Range Rover had veered off course and was wallowing badly in the marsh, its passenger still hanging out of the window trying to fix the Mazda in his gunsights. Then, just as suddenly, the Range Rover slewed into a high-speed skid and hit the blackened stump of a tree.

The impact flipped the vehicle over sideways. Ben caught a glimpse of the passenger opening his mouth to scream as he was half thrown from the window and the Range Rover overturned on top of him, crushing him deep into the mud and smearing him like an insect under its weight. It slid for a few yards and then smacked into another tree stump, head-on, with enough force to kick the rear wheels high up in the air. The windscreen exploded outwards, and through the spinning shards of glass the body of the driver was shot like a missile over the bonnet and into the soft marsh.

Ben brought the Mazda round in a handbrake turn, sending up a wave of watery mud as it came to rest among a thick bank of reeds. 'You okay?' he asked Jude.

'I think so,' Jude mumbled. Ben grabbed the shotgun, stepped out of the car and immediately felt his feet sinking into the ground. *This isn't a marsh*, he thought, stepping quickly back towards the firmer ground on which the Mazda was resting. *This is a bog.*

The Range Rover had come to a stop right in the softest part of it. One of its headlights was still intact, and in its beam Ben could see the sucking brown mud working its way up the crumpled bodywork as the vehicle began to sink.

'Help me,' the Range Rover's driver croaked. He was a few feet in front of the overturned vehicle. His legs had already sunk deep into the bog. He reached out a hand in supplication. The other arm was mangled and twisted at his side. His ski mask had been ripped away in the crash. Most of his face was covered in the blood that was pouring from an open gash across his scalp, but Ben could see the look of utter horror in his eyes as the bog squelched and sucked at him, drawing him inexorably down inch by inch. 'Help me. Please.'

Jude had climbed out of the car and stood at Ben's side. 'We can't just leave the guy to drown,' he said shakily. 'It's awful.'

Ben spotted the half-submerged remains of an old tree that lay crossways like a bridge between him and the sinking driver. Slinging the shotgun across his shoulder, he placed his foot on it. The bog heaved around the rotten wood like a living thing, but the trunk took Ben's weight. He took a step towards the man, then another. It was unsteady beneath his feet. One slip, and he'd be next in line crying to be rescued.

'Help me,' the man moaned again, stretching out with his clawed hand.

Ben took another step forwards. He looked at the hand. 'Pull him out!' Jude called across from firm ground.

Ben looked at the man's pleading face. He took in the lean features under the mask of blood, and the scar over the eye. He knew that face. He'd seen it before. And he remembered where.

The man had sunk in almost up to his chest now. He was beginning to gibber in panic. 'Ben!' Jude yelled. 'Grab his hand! You've got to help him. for God's sake!'

Ben didn't grab the hand, not for God's sake or anyone else's. He reached into his jacket pocket for the printout of the photo from Petra Norrington's camera. He unfolded it, studied it briefly in the glare from the Range Rover's rapidly-disappearing headlight. Then he crumpled the printout into a ball and lobbed it over to Jude.

Jude caught it, uncrumpled it and stared at it mutely.

Slowly, calmly, Ben unslung the shotgun from his shoulder. His injured arm hurt as he worked the pump. The empty shell spat out and landed with a plop in the mud. The last round in the magazine fed into the chamber. Ben pointed the gun at the sinking man.

'What are you doing?' Jude yelled, still clutching the crumpled printout.

'That picture was taken the night your parents died,' Ben told him, not taking his eyes off the whimpering, groaning man in the bog. The mud was almost up to his neck now. He was flailing with his free arm. The other was well beneath the surface. A few feet away, the Range Rover was almost completely submerged.

'This is the man who ran them off the road,' Ben said.

'I'm begging you. Pull me out!'

'What's your name?'

'Napier,' the man moaned. 'Vincent Napier.'

'Is that your real name? Not that it matters any more.'

'Don't let me die like this!' Napier sobbed. His free hand clawed desperately at the air. His head thrashed from side to side.

'The more you struggle,' Ben said. 'The quicker you'll go down.'

'Ben!' Jude shouted from firm ground. 'Help him!'

'Please,' Napier wept. 'Look, I only do what I'm told to do.'

'Just business,' Ben said.

'Yes! You've got to understand.'

'I understand you've got less than half a minute left, Vincent,' Ben said. 'Tell me who you people are working for.'

'I don't know his name! He's just the boss! I've only met him once!'

Ben believed him. People in these kinds of situations generally didn't tell lies. 'Then that doesn't make you very useful to me, does it?' he said.

'Please don't let me drown.' The mud was up to Napier's chin and the arm reaching out was submerged to the elbow.

'Ben!' Jude shouted.

Ben didn't look back at him. 'Turn around, Jude,' he said.

'For fuck's sake!' Jude yelled hoarsely.

Ben edged a few more inches across the tree trunk and reached out to the drowning man. Not with his hand. With his foot. He planted the sole of his shoe on Napier's bloody forehead and pushed.

'No!' Napier screamed. Then the mud filled his mouth and his cry became a bubbling gurgle. His eyes stared upwards in horror in the last light of the Range Rover's sinking headlamp. Then the light was gone, and so was the top of Vincent Napier's head as Ben pressed him under with a final shove of his heel. A few bubbles clustered and popped on the surface of the swirling mud.

Ben watched for a few seconds until the bubbles stopped, then turned and started making his way back to firm ground.

Chapter Twenty-Nine

'I can't believe what I just saw you do to that guy,' Jude said sullenly as Ben returned to the Mazda.

'I told you not to look,' Ben replied.

Jude was too shocked to reply. He breathed heavily for a few moments, then suddenly took out his phone and started punching in a number.

'What are you doing?'

'What do you think I'm doing? I'm calling the police.'

Ben stepped up and grabbed the phone from him. 'I don't think so.'

'Hey. Give me that back.'

Ben tossed the phone into the bog where the Range Rover had now completely vanished. It hit the mud with a splash and sank almost instantly.

'That was my Nokia!'

'You never answer it anyway,' Ben said.

'This isn't happening,' Jude groaned, sitting on a grassy mound and rubbing his face. 'It's all a nightmare.' He glowered up at Ben. 'Just who the fuck are you?'

'You keep asking me that. I told you. I was at college with your parents. I was on the same course your dad did.'

'Theology? *You*?'

Ben nodded.

'What kind of theologian guns people down in cold blood and drowns them in bogs?'

'One who's spent too many years doing stuff you don't want to know about,' Ben said.

Jude grunted. 'Oh, right. So now you're going to tell me you were in the SAS or something.'

Ben said nothing. He examined the car. There wasn't a single window intact and much of the bodywork was riddled with holes. It mightn't have looked out of place in war-torn Kabul or Tripoli, but driving it on the public roads of Britain was asking for more trouble that Ben didn't need.

He took the shotgun and his bag out of the car. His heart sank when he saw the bullet holes in the green canvas, thinking of Simeon's laptop inside. His fears were confirmed when he examined the machine and found that the bullets had punched right through it. He had a feeling that Toshiba's service warranty didn't extend to their products being strafed with 9mm full metal jacket rounds. The casing fell apart in his hands, twisted wires and bits of shattered circuit board falling out into the dirt. The hard drive was history, and so were Ben's chances of ever getting into Simeon's research files.

'Shit,' he said. There wasn't much point in putting the thing back in his bag. He tossed its remains into the Mazda, then climbed in behind the wheel, fired up the engine and slammed it into gear. The car lurched forward.

'Hey!' Jude shouted as Ben drove the car straight into the middle of the bog, where the Range Rover had now completely sunk. As the mud began to pull greedily at the Mazda's wheels, Ben clambered out, jumped up on the roof and ran down the length of the car to make the leap back onto solid ground.

It didn't take long for the bog to engulf the car, along with Simeon's laptop.

'Mum loved that car,' Jude said reprovingly, as if Ben had wrecked and sunk it out of sheer badness.

'This place will be crawling with police come morning,' Ben told him, folding the shotgun stock and stuffing it into his bag. 'I don't think you want them finding her car in the middle of it, do you?' He slung the bag over his shoulder and started walking away across the moor. The dog followed at his heels. Jude hung back for a few moments, then muttered, 'Oh, bollocks,' and reluctantly followed too.

There weren't too many roads cutting across the wilderness of Bodmin Moor, and it was a long trudge through the cold and dark before Ben and Jude came across another and began walking along it. There wasn't a car or a light in sight. Ben led the way, with Scruffy trotting along happily at his side. Jude lagged behind, silent and brooding.

Ben didn't blame him.

It was after 1 a.m. by the time they came to the isolated cottage. The place was all in darkness, but somebody was obviously home, judging by the two vehicles parked outside, a year-old Nissan Outlaw off-roader sitting next to a badly rusted-out Vauxhall Astra. The red light of an alarm system flashed in the window of the Nissan. The Vauxhall had none. Ben tried the door, and found it open.

'Don't tell me you're going to steal it,' Jude whispered at his shoulder.

'I'm not stealing it,' Ben answered. 'I'm buying it.' He reached for his wallet, took out five twenties and tucked them under one of the Nissan's windscreen wipers. A hundred pounds was probably more than the Astra was worth.

'That makes it right?' Jude said, frowning.

Ben climbed into the car, felt behind the plastic fascia under the steering wheel and started tugging at wires. In

194

moments, the engine spluttered into life. It didn't sound completely terminal. 'That'll do,' he said.

Lights came on in the cottage. An upstairs window flew open and a man's voice let out a yell.

'Shit!' Jude clambered quickly into the passenger seat. 'Scruffy, come on!' The dog finished urinating on the tyre of the Nissan Outlaw and bounced up into Jude's lap. Ben hit the gas and they sped away down the road in a cloud of blue smoke.

When Jude was assured that the owner of the Nissan wasn't in hot pursuit, he turned to Ben. 'So now we're off to France in this stolen rustbucket? I suppose I don't have much choice except to come with you, do I?'

'No, you don't,' Ben said, driving fast through the darkness. He was already figuring out his next move. 'But we need to make a stop-off first.'

'You owe me an explanation. A very long explanation.'

'I know.'

'What's this all about? What was my dad involved in? I mean, was he some kind of crook or something? It sounds crazy, just saying it.'

'Your father was a good man,' Ben said. 'The best. None of this was his fault. But there was something he was working on that got him into a lot of trouble. Not just him, but the people who were working on it with him.'

'I don't understand. How could someone like him get into this situation?'

'Did he ever mention anything to you about a sword?'

Jude looked baffled. 'No? What sword?'

'This was a particular one. A sacred sword.'

'What's that supposed to mean?'

'Right now,' Ben said, 'I have absolutely no idea.'

Jude shook his head. 'I'd definitely have remembered if

he'd mentioned something like that. He never said anything to me. Did Mum know about it too?'

'She knew very little,' Ben said. 'Only what she told me, that he was writing a book about it. There were at least three people involved in the research project. Did you know about his trips to America and Israel?'

'I knew he went there. That's about it.'

'So he never talked about his reasons for going? People he travelled with, or people he might have met up with there?'

'We never talk . . . I mean we never talked about anything to do with his work, or religion, or any of that stuff,' Jude said. 'We always ended up arguing about it, and Mum would get upset . . .' His voice trailed off. He wasn't far from tears.

Ben gave him a moment, then asked, 'How about somebody called Lalique? Fabrice Lalique? Did your dad ever mention that name?'

Jude sniffed. 'No. Who is he?'

'He *was* a Catholic priest in Millau in the south of France,' Ben said. 'He and your dad went to Israel together in connection with this sacred sword business.'

'Well, if we're going to France, why don't we ask this Lalique guy what's going on?'

'Because he's dead, Jude. He fell off a bridge. Or was pushed.'

Jude swallowed hard. 'So these other people who were involved in this thing with Dad. Are they . . . are they all dead?'

'They weren't yesterday, when one of them phoned the house. An American called Wes.'

'You talked to him? What did he say?'

'He wasn't very forthcoming,' Ben said. 'He sounded scared. I think they're after him too.'

'And now they're after us,' Jude said. 'But I don't know anything about this! I've never even heard of this sacred sword thing before.'

Ben looked at him. 'First, they don't know that. Second, you're a witness now. Believe me, Jude. I know these kinds of people. If they find you, they'll torture you until they're satisfied that you know nothing, and then they'll kill you.'

Jude swallowed again, harder. 'But why? What the hell is so important about some crummy old sword?'

'That's what I'm going to try my best to find out, starting with a visit to Saint-Christophe, the village near Millau where this Lalique lived.'

'While I sit tight at your place in Normandy, is that it?'

Ben shook his head. 'I've changed my mind about that. These people must know who I am by now. It'd be easy for them to find you at Le Val. All they'd have to do is look up my business website.'

'So where are you taking me?'

'Paris,' Ben said.

'You have a place in Paris as well?'

'Just an apartment where you can hole up for a while.'

'What are you, a millionaire or something?'

'Hardly that,' Ben said. But Victor Jeunet, the place's former owner, had been one many times over. Some years earlier, his wealth had made him the target of kidnappers who'd snatched his child for ransom. When the money had been duly paid, a small finger had arrived in the post with a demand for five times more. Soon afterwards, Ben had become involved in his capacity as a 'crisis response consultant'. The child had come home with nine fingers, but safe. The kidnappers hadn't fared so well. The overjoyed Jeunet had given Ben the apartment as a gift, and for a time it had become his safehouse in Paris while taking on kidnap and ransom jobs across Europe and beyond. It had never been registered in his name. Nobody would be able to find Jude there.

'Paris sounds good,' Jude said, nodding. 'Great. Cool.'

Ben heard the phoney tone in Jude's voice and knew he had a problem. It wasn't the security of the safehouse. It was a question of whether he could trust this young hothead to stay put for five minutes while he tried to get to the bottom of this. Somehow, he didn't think so.

Chapter Thirty

'How can they have *disappeared*?' Penrose Lucas shouted, thumping on the desk. He was still bleary from being woken up in the middle of the night with this appalling news. He slumped in his desk chair, hair awry, his satin dressing gown hanging open to reveal the butt of the .357 Magnum protruding from the waistband of his boxer shorts. He'd now taken to sleeping with the gun at night, clutching it as he dreamed.

'That's all I can tell you.' Cutter replied. 'Napier called me to say they'd followed Hope to Cornwall. That's where they planned to take him out. There's been nothing since. None of them are answering their phones.' His voice was showing the strain of worry. 'If Vince Napier hasn't got back to me, something's wrong.'

'You sent six men after one and you tell me something's wrong?! You told me Napier was one of your top people!' Penrose screeched.

'He is,' Cutter said, resting his balled fists on the desktop and looking Penrose in the eye. The dressing on Cutter's brow had been removed, showing the nasty gash that Ben Hope had administered with the shotgun barrel. The split lip hadn't fully healed yet, and it hurt when he talked. He was still fully dressed, too edgy to sleep.

'Or *was!*' Penrose yelled. The migraine punched through his head like a spear blade. He screwed his eyes shut and dug the balls of his thumbs into his temples, thinking of all the money and treats he'd expended on these men, only for them to be snuffed out just like that, thanks to this Ben Hope. It was becoming a nightmare.

'And I suppose you have no idea where Hope is now?' Penrose grated. He glanced across at O'Neill, who just shook his head. Like Cutter, O'Neill hadn't been to bed that night.

'We'll find him,' Cutter insisted.

'That's what you said about Holland, too,' Penrose snapped. 'And even if you do find him, what then?'

'I'm calling in more men,' Cutter said. He'd already made the call to his old associate Linus Gant. They'd worked together in Somalia. 'But it's going to cost more. They don't come cheap.'

Penrose stared at him. 'Cheap? You call what I've been paying you cheap?'

'How much more?' O'Neill asked.

'A grand a day. That's the new price for all of us.'

'Fine, fine,' Penrose said, waving his arms. 'Whatever it takes.'

But O'Neill was stony-faced. 'I feel we're drifting off target here,' he ventured after a moment's silence. 'In my opinion it's time to re-evaluate the whole plan. This is not in line with our objective. Which I thought had been made clear to you.'

Penrose's face paled white. He bared his teeth. There was a fleck of foam at the corner of his mouth as he tore himself away from the desk, paced across the room towards O'Neill and stabbed the air with a trembling finger. 'Are you questioning my orders?'

As well as your rational judgement, O'Neill wanted to reply.

But he could see the fire burning in Penrose's bulging eyes and was watching the hand that might at any second dart inside the folds of the satin gown and come out shooting. He thought of his wife back home in London, and said nothing.

Penrose glared at him in disgust, then whipped back around to face Cutter. 'You tell your contacts I'll pay twelve hundred a day, damn it. And I'm offering a million bounty to whoever brings me Ben Hope's head on a plate.'

Chapter Thirty-One

Three and a half hours later, with the fuel gauge deep into the red and Jude slumped fast asleep in the passenger seat, Ben pulled up at a frosty truck stop off the M4 motorway before London to grab some rest. He'd slept in a lot more uncomfortable places than the dank interior of a half-decrepit Vauxhall on a freezing December morning, but his mind was too agitated to let him drift off. Dawn was still some way away when he finally gave up on the idea of sleep, and drove to the nearby Murco filling station.

While Ben attended to the fuel pump, Jude let Scruffy out of the car and wandered around the forecourt, stretching his legs and flapping his arms to stay warm, and then went inside the filling station shop to stand in the blast of the fan heater.

Ben had just finishing fuelling up and was about to go to pay when he heard the commotion from inside the shop. He hurried over to find Jude in an argument with the fat guy manning the counter, under the eye of the CCTV cameras. A newspaper stand had been knocked over and there were crumpled tabloids scattered on the floor. The fat guy yelled as Jude kicked over another one. 'Fucking lies!' Jude was shouting. There were tears in his eyes.

'What is it?' Ben said, bewildered, and Jude thrust one

of the crumpled newspapers into his hands. 'Look at this shit.' It was that morning's paper, dated December 20th.

'Is he with you?' the shopkeeper raged at Ben. 'You're going to pay for this damage, mate.'

'Step back, pork chop, or I'll do some more,' Jude growled. The guy flushed purple and made a grab for him. Ben gently nudged the shopkeeper back a step and gave him a look that quietened him for a moment. 'Now what's this about?' he said to Jude. Then he looked at the headline Jude was showing him, and his heart skipped two beats.

JOYRIDING VICAR IN LOTUS DEATH PLUNGE.

The colour photo underneath the huge bold print showed the crumpled car being winched out of the river. The partially demolished bridge was clearly visible in the background.

'What the—?' The pages crumpled in Ben's fists as he scanned the text below. Jude had snatched another copy off the floor and began to read out loud, barely able to speak for fury. 'Reverend Arundel was well known locally for being a playboy and a reckless driver. According to a witness at the scene of the crash, "Thank God there was nobody else on the road, the speed he was going at. They wouldn't have stood a chance."' Jude's face contorted in anger. He screwed the newspaper into a tight ball, hurled it down and started stamping on it.

'That's it. I'm calling the police,' the fat guy said, hovering warily a few yards away.

'Listen,' Ben told him. 'The article's about somebody close. He's just upset.' Shelling out a fifty and a twenty from his wallet, he handed them over. 'The twenty's for the fuel. The rest is for you. Take it easy, my friend.'

The fat guy's mouth twisted. He wasn't convinced.

'Come on,' Ben said. 'It's Christmas.'

The fat guy was breathing heavily and clutching his money

as Ben picked up the fallen stands and tidied up the mess. Jude had stormed outside. Ben found him pacing furiously near the car. 'Let's go.'

'How can they print that stuff?' Jude raged as they drove away. 'How can they say those things?'

'You know it's not true,' Ben said quietly. 'That's what matters.'

'It does matter. It matters a lot. They said there was a witness. What witness?'

'There was no witness,' Ben said. 'I told you. I was the first on the scene.'

'These people can fabricate a witness and write a load of lies in the press?' Jude punched the dashboard with such force that it cracked the plastic and left a smear of blood.

'They can do whatever they want,' Ben said. Like plant paedophile filth on an innocent man's computer before hurling him off the world's tallest bridge, he thought. He said nothing more. Jude raged on a while longer and finally flung himself back in his seat and lapsed into a simmering trance, nursing his torn knuckles. The dog hopped up onto Jude's lap, sniffed at his hand and gave it a lick.

A gloomy dawn was beginning to break over the London skyline as Ben pulled up in the familiar quiet street in Richmond. 'What is this place?' Jude asked. 'Hey. Where are you taking Scruffy?'

'He'll be fine. You stay here.' Ben scooped the dog off Jude's lap and got out of the car. He felt stupid and embarrassed as he walked up to the familiar red-brick Victorian house clutching the dog under his arm. Quarter to seven in the morning. He hoped Amal was an early riser. Ben barely knew the guy, and here he was about to lumber him with an unwanted temporary pet. 'I should have left you on the moors,' he muttered.

Scruffy looked at him and wagged his tail.

'Just kidding,' Ben said.

He was about to ring the bell when the door abruptly jerked open. He blinked as he found himself suddenly face to face with Brooke.

She stood rooted in the doorway, her tartan dressing gown wrapped tightly around her. Her unsmiling gaze pierced right through him. 'I saw you out of the window. What are you doing here, Ben?'

'I thought you weren't here,' he replied lamely.

Brooke crossed her arms. She gave a little snort. 'Is that why you came?' she asked. 'Because you thought I wasn't here?'

'No,' he said, flustered. 'I came about this dog.'

Brooke stared at Scruffy. Her expression didn't change. 'What are you doing with that dog?'

'He's not mine.'

'I know that, Ben. So you're picking up strays now?'

'I think I've kind of inherited him.' Ben paused. 'You look good, Brooke.' In fact she looked spectacular. Her auburn hair was longer than it had been, and she was wearing it loose over her shoulders.

'Thanks,' she sniffed. 'You look like someone who's spent the night in a car.' She glanced down at the dried spatters of Cornish mud that flecked the bottoms of his jeans. 'Have you been wading in a mire or something?'

'Or something,' Ben said. This didn't seem to be going too well.

'What's with the banger?' she said, peering over his shoulder at the Vauxhall. 'And who's the guy with you?'

'It's a long story,' he said.

'It always is with you, isn't it?'

'So what about the dog?' he asked.

'What about him?'

'I was going to ask Amal if he'd take him.'

'Amal's allergic to animals.'

'Then would you? He's Scruffy.'

'Not as scruffy as you are,' she said. 'What is this, another present? I didn't want the last one.'

'I need the favour. It's only for a little while.'

'This isn't the Brooke Marcel boarding kennel,' she said. 'Fine.'

'Why don't you ask your friend Darcey Kane?'

That hurt like a punch in the guts. Ben said nothing for a few moments, then turned to walk away.

'All right. I'll take the ruddy dog,' Brooke said. 'He's not going to pee all over my flat, I hope?'

'He's a vicarage dog,' Ben said, setting Scruffy down on the ground.

'Oh, well, in that case. What does His Worship eat?'

'I don't know. Dog food, I suppose.'

'That's helpful. I have some stewing beef in the fridge.' She paused, eyed the dog for a moment and then glanced back up at Ben with a softer expression. 'I'm sorry for what I said before. It wasn't fair of me to mention her.'

Ben didn't reply.

'It's cold out here. Do you and your friend want to come inside for a cup of coffee or something? You can wash up in my bathroom.'

Ben paused a second, then shook his head. 'I'd better make a move.'

'Just like that?'

'Just like that,' he said with a shrug. 'I'm sorry I can't explain. I really appreciate this, Brooke.'

Brooke reached down to pat Scruffy on the head, and he trotted inside the flat as if he'd lived there all his life. 'You're not in trouble, are you?' she asked Ben. The flash of concern he thought he saw in her eyes made him feel strangely comforted.

'Don't worry about me,' he said.

'I'll always worry about you, and you know it,' she said. She stepped back into the hallway to where her handbag hung from a Victorian coathanger, took out her purse and produced a business card. 'My new number's on here. In case you need it,' she added hesitantly.

Their fingers brushed as he took the card from her hand. They parted with a few more lame words. Ben felt her gaze on him as he walked towards the car. *Don't look back*, he thought.

But he did. Brooke was still standing in the doorway. She gave him an uncertain wave as he opened the car door, and a drum began to beat triumphantly in his heart. He managed to conquer the urge to run back through the gate and take her in his arms. It somehow didn't seem appropriate.

'Who was that?' Jude said as Ben got back in the car. 'She looks nice.'

'Never mind,' Ben said, starting the engine. He glanced back towards the house and saw that Brooke had shut the door.

'Your girlfriend?'

'Leave it, Jude.'

'What's wrong? You two have a fight?'

Ben said nothing and sped away.

Chapter Thirty-Two

After managing to make a last-minute phone booking en route, Ben screeched the Vauxhall into the car ferry terminal at Dover with just minutes to spare before the 10 a.m. crossing. They were the last car to board.

A few days closer to Christmas than Ben's outward journey from France, the ship was more crowded. As the cliffs of Dover sank into the leaden sea, he wandered out on deck and leaned against the stern railing. Jude came out to join him. 'I still don't understand why you didn't want to take a flight,' Jude said, gazing down at the ship's wake.

'I thought you liked the sea,' Ben said.

'I do. A lot. But you seemed in such a hurry. The ferry seems like an unnecessary hassle.'

'Some things are worth the hassle,' Ben said.

Jude frowned at him. 'You're a complete mystery to me, you know that? I always get the feeling you're holding stuff back. Don't you trust me?'

Ben didn't reply. He took out his cigarettes.

'We're not going to make it through this, are we?' Jude said, gazing fixedly down at the ferry's broad white wake. 'We're going to get killed. I am, at any rate.'

'You're not going to get killed,' Ben said. 'A few weeks from now you'll be back at university and getting on with your life.'

Jude shook his head sadly. 'If I make it through this, I don't think I'll be going back there. I'd already kind of decided to quit. Dad and I argued about it a lot. I suppose you're going to give me a hard time about it too?'

'Not a bit of it. Quit to do what?' Ben asked.

'I don't really know yet. I always wanted to do something to help the environment. Maybe I'll join up with Greenpeace, try to get crew work on board one of their ships.'

Ben lit a cigarette and offered him one. Jude waved it away. 'Don't smoke.'

'You mean you don't smoke tobacco,' Ben said.

Jude shot him a glance. 'I don't smoke anything else either, unlike a lot of the deadheads that hang around Robbie's folks' place. Not that it's any of your business.' He went quiet for a while, turned his back on the deck rail and gently rubbed his torn knuckles. They looked painful. Ben knew from experience how much it hurt to vent your anger against solid objects, like brick walls and car dashboards.

He knew how other kinds of pain felt, too.

'If it's any consolation, I've been there myself,' he said, letting a stream of smoke blow away on the sea breeze. 'I lost my parents, a long time ago. I was a bit younger than you when it happened. I know exactly what it's like to be left all alone in the world.'

'Did they die in an accident?'

Ben shook his head. 'I almost wish they had. No, my mother killed herself. My father went soon afterwards. He couldn't go on.' He could talk about these things now, though it still pained him after so many years.

'I'm sorry,' Jude said. 'So you've got no family either.'

'I didn't, for a long time. Until I found my sister Ruth.'

'Found her?'

'Ruth was kidnapped as a child, during a family holiday

209

in Morocco. For years, everyone assumed she was dead. We all lost hope. It was what tore the rest of the family apart.' Ben puffed out a cloud of smoke. 'Except that she wasn't dead at all.'

'How come?'

'That's a long story,' Ben said, and immediately heard Brooke's voice in his mind.

It always is with you, isn't it?

'She lives in Switzerland now,' he went on, 'running her own mega-corporation. You'd like her. She's another Greenie, like you.'

'Crazy shit,' Jude said, gazing out to sea.

'I suppose it's been a crazy life,' Ben said.

It was 12.30 p.m. local time when the ferry docked at the cold, sleety port of Calais and they disembarked and breezed through customs. 'Are you sure we'll make it to Paris in this thing?' Jude asked uncertainly as Ben fired up the Vauxhall and a cloud of black smoke belched from its exhaust.

Once they were safely away from the watchful security officials at the port, Ben pulled into a side street and got out of the car. Ignoring Jude's nonstop questions as to what the hell he was doing, he crouched down on the pavement to peer at the filth-crusted underside of the Vauxhall, produced a small clasp knife and slit the winding of duct tape that secured the two-foot-long plastic-wrapped item to one of the rusty chassis tubes.

'I think I know what that is,' Jude said suspiciously as Ben detached it from the bottom of the car, glanced quickly up and down the street and then slipped the object into his bag.

'There,' Ben said. 'Now you know why we didn't take a flight.'

'You just smuggled a dirty great gun through customs!'

Ben shrugged. 'Let's hope the nasty terrorists don't get the same idea. Now grab your rucksack. This car's scrap. There's a Hertz place two minutes' walk from here.'

They picked up a silver Renault Laguna at the car rental office and quickly left the north coast behind them, cutting down through the Pas de Calais and Picardy towards Paris, three hours' drive to the south. Ben pressed the Laguna on hard, carving through the motorway traffic and keeping an eye out for police.

Sometime after Amiens, he turned on the radio to escape the monotonous roar of the heater, only to find a classical music station playing Chopin's *Marche Funèbre*. As if he needed a reminder that Simeon and Michaela's funeral could be, for all he knew, taking place at that very moment. He quickly hit the tuner button, scanning through a jumble of music and talk until he landed on a jazz station and turned up the volume.

Nearly four hours had gone by since leaving Calais when Jude stretched, yawned and glanced at a passing road sign for Orléans. 'My French geography isn't exactly up to scratch, but as far as I can tell we seem to have passed Paris some time ago.'

'Well spotted.'

'Thought you were planning on leaving me there?'

'That was the plan,' Ben said. 'But remember what you said before about me not trusting you?'

'I remember,' Jude said warily.

'You were right. It seems to me that if I leave you in Paris, the moment my back's turned, you'll be haring after me across France. Correct?'

Jude threw up his arms in protest, then relented. 'I've as much right to find out what's going on as you have. They were my parents.'

'I understand,' Ben said. 'But I'm serious. You stick close by me and do exactly what I say. No more messing around, or I'll truss you up like a Christmas turkey and you can spend the rest of the journey shut in the boot.'

'You'd do that, wouldn't you?'

'Like I said, we handle this my way. Promise?'

'Promise,' Jude said reluctantly. 'Does this military regime extend to stopping anytime soon for a bite to eat? I'm starving.'

Lunch was a cold ham baguette and a bottle of mineral water at a motorway service station. They said little, and listened to the drumming of the freezing rain on the car roof. Ben used the Laguna's sat nav to check his route southwards: the motorway would carry them straight down past Bourges and Clermont-Ferrand, cutting through the Auvergne region and the Massif Central, then finally into the Midi-Pyrénées.

Meanwhile, wheels were in motion and the powerful information-gathering machine that was the Trimble Group was doing its work, sucking in data from contacts most government agencies could only dream of, processing it at light speed and siphoning it directly through the appropriate channels. The encrypted email landed with a little *ping* on Rex O'Neill's screen on his desk in Capri at precisely the moment Ben Hope was using his credit card to pay for the rental car at the Hertz office in the Port of Calais. O'Neill opened it and saw the names Hope and Arundel, together with the details and exact times of their clearing passport control into France.

He had a decision to make. He could either keep this information to himself, refuse to cooperate with the plans of a man he now believed to be a lunatic, or else he could do what his job required him to do and notify his boss that his current number one target had just reappeared on the radar along with a very interesting travelling companion.

O'Neill stared at the screen for a long time, undecided and wishing fervently that he had never been given this assignment. He reached across his desk, picked up the little framed portrait photo of Megan and gazed tenderly at it for a moment, thinking how beautiful she was and how much he longed to be back in London with her instead of stuck in this gilded cage serving the egomaniacal whims of a man like Penrose Lucas.

'What should I do, Megan?' he said out loud. There was no reply. Rex O'Neill sighed, then stood up, walked out into the cool sunlight and made his way across the villa complex towards Penrose's office.

Chapter Thirty-Three

It was getting on for eight o'clock in the evening as they approached their destination. The rain had stopped, and snowclouds were gathering thickly in the night sky. Ben bought a local map from a service station outside Millau, then drove on a little way to the tiny village of Comprégnac where a quick enquiry at a bar-restaurant yielded two key pieces of information: firstly, it provided him with directions to the late Father Fabrice Lalique's nearby home; secondly it confirmed what Ben had already suspected, that the priest's name had become virtually unmentionable locally since the child porn outrage had erupted across the media.

The village of Saint-Christophe nestled at the foot of towering cliffs close to the bank of the River Tarn. The oldest buildings dated visibly back to medieval times, when the village's population had probably never exceeded a hundred people. Some centuries later, the village had begun to sprawl outwards along the banks of the river, sprouting a latticework of narrow cobbled streets. But Saint-Christophe's most striking and least picturesque architectural development hadn't happened until much, much more recently. The illuminated span of the massive, towering Millau Viaduct, cutting across the valley several kilometres away, dominated the entire landscape. As Ben drove around the outskirts of

214

the village, he kept glancing at the distant bridge. Its ugly presence was inescapable, and a constant brutal reminder of what had happened there just weeks earlier. It would be years before the local community would be allowed to forget the scandal of their disgraced priest.

Less than a kilometre outside the village limits, ringed by an ivy-covered stone wall, was the simple eighteenth-century country residence where the now infamous Fabrice Lalique had spent most of his life. Ben drove the Laguna in through the pillared entrance. He'd half-expected the place to be deserted, but a light in a downstairs window prompted him to walk up to the old house and rap the heavy iron door knocker.

Several chilly minutes went by before his repeated knocks finally drew the attention of whoever was inside. The door opened, and Ben found himself looking down at a tiny, gnarled old woman in a black gown that did nothing to disguise her dowager's hump. Her face was as brown and wrinkled as a walnut shell, and its expression was openly hostile. 'Qui êtes vous? Qu'est-ce que vous voulez?'

Ben told her his name and explained in French that they were very sorry to disturb her at this time of night, but that they were friends of one of Father Lalique's most trusted colleagues. The old woman seemed utterly unmoved by this, but Ben pressed on, saying that he had a few questions about Father Lalique's work and that he'd be very grateful for a few moments of her time.

'Allez,' the old woman rasped. 'Allez-vous-en!'

'What's she saying?' Jude asked.

'That's French for "piss off",' Ben told him.

'I get it now,' Jude said as the old woman began shooing them away from the doorstep, threatening to call the gendarmes and doing everything but hawk and spit at them. 'Charming wife this guy had.'

'He was a Catholic priest, Jude. They remain celibate. She must have been his housekeeper.'

'Whatever,' Jude said, backing away from the ferocious old woman. 'I think I can grab her, if you find something to tie her up with.'

Ben looked at him. 'What do you think I am?' He graciously thanked the housekeeper for her time, apologised again for the disturbance and said he'd be staying locally for a few days in case she changed her mind. He knew she wouldn't.

'That wasn't much use, was it?' Jude said as they drove off. 'All this way to be scared off by the priest's resident bulldog.'

'I don't blame her,' Ben said. 'I'd have done the same, in her position. She's probably had a million journalists sticking their noses into her life since her employer's death. She's alone and vulnerable.' The truth was that he had every intention of returning to the house, but he wanted to do it alone, and discreetly. His way.

'I'd hardly describe her as vulnerable. So what now, boss?'

'Don't call me "boss",' Ben said.

The late priest's housekeeper, Cécilie Lamont, peeked through the window at the disappearing taillights of the car, then tutted loudly in disgust and marched over to the phone to call her elder sister in Perpignan. 'Can you believe what the world's coming to, Claudette?' she complained bitterly. 'Now it's two *rosbifs* coming round here to pry into poor Father Lalique's affairs. As if there hadn't been enough injustice done to that man already!'

'You should report them,' Claudette croaked. She was eighty-seven and full of emphysema. 'Did you get their names?'

Cécilie thought for a moment and said yes, the older of

216

the two had given his name – she pronounced it 'Ope'. Spoke almost perfect French, hardly a trace of accent, and it had only been when they'd started talking English that she'd realised they were rosbifs. They'd told her they were staying nearby, and perhaps she should call her grandson Philippe at the gendarmerie in Millau. Philippe would know how to deal with their kind.

Cécilie ranted on a while longer about foreigners, then returned to the subject of all the terrible intrusions she was having to endure now that dear Father Lalique was gone. She couldn't wait until January, when his replacement Father Girard would arrive along with a new housekeeper, and she could finally retire and move to Perpignan to be with Claudette. There was nothing like family, the two sisters agreed.

After a few minutes, the operative monitoring the phone call from much further away than Perpignan decided he'd heard all that was going to be useful. He turned off his earpiece and let the two old ladies natter on. The details of Madame Lamont's two foreign visitors were information he needed to relay immediately.

Earlier that day, the team had acquired the details of the ferry booking made by Ben Hope, minutes after it had been made; just over eight hours ago, they'd learned that Hope and Arundel had cleared passport control into France and duly passed that information over to Rex O'Neill. Since then, the team had been frantically trying to pick up a trace of their targets. Now all of a sudden the trail was live again.

The operative picked up a phone and quickly stabbed in a number.

Things would move quickly from here.

Chapter Thirty-Four

The village's only hotel was the Auberge Saint-Christophe, a medieval inn that seemed to be undergoing its first major overhaul in about seven centuries and was half-hidden behind a tower of scaffolding. The owner was apologetic, but the renovations meant all he could offer Ben and Jude was a small twin room. Sadly the restaurant was closed too, but the owner could heartily recommend Chez Moustache at the other end of the village. Ben took the room anyway.

The snow was floating down and beginning to line the cobbled streets as Ben and Jude left the Auberge in search of Chez Moustache. They found the old stone building down a winding alley, with a sign that swung in the wind. A battered red Peugeot 504 pickup was parked outside, empty bottle crates littered on the back.

Ben led the way inside the bar. In contrast to the sleepy street the place was lively, noisy and crowded. He saw right away how it had got its name. The barman was a broad, bear-like character sporting a formidable set of grizzled whiskers that he must have spent the last thirty years pampering.

'Bonsoir, messieurs. Je suis Moustache,' he welcomed them proudly, the bush parting in a toothy grin. There was a door open behind him leading through to a busy kitchen, two women scurrying here and there amid a lot of steam and smoke, leaping flambée flames and some wonderful odours of frying meat, garlic and shallots.

Ben asked Moustache if they could cook up a couple of steak-frîtes for him and his friend. No problem, Monsieur. Ben ordered a whisky aperitif. 'You want a drink?' he asked Jude.

Jude wrinkled his nose. 'Not one like that. Whisky tastes like shit.'

'Says the connoisseur. I'm sorry they don't serve Guinness, red wine and vodka cocktails in this place.'

'Ha, ha. I'll have a beer,' Jude said.

'Un demi pour le gosse,' Ben said to Moustache, jerking his thumb at Jude.

'What's a gosse?' Jude wanted to know.

'It means a snotty-nosed brat.'

'Oh, thanks. Keep them coming, why don't you?'

Some guys at the other end of the bar had picked up on their English conversation and were looking over. One of them was bony and acne-scarred with greased-back hair, slumped on a high stool with his elbows on the counter. Leaning against the bar next to him was a thick-chested, bearded man of about fifty, who wore a heavy chequered work shirt with the sleeves rolled up. They were all knocking back shots of some kind of clear liquor. Whatever bottle it had come from was out of sight under the bar. 'Eh, les rosbifs,' Ben heard the bony one call out. The bearded one grinned. Someone else let out a cackle.

'Did that guy just call us something?' Jude asked, staring back at them.

'He called us rosbifs. Like roast beef,' Ben explained. 'It's one of the kinder terms the French use to describe the Brits.'

'I don't even like roast beef,' Jude muttered, maintaining eye contact with the guys at the bar. 'Hey. You got a problem?' he said more loudly.

'Take it easy,' Ben told him. 'We didn't come here for a bar brawl.'

'Oh, I bet you never got in a fight in your life.'

'Never once,' Ben said.

Moustache had taken in the situation. 'They're not bad lads,' he said in French as he finished pouring Jude's beer. 'Just having some fun.'

'I have no problem with that,' Ben said. Jude picked up his beer and took a gulp. The guys at the bar had lost interest and started chatting among themselves, laughing as they drank their colourless drinks.

'You're not a tourist,' Moustache said to Ben with a half-smile.

'No, I live in France,' Ben told him. 'I'm here because of Fabrice Lalique.' Might as well throw it out and see what comes back, he thought.

Moustache narrowed his eyes and clunked the brimming beer glass down on the bar. 'You mean Father Lalique?'

Ben nodded.

'He's dead.'

'I know,' Ben said. 'I read all about it.'

'Your steaks'll be ready soon,' Moustache rumbled, suddenly less than friendly. 'You want to take a seat over there? Corinne will bring the food over to you.'

'I was just wondering what local people might have thought about what happened to him,' Ben said.

'He killed himself. He was sick. That's it. *Fini.*'

Moustache seemed about to turn away, so Ben pressed on while he still could. 'He must have known a lot of people, made a lot of friends around here over the years. Does everyone feel that way? Doesn't anybody find what happened a little odd, a little out of character?'

'People here have had enough of talking about Fabrice Lalique, okay? Now, if you'll excuse me, I'm busy.'

'You know what I think?'

'Monsieur, nobody is interested in what you think.'

'I think a lot of people around here don't buy the stories about Father Lalique. That's why I'm here, because I'm looking for the truth about what happened to him.'

'You are from the police? A detective?'

'I'm just a concerned member of the public,' Ben said. He laid a business card on the bar. 'This is my number if anyone wants to talk to me.'

The guys along the other end of the bar had stopped chatting among themselves and were all silent. The bearded one in the work shirt was looking at Ben intently. The expression in his dark eyes wasn't easy to read.

The kitchen door swung open and a harried-looking young blonde emerged carrying two steaming plates, calling out shrilly, 'Deux steak-frites!' Moustache pointed at Ben and Jude, and then the bar conversation was over as their evening meal was served to them at a corner table.

'What was all that about?' Jude said through a mouthful of fries.

'Just some basic reconnaissance,' Ben said.

'You think people round here are going to talk to us? You see their faces whenever you mention his name.'

Ben glanced at his watch. It was just after ten. He wanted to wait a few more hours before paying another visit to Lalique's house, in case his defensive housekeeper was in the habit of staying up late.

While they were eating, Ben noticed the group of men at the bar break up. The bearded guy and Moustache

221

disappeared into a back room together for a moment. When the bearded man emerged, he was counting through a roll of notes with a wetted fingertip. He stuffed the cash in his back pocket, threw a last curious look at Ben, bade goodnight to his pal Moustache and then batted through the door and out into the snow. A few moments later, Ben glanced through the window and saw the taillights of the Peugeot pickup disappear up the alleyway.

Chapter Thirty-Five

After their meal, Ben and Jude headed back to the Auberge and climbed the stairs to the twin room. It was small and basic, but everything worked and it was warm. The twin beds were neatly made and each covered with a hand-knitted woollen spread. Jude flattened himself on the bed nearest the door, let out a loud sigh and closed his eyes. For all his bravado, Ben could tell he was still completely overwhelmed by the events of the last couple of days.

Ben dumped his jacket on the other bed next to where he'd left his bag earlier, settled himself in an armchair and cast his eye around the room. He liked its simplicity. No television, no radio, no internet connection. No smoke alarm. He liked that too. Civilised. He took out his Gauloises and Zippo. Thumbed the lighter's flint striker wheel and relished the smell of burning petroleum-based fluid from the flickering orange flame.

There was nothing quite like a Zippo. Made in Bradford, Pennsylvania, U.S.A. since 1933. Simple, rugged, battle-tested, as timeless and dependable as a Browning Hi-Power automatic pistol. Ben touched the flame to the tip of the Gauloise and tasted the welcome sting of the strong smoke at the back of his throat.

'You shouldn't smoke so much,' Jude's voice came from across the room.

Ben clanged the lighter shut and took another draw on the cigarette. 'Why?' he said.

Jude shrugged his shoulders against the bedspread, still lying flat on his back with his eyes shut. 'You'll die,' he said simply.

'I'm truly touched by your concern.'

'Who said I was concerned? I just said that people who smoke will die.'

Ben looked at him. 'So if I stop smoking, I won't die?'

Jude gave another shrug. 'No, obviously you'll still die,' he said after a beat.

'So I can either die doing something that gives me pleasure,' Ben said, 'or I can die avoiding it out of fear. I think I know which way I'd rather live my life, thanks.'

Jude didn't say any more. After a while, his breathing settled into the slow, steady rhythm of sleep. Ben turned off all the lights except for the little lamp near his armchair. He finished his cigarette and sat thinking for a few minutes. 'Fuck it,' he murmured to himself, tempted by another cigarette. He put one to his lips. Reached for the Zippo. Thumbed the wheel. There was a spark from the flint, but no flame. He tried again. 'Fuck it,' he repeated. So much for classic design and utter dependability. The damn thing had run out of lighter fluid.

Remembering that he carried a spare can, he sprang up out of the armchair and went over to root in the depths of his bag.

The first thing he found was the Bible he'd taken from the vicarage. He gazed at it for a moment, then put it back in the bag and continued rummaging. His fingers closed on something small and solid. It wasn't the lighter fluid, either, but he took it out and held it tightly in both hands.

Until now, he'd completely forgotten about the present Michaela had given him. He carried it over to the armchair, dropping any notion of another cigarette as he turned the Christmas-wrapped object over in his hands and felt a fresh wave of sadness wash over him.

Jude was fast asleep on the bed, snoring gently.

Ben heard Michaela's words in his mind. *Promise me that you won't open it until you're back in France.* He was in France now. He quietly, carefully pulled away the prettily tied ribbon, then tore open the wrapping.

As he'd thought, the present was a book. Not another Bible, but a very handsome antique miniature leather-bound edition with *Works of John Milton* embossed in fine gilt letters on the cover.

There was a lump in Ben's throat as he opened the book. To his surprise, a little envelope fell out from between the pages and dropped in his lap. He popped the seal, expecting a Christmas card. He didn't know if he could bear to read the cheery inscription Michaela and Simeon would have written inside.

But there was no Christmas card inside the envelope. Instead he found two sheets of neatly folded letter paper. The paper was a delicate shade of sky blue, and smelled faintly of the same perfume Michaela had worn. When he unfolded it, he saw that both pages were filled with her elegant, curvaceous handwriting.

Dear Ben,

Simeon and I hope you had a safe journey back to France. I expect you're tucked up all warm and cosy at home with a nice glass of wine reading this.

*It was a joy to meet up with you again so unexpect-
edly, Ben. Simeon and I have been so delighted to see
you after so long.*

Ben couldn't stand any more. He scrunched the letter
up and tossed it on the ground. A few seconds later,
with a stab of shame, he picked it up again and went on
reading.

And his mouth dropped open.

*Twenty years is a long time to wait to tell someone
a secret. Simeon and I have often talked about how,
when and indeed whether we should reveal to you
what I'm about to say. When we met up with you
again at the concert, we both agreed that the time had
come. You were never one for beating about the bush,
Ben, so here goes.*

Jude isn't Simeon's child. He's yours.

*There. I've finally told you what nobody else in the
world knows.*

*I'm not quite sure how you'll react to the news. All
I can tell you is, Ben, I know it for a fact. There's
absolutely no doubt about it, for reasons I'm sure I
don't need to explain to you.*

*You must have suspected all those years ago, as I
did, that even when you and I were an item, Simeon
secretly liked me more than just as a friend. When you
and I split up – that is, when I dumped you in the
awful way I did – and you disappeared from
University soon afterwards, Simeon was there for me.
He's known since before Jude was born who the real
father was, and been honoured to raise him as his own
son. We always hoped that a brother or sister might*

226

come along for Jude one day, but sadly that wasn't God's will.

Please never think that either Simeon or I would dream of placing any responsibility, legal or otherwise, on you. We just thought it was right that you should be told the truth. I hope you'll want to meet Jude one day, and that you'll see what a wonderful and charming young man he's turned out to be . . . when he puts his mind to it, that is. If you ever felt he should know who his biological father is, well, that's a choice we freely leave to you.

Either way, we hope you'll keep in touch with us all now that we've made contact again. If you prefer not to, and don't want to meet and get to know Jude, we'll understand. If we don't see you again, may you have the peaceful and joyous life you've always wanted.

Thank you for having spent this Christmas with us. Your presence has made it feel special, and it's been a long time since I've seen Simeon so happy.

Love, and God bless,

Michaela (and Simeon) Arundel

Chapter Thirty-Six

Ben read the letter three times, open-mouthed, then a fourth just to make sure he hadn't dreamed it. There was no mistake. He stared at Michaela's handwriting until the words swam before his eyes and lost all meaning.

He was still sitting there gaping at it in utter disbelief when Jude's voice broke in on his thoughts and startled him. 'What's that you're reading?' Jude asked, yawning. He kicked out his legs and bounced off the bed.

Ben quickly slipped the letter in between the pages of the book. 'Poetry,' he said in a dry, raspy voice. He cleared his throat.

'Poetry. Give me a fucking break.' Jude peered at the book cover and let out a snort. 'Milton. I tried to read that once. Couldn't be bothered with it. Load of old tat, if you ask me. Where did you get that book from, anyway?'

Ben looked at him for the longest time.

'What?' Jude said.

Ben didn't reply. He didn't have the words.

'So I didn't like Milton. What's the big deal?'

'Milton?' Ben said. His mind wasn't working. His thoughts were a spinning jumble.

'Why – are – you – staring – at – me?' Jude said, making bug eyes. 'You're freaking me out.'

'I wasn't staring at you,' Ben said.

'Yes, you bloody well were.' Jude flapped his arms impatiently. 'Anyway. It's almost midnight. What are we doing? I'm tired of sitting around here waiting for nothing to happen.'

'Get some sleep,' Ben said, forcing himself to return to the present moment. 'Tomorrow might be a long day.'

'I just was sleeping. I'm not sleepy any more.' Jude crossed over to the window and pressed his nose to the glass, watching the snow fall over the village street.

Ben suddenly realised that the Christmas wrapping from Michaela's present was still lying on the rug. Jude only had to turn round to see it there. Feeling suddenly heavy and weary, he levered himself out of the armchair, bent down and scooped it up and stuffed it in his pocket before Jude could notice. He slipped the Milton into his other pocket and grabbed his jacket from the bed. It felt as if it was weighed down with lead. 'Do what you want. I need some air. Going out for a walk.'

Still in a daze, Ben left the room and stumbled downstairs to the empty foyer. Outside, the cobbles were beginning to disappear under a blanket of white. Large snowflakes drifted down in the glow of the street lamps and flecked his hair and shoulders as he set off aimlessly through the winding village streets. Saint-Christophe was mostly asleep, just a smattering of lights on here and there.

Could the letter have been some kind of joke? he thought in bewilderment as he walked. No, Michaela and Simeon would never have done that. Nor would they have lied about such a thing.

Could Michaela have made a mistake? If the baby hadn't been Simeon's, perhaps it had been someone else's entirely. Ben pondered the idea for a moment, then felt ashamed for thinking it. No. There had been nobody else during those days of his and Michaela's brief relationship.

Ben pictured Jude's face in his mind. His eyes, his mouth, his nose, the shape of his cheekbones and forehead, the colour of his hair. With a sudden certainty that made him draw a sharp breath, he realised he could see his own features reflected in the younger man's. Once you knew, it was obvious.

Then it was real. It was true. *He's my son.* Ben slowed his stride, turned and gazed back towards the Auberge Saint-Christophe. His eyes picked out the window of their room, a rectangle of dim light behind the latticework of scaffolding.

My son is in that room.

He shook his head in amazement. Thoughts tumbled through his mind as he walked on. *Could they not have told me sooner? Could they not have tried to find me?* For a few moments he felt indignation rising up inside him. Resentment, almost, that his oldest friends could have kept something like this from him for so many years.

But then he tried to imagine what the decision would have been like for them. It couldn't have been easy. Michaela's letter made it clear that it was something they'd discussed for a long time. And Ben hadn't missed the implication in her words that some part of them hadn't wanted to tell him at all.

But it was the truth. The truth.

I have a son.

Ben had reached the deserted village square. Snow was settling on the benches and iron railings that surrounded the 1945 Liberation Day monument, a marble plinth bearing a bronze statue of two French soldiers struggling under the burden of a wounded comrade. Their helmets and the folds

230

of their clothing were rimmed with white. Ben stopped and gazed at the statue for a moment. Then a thought hit him like a punch in the stomach, making him sit down heavily on the nearest bench. He sank his head in his hands, suddenly filled with horror.

Bodmin Moor. The man in the bog. The way Ben had drowned him. Callously, deliberately. Inflicting a cruel, slow death on a defenceless enemy. Jude's face afterwards.

What kind of man are you? Ben asked himself. What kind of man could kill like that, in cold blood, with his own son watching? Ben knew what kind. A trained assassin. Someone who'd devoted much of his life to war and bloodshed, who'd learned to suppress every shred of his own humanity in order to inflict injury and death on other men, simply because he'd been told to.

That was who he was. Perhaps that was all he ever would be. Perhaps it was why he didn't deserve happiness, or love. Or Brooke.

Jude had grown up and spent his whole life believing that he was the son of a good man. They'd had their quarrels and disagreements like any other father and son, but Jude would look back on Simeon's life and forever regard him as a decent human being, kind and gentle and just, who'd done his best to instil higher values in his only child. Could he ever say that about Ben Hope? How could he respect a man who'd done the things his real father had done?

Michaela's words returned to Ben as he sat there on the snowy bench, trembling in the cold. *'If you ever felt that he should know . . . that's a choice we freely leave to you.'*

'Never,' Ben said out loud. 'I will never tell him whose son he really is.'

Chapter Thirty-Seven

Ben was heading slowly back through the empty streets, still dazed, still in shock, when he felt the pulsing vibration of his phone in his trouser pocket. Answering it with a muttered 'Hello?' he heard an unfamiliar voice. Male, French, thirties or forties, speaking quietly and furtively as if he didn't want to be overheard.

'Is this Monsieur Hope?' the voice said.

'Yes,' Ben said. He blinked snow out of his eyes and struggled to focus mentally.

'The Monsieur Hope who was asking about Father Lalique?' the voice said.

Very quickly, the fog in Ben's mind began to clear. 'Who is this?'

'I have information for you,' the voice said after a pause. 'Father Lalique's suicide was set up. He was involved in something.' Another pause. 'This is not something to discuss on the phone. We must meet in person. Can you manage it tonight?'

'Give me your address,' Ben said. 'I'll meet you there right away.'

'Not here,' the voice said. 'This is a small village and I have no desire to be openly associated with the scandal of the paedophile priest. Do you know the ruined church? It is easy to find, about two kilometres west of the village, heading towards St Affrique. I will meet you there in thirty minutes.'

Ben had noticed the broken-down steeple on the drive in. It had reminded him of Simeon and his efforts to fund the repair of ailing ecclesiastical buildings. 'I'll be there,' he told his anonymous caller.

Completely focused and alert now, Ben raced back to the Auberge. 'What's going on?' Jude asked as he marched into the room.

Ben didn't want to look at Jude in case he started staring at him again. 'You stay put a while,' he said, snatching the Renault keys from the stand inside the door. 'I'm going back out.'

'At this time of night, in the snow?'

Ben discreetly slipped the book out of his pocket and bundled it into his bag under his spare clothes, well out of sight. The last thing he wanted was for Jude to develop a sudden interest in the literary works of John Milton. He was going to have to ditch the letter soon, although he'd be reluctant to lose it.

'Where are you going?' Jude demanded. 'You've had a call from someone, haven't you?'

'Yes. Someone in the village has information and we've set up a rendezvous. But I don't want you there.'

'You try and stop me,' Jude said, bristling.

'Didn't you hear me?'

'Didn't you hear *me*?' Jude retorted angrily. 'They were *my* parents.'

Ben froze for a second.

'I said—'

'I heard you,' Ben said. What was he supposed to do, shut Jude in a cupboard? Tie him to a chair? 'All right. You can

233

come. But remember our deal. You stay out of the way and keep your mouth shut.'

'I remember the deal,' Jude said. 'Not like I speak French anyway.' Seeing Ben slinging his bag over his shoulder and knowing the gun was inside, he asked anxiously, 'Are we expecting trouble?'

Ben shook his head. 'No reason to. But there's no way I'm leaving a firearm unattended in an empty hotel room.'

In the tiny car park behind the Auberge Saint-Christophe he scraped the fresh snow off the Laguna's windscreen. 'Where's the RV?' Jude said, getting into the car. 'That's what you military types call a rendezvous, isn't it?'

'Remember that ruined church we passed on the way in?' Ben said.

'Seems like a funny place to meet someone.'

The snowclouds had dispersed since the last flurry, and the moon was bright as Ben made his way carefully out of the village. After about a mile and a half he spotted the remnants of the old spire silhouetted above the trees, and turned off the road onto the short bumpy track leading to the tumbledown entrance of the churchyard.

There was no other vehicle in sight. Ben climbed out of the car and Jude followed him under the doorless archway into the ruined church. Moonlight streamed down through great holes in the roof, casting eerie shadows across the interior.

'This place has seen better days, that's for sure' Jude observed, sniffing at the smell of damp and rot. Little remained except the empty stone shell of the building. The altar was missing, probably looted decades ago. Even the flagstones had been prised up. Ben guessed they'd found their way into a lot of the local houses and cottages over the centuries. The bare earth floor was littered with dead leaves and the decayed remnants of the old wooden pews. A dusting of snow had fallen in through the holes in the roof.

'There's nobody here,' Jude said. 'I think your caller's playing a prank on us.'

'Be patient.'

Jude paced around the inside of the moonlit ruin as Ben sat on a pile of broken stone with his bag at his feet. He fished out his spare can of Zippo fuel and busied himself refilling the lighter. He resisted the urge to re-read Michaela's letter, and instead put the fluid canister away and rebuckled the bag's leather straps. Ten minutes passed. Fifteen. Ben began to wonder whether his mystery caller was going to make an appearance or not. Maybe Jude was right.

Jude stopped his pacing. 'Why do you keep looking at me that way?' he asked suspiciously.

'Was I?' Ben realised he had been. It was completely involuntary.

'You're not going queer, are you?' Jude said.

'You should get a haircut,' Ben said. His own thick hair would scarcely have passed military muster these days, but he'd known many an RSM who would have delighted in ordering Jude's unruly mop to be shorn to the roots.

'Girls like it,' Jude retorted.

More minutes passed. Jude stamped around the ruin, clutching at his sides and shivering. 'It's bloody cold out here. How can you sit still like that? Let me guess. Arctic training.'

'I did say you should have stayed at the guesthouse. The flask's in the bag. A nip of whisky will warm you.'

Jude made a face. 'No, thanks. You sit and freeze your balls off if you want. I'm going to wait in the car.'

As Jude left the church, Ben glanced impatiently at his watch. His contact was almost twenty-five minutes late. The guy either hadn't been able to get away, or he'd had second thoughts. Ben was trying to decide whether to give it one more minute when he heard a sound from the archway and looked up.

Jude had reappeared in the entrance. He was struggling in the clutches of a strong, bulky man in a woollen hat. One gloved hand was clamped over his mouth, muffling his protests. The other held a double-edged combat dagger to his throat. A moonbeam glittered off the slim, leaf-shaped tongue of steel.

Chapter Thirty-Eight

Three more dark figures burst into the church. More hardware flashed under the moonlight, two long silenced pistols and the unmistakable shape of a Heckler & Koch MP5 submachine carbine swivelling Ben's way as he jumped to his feet in alarm. He looked down at his bag, just a few inches from his feet. The shotgun was inside, a round already chambered and waiting. But it might as well have been in Hanoi. The odds of getting the straps unbuckled and the weapon clear of the canvas before a bullet found him, or Jude got cut, were vanishingly remote.

'I advise you to stay very still, Major Hope.' The tall figure clutching the MP5 stepped forward. He was in his mid or late fifties, lean and gaunt. The moonlight cast deep shadows in the hollows of his cheeks and sunken eyes. His lips were thin and tight, his hair cropped into a sharp V over his brow. Ben tried to place the accent. It wasn't quite Afrikaaner. Maybe old-school Rhodesian. One thing was for sure, the guy wasn't a local. Or an amateur, for that matter. The muzzle of the MP5 was pointed rock-steadily at Ben's chest. The man came on two steps and then stopped. Close enough to have no possibility of missing his mark if he squeezed off a burst. Too far away for Ben to be able to do a damn thing about it. Any attempt at a disarming move would be utterly suicidal.

The tall man took out a phone. He kept his eyes on Ben as he thumbed the keys. The call was short. 'This is Gant. We have him.'

Gant. Professionals didn't reveal names to men they intended to let live.

Ben looked at Jude. The big guy in the wool hat had the knife pressed hard against his throat. Jude's eyes were wide and bright with fear. He let out something muffled and indistinct from behind the glove over his mouth.

Ben felt his skin tingle and the blood chill in his veins. 'Let him go,' he called out. 'He's nothing to do with this. Just a hitcher I picked up on the road.'

The tall man called Gant smiled. 'You normally bring hitch hikers into your hotel room, Major?'

Ben said nothing. His eyes flicked from one man to another. The pistols were pointed at him in firm two-handed grips. They had him cold.

'We know who he is,' the tall man said, without looking back at Jude. 'Arundel's boy. Either he's going to tell us what we want to know, or you are. And don't waste time, Major. You may not have a lot of it left. Now, kick aside the bag, please. We know how tricky you can be.'

Ben hesitated, then swept his foot to the side and sent the bag, with the shotgun inside, tumbling away a couple of yards.

Without letting the MP5's muzzle flicker a millimetre, Gant took his left hand from the forend of his weapon and gestured back over his shoulder to his colleague with the knife. The big guy smiled and pressed the knife harder to Jude's throat. Any more pressure and it would split the skin. The slightest lateral movement and it would slice deep. Ben's heart hammered uncontrollably. Jude's eyes opened even wider in alarm and his muffled protests rose a notch.

'Now,' Gant said. 'Who wants to tell us where the sword is?'

Ben considered his options. He could tell the truth, and reveal to these people that he knew next to nothing at all, in which case Jude and he were pretty much guaranteed not to emerge alive from this situation. Or he could play along, in the desperate hope that if he kept them talking as long as he could, some opportunity might appear. It wasn't much, but under the circumstances it was everything.

'Wes has the sword,' he said. As far as it went, he was pretty certain that much was accurate.

'Its location?' Gant asked impassively.

So they obviously hadn't caught Wes yet, or if they had, he was dead. Either way, their target still eluded them.

Ben hesitated with his next reply. Just a fraction too long. Gant waved at his colleague again. The big guy grinned. Jude let out a cry of pain. Ben saw a trickle of blood run from the blade and his whole body jolted in horror. 'Don't do it!' he shouted. His throat was so tight he could barely speak.

The gesture again. The big guy looked disappointed and slackened the pressure on the knife. The blood ran down Jude's neck, but the cut didn't look as if it had broken all the layers of skin.

'I won't ask you again, Major,' Gant said.

'The name is Ben,' Ben said, not taking his gaze off Jude. 'Since you know anyway.' *We're going to get out of this*, he said with his eyes. *Just keep watching me. Everything's going to be okay.*

He was terrified that it might be the biggest lie he'd ever told.

'I was an officer too, you know,' Gant said, almost conversationally. 'Back in the day. I fought for my country.'

'But these days you just kill for whoever pays the most,' Ben said. 'Nice.'

Gant gave a thin smile. 'We're running out of time. The sword.'

'You'd never find it,' Ben said. 'But I can take you to where Wes has hidden it.'

Gant shook his head. 'Doesn't work that way. You tell us where it is. Last chance.'

Ben nodded. 'All right. Fine. I have a map here in my pocket. The location's marked on it.'

'Map?' Gant repeated suspiciously.

'The night Simeon Arundel's home was raided,' Ben said. 'I took the map from his safe. It tells you all you need to know.'

Gant remained poker-faced. 'Pass it over.'

'If I reach for it, you'll shoot me,' Ben said. 'You come over here and take it from my pocket.' In his mind he was already playing out the scenario. He pictured Gant's tall figure stepping up close to him. Reaching out a hand to frisk him for the map. The other hand taking the weight of the weapon. Ben making his lightning move to deflect its angle of aim away from him. A shot might go off. Maybe a whole burst, the muzzle flash lighting up the church. But within the next second, Ben would have delivered the lethal blow to Gant's throat or the base of the nose with the edge of his hand.

Once he'd seized control of the MP5, he'd have to neutralise the knifeman without touching Jude. Difficult. Not impossible. Ben had spent countless hours of his past in the killing house at Hereford training with the MP5 for exactly such contingencies.

The two pistol shooters would have time to fire in the exchange. Ben would take at least two bullets before he could cut them down. He was realistic about that – but at this point, he was past caring about his own skin. Only Jude's mattered.

Gant gave a curt shake of the head, and Ben's plan fell apart in an instant. 'Do it properly and I won't shoot. Thumb and forefinger. Nice and slow. Slide the map out and toss it on the ground.'

Ben did as he'd been told. Very cautiously and deliberately, he opened the left side of his jacket, reached to the inside pocket and slipped out the local map he'd bought on the way to Saint-Christophe. He dangled it between thumb and forefinger, then skimmed it across the floor towards the tall man.

It fell short. Exactly as Ben had intended it to.

Gant tutted reprovingly. 'Bad throw.'

'Sorry about that,' Ben replied.

Gant moved forward a step. Then another. His eyes flicked down towards the floor, and he began to stoop to pick up the map. He was within range now, just.

This was it. Ben had played his last and only card, and once Gant got a close-up look at the map and realised what it was, it would be over. Jude would die. Ben would too, if he was lucky. Otherwise, they might just take him away to be tortured and then dump his ravaged body in a ditch somewhere.

Ben's body tensed as he watched Gant bend to pick up the map. It would have to be a frenzied assault, several moves blurred seamlessly into one, the fastest he'd ever moved in his life. Faster than razor-honed carbon steel could slash through human flesh, faster than fingers could twitch against triggers.

Ben realised he was trembling in fear. Not for himself, but for Jude.

He's your son.

Gant's sharp eyes were off him and he was too intent on the map to see the attack coming.

Ben lashed out. Felt the toe of his shoe connect against Gant's face. Heard the grunt of pain as the man's head snapped back and sideways. Ben launched himself at the MP5.

And the inside of the church exploded in a flurry of gunfire.

Chapter Thirty-Nine

It was in moments like these that the principles of physics fell away, milliseconds suddenly became like hours and you really did have time to review your entire life in the time it took for a bullet to cross the space between a gun muzzle and your brain. In stop-frame slow-motion, Ben saw Gant's face split open and the blood fly from the impact of the kick. Felt his knee connect with his enemy's ribs and the cold steel of the submachine gun in his hands as he wrestled it violently from the man's grip. He heard the report of the first silenced pistol shot and the searing whistle of the bullet pass his ear. And heard Jude's scream from somewhere a million miles beyond his reach at the other side of the church.

Gant kicked and struggled. Ben ripped the gun from his hands and rolled across the floor. *Whumph. Whumph.* The silenced pistols letting fly.

In a semi-instant snatched in his peripheral vision Ben thought he saw a figure standing in the church archway. Then through the mayhem sounded a percussive, ear-shattering boom. A flash of white-orange flame and a rolling mushroom of smoke. Then another, crashing through Ben's eardrums like a clap of thunder.

Ben didn't know what was happening. He only knew that

he had control of the MP5 now. He could virtually feel the dreaded knife blade cutting into Jude's flesh, as though it were his own. Driving another pitiless blow into Gant's bloody face he raised the submachine gun and took instinctive aim at the big guy with the knife. In the semi-darkness, disorientated by the explosions and the flashes, he couldn't even see the sights. He felt the trigger break under the pressure of his finger and the weapon gave a judder in his hand as it spat a three-round burst of 9mm shells in less than a fifth of a second.

Jude fell to one side, the knifeman to the other. Jude hit the floor with his shoulder and rolled. The knifeman hit the floor flat on his back and didn't move.

Ben whipped around to see one of the two pistol shooters lying twisted on the ground. The other squeezed off a shot that ricocheted off the stone wall. Ben realised he was shooting at the figure who'd appeared in the archway and was half-hidden in swirling white smoke.

A third crashing fiery blast filled the church. The pistol shooter was lifted off his feet and sprawled backwards in the dirt.

By then, Ben had was already running over to Jude, calling his name. He saw the blood soaking Jude's clothes – then realised that almost all of it was spatter from the dead knifeman. The cut on Jude's neck was superficial. Ben dropped the MP5 and helped him to his feet.

As quickly as it had kicked off, the fight was over. Three men lay dead on the floor of the church. One killed by Ben, two by the mysterious new arrival, who was still standing near the archway, holding a large revolver. White smoke trickled from its barrel and floated up to join the pall that drifted in the air. It smelled pungently of rotten eggs.

Old-fashioned gunpowder, the stench that had filled a million battlefields of days gone by.

Gant, the leader of the men, was on his knees and elbows groaning and bleeding liberally from his smashed nose and teeth. Injured and groggy, but still a threat. Seeing one of the fallen pistols nearby he made a sudden and surprisingly fast lunge for it.

'Ah, non, non. Pas si vite,' said the figure in the archway, raising the smoky revolver and deftly cocking the hammer with his thumb. Flame burst from its barrel. The gunshot flattened Gant into the dirt like a crushed beetle.

Ben left Jude standing propped against a stone wall and turned to face the new arrival. 'Thanks, but I might have wanted to talk to him,' he said sternly, pointing at Gant's bleeding body.

The man shrugged. 'That is no way to greet someone who has just saved your life,' he said gruffly in French.

Ben peered at him. Where had he seen him before? He was about Ben's height, ten or a dozen years older, bearded and dark and wearing a chequered work shirt. Then Ben remembered: he'd been one of the group standing at the bar in Saint-Christophe that evening. The guy who'd been doing some kind of business with Moustache and left counting his money.

'Who are you?' Ben asked.

'My name is Jacques Rabier. I knew Fabrice Lalique, and like you, I would like to discover the truth about what happened to him.' He kicked one of the corpses as if it were a sack of grain. 'It seems I was not the only person interested in talking to you tonight.'

'Was it you who called me?'

Rabier shook his head. 'I think perhaps it was one of

your friends here, no? You have walked into a trap, *mon vieux*.'

'How did you find us?'

'This is a small village. I knew where you and your son were staying.'

'He's not my son,' Ben replied with a total lack of conviction.

Rabier raised an eyebrow. 'He looks like you.'

'What's he saying?' Jude groaned in the background, nursing his cut neck. He looked pale and shaky.

'Nothing,' Ben told him. 'Keep talking,' he said to Rabier in French.

'I was coming to speak with you when I saw you leaving the hotel in a hurry, and I followed you here. I thought this was a strange place for you to come, so I watched to see what you were doing. Then these men appeared from the trees. I thought that was strange too. Then when I saw them make a grab for the boy there, I thought perhaps it was time for old Jacques to give you some help.'

'I'm obliged to you, Jacques. One thing, though. If you were just coming to talk to us, why the six-gun?'

Rabier hefted the revolver in his fist and gave a crooked smile. Ben had never seen a weapon like it in action before, the type of old-fashioned cap and ball pistol that harked back to the 1860s and the days before modern cartridges and smokeless gunpowder. In Britain you needed a stack of authorisations to own one; in France they were completely unrestricted. 'I carry this everywhere with me now,' Rabier said. 'It is a precaution I have been taking ever since those men threw Fabrice off the bridge.'

'That's what you believe?'

'You do not?'

Ben took out his pack of Gauloises, offered the Frenchman

one, took one for himself and lit them both up with his Zippo. 'I'm taking it that you're not the kind of guy to be calling the gendarmerie in such situations,' he said, motioning at the dead men on the ground.

Rabier let out a short laugh. 'Bernard, the Chief of Police, is one of my best customers.' He spat on the ground. 'But the rest of them are no better than the Nazis who butchered my grandfather and grandmother during the occupation. We have the new Gestapo now, only their masters are in Brussels instead of Berlin.'

Ben didn't ask in what capacity Bernard was one of Rabier's best customers, but he had the impression that his new friend was in the illicit booze business. Ben had lived in rural France long enough to know that black market alcohol was a growth industry there.

'You have no more social engagements planned for this evening?' Rabier asked.

'This was it,' Ben said.

'Then come back with me to the farm. We can dispose of these *connards* there, and we will talk. You can stay the night.' Rabier went to fetch his pickup truck from where he'd left it hidden among the trees, and backed it up to the entrance to the church. Jude retreated to the far side of the ruin and didn't watch as Ben and the Frenchman grabbed each corpse in turn by the collar and ankles and flung them in an undignified heap on the flatbed of the pickup. Rabier seemed quite unperturbed by the grisly work, and puffed happily on his cigarette. 'You have done this before?' he asked Ben. That crooked smile again.

'Funny, I was just about to ask you the same,' Ben said.

'The answer is no, but I have often thought about where I would bury any *salopard* who fucks with me,' Rabier said. He covered the bodies with a tarp, lashed it down at the corners, and the load was secure.

They agreed to drive back in tandem to Saint-Christophe so that Jude could pick up his rucksack from the hotel. 'Are you all right?' Ben asked him as they drove towards the village, Rabier's pickup truck leading the way. Jude had gone very quiet and was holding a handkerchief to his neck. The knifeman's blood was still dripping off his clothes. The folks at Hertz weren't going to be overjoyed about the state of their seats.

Jude let out a grim laugh. 'My parents have been murdered and I can't go to their funeral. I'm on the run from bad guys who want to kill us because of some stupid sword. I'm covered in the blood of yet another person that's just been slaughtered in front of me. Is it eight now? I lose count. I've stolen cars and smuggled guns and now I've had my throat cut. I'm doing just great since I met you.'

The count was ten, Ben thought, but he kept that detail to himself.

Jude pointed through the windscreen at Rabier's pickup. 'And you do realise that this guy is insane?'

'I've known worse.'

'Unfortunately, I can believe that.'

Once they'd retrieved Jude's things from the Auberge, they rejoined Rabier where he was waiting for them on the edge of the village, and followed him to his place. It was a half-hour drive through the lanes before the pickup truck veered in through a gate and bounced up a track towards a large house and clustered outbuildings. The stonework of the house was badly in need of repair, and one of the window shutters was flapping loose in the breeze.

'It's worse than Black Hill Farm,' Jude said.

'I don't think there's a Madame Rabier,' Ben said.

Rabier led them inside. Wooden crates were piled high in

every corner. Ben decided his guess about Rabier's occupation had been correct. The Frenchman directed Jude towards a bathroom and offered him a pair of overalls to change into. His clothes were ruined. 'We will burn them later,' Rabier said, then turned to Ben. 'Come. We have some dead rats to bury. Then we will talk.'

Chapter Forty

After unloading the bodies from the pickup truck, Ben checked all three for any kind of ID and found none. Rabier sloshed the blood out of the back of the truck with a hose-pipe, then strode over to a storage shed. A moment later there was a clattering roar and a squeal of caterpillar tracks, and he drove out in a small mechanical digger. The two of them heaved the bodies into the digger's shovel. Ben climbed on board and Rabier drove him across the farmyard to a sprawling manure heap that was at least ten feet high in places. Rabier yanked a lever and the digger dropped the corpses on the ground like so many garbage sacks before getting to work gouging out a massive hole in the middle of the stinking manure.

Ten minutes later the hole was filled in, with the dead men inside it. 'After a few seasons they will make excellent fertiliser,' Rabier yelled over the clatter of the engine as he drove the digger back to its storage shed.

When they returned to the house, Jude had finished cleaning himself up and was changed into a pair of jeans and a bright yellow tracksuit top from his rucksack. He smelled of antiseptic lotion and there was a sticking plaster over the cut on his neck. Looking a little pale, he sat quietly in the kitchen as Rabier slammed three shot glasses down on the table and grabbed an unlabelled bottle containing some clear liquid that Ben suspected wasn't water. Rabier wrenched the cork from the bottle with his teeth and glugged out three brimming glasses.

Ben took a sip and his tongue was instantly ablaze. Swallowed, and a burning trail ignited violently all the way through his body like a length of high-explosive detonation cord going off. Another sip too soon afterwards would probably be fatal. It was like the moonshine he'd tasted once in Montana, only about double the strength.

'You make this stuff yourself?' he asked Rabier when he could speak again.

The Frenchman shrugged. After helping to kill and bury four men tonight in front of Ben and Jude, he didn't have a lot more to hide. 'It is my business. Not strictly legal, *naturellement.* But very popular with the after-hours clientèle, when the bars have closed and the fascists are at home in their beds.'

Ben took another sip and decided he could get to like this stuff. 'Let's talk about Fabrice. You knew him well?'

'He was my best friend,' Rabier said. 'We grew up together. I knew him like nobody else. Well enough to know that he was no child molester. He loved children, but only in the proper way, and any man who says otherwise is a lying piece of shit.'

'The night he was killed, he telephoned his colleague in England, my friend, Jude's father. He left a message saying he was being followed.'

Rabier nodded. 'This is correct. He was being followed, and in his panic he came here to the farm, hoping to hide from his pursuers.'

Ben was surprised by the confidence of Rabier's assertion. 'You saw him?'

'If I had seen him, he would still be alive now. I was not here.' Rabier reached into his pocket and drew out a little silver crucifix on a broken chain. He laid it gently on the table. 'This belonged to Fabrice. It was a gift from his mother when he was nine years old and he had worn it ever since. He would have been buried with it.' He paused a while, gazing at the tiny cross. 'That night I had been making my delivery to some of the local bars. To avoid the police, my customers prefer to carry out such business after nightfall, so it was not until late that I returned home and noticed something unusual. Come. I will show you.'

Rabier led them outside and across the yard, towards a large wooden barn that stood behind the house. 'Here,' he said, pointing at the ground, 'I found the tracks of a car. Also in the dirt were the footprints of several men, and some marks made by another man's shoes as he fought them and was dragged to the car from over here.' Rabier pointed at the barn. He stepped up to the tall wood-slat doors and pushed them open with a creak, switching on a light as he led Ben and Jude inside.

Rabier pointed at the straw-covered floor of the barn. 'The same signs of struggle were also in here. And here,' he said, reaching down and hauling up a trapdoor set into the floor, 'is where I found Fabrice's chain.'

Ben stepped to the edge of the trapdoor and looked down at the space below the floor.

'I have lived on this farm all my life,' Rabier said, crouching by the square hole. 'As children, Fabrice and I used to hide down here for many hours; as young men, to smoke and fool around with girls.' He smiled his crooked smile, which then dropped to a look of sadness. 'Fabrice returned to the same place to hide from his enemies, but they found him and took him away. There is where I found his cross, on the floor inside the hole. It is as if he had left me a sign.' Rabier straightened up and closed the trapdoor.

Ben started explaining to Jude. 'He said he found—'

'I get the gist,' Jude said. 'Why didn't he call the police?'

Rabier picked up on the word 'police'. '*Le jeune* doesn't understand,' he said in French. 'If these men could murder my friend and make it appear like suicide, what could they do to me? It was not safe to speak a word to anyone. Besides, I cannot afford to have the bastard cops crawling all over my place. They discover my distilling equipment, it's prison for old Jacques Rabier.'

'Was Fabrice's home broken into that night?' Ben asked as they headed back towards the house.

'If it was, it was done without leaving a trace,' Rabier said. 'You are thinking of the porno? How it found its way onto his computer?'

'The people who murdered Fabrice are as interested in discrediting their victims as they are in killing them,' Ben said. 'Take away a man's life, questions get asked. Destroy his reputation at the same time, everyone goes quiet. The bigger the scandal, the better the smokescreen.'

'Putain de salauds,' Rabier muttered in disgust. 'What is going on here? What had poor Fabrice got himself mixed up with?'

'Fabrice was a member of an international group, based in France, England and America and maybe also in Israel. They were working together on some kind of research project, for which they travelled out to the Israeli desert together.'

'I knew that Fabrice had gone there,' Rabier said. 'He was gone for two weeks, but he never explained why, as though he was unwilling to discuss it. He also went to America. Again, he seemed anxious to keep the reasons for his journey there to himself.'

Ben remembered Michaela had said that Simeon had twice travelled to the States to see an 'expert'. Ben wondered if the expert had been this man called Wes. 'Did Fabrice say what part of America he'd gone to?'

'No, he was evasive about it. I thought at the time that it was unusual he would not share it with me. The only secrets he kept otherwise were the ones he was told in the confessional.'

'The project had to do with a sword,' Ben said. 'A sacred sword. He never mentioned that either?'

'Une épee sacrée,' Rabier muttered, shaking his head. 'No, I have no idea about that.'

'What about the names of the other members of the group?' Ben asked. 'Simeon Arundel in England? An American named Wes, a woman called Martha, and an Israeli who travelled with them to the desert?'

Rabier shook his head again. 'He never spoke of them. This Simeon in England – you said he is your friend.'

'He's dead,' Ben said. 'They killed him, too, along with his wife. That's why I'm here.' He motioned to Jude, who was sitting staring into space, lost in his own thoughts. 'This is their son.'

'Merde,' Rabier breathed. 'I am sorry. But these people, they are after this sword? Why?'

'I don't know why. All I know is that they're organised and they mean business. They knew that my friend Simeon was in possession of the bulk of the research material, which means they most likely had been tapping his phone conversations with Fabrice and his other associates. The moment

Simeon was out of the way, they tried to steal the material from his home.'

Rabier thought for a moment. 'This is why there was no robbery from Fabrice's house.'

'And it's the reason why they killed him the way they did,' Ben said. 'If they'd needed to rob his home, a suicide at almost exactly the same time would have looked suspicious. They'd have done what they did to my friend, stage an accident instead. I'm sure that's also what they were planning for me and Jude, if they'd managed to get us yesterday. Tonight wasn't the first time they tried.'

Rabier raised an eyebrow. 'You are taking risks, my friend. These men we buried, they were professional killers, no?'

Ben nodded. 'At least one was ex-military. Possibly all of them. I'd say they were hired on a private contract.'

'Des mercenaires? Putain de merde.' Rabier looked at Ben and his eyes narrowed. 'And you intend to pursue them. Which tells me something about you. You are not afraid. You are *soldat*?'

'I was, once.'

'I can see it in you,' Rabier said. 'But one man against so many . . . How do you intend to go about it?'

'My best chance of tracking them down is through the sword,' Ben said. 'If I knew what it was, where it was, why it was so important, it might tell me who's after it and is prepared to kill to get it. That would give me the advantage I need.'

'And then it is payback time, yes?' Rabier said.

Ben said nothing.

'What about this boy here?' Rabier said, pointing at Jude. 'Can you take him with you?'

Garçon was a word Jude understood, and it snapped him

out of his reverie. 'Will you tell him I am *not* a boy?' he said, flushing.

'I don't have a lot of choice,' Ben said to Rabier in French, ignoring Jude. 'He's headstrong. Like his father was at his age,' he added wistfully. 'I can't trust him to stay put.'

'You want to leave him with me? I will make sure he comes to no harm.'

'I appreciate the offer,' Ben said. 'And I'll certainly take you up on it for tonight.'

'Tonight?'

Ben nodded. 'If the killers didn't steal anything from Fabrice's house, that means there's a chance I might find something there, some information that could be useful. I'm going to pay the place a visit.'

'There is the matter of Madame Lamont,' Rabier said. 'She is as alert as a guard dog, even at the age of seventy-two.'

'We've already encountered Madame Lamont,' Ben said, and smiled. 'She seems quite a robust lady.'

'Robust? She is a force of nature. For over twenty years, Fabrice lived in fear of her. The woman is evil. Worse, she has a grandson in the gendarmerie.'

'Does she have a gun?'

'I would not put it past her. It will have to be done very carefully.'

'House-breaking isn't exactly new to me,' Ben said.

Rabier grinned. 'Did you say you were a soldier or a thief? In any case, there is no need to break in. The time Fabrice went to Israel, Madame Lamont had to visit her sick sister in Perpignan. Fabrice asked me to go over to the house to feed his cat, Lafayette. The cat was old. It is dead now. But I still have the back door key.' He went over to a drawer and fished out a large iron key. 'Then it is agreed? We go tonight.'

'Not we,' Ben said. 'I do this alone. Jacques, I need you to draw me a plan of the house.'

Chapter Forty-One

It wouldn't have been the first time Ben had broken into a house in the dead of night, but having a key to the place did make matters far easier. After coasting the Laguna to a halt a long way down the road, he crept silently through the garden of Fabrice Lalique's former home. He was wearing a pair of tight-fitting calfskin gloves borrowed from Jacques Rabier, and carried a small flashlight in his pocket. His bag, containing the precious letter that he was determined to keep from Jude's eyes, was hidden under the driver's seat of the Laguna.

Crouching in the shadows of the bushes, Ben peeled back his sleeve and checked the luminous dial of his watch. It was just after three. The wind was coming up, blowing cold from the north and rustling the trees. Ben paused under cover for a moment to scan the top floor windows which, according to Rabier's detailed sketch of the house's layout, were those of the formidable housekeeper's quarters in the converted attic. The windows were all in darkness. Cerberus was, seemingly, tucked up for the night and fast asleep.

Ben padded across to the back door. The old iron key Rabier had given him was heavily greased to deaden its sound in the lock. He slipped it in and turned it slowly, easing the lock open millimetre by millimetre. The door opened without a creak. Ben let himself inside and waited a few moments for his eyes to adjust to the near-total darkness. He listened. Except for the ticking of a grandfather clock in the hallway and the whistle of the wind around the eaves outside, the place was in utter silence.

Ben had the layout of the house committed to memory. At the end of the hallway was a back staircase flanked either side by two doors. The door on the right led through to the salon, the one on the left to another staircase that descended to the wine cellar, part of which Fabrice Lalique had converted into his office. That was where Ben was heading. With the door closed silently behind him, he turned on the flashlight and crept down the well-worn stone steps.

The cellar still housed an impressive collection of wine, with well-stocked racks of dusty bottles stretching away into the shadows. Old Lalique had certainly enjoyed a tipple, Ben thought, casting the beam of his torch on an empty glass and a half-full recorked bottle of Bordeaux sitting on a little table next to a chair among the wine racks. The dead man's last drink.

At the other end of the cellar was the priest's home office, which had been decorated with typical French flair. The desk was a fine old oak antique, the sofa was luxuriously scattered with cushions, and the Persian rug was tastefully frayed around the edges. An ornamental velvet curtain was tied back with a tasselled rope.

Shining the flashlight around the office, Ben noticed the collection of framed drawings that hung on the walls – a pastel of some horses in a meadow, a charcoal sketch of a country church, a couple of landscapes – which all bore the same signature, F. Lalique. The priest had been quite a gifted artist. The same couldn't be said for the painter of the gaudily-mounted portrait of the Pope that hung over the desk, next to a large crucifix.

Ben shone the torch down to the desk. Its top was bare apart from a portable phone, but the marks were visible where the rubber feet of the priest's computer had worn against the varnish on the oak surface. The machine was probably still sitting in an evidence room in the nearest Préfecture de Police, thoroughly fingerprinted, gutted of its hard drive, the offending material all logged and stored as a testament to the deceased's undying shame.

At that moment, Ben thought he heard a sound from upstairs. He instantly turned off the torch and froze immobile in the darkness, listening. Had it been the sound of a door, somebody moving about in the house? Or just a loose shutter banging in the wind? He waited several minutes and heard no more, then turned the torch back on and continued examining Lalique's desk. It was a double-pedestal type, with a wide middle drawer and four smaller ones in columns either side. Nine in all. He slid open the middle drawer and spent a while combing through the papers untidily stuffed inside. Nothing of interest there.

The next seven drawers Ben tried were just as messy. Either Lalique had been the world's worst organiser, or the cops had already rifled carelessly through his stuff, searching for further evidence relating to his crimes. But if they'd thought they were going to uncover hot leads to the paedophile networks of the entire Midi-Pyrénées region among all this routine church paperwork, letters from parishioners, bills and receipts and a ton of miscellaneous rubbish, they must have been bitterly disappointed. It looked as if they'd taken virtually nothing away except the computer.

The last drawer Ben tried was the bottom left. It was stiffer than the others, and he had to give it a jerk to open it. The drawer was comparatively empty. As it slid open, a handsome old ebony fountain pen rolled to the front. The drawer contained a few other miscellaneous items like a spare pair of bifocal spectacles, a box of ink cartridges for the fountain pen and another of paper clips. Among the junk was a slim leather wallet containing the dead man's passport and national identity card. Shining his torch on the pages of the passport, Ben found the Israeli customs and United States Immigration stamps in the back, showing the dates of Lalique's visits. He hadn't been anywhere else out of Europe in the eight years since the passport had been issued.

It was interesting information, as far as it went – which wasn't nearly far enough and didn't tell Ben anything he hadn't already known. He was beginning to worry that he wasn't going to find anything helpful here. He put the passport and ID card back in their wallet, replaced them where he'd found them and pushed the stiff drawer firmly shut. There was a soft rumble and *clunk* as the fountain pen rolled to the back of the drawer and came to a rest against the rear partition.

Ben was about to move away from the desk – frustration rising as he thought about where to look next – when he stopped. *Hold on*, he thought. Something odd there. He opened the drawer again. The fountain pen rolled forwards again to the front. He shone the torch inside, then reached in with his hand, all the way so that his fingers touched the back partition. It was a deep desk and he could get his arm into all the other drawers right up to the elbow. Not this one. For some reason, the bottom left drawer appeared to be about four inches shorter.

When Ben tried to slide the drawer out completely, he found that something was preventing it from coming free. Groping blindly around inside, his fingers touched against a little spring catch. When depressed, it allowed the drawer to be removed completely from the desk.

And now Ben saw why the drawer was shorter than the others. At the back was a hidden compartment, four inches deep. He smiled to himself. Good old police inefficiency could be a blessed thing sometimes.

The secret compartment contained just two items. One was a pocket-sized artist's sketch pad, the other a little address book. Curious, Ben picked up the sketch pad first and opened it. On the first page was a rough version of Lalique's drawing of the horses; on the second an early draft of one of his landscapes. Thinking he'd hit another dead end, Ben flipped one last page before giving up.

The next sketch was something very different. It was a simple pencil line drawing of an object that was unmistakably a sword, but one of a kind Ben had never seen before. A strange-looking weapon, plain and simple in design, with a definite Middle-Eastern style to its peculiar sickle-shaped blade and curved hilt. He was by no means an expert, but from the proportion of handle to blade he guessed the real-life sword wasn't huge, perhaps three to four feet long overall, not much larger than some big machetes he'd seen.

Ben turned over another page and found another sketch of the same weapon, this time drawn in more careful detail, down to the tiny inscriptions running the length of the blade. He peered closely at them, but couldn't make them out.

It couldn't be a coincidence. This had to be *the* sword.

As Ben was staring at the drawing, he heard the sound again. This time, it definitely wasn't the wind. Somebody was moving about in the house. Approaching the cellar. He killed the flashlight and ducked behind the desk. There was nowhere else to hide.

The cellar door opened and the light came on. Footsteps

sounded on the stone staircase. Peering cautiously over the top of the desk, Ben saw that it was Madame Lamont. She was wrapped in a dressing gown, her grey hair tousled and her feet encased in furry slippers. He half expected to see a .38 in her hand. Small woman, big trouble.

But as the housekeeper reached the bottom of the steps, Ben heard her singing to herself and realised the old woman was half drunk. She must have been boozing all evening and then passed out for a while in her room; now she'd come looking for some more. Madame Lamont shuffled across the floor in her slippers, making her way to the little table between the wine racks. She settled herself in the chair, ripped the cork out of the bottle and poured a brimming glassful, which she knocked back in a gulp.

Hell, Ben thought. So much for the dead man's last drink. What was he going to do? The old dipso could be here for hours. He didn't have time to wait for her to drink herself unconscious again.

Madame Lamont was about to launch into her second glass when Ben came up behind her chair and hooded her with the cover of one of Lalique's cushions. The old woman began to screech and struggle. If Jude could see me now, he thought grimly as he lashed her securely to the chair with the curtain tieback rope. But Madame Lamont was a tough old bird, and from the fury of her struggles, he didn't think she was about to expire from a heart attack any time soon.

Ignoring the muffled cries, Ben ran back to Lalique's office and started leafing through the little address book that the priest had kept hidden in his secret compartment. Its pages were virtually empty, other than for a small handful of contacts that Lalique had entered by their first names only, either to conceal their full identities from prying eyes or simply because they were familiar to him. Under S, Ben found 'Simeon' listed alongside his Oxfordshire phone number; under W was the name 'Wesley', together with a number bearing the international prefix for the U.S.A. Flipping through the pages, the only other name Ben could find was someone called Hillel, with an Israeli number.

Hillel. Could he have been the burly Middle-Eastern-looking man in the photo? If so, Lalique must have kept this address book solely as a record of the group of associates involved with the sword. Remembering the woman called Martha, Ben searched under M. There was no trace of her, which seemed to confirm his suspicions that Martha, whoever she was, must have been peripheral to the group.

Across the cellar, Madame Lamont was still in full voice and she was fighting her bonds like a tigress. Ben's knots were good. He was confident she'd settle eventually.

Laying the address book aside he returned to the sketch pad. The fact that Fabrice Lalique had drawn the sword told him a number of things. One, it was a lot quicker and easier to take a photo than to do a detailed line drawing, however talented the artist. That implied to Ben that Simeon and his colleagues might have been unwilling to photograph the sword, in case the images fell into the wrong hands and aroused the wrong kind of curiosity. Had Fabrice perhaps sketched it without the others' knowledge, maybe working from memory afterwards? Such extreme secretiveness begged even more questions. Just what was this sword?

Two, it suggested that Fabrice must have been in the sword's presence at some point. Had that been in Israel? In America? Where was it now?

Three, given Lalique's skill as an artist, Ben had to suppose that the drawings were a good likeness. With that in mind, it wasn't the strange sickle shape of the weapon that perplexed him. It was its plainness, the absence of any kind of adornment. In his experience, and the experience of all history, when men killed one another in order to possess an object, it was generally because that object held some significant value. And value generally boiled down to hard cash. A sword of serious historical importance – perhaps once having belonged to a king or an emperor – could be expected to be heavily encrusted with precious stones and bear the flourishes of the most proficient craftsmen of its time. But this one had nothing of the sort.

Maybe it was made of solid gold, Ben thought. It was impossible to tell from the sketch. But then, gold was just gold. Once melted down, it might as well have come from anywhere. Someone with the cash to hire professional gunmen and organise phone taps and elaborate fake suicides and accidents could buy all the gold they wanted. Why this particular sword?

Ben still had too many questions, but he didn't think he'd get any more answers here tonight. Pocketing the sketch pad and the address book, he picked up his flashlight and Lalique's desk phone. He turned off the cellar light at the switch near the steps, then switched on the flashlight and walked back over to where Madame Lamont was still struggling to get free. He obliged her by liberating one hand, into which he pressed the phone. The old woman squawked obscenities at him as he removed the cushion cover from her head.

'Call your grandson,' he said in French, then headed up the steps and left the darkened cellar, shutting the door behind him. By the time the police arrived to rescue her, he'd be far away.

Chapter Forty-Two

Jacques Rabier had fallen asleep on the tatty sofa in the kitchen and was snoring loudly as Ben returned to the farm. Ben could barely remember when he'd last slept himself. He sat down wearily at Rabier's grimy kitchen table and took out his phone and the address book he'd recovered from Fabrice Lalique's office. He flipped the address book open to the letter W, and dialled the number Lalique had written for the American called Wesley.

Four a.m. in France; it would be late afternoon to late evening in the States, depending on which time zone Wesley lived in. The dialling tone droned on until it eventually cut off. There was no answerphone. Ben shrugged and leafed back through the address book to H for Hillel. Again, he stabbed out the number and waited. It would be around dawn in Israel, so there was a good chance somebody would be up and about to take the call.

After several rings, a woman's voice replied in rapid-fire Hebrew. Thanks to his theology studies, Ben's knowledge of biblical and classical Hebrew was sharper than his understanding of the modern language, and he missed most of what the woman was saying to him. He was a lot better at Arabic.

'I was looking for Hillel,' he said in English, and the

woman switched to English with the same transatlantic twang of nearly everyone who'd learned the language outside of Britain. 'This is Hillel's Coffee House, Zion Square. He's not here right now.' There was music playing in the background, and a buzz of chatter and activity. Ben knew that these kinds of places were often open twenty-four hours a day. He'd been in a thousand coffee bars like it in his time, all over the Middle East and Africa, and he could well imagine the scene – the poky interior, fading decor, smoky atmosphere, harried waitresses run off their feet for twelve hours at a stretch.

'Zion Square in Jerusalem?' he asked, remembering the name from his last visit to the place.

'Sure,' the woman said nonchalantly. 'Can I help you?'

'Will Hillel be in later?' Ben asked.

'He doesn't come in that often. Might pay a visit late afternoon. Who's calling?'

Ben ended the call without replying, and immediately started hunting for Hillel's Coffee House online. Its colourful website quickly confirmed that it was a popular all-hours café in Zion Square, off Jaffa Road in downtown West Jerusalem, owned and run by Hillel Zada and his wife Ayala.

When Ben saw the photo of the place he realised he couldn't have been more wrong about it. The coffee house was as upmarket as any five-star restaurant in London, Paris or Rome. Its smiling owners were pictured standing in front of the bar, surrounded by glitzy decor that had quite obviously had a ton of money thrown at it. Ayala was in her fifties, tiny and trim, much-bejewelled, dark-haired with streaks of grey. Her husband was a large, burly guy around age sixty, decked out in a loud flowery shirt that had four buttons open and revealed two gold neck-chains, each as

267

thick as a rope. An even chunkier gold identity bracelet dangled from one thick, hairy wrist.

It wasn't the first time Ben had laid eyes on the Israeli. He was the same man who'd been photographed in the group shot with Wesley, Simeon and Fabrice Lalique. 'Got you,' Ben muttered under his breath.

A groan came from the sofa, and Ben turned to see that Rabier had woken up. 'You're back,' the Frenchman muttered. 'What time is it?' He glanced at his watch and swore, then got up stiffly and yawned and stretched his way over to the surface where he kept his tray of shot glasses and one of his nefarious unlabelled bottles. 'So how did it go? Did Madame Lamont give you any trouble?'

'She was as good as gold,' Ben said.

Rabier filled two glasses, slid one across the table to Ben and sat down heavily in a chair with the other. He raised his glass. 'Salut.'

'Salut.' It wasn't really what Ben needed, but he took a sip anyway and felt a trail of fire melt downwards through his body. 'Where's Jude?' he asked when his tongue regained sensation.

Rabier smacked his lips and jerked his thumb at the ceiling. 'In the spare bedroom. Sleeping like a baby, last I saw him.'

'I'll go and check on him.' The bare wooden stairs were near the kitchen door. Ben climbed them softly and peered in through the door of the room where Jude was still fast asleep. He hovered in the doorway a moment longer than necessary, then quietly shut the door.

'Out for the count,' he said as he returned to the kitchen.

Rabier smiled. 'I have never seen anyone so exhausted.'

'He's been through a lot the last couple of days.'

'You don't look too fresh yourself, my friend. You should rest.'

'There'll be time for that later,' Ben said.

'Yes, in the grave,' Rabier chuckled. 'Then have another drink. This stuff of mine clears your head.'

Ben somehow doubted that. He showed Rabier the sketch pad. The Frenchman gazed sadly at his dead friend's artwork, then his brow furrowed as he turned the pages to the drawings of the sword. 'What kind of sword is this?' he murmured, scratching his beard.

'One I don't think you'll find in the war museum in Paris. My guess is it's eastern. Let's see if we can find anything like it.' Ben ran another web search on his phone, entering 'middle eastern sword' and clicking 'images'.

A host of material came up on the tiny screen. He scrolled down through dozens of pictures featuring Islamic shamshirs and mamelukes, wicked-looking Afghan warrior sabres and daggers; there were several images of scantily clad female belly dancers, some thin, some fat, performing with a variety of great curved scimitars balanced on their heads. He saw nothing that very closely resembled the sword in the priest's sketches, the nearest match an ancient Egyptian sickle sword called a khopesh.

'I don't know,' he said, returning to study the more detailed of Lalique's two sketches. 'Whatever it is, it's old. Really old. Nobody's used swords like this for a thousand years, or maybe even longer.'

They sat and smoked a while, and talked about dead friends, lost wives. 'My Brigitte was eaten by the crab, you know, cancer,' Rabier said. Ben told him a little about Leigh. It felt good to talk. Finally, it seemed that even Rabier's appetite for his homebrewed rocket fuel had abated, and he bubbled up a pot of espresso on the gas stove. Ben gratefully accepted a cup of the scalding coffee. 'About your offer, Jacques. To look after Jude for a while. If it still stands . . .'

'He can help me on the farm. There will be plenty to occupy him here. You were thinking of going somewhere?'

Ben nodded. 'This isn't over yet. And it's not going to get any easier or less dangerous.'

Rabier reached across to a fingermarked drawer of the kitchen dresser, yanked it open and lifted out the black powder revolver. 'Take it,' he said, sliding the gun across the tabletop.

'Thanks, Jacques, but I can't take that where I'm headed. Nor the shotgun. You can hang onto it for me.'

'Where are you going?'

'Toulouse airport, then Jerusalem via Paris. But say nothing about that to Jude. He's liable to come after me and I don't want him any more involved in this than he has to be.'

Rabier grinned. 'I have already forgotten. And now, my friend, I am going to bed.'

'In which case I'll say au revoir, Jacques. I won't be here when you awake. And thanks again.'

Ben napped for an hour on a lounger in Rabier's living room, resting his head on a mildewy cushion and covered with an old blanket that smelled of mould. When he awoke and returned upstairs to the spare bedroom, he found Jude still sleeping off the trauma of the last two days. He said a silent goodbye and left.

Ben slipped outside into the pre-dawn gloom to the Laguna, rolled quietly down the track to the road and set off on the eighty-mile journey to Toulouse airport. The snow had stopped and the roads were clear, piles of brown slush caked high at the roadsides. Traffic was heavy in the lead-up to Christmas.

Ben regretted having gone off without offering any explanation to Jude, but it was the only way. He would have insisted on coming along. Ben had already placed him in too much danger, and the risks were mounting. The farm was the best place for Jude while Ben followed the trail. Thanks to Jacques Rabier, the only potential witnesses to the incident at the ruined church were now languishing under several tons of well-rotted manure. Nobody could implicate Rabier, and nobody could have any idea where Jude was. The Frenchman might be a bit crazy, but Ben trusted him.

Twenty minutes from Toulouse airport, a strange irregular knocking sound started up from the back of the car. It paused for a moment, then started up again. Ben pulled off the busy road into a layby, got out and walked around the car. He could see nothing. Then he heard it again: thump, thump. Coming from inside the boot. Ben stared at the back of the car for a moment, then swung open the boot lid.

Jude's face peered up from inside. 'You bastard, you were going to leave me behind, weren't you?' He jumped up and hopped out onto the slushy verge. Traffic whooshed past as he squared up to Ben at the roadside. 'Now who can't be trusted?'

'What the hell are you playing at?' Ben said angrily. He felt like stuffing Jude back in the boot and returning him to Rabier's.

'Don't you get it yet? I'm going to see this through. I don't care about anything else.'

'How did you know I was leaving?'

'I heard you and Rabier talking.'

'You were asleep.'

'Oh, sure. And just because I don't speak French, doesn't mean I'm stupid. I got the gist. Jerusalem?'

'You're not coming,' Ben said, though he already knew it was futile. 'No chance.'

Jude ripped his passport out of his pocket as if he were

271

drawing a knife. 'You can't stop me. I'll pay you back the cost of the ticket. That's if we get out of this alive,' he added darkly.

The traffic streaked by. Ben gazed up the road in the direction of Toulouse, then turned and looked back the other way. He'd come too far to double back to the farm, and there was no time. Jude had him. He let out a long sigh. 'There's no need to pay me back.'

'So I'm coming?'

Ben looked at him. 'You really are a stubborn sod.'

The worst thing was knowing exactly where Jude had got it from.

Chapter Forty-Three

The water was roaring in Ben's ears and the current threatened to drag him away as he struggled across the bonnet of the sinking car to tear away the shattered windscreen. The two figures sat immobile before him, strapped into their seats. Michaela's hair floating around her face in the murk. He called their names, but all that came out of his mouth was an explosion of air bubbles. He felt the car sinking deeper, deeper, under him. Reached inside to take his friends' hands and haul them to safety.

Their eyes opened and stared into his.

'Ben,' they said, their echoing voices merging into a single plaintive moan that filled his head. 'Beeeeen . . .'

Ben woke with a start. For a few moments he glanced about him, disorientated, as the shockingly vivid dream rapidly faded away and the reality of the present came flooding back. He could feel the soft rumble of the aircraft through his seat and the soles of his shoes; the presence of Jude sitting next to him, gazing down into his lap, ignoring the clouds passing by outside the window. People all around. The flight from Paris to Jerusalem was crowded with travellers flocking to Bethlehem for the festive season.

An Air France hostess passed by with a smile and asked Ben if everything was all right. He mumbled a reply, then

273

checked his watch. It was almost three in the afternoon, nine hours since he'd slipped away from Jacques Rabier's place thinking he was setting off alone.

Jude slowly turned around to face him, and Ben saw that his eyes were rimmed with red. 'My dad,' Jude said.

Ben just looked at him. He felt panic stab through his guts. Did Jude know? How could that be? What was he going to say?

'My dad,' Jude said again. 'He was a good man, wasn't he?'

Ben's panic subsided. He blinked and tried to shake away the last remnants of his stupor. 'Yes, he was, Jude.'

'And I was a shit. To both of them. But especially him.'

'You shouldn't think that way.'

'It's true, isn't it? He always supported me. Even when we argued, he was there for me. And I knew how much it meant to him to have me home for Christmas. I wasn't even going to go. All I wanted was to get pissed with that arsehole Robbie and his stupid friends.' Jude's voice thickened as he went on. 'I didn't even get to say goodbye. I didn't care. While they were dying I was having a good time. And now I'll never see either of them again. What did they do to deserve a son like me?'

'They loved you very much,' was all Ben could think to say, and then he said no more.

Some time later the plane dropped out of the clouds and began its descent towards Ben Gurion Airport, some thirty miles to the west of Jerusalem. By the time they'd landed and taxied to a halt, Jude's dark mood seemed to have lifted somewhat.

After passing through the airport they boarded a crowded service taxi minibus that shuttled them towards Jerusalem, high up into the Judean Hills. On the approach to the city the limestone high-rises of the modern city sparkled in the pale sunlight. Olive groves and fields stretched out to the west. To the east lay the endless desert expanse of the Jordan Valley.

Downtown West Jerusalem was a bustling welter of cafés and restaurants, shopping precincts, tourist attractions and souvenir shops, banks and airline offices, cinemas and nightclubs, and a constant hubbub of traffic.

'It looks just like any other city,' Jude observed as they stepped off the taxi and were engulfed in the crowds. Ben was already looking to hail a private cab to take them to their destination in Zion Square.

'What did you expect, Bedouin camel trains parading through the sand dunes?'

'You've been to Jerusalem before, haven't you? What were you doing here?'

Ben shrugged. He recalled a wild motorcycle chase through the city with half of Jerusalem's police after him. Racing to stop a hired killer from detonating a huge bomb at the heart of the Temple Mount and sparking off World War Three. 'It was just a short holiday,' he said, and stepped out to flag down one of the city's ubiquitous battered Mercedes taxicabs.

Hillel's coffee house was an even bigger and glitzier place than it had looked in the photos on its website. The buzz of chatter and the mixed aromas of roasted coffee and fresh-baked bread hit them as they wandered inside and took a tiny table near a window overlooking the thronging square. The menus offered snack foods of all kinds, homemade hummus, salads, pitta breads and sandwiches, omelettes. Jude declared himself to be starving, and had his eye on a falafel sandwich like the one the man at the next table was eating. Ben ordered a Turkish coffee for himself and asked the pretty dark-haired waitress if Hillel was in. He wasn't, the waitress said, but he was expected to make an appearance sometime before long.

Ben and Jude spoke little as they waited. Jude devoured his sandwich and asked for another. Ben wasn't in the mood for eating, but toyed with a plate of tabbouleh and cold meats, which he washed down with another cup of the fortifying coffee, just about strong enough to stand a spoon in.

Then, just after six, a gleaming gold Jaguar Sovereign pulled up outside the Coffee House. The driver's door swung open and a large man stepped out and strode purposefully towards the Coffee House.

Ben recognised him instantly as the owner, Hillel Zada. The florid open-necked shirt from the website photo had been replaced by a Ralph Lauren overcoat and shoes that looked handmade. Business was obviously better than ever at Hillel's. He breezed through the door and was immediately all smiles as he greeted regulars, pausing at one table and then another to chat as he made his way towards the bar where a member of staff awaited him.

'Aren't you going to talk to him?' Jude whispered to Ben as Hillel strolled past their table. Ben sipped the last of his coffee and watched Hillel speak to the member of staff, then disappear through a door. 'You wait here,' Ben said, getting up.

'Usual story,' Jude muttered. 'I never get to do anything.'

Ben made his way between the tables and headed towards the door that Hillel had gone through. Before he got there, a waiter spotted him and intercepted him, holding up a hand and saying in English, 'I'm sorry, sir, you can't go in there.' Ben smiled politely and brushed past. The waiter chased after him, protesting as he reached the door and opened it.

Behind the door was a storeroom, with shelving stacked

from floor to ceiling and heaped with boxes and crates, sacks of chick peas, coffee beans and rice. Four huge refrigerators hummed in one corner. Across the far side of the storeroom stood Hillel, pen in hand, surveying the shelves and checking off entries on a stock inventory. The door batted shut behind Ben. Hillel turned round and stared at him.

'Hillel Zada?' Ben said.

The big Israeli frowned at him but didn't look especially perturbed at the sudden appearance of a complete stranger. He would have been, Ben thought, if he'd known there were people out there ready to kill anyone connected with the sacred sword.

Hillel was about to speak when the waiter burst through the door and began pointing at Ben and rattling off an apologetic stream of Hebrew that was probably along the lines of 'I tried to stop him. He just shoved past me.' Hillel listened calmly, then gave Ben a piercing, authoritative stare. 'This room is for staff only,' he said in English. 'Private.'

'That's good, Mr Zada,' Ben said, 'because I have private business to discuss with you. Alone,' he added, throwing a sideways glance at the waiter.

Hillel Zada's frown deepened. He motioned to the waiter and muttered something in Hebrew. The waiter glanced nervously at Ben, then left. 'Are you selling something?' Hillel said to Ben when they were alone. 'I am a busy man.'

Ben got to the point. 'Simeon Arundel and Fabrice Lalique have been murdered. Wesley might be dead too, or he soon will be. And I think you can tell me why.'

There was a long silence. Hillel's face dropped. He seemed to weaken momentarily, and had to rest his bulk on a stack of boxes. Ben could see from his shocked expression that this news came as a complete surprise. Hillel had had no idea until that moment of the trouble that had descended on his associates. If anyone was following him with harmful intent, he wasn't aware of it yet.

After taking a few moments to digest the news, Hillel looked up at Ben. 'Who are you?' he demanded, a note of suspicion creeping into his voice.

'My name's Ben Hope. I was a friend of Simeon's. I need to know what this is about, and exactly what it was you were all into.'

'What are you talking about?' Hillel said, still just as suspicious. His English was heavily accented but very correct, and he spoke every word carefully.

'Let's not waste time, Mr Zada. I'm talking about the sword. I've seen the photograph of you with Simeon, Fabrice and Wesley. I know they came here last year. And I know that other people are in great danger. You may be too.'

Hillel's expression was stony and full of doubt. 'Ben Hope. You say you were a friend of Simeon's?'

'And of his wife, Michaela,' Ben said. 'I was staying with them at their home in England when they were killed.'

'How did they die?' the Israeli asked sadly.

'In an accident that wasn't, caused by someone who wants the sword.'

Hillel absorbed this gravely, then peered at Ben with renewed suspicion. 'And why should I believe you were Simeon's friend? He never mentioned anybody called Ben Hope.'

The storeroom door burst open again. Half expecting it to be more members of staff come to rescue their boss, Ben turned. It was Jude.

'Were you going to leave me sitting there all day?' Jude said indignantly.

Hillel's face darkened at this further intrusion into his privacy – then he did a double-take and peered at Jude with narrowed eyes. 'I know you,' he said, pointing. 'You are Simeon's boy. He showed me a photograph of you.' He glanced from Jude to Ben, the suspicion melting away.

'My father's dead,' Jude said. 'If you know anything that could help us understand why, we'd be very grateful to you, sir.'

'I truly grieve for your loss,' Hillel said, clutching Jude's arm with a big hand. 'Your father was my friend.' He turned to Ben. 'Please forgive my rudeness. Tell me about Fabrice Lalique and Wesley Holland. What has happened to them all?'

It was the first time Ben had known the American's surname. 'Lalique was thrown off a bridge near his home in France. It was made to look like suicide. As for Holland, as far as I know he's somewhere in America, running for his life.'

'But how is it possible that a sword could bring such trouble?' Hillel asked.

'Mr Zada, the clock is ticking. The more I know about this thing, where it came from, what it is and who wants it so badly, the easier it'll be for me to find these people before it's too late. Right now I'm in the dark. You need to tell me everything.'

'Are you a detective?'

'I'm just someone who wants to help,' Ben said. 'And I need yours.'

Hillel nodded solemnly. 'It will take a long time and I have a family engagement this evening.' He reached inside his coat, slipped out a business card and handed it to Ben. 'Meet me tomorrow morning at eight, at my home. And I promise you, you will hear the whole story.'

Chapter Forty-Four

'I want words with you, Ezekiel.'

When his father said 'I want words with you,' there was always bound to be trouble. And trouble meant pain. The boy readied himself. He could handle pain. He'd handled it before. Nothing his father could do to him physically hurt him as much as the sound of his own name. Ezekiel Penrose Lucas. A cruel affliction that had tormented him every day of his young life.

Ezekiel Squeakiel, his classmates called him, in mockery of his still-unbroken voice that had the habit of shooting up an octave when he was nervous, which was much of the time. 'Ezekiel Squeakiel!'

'You were fidgeting in church again today,' his father pronounced in the solemn tone of a judge about to deal out a death sentence.

'I was not fidgeting,' the boy replied hotly.

'You may think you can lie to me, but God sees everything. And so did Mrs Woods. She was horrified.'

'Mrs Woods is a dirty old cockroach!' Penrose screamed at his father. 'I hate her and I wish she was dead!'

'Hell rip and roast you for a bastard, boy!' his father shouted back, turning dark red. With a terrible slowness, he reached behind him and opened the hated cupboard door, and the speech began. 'Those who are tainted shall drink the wine of the wrath of God . . .' he intoned as he took the belt from the jar of vinegar. He cracked it once, and a spatter of the foul-smelling liquid hit the wall. He beckoned to the boy. It was time for the punishment.

'. . . and they shall be tormented by fire and brimstone in the presence of the holy angels . . .'

Whack. Whack. The belt falling and rising. The sharp lash of leather against bare buttocks.

Penrose's face streamed with tears. He would not scream.

'. . . and in the presence of the Lamb.'

He bit so hard on his lip to hold it in that he could taste blood in his mouth, but the pain was so strong that he couldn't stop himself and a wail burst from his throat. 'Mummy! Make him stop!'

But Mummy would not make him stop. Mummy was in the next room, too terrified to say a word to the tyrant, lest he turn the belt on her, too.

Then it was over, and Penrose could do nothing but whimper in pain and rage and wish his father the most terrible suffering a young boy could dream of.

'Now get down on your knees and pray to God, that He may show you forgiveness.'

'I hate God,' the boy thought. 'I wish God were dead, too.'

The next day, Penrose sneaked out of the house with something long under his arm, wrapped inside a plastic bag. Still aching from the beating, he made his way furtively up the street towards Mrs Woods' house, half a mile away. The old cockroach lived alone with her beloved cat. The cat was fifteen or sixteen, had only one eye and was named Thomas O'Malley.

Penrose crouched hidden among the evergreens at the edge of her rambling garden. He slipped the plastic bag away to reveal his air rifle. With murder in his heart he quietly cocked *the gun and slipped a .22 pellet in the breech. And waited, silently.*

After a long time, there was a movement in the long grass. It was Thomas O'Malley. Penrose watched and his heart began to beat harder as the old cat moved slowly and stiffly through the garden.

Very carefully, the boy levelled the rifle. He found the cat in his sights and pulled the trigger. There was a crack as the spring mechanism fired the pellet from the barrel. The cat leaped in the air with a yowl and began thrashing on the grass. He'd got it in the stomach. Penrose jumped up from his hiding place and ran over to the suffering animal, clutching his rifle. 'Hell rip and roast you!' He raised the rifle up and brought the butt end of its stock down hard on the cat's head. There was a crunch, and a lot of blood. He raised the rifle and did the same again.

'Hell rip and roast you!'

The cat stopped moving, broken and squashed on the bloody grass. Penrose stood staring at it. He felt no remorse for having killed it. A smile spread over his face.

A voice made the boy turn. It was Mrs Woods up by the house, calling the cat's name. Penrose was frightened she might come looking for it. He slipped away into the bushes.

Penrose faintly registered the knock at his office door and raised his head slowly off his desk. He unglued one gummed-up eye, then the other, and blinked at the light streaming in through the office window. In front of him on the desk's littered top were his beloved pistol and his bottle of pain-killers. He felt woozy from the pills. The surface of the desk seemed to tilt before his eyes.

Rex O'Neill knocked on the door once more, and then walked into the room without waiting for a prompt. 'How's the headache?'

'What do you want?' Penrose demanded, livid at the interruption.

'To give you the latest update on Hope.'

Penrose's face lit up. At last. When the call from Cutter's man Gant had come in from France some eighteen hours earlier, saying that they'd captured Hope and Arundel, it had been cause for wild celebration and the opening of several cases of vintage Dom Pérignon, many bottles of which had been consumed by the team. Even Penrose had deigned to take a sip or two in the spirit of the moment. O'Neill had, of course, abstained, disapproving as always.

But as the hours had begun stacking up since the call without any further feedback from the team in France, Penrose had been growing increasingly anxious to know what was happening. He'd been convinced for a while now that Hope knew where the sword was. He'd probably had it himself, all along. Why else would Simeon Arundel have brought a man like him on board, if not to entrust the precious cargo to him? Why else would Hope be travelling with Arundel's son?

Penrose quivered with anticipation. 'Well? Did we get them? Do we have the sword?'

'I'm afraid not. It isn't good news.'

Penrose turned suddenly white.

'There's been no further contact from Gant,' O'Neill went on. 'And I've just received word that Hope and Arundel's son cleared passport control at Ben Gurion Airport in Jerusalem this afternoon.'

Penrose's face went from white to puce. 'But how could that be?' he exploded. 'We had them.'

'Evidently we don't have them any longer.'

Penrose's fury knew no bounds. He hurled his heavy leather recliner desk chair against the wall. Overturned the desk itself, sending papers and phones, his computer, his drugs and his pistol crashing to the floor. He shook his clenched fists, raised his face to the ceiling and let out a howl. Hope! The man was a vile scourge. He had to be stopped. 'What are they doing in Jerusalem?' he shouted.

'We don't know,' O'Neill replied calmly.

'Where's Cutter? Get me Cutter.'

'I don't think he'll be much use to you at the moment. He's still comatose, along with most of the others. What did you think would happen if you let them loose on so much champagne?'

'I keep my troops loyal to me,' Penrose hissed defensively.

With unlimited booze, boatloads of whores and a mountain of cash that doesn't belong to you. You think they wouldn't cut your throat in a second if a better deal came along? O'Neill wanted to say, but had the wisdom not to. He knew that Penrose secretly regarded himself as some kind of emperor – Caligula came to mind – and Cutter's moronic thugs as his personal Praetorian Guard. The man was slipping deeper into his own little fantasy world.

Penrose would not, could not, accept that his precious plan, so scrupulously and lovingly orchestrated, was slowly beginning to unravel before his eyes and there was not a damned thing he could do about it. He stamped up and down, flailing his arms and issuing orders like sparks flying off a Catherine wheel. 'Go and wake Cutter up. Force-feed him black coffee or whatever it takes to get him sober. Tell him to gather as many men together as we have available. Get the Cessna ready for takeoff. Call Naples and have the jet put on standby. I want a team heading for Israel within the hour.'

O'Neill stared at him. 'Have you any idea how hard it'll be to find Hope in Jerusalem? He could be anywhere.'

'I don't care!' Penrose screamed. 'I want him found and I want him dead. Do I have to do it myself?'

O'Neill left the office without another word. When he was some distance away, he took out his phone and began to key in a number that, if dialled, could change everything for Penrose Lucas. His finger hovered over the last digit as he suddenly had second thoughts.

This was his job. He was well paid for what he did, and he had the fine home in London and the enormous mortgage hanging around his neck to show for it, as well as his growing family and the impending responsibility of fatherhood to think of. Could he afford to take a gamble on how the Trimble Group would react if he spilled his concerns to them? He knew virtually nothing of their deeper agenda. Who would they most likely favour: an expendable, replaceable mid-ranking operative like Rex O'Neill, or the prize racehorse into whom they'd already invested millions?

O'Neill thought better of making the call. He put the phone away and went to see if he could rouse the drunken Steve Cutter.

Chapter Forty-Five

Ben and Jude had managed to beat the Christmas rush and snatch the only connecting rooms at the Golden Jerusalem hotel on Jaffa Road. The carpets were wearing thin in places, but Ben didn't care and his room had a balcony overlooking Zion Square where he could smoke and watch the city. He resisted the mini-bar, convinced he could still feel the after-effects of Jacques Rabier's moonshine dissolving his innards. After a quiet dinner in the hotel, during which Jude was very morose and reticent, Ben returned to his room, sat on the bed and used his phone to go online and check out the name Wesley Holland.

The simple addition of a surname was all it took to transform a completely obscure lead into a font of information; in fact a bewildering excess of it for Ben's purposes. Holland was all over the internet, although by all accounts the man himself was notoriously camera-shy and somewhat given to reclusiveness. Of the hundreds of articles Ben came across, nearly all focused on the American's wealth, with estimates of his personal worth veering between nine hundred million to over a billion and a half.

Wesley Bartholomew Holland had been born in a small town in rural Idaho during the Second World War, the only child of a hardware store manager and a schoolmistress, his mother having instilled in him a passion for history that had stayed with him all his life. His father had been one of so many U.S. Marines slaughtered as they came off the landing craft at Omaha beach, when Wesley was an infant. Raised by his devoted mother, the boy had grown up to be a brilliant young man with an uncanny knack for business, and gone on to make his first fortune in real estate. By the age of thirty, he'd become one of the richest men in America.

Wesley Holland was currently believed to have major business interests in more than sixty countries, in industries ranging from electronics to aviation to publishing and many more besides. He owned silver mines in Mexico and gold mines in Australia, copper mines in Chile, steel foundries in Japan. Pipelines, airlines, factories, private colleges, chain megastores. At one time he'd owned a Major League baseball team, though he had little interest in sport. Married four times, never successfully or for very long. In recent years, Holland's passion for all things antiquated had inspired him to pour millions into the restoration of crumbling historic buildings, churches and cathedrals across the U.S.A. and Europe.

Ben thought about that. Was it possible Holland's and Simeon's paths had crossed with regard to a church restoration?

He read on. Holland had supported the arts, made gigantic donations to galleries and museums, rescued scores of formal gardens from the hands of developers. But most of all he was known for his vast and enormously valuable private collection of antique arms and armour, the fruit of a half-century-long love affair with the weaponry of bygone times, that had made him one of the world's pre-eminent collectors of ancient swords.

Now Ben began to understand what connected the American to Simeon's mysterious research. Had the sacred sword, whatever it was, in fact been Holland's own discovery? That might account for the trips Simeon and Fabrice Lalique had taken to the States. But why had Holland shared it with two clergymen? Moreover, two who were from different branches of the church? How had Lalique become involved? And what about the Israeli connection? Maybe tomorrow's meeting with Hillel Zada would answer those questions.

Tracking through recent articles on Holland, Ben finally came across the unfolding news story of the recent attack at his home, the Whitworth Mansion near Lake Ontario. He looked at photos of the enormous house and read every scrap he could find about the incident. Three members of Holland's staff had been shot dead in what was believed to have been an attempted robbery by an armed gang, who had left apparently empty-handed after the billionaire had managed to escape to a panic room and call the police. Holland himself had disappeared shortly after the incident, and sources close to him had expressed great concern at the lack of contact from him since. It was not believed that Holland was under suspicion for the crimes committed at his home.

There had been two possible sightings of the billionaire soon after his disappearance, one from a freight trucker named Maynard Griggs who claimed to have picked up an elderly hitchhiker a few miles from the Massachusetts state line and only recognised him later from the television news; and one from a forty-seven-year-old waitress named Sally-Ann Ryerson who'd served coffee to a lone traveller closely matching Holland's description at the diner where she worked outside Lunenburg, MA. The man had told her he was heading towards Boston, possibly by bus. No further sightings had been reported. The investigation was continuing.

Ben went on searching for more material.

*

Cutter, Grinnall, Mills and Doyle thundered up the stairs to the floor where the hotel manager had told them the foreigners were staying. The manager was now lying comatose on the floor of the office behind the lobby, bleeding profusely from a pistol-butt blow to the head. The old guy might have had a heart attack, they weren't sure. He'd collapsed before they'd managed to get all the information out of him.

It was almost midnight. A busy few hours had gone by since the Trimble Group jet had touched down at the private terminal at Ben Gurion Airport. Cutter was under pressure to get results, and he wasn't messing around. A few heads had been broken before one of the airport shuttle service minibus drivers had finally come up with something. Two foreigners answering Hope and Arundel's descriptions had got off his bus in Jerusalem centre and been seen hailing a cab. At first the minibus driver couldn't remember which taxi firm it had been, but it was amazing how a knife to the testicles focused the mind. From there, it had been a straightforward matter of bribing and brutalising as many people as it took until a taxi driver spat out the name of a hotel.

'This is the floor,' Cutter said as they emerged at the top of the stairs. He started off in long strides down the corridor. Grinnall walked a step behind, his leather coat swishing. At the rear, Mills and Doyle were deep in debate.

'He's fucking nuts, though, ain't he? See it in his fucking eyes.'

'That's not the fucking point, though.'

'Shut it,' Cutter threw back over his shoulder, and the conversation ceased. Up ahead, a pretty, plump Israeli girl in a cleaner's uniform emerged from an empty room carrying a mop and bucket. She was working very late tonight, and looked as weary as she felt. Her polite smile faded when she saw the looks on the four men's faces. Before she could let out a scream, Grinnall clapped a hand over her mouth. 'Take her in there,' Cutter said softly, glancing up and down the corridor. They dragged her into the room and shut the door.

Inside the room, Grinnall kept his hand tightly over her mouth, clutching her head to his chest with a pistol at her temple. She squirmed and rolled her eyes in terror at the sight of the gun. He hadn't had this much fun since plugging the motel reception girl back in America. It made up for the humiliation of losing Holland's trail and returning empty-handed.

Cutter took out the photo prints he'd shown the manager downstairs. Hope's was taken from his business website, Arundel's from college records. 'You seen these men?' he asked the girl, flashing the pictures in front of her. She didn't understand a word of English, but his meaning was very clear. She squinted at the pictures. She'd only seen the foreigners a couple of times since they'd checked in, but she was fairly certain it was them. She nodded.

'You fucking sure?' Cutter demanded. On cue, Grinnall's pistol muzzle ground harder against the side of her head. She let out a little squeal of pain and fear, then nodded frantically a second time.

'What room?' Cutter hissed. 'Let her speak, Terry.'

'She'll scream.'

'No, she won't.' Cutter slipped out a double-edged stiletto knife and pressed it lightly against her trembling throat. 'What room, darling?' The girl babbled something in Hebrew.

Cutter grabbed her hand impatiently. 'Use your bloody fingers, girl.' Understanding, she held up seven trembling fingers, then eight.

'Room 78. Move.'

'What about her?' Grinnall asked.

'Let's do her,' Doyle said, glancing at the neatly made bed. 'We got time.'

'We're not going to do her,' Cutter said. He drew back his fist and punched the girl hard in the face, knocking her out. Grinnall chuckled. They left her sprawled on the carpet, shut the room and continued up the corridor. Reaching the door of Room 78, they paused a moment to check their weapons one last time.

Then kicked in the door with a splintering crash.

The blond-haired man who'd been reclining on the bed jerked bolt upright in panic as the four armed intruders burst into his room. He was wearing only a pair of Calvin Klein boxer shorts, and his legs were scrawny and shaved smooth. He had silver rings in both nipples. He scrabbled for his spectacles on the bedside table, jammed them onto his nose and gawked up in speechless horror. His younger travelling companion had just emerged from the shower, naked except for a pink bathrobe draped over his narrow shoulders. He froze, terrified, and seemed about to burst into tears.

'Ah, *fuck*,' said Cutter, lowering his gun.

Chapter Forty-Six

Ben managed to sleep a while despite the thoughts and questions that filled his head. He was awake early the following morning and met Jude downstairs for breakfast. Jude ate voraciously but Ben wasn't hungry. He demolished a pot of coffee, then the two of them headed out of the hotel to hail a taxi. Ben showed the driver the address on Hillel Zada's card, and the car took off. They headed west, with road signs pointing north for Ramallah and southwards towards Bethlehem.

Jerusalem is one city in two countries. Hillel's home was in the suburbs west of the Green Line, the 1949 armistice demarcation line that marked the division not just between West and East Jerusalem, but also between Israel and Palestine, where heavily armed customs officials stopped all traffic and checked passports. Ben and Jude were waved through into a very different section of the city. Suddenly the shop signs were all in Arabic instead of Hebrew, and the Islamic influence was noticeably stronger. A gang of youths hurled stones at the passing Israeli-registered taxicab. The driver pressed on with barely a glance at them.

It was just after eight when they reached Hillel Zada's home, a large, sprawling villa set among gardens ringed by a high wall. A tall arched entrance was closed off by wooden gates. Ben let the taxi driver go, then pressed the buzzer by the entrance. Moments later, he and Jude heard a powerful engine fire up from inside the wall. The gates swung open automatically and a Toyota Land Cruiser with oversized wheels, grilles over the headlights and clusters of spotlamps on the roof and radiator came roaring out of the entrance. From the noise, the exhaust was either some kind of high-performance add-on, or it was about to drop off. Hillel Zada's bearded face appeared at the driver's window. 'I have been waiting for you,' he said solemnly. 'Get in.'

As they charged off at high speed in Hillel's tank, he explained that he had all seven of his children currently visiting, with all sixteen of his grandchildren. With a full house, it was easier for them to talk elsewhere. Besides, he added enigmatically, there was something he wanted to show them.

'Where are we going?' Ben asked over the bellowing racket of the Land Cruiser.

'I will take you to where it began,' Hillel said sadly. 'Where I first made my discovery, nearly fifty years ago.'

As Hillel went carving back through the city with very little regard for other traffic and none at all for red lights, Ben gripped the handle of the passenger door and wondered if he drove his pristine Jaguar this way too. The Israeli seemed perfectly calm, but there was a look of deep sadness in his eyes and he looked drawn, as if he'd been up for much of the night grieving for his dead acquaintances.

Finally, the Land Cruiser broke free of the outskirts of Jerusalem and hit a winding sand-dusted road that led eastwards into the desert. Conversation was almost impossible over the engine noise, so Ben leaned back in the passenger seat, cracked the window open a few inches and smoked in silence. Jude was quiet in the back seat. From time to time Ben glanced over his shoulder at him, and the content of Michaela's letter would come flooding back into his mind, leaving him with a knotty feeling in his stomach.

The Land Cruiser wasn't the only vehicle heading into the desert. A thin stream of cars and vans, as well as a tour bus, were venturing out in the same direction. The road carved its way onwards across an ocean of sandy rubble that stretched out to the rocky escarpments in the distance. A few lonely shrubs and small trees lined the roadside. Road signs flashed by in Arabic and English.

After almost an hour's driving, the snaking road cleared a rise and Jude let out a whistle as a spectacular vista opened up ahead. 'The Dead Sea,' Hillel said over the engine noise, motioning grandly through the dusty windscreen towards the vast expanse of salt lake that stretched out ahead of them in the middle distance, before the seemingly limitless desert closed in again. Somewhere across the sands lay the Jordanian border.

'And there,' Hillel said, pointing up at a huge sandy mountain that towered high over the water, casting a giant shadow across the sands, 'is Masada.'

'What is this place?' Jude asked in fascination, leaning forward between the front seats and craning his neck upwards as high as he could to see the top of the mountain.

'Masada was a fortress,' Ben told him, speaking loudly to be heard, 'where the great Jewish rebellion against the Roman Empire made its last stand, forty years after the death of Christ. Nine hundred men, women and children, who'd fled from the sack of Jerusalem and the Roman purge against their race. They held out here for three years while a massive Roman army camped at the foot of the mountain and built a siege embankment and an assault ramp to storm the fort.'

'I'm guessing the Romans killed them all,' Jude said, straining to make out the fortress on the very top of the rocky crag far, far above the desert.

'They didn't get the chance. According to the Roman historian Josephus, when the soldiers eventually breached the stronghold, all they found were mounds of dead bodies. The Jewish resistants had committed mass suicide rather than let themselves be taken. Each man slaughtered his own wife and children, then a team was elected to kill everyone remaining before finally falling on their own swords.'

'Shit,' Jude said, shaking his head. 'Nine hundred people.'

'That's what the history books say,' Ben said.

'What would the Romans have done to them if they'd captured them?'

'Probably a lot worse.'

'Those Romans were mean mothers.'

'You are a historian?' Hillel asked, glancing at Ben as he drove.

'Hardly. I studied theology with his father,' Ben replied, motioning back at Jude. 'I've read a few background texts about this place, that's all.'

'Then you must know that for many centuries, the site of the great martyrdom was lost to knowledge,' Hillel said. 'Masada was rediscovered in 1842, and it was not until 1963 that excavations began, led by an Israeli archaeologist called Yigael Yadin. Such a huge task required a very large work-force. They hired men by the truckload. One of them, a boy of sixteen who was willing to do the hardest work to help support his family.' Hillel prodded his chest with his thumb. 'Me. That is where my story begins.'

'What is it you want to show us, Hillel?'

'The same thing I showed to Wesley, and then later to Simeon and the Frenchman.'

The Land Cruiser followed the other traffic into a parking lot near to a cable car station, from which thick steel cables soared skywards towards the looming mountain. Along with a mixed handful of tourists, the rowdiest of which was a contingent of Italians, Ben, Jude and Hillel boarded the next cable car. There was a delay while a corpulent American family squeezed themselves aboard, adding drastically to the cable car's payload. It was the size of a minibus, offering all-around views as it glided up the mountain on a track running parallel to a second cable car bringing visitors back down to earth.

Jude shivered. 'You wouldn't expect it to be so chilly in the desert.'

In SAS desert operations in the Gulf, Ben had seen sleet, snow and soldiers suffering from frostbite and hypothermia. It wasn't a memory he wanted to share with a cable car-load of tourists.

Despite the cold, Masada evidently attracted its fair share of seasonal visitors. Hillel informed Ben and Jude, not without a measure of pride, that it was Israel's most visited archaeological site. The tourists noisily expressed their appreciation as the cable car made its way up the side of the mountain. Even Ben was struck by the sight, realising for the first time the incredible scale of the Roman military operation to take such an inaccessible fortress.

As they climbed, the traces of the Roman military camps dotted around the base of the mountain were clearly visible. Ahead, the great russety-red sandstone mountain loomed closer and closer under the cloudy sky. They glided over the tiny matchstick figures of people ascending the mountain on foot via a winding path, like pilgrims from some bygone age.

The cable car neared the fragile-looking docking station precariously erected on the face of the cliff. Finally, and to Jude's obvious relief, they made it all the way to the top without being brought crashing down to the rocks by the weight of the lardy American family.

'Holy shit, get a load of this,' Jude breathed when they stepped out on the wide flat summit of the mountain and the full panoramic breadth of the view opened up. They were so high above the sweeping vista of the desert and the hazy Dead Sea that it was like looking down from the windows of an aircraft.

Ben gazed around him at the extensive stone remains of the fortress and could see that the modern-day excavation work had been almost as massive in scale as the Romans' attempts to destroy the place nearly two thousand years earlier.

'It did not look like this back in 1963,' Hillel said. 'Then it was only a field of rubble, half erased by time and the hand of nature.' He pointed out the black painted lines that were visible on many of the buildings, archways and columns. 'Those mark where the original stonework ends and the reconstructions begin.'

'It's very impressive,' Ben said. 'But as you know, we didn't come here to do the tourist thing.'

Hillel nodded. 'This way,' he said, leading them through the ruins. As he walked, he began to tell his story.

'I was the eldest of ten children. My family were very poor. My mother worked in a factory where the conditions were very bad and the pay was even worse. My father worked as a stonemason, until one day, when I was thirteen years of age, he fell from a ladder and his legs were smashed. He never walked again and was always in great pain. With my poor father crippled and no longer able to earn any money, much responsibility fell on me. I worked delivering goods for Jerusalem merchants. I stole eggs and resold them. I even stole a chicken once. We struggled every day just to stay alive and pay the rent for a tiny hovel that was not fit for a dog to live in.'

Hillel paused to run his hand admiringly along a wall, as if he'd built it himself. 'When I heard of the huge workforce that was being gathered for the excavation of the Masada site, I signed on. I was big and strong and already used to hard work. Now, follow me through this set of arches, and I will show you.'

A few yards on, Hillel stopped to contemplate a section of the thick, craggy rampart wall. Beyond it was a sheer drop protected by a modern-day steel railing, and the dizzying view for miles towards Jerusalem. He crouched down low and delicately brushed some sand away from a crevice near the foot of the wall. 'This is the place,' he said, twisting his head up to look at Ben. 'Come. See.'

The crevice was a horizontal gap in the ancient masonry where stones of uneven size had been used to build the wall. It was about four feet long and only just wide enough for a man to insert his fist.

'It was June, 1963. I was assigned to this section with two other workers,' Hillel said. 'We were dying in the heat, tired and thirsty, while our foreman, a man called Samir, gulped water from his canteen and shouted at us whenever we stopped. I remember how much I hated him.' Hillel scraped a small handful of sand and stones from the crevice and let it slip through his fingers.

'Each man had his own piece of wall to work on. Mine was almost buried. I was digging away sand and stone with my bare hands when I found the hole and, deep inside it, something wrapped in a bundle of cloth. We had orders to report any find immediately to the foremen. I turned towards Samir and was about to call him when I saw that he was swallowing more water from his canteen, drinking like a hog so that it was pouring from his mouth and splashing on the ground. I was so thirsty, and so angry, that I did not call him. Instead, I pulled out the bundle and, careful to let nobody see me, I unwrapped it.'

'And it was a sword,' Ben said.

Chapter Forty-Seven

Hillel stood up and dusted the sand off his hands. 'Yes. A very beautiful sword. Its handle was made of bronze that shone like gold in the sun, the blade shaped like this, and so long.' He traced a curved line through the air, then spaced his palms a distance apart. Ben saw that his measurement estimate from Fabrice Lalique's sketch had been more or less right, about three and a half feet overall.

'I could see it was very, very old,' Hillel went on, 'and that it must have been hidden here for longer than time itself. I knew nothing of history, but this was surely an object of great value. Again I turned to Samir, but he was now standing talking to another foreman, sharing a joke and smoking cigarettes. I looked at Samir's fat belly, and thought of my poor crippled father at home, and my mother working like a slave in the factory.'

'You decided to keep it for yourself,' Jude said.

'When times are hard and you have a family to care for, you are sometimes forced to do things that you may know are wrong,' Hillel said. 'Yes, I wrapped the sword back in its bundle and replaced it where I had found it. For the rest of the day I was terrified that another worker would find it. But they did not, and as the day came to an end I managed to bring it onto the lorry that was taking the workers back to Jerusalem. There were so many of us that the foremen did not take notice of what one boy was doing.

'Returning to the city, I went straight to Ali the pawn-broker on Jaffa Road. He examined the sword and asked me where I had found it. I told him some lie that I do not remember now. We haggled over its value, and then Ali told me I was a son of a baboon and tossed me a handful of coins, enough to feed my family for a week and buy medicine to ease the pain in my father's legs. I remember how proud I was, for a long time afterwards. Samir and the other foremen never knew my secret.'

'So you no longer had the sword,' Ben said, trying to understand.

'No, I never saw it again. My life went on. I grew up and became a taxi driver in Jerusalem. My father died, and soon afterwards my poor mother too. I married Ayala. One by one, my brothers and sisters all went their own ways. Many years went by and my family grew. I worked hard to ensure that they never had to suffer the poverty I had known in my childhood. Eighteen hours a day. Everybody in Jerusalem knew me. When I was not driving around the city, I was learning to speak English so that I could talk to the rich foreigners who got in my taxi. I dreamed of having a busi-ness of my own, that I could pass on to my children. But my dream never happened.' Hillel paused, gazing across the desert as he replayed his life's events inside his head.

Ben was growing impatient with the story and could sense Jude's increasing restlessness, too. 'Is any of this heading our way, Hillel?'

'I am sorry. Let me go on. Then, one day two and a half years ago, a rich American appeared at my taxi company offices. He said he wanted to book Hillel Zada to be his driver for the day. Just me, nobody else, and he was offering to pay double the normal rate. So we got in the car. I asked him where he wanted to go. He said nowhere. He just wanted to talk to me about a sword.'

'It was Wesley Holland?'

Hillel nodded. 'Of course, I had not forgotten the sword, and at first I was worried that I was to be punished for the crime of my youth. I thought perhaps this American was a detective who had tracked me down. But I was wrong.'

'How did Holland find you?'

'Ali the pawnbroker. More than ninety years old, and still carrying on his trade, that jackal.' Hillel smiled. 'As Mr Holland explained to me, Ali had sold the sword many years earlier to a man named Fekkesh, for fifty times what he had paid me. Fekkesh kept it for thirty years before he also sold it on. It finally found its way to Saudi Arabia, where it belonged to a prince. It was there, three years ago, that Mr Holland saw it and told the prince he wished to buy it. He has many swords. There are men who collect them.'

'I know,' Ben said.

Hillel raised his eyebrows. 'I did not know. I thought it strange. But who am I to question what men do?'

'Go on.'

'Mr Holland took the sword back to America. He was very fascinated with it and wanted to trace it back to where it had come from. A man like him, with the money and power to do anything he desires, was soon able to follow the trail back from Saudi Arabia to Fekkesh, then to old Ali, and finally to me. As I told you, everyone in Jerusalem knows Hillel Zada. And in this city people are quick to give information when a man like Wesley Holland is offering cash.'

'What did he want from you?'

'He told me he had spent much time studying the sword and speaking about it with other experts. He was eager to know where I had found it, so I brought him here to Masada. He was very excited when I showed him this spot and described how I came across the sword. He asked me if I knew how valuable it was, or if I knew anything of its history. I said I did not. That was when he told me that I had done a wonderful thing in finding it, and that he wished to reward me for my deed.' Hillel couldn't repress a broad grin. 'Before I knew what was happening, Mr Holland took me to a bank and opened an account for me containing three million dollars.'

'Three million!' Jude burst out.

'Just a reward? Nothing else?' Ben said, mystified that one sword could be worth so much, even to a man for whom three million was pocket change.

'He wished only to thank me for finding the sword,' Hillel said. 'I went home to Ayala. I said "Wife, we are rich. Quit your job. We are leaving this apartment". And so we did.'

He shrugged. 'We were not rich enough to go and live in the very exclusive quarters like Yemin Moshe, but thanks to Mr Holland's generosity we are very comfortable. And now I have my dream, my own business that I can pass to my sons when I am gone. Four of them work there already. We will soon be opening another, in King George Street. Then perhaps London. Or New York,' he added excitedly, running away with himself.

'Where does my dad come in?' Jude asked. 'And Fabrice Lalique?'

Hillel suddenly looked grave. 'About a year after Mr Holland's visit, he contacted me again to say that he wanted to bring two other men to view the spot where I had found the sword. He introduced them as Reverend Arundel and Father Lalique from England and France. They were very kind, very decent men.'

'How did they become involved?' Ben asked.

Hillel shook his head. 'That I cannot say. Their business was with Mr Holland, and they told me little. They apologised for being secretive, but Simeon told me that one day, when their research was over and the truth about the sword was proved, I would be the first to know before they revealed it to the world. Those were their very words.'

Ben knew that Simeon Arundel would never have used such grandiose terms lightly. 'Revealed it to the world? So we're talking about something extremely important.'

'Mr Holland said this was a very special discovery. One of the most special anyone could imagine.'

'I wish you'd never found it,' Jude said. 'I'm glad you found your dream, Mr Zada. But my parents died for it.'

There was a silence, just the wind whistling over the ramparts of Masada. Hillel hung his head sorrowfully. 'I am so sorry for what happened to your father and mother,' he murmured. 'I am sure she was a wonderful woman. Simeon was a fine man, and he was so proud of his only son. He spoke of you often.'

Jude looked away. He wiped his eye quickly, as if he didn't want anyone to notice.

'Hillel, I'm concerned that whoever is chasing after this sword might also come after you,' Ben said. 'Has anyone been following you or hanging about the Coffee House? Any odd phone calls?'

Hillel looked blank. 'I have noticed nothing.'

If Hillel had been left alone, it could only be because Wesley, Simeon and Fabrice had kept the Israeli somewhat in the dark and not involved him too closely in their plans. Whoever had been listening in to their phone conversations had either considered Hillel not worth chasing, or perhaps not known about him at all. Nonetheless, Ben advised him to keep his eyes open. 'Tell your wife to do the same. These people are determined.'

Hillel's face flushed with anger. 'Who are these filthy dogs?'

'That's what I aim to find out.'

'I pray you can before too long,' Hillel said. 'I fear for Mr Holland's life.'

'He was alive when he called Simeon's home three days ago,' Ben said. 'Before he realised I wasn't Simeon, he said a few things. One was that he was travelling to meet somebody called Martha. He mentioned her again in a phone message he left. It's possible that she might be looking after the sword. Does the name mean anything to you?'

Hillel thought long and hard, then shook his head. 'I am sorry. They never spoke of a Martha to me, nor did I ever meet such a person. Did Mr Holland not give any clue who this woman was, or where?'

'None. A witness thinks they saw him heading for Boston, on the east coast. My guess is that Martha lives somewhere around there.'

Hillel shook his head again. 'I wish that I could help you, but I have no idea about Martha. And I do not even know where Boston is.'

Nobody spoke for a few moments. The wind whipped up flurries of sand from the crumbled ramparts of the fortress. Ben lit a Gauloise and sucked smoke, fighting back the dark suspicion that the two-thousand-mile journey to Israel had ultimately taught him very little. Jude leaned against the safety rail, gazing wistfully towards the Dead Sea, occupied with his own thoughts.

'Your father told me that you love the sea very much,' Hillel said fondly to Jude, joining him at the rail.

'He was right,' Jude replied. 'I do.'

'You and Mr Holland would get along well. He has a home by the ocean. What a palace it must be. With great tall windows, taller than a man, he said to me. He told me how he often stands there and watches the waves for hours at a time, and the tower of light shining across the water at night.'

Ben looked at Hillel. Tower of light? He wondered about it for a moment, but said nothing, and it soon passed out of his mind as they left the ruins and made their way back towards the cable car.

Chapter Forty-Eight

Her name was Daria Pignatelli. She was twenty-eight, and a native of Naples. She was very dark and very beautiful, with flashing eyes and perfect teeth and a figure that should have carried an Italian government health warning for its ability to cause major traffic pile-ups as she walked down the street.

Daria had learned almost ten years ago that she could make more money from men who were drawn to her for her beauty than she ever could from helping her parents to run their little purse-making business from a converted garage. She was not – not yet – the most expensive prostitute in Naples, but she was a far cry from the poor drug-addled waifs who lined the backstreets and would give it away for a song to anybody. Daria was sensible and careful. She maintained her self-respect, could afford to be reasonably picky about her clientele, and would do nothing she wasn't comfortable with. She was also a devout Catholic who saw no particular conflict between her faith and her chosen profession.

The Englishman had first noticed her when she'd been among several other girls brought to the island by motor launch to visit a group of clients in what seemed like a kind of shared apartment attached to the secluded villa. She'd

307

seen him watching from a window of the main house, and been able to tell right away that this somewhat older, somehow sad and lonely-looking man wasn't like the hard, crude brutes for whom she and the other girls were intended. The way he was scrutinising her, seeming to single her out from the others, she could see he liked her. She'd overheard someone refer to him as 'Mr Lucas'. He was clearly the owner of the villa and in charge of whatever kind of business went on there. Like the other girls, Daria had the good sense not to concern herself with such matters.

The little contingent had made the boat trip across to the villa several times since. They were well enough looked after, extremely well paid in crisp banknotes, of which there seemed to be no shortage, and there was always lots of wine and champagne. She was always with a different man. They seemed to come and go. Again, she never asked why.

The phone call yesterday had come as no real surprise. Mr Lucas wanted to see Daria, alone. A car had come to pick her up at her apartment and taken her to meet the boat. The December weather was mild enough to wear a dress that was light without being too revealing. Mr Lucas had come to greet her at the gate of the villa. He was wearing a monogrammed satin dressing gown which she told him looked very *raffinato*.

He appeared nervous at first, and Daria thought he seemed a little wired, as if he hadn't been sleeping properly. A lot of her rich clients were highly stressed businessmen seeking a little relaxation. When she slipped her willowy arm through his and let herself be led into the cool white interior of the villa – plants and artwork and expensive antiques everywhere – he seemed to unwind. *Meester Lucas* – he loved the way his name tripped deliciously off her tongue. She giggled and apologised for her bad English. He smiled charmingly. 'No, I adore the way you speak. And please call me Penrose.'

Deep inside the villa, he took her to a plushly furnished office complete with a broad desk and a giant leather recliner chair. Kinky, she'd thought at first, until he showed her through a door into the adjoining bedroom. Daria got the strange impression that Mr Lucas spent most of his time in these two rooms. Who were all those other men? What did they do for him? He was obviously terribly wealthy and important. The bedroom was very luxurious, with a king-size bed and marble floor, beautiful things all around.

Penrose sat on the bed and motioned at her dress. 'Take it off,' he said. She duly obliged. The silk pooled around her ankles and she stepped out of it in one of her many sets of lacy underwear. For this occasion she'd chosen red, to go with the red high heels.

Penrose felt his heart quicken as he ran his eyes up and down her appreciatively. What a body. He'd already decided that he wanted to cover her with money first, stacks and stacks of lovely cash from one of the stuffed holdalls that were currently hidden under the bed, then make her take off the rest of her clothes, very very slowly, and then—

The fantasy abruptly popped like a bubble. Penrose's brow creased. He leaned forward on the bed, craning his neck to peer more closely at her. Was that . . . ?

Yes, it was!

He pointed. 'Take that off,' he said more sternly. 'Take it off immediately.'

Daria smiled, reached behind her and began undoing the clasp of her lacy bra.

'No! Not that!' he shouted. 'That! That *thing!*' Suddenly all the charm and refinement were gone. His face was turning red and he was scowling at her. Daria was confused. What had she done wrong? He kept pointing at her. 'Get that bloody thing out of my sight!' Frowning, she realised that his accusing finger was aimed at the little gold cross that she wore on a chain around her neck. She'd had it for most of her life, and believed that it protected her from evil.

And maybe she needed protection today. Daria was beginning not to like the look of this Englishman at all.

'Do you hear me, whore? You do what I tell you to do! Take it off!'

Just because she was a whore, didn't mean she let herself be treated like a dog, and she'd damn well wear her cross if she wanted to. Daria had a pretty fiery temper of her own, and she was happy to give him a healthy dose of it. She let off a rapid and very loud burst of Italian, telling him to watch his fucking mouth and she wouldn't take her little cross off for anyone. If he wanted to screw her, he'd screw her with it on or else go and screw someone else, all right?

Penrose couldn't take his eyes off the cross twinkling against the honey skin of her throat. His face twisted. How dare this filthy Christian slut talk to him like this? A paroxysm of fury gripped him and he launched himself off the bed and straight at her, slapping her arms aside with one hand and making a grab for the necklace with the other. His fingers closed around the gold chain and he yanked hard, trying to rip it off her neck.

Daria let out a cry as the chain bit into the back of her neck. She instinctively jerked away from him, tearing the little chain out of his fingers before he could snap it. She hurled another stream of Neapolitan invective at him. 'That's it. I'm leaving this place right now. Who do you think you are, you piece of shit? Take me back to the boat!'

Penrose held his shaking hand up and stared at the blood

running down his palm from where the chain had cut his fingers. The whore was screaming at him. She was crazy.

She was a bitch. A filthy, filthy, repulsive little—

Penrose's eyes bulged. His jaws clamped tightly together so that the muscles bunched up in his cheeks. He thrust his bloody hand inside the folds of his dressing gown. It came out clutching his Coonan .357. The pistol gleamed under the lights. He'd been playing with it earlier, lovingly cycling rounds through its action and replacing them in the magazine, then oiling and polishing the stainless steel with a silk handkerchief, thinking of the power that he had, how he could do anything he wanted and nobody could ever stop him.

Daria screamed when she saw the gun in his fist and the madness in his eyes as he pointed it at her. She tried to run for the door, but even as she turned to get away from him, the blast of the gunshot filled her world and the impact of the bullet hurled her brutally against the wall. She tumbled to the floor, her whole body quaking. She screamed again as she saw the dark blood welling fast out of the ragged hole in her side.

It wasn't a very good shot, Penrose thought, but then it was the first time he'd ever fired the gun. Now he knew what it felt like, and he decided he very much enjoyed the kickback of the recoil against his hand and up his arm. He'd like to feel that again. He stepped up to the screaming woman, held the gun closer this time so that he couldn't miss, and pulled the trigger. The gun flashed and boomed. The spray of blood hit him in the face.

The point-blank shot had blown Daria's throat apart. Suddenly the screaming was a tortured gurgle. Her eyes rolled whitely in the mask of blood. Penrose fired a third shot and her head snapped back against the floor with a clean round hole between her eyes.

Getting more accurate already. It just takes practice, he thought.

A high-pitched tinnitus whine was singing in his ears from the gunshots and he could smell cordite in the air. He leaned over the body and gazed down in fascination at the way the third bullet had crumpled in her whole skull. Wow. Incredible. He smacked his lips and tasted the salty tang of Daria Pignatelli's warm blood.

Now, who was going to clean up this mess? Not him, that was for sure.

Rex O'Neill had just been talking on the phone to Steve Cutter, who'd called from Jerusalem to say, predictably, that they couldn't find any trace of Hope and Arundel. 'Just come back,' O'Neill had told him resignedly. What a stupid mess. He'd stopped even trying to calculate the astronomical daily wastage of Trimble Group funds.

As he was putting down the phone he could hear shouting coming from the direction of Penrose's office. 'What is it now?' he muttered to himself in exasperation. Then came the sound of a woman screaming. O'Neill tensed, listening.

It was the unmistakable and very loud noise of a gunshot that brought him running in a panic. What the hell was happening? He was racing along the corridor towards Penrose's office when the second shot went off, and tearing through the door moments after the third deafening explosion erupted from inside the adjoining bedroom.

His mind awhirl, he crashed through into the bedroom. He stopped. Looked down and saw the blood pooling around his shoes. Looked across and saw the bloodied corpse of the beautiful young woman spread out on the floor. Looked up and saw Penrose Lucas standing there, eyes and hair wild, his face spattered red.

'You . . .' O'Neill began. 'Oh, no. No.' Words failed him. He backed away a step, feeling the slick blood under his feet.

'It's very simple,' Penrose said, waving the gun in the air. 'I told her to take it off and she refused. What else was I . . . Hey! O'Neill! Where are you going?'

Rex O'Neill stumbled out of the bedroom and across the office, fighting the urge to vomit. He slammed the door behind him and ran off down the corridor, leaving a trail of bloody shoeprints behind him. When he got back to his room, he leaned against the wall and breathed hard for a few moments. Then he locked the door. Took out his phone.

And this time he did dial that number.

Chapter Forty-Nine

Back at Zion Square, Hillel insisted on dragging Ben and Jude into the coffee shop to instruct his staff that these honoured visitors were to have anything they liked, any time they wanted it, and without charge. 'It is the least I can do,' he said.

Ben thanked him for his time and his help, warned him once again to be careful, and promised to call the moment he had news about Wesley Holland.

They watched Hillel roar off in his Land Cruiser, then headed back across the square to the hotel. Jude said something about taking a shower, and disappeared through the connecting door from Ben's room into his own.

Ben threw open the windows and gazed out across the square. None of this made any sense to him, but maybe it was because he wasn't thinking straight. He felt as if his brain was misfiring on one cylinder – or maybe a couple of cylinders, unable to focus properly. And he knew the reason why. He marched over to his bag, tore it open and took out the letter.

He slumped in an armchair to read it once more, as if somehow after a dozen readings it might now suddenly mean something completely different and he'd be released from the perturbing responsibility that weighed so heavily on him.

But no, Michaela's words told him the same incredible things as they had before. If it was all a dream, it was taking a hell of a long time to finish.

Ben felt quite lost.

He didn't hear the connecting door open and Jude walk into the room.

'What's that?' Jude asked.

With a jolt like an electric shock, Ben stuffed the letter away into the bag. 'Just looking back at some of the stuff I found in Lalique's place,' he said as casually as he could, glancing at Jude out of the corner of his eye.

'Right,' Jude said uninterestedly. He flopped on the bed. 'So what do we do now?'

Good question, Ben thought. He didn't like to admit it even to himself, but he was running out of road. They'd just exhausted their last lead. Except for one. 'If we knew who this Martha was, we'd be able to trace Holland. Trace Holland, and we'd get to the bottom of this thing. The problem is, we don't.'

'Maybe she's his wife. Have you done a search on Martha Holland?'

'Holland doesn't have a wife,' Ben said impatiently. 'I spent an hour looking him up online last night. He quit after the fourth marriage went south. In any case, I assume he wouldn't be travelling across America to visit Martha if he was married to her, would he? They'd be living together.'

'You're just old fashioned.'

'Maybe I am,' Ben said, 'but not as old fashioned as Wesley Holland. I'm pretty sure of that much.'

'Fine. Ex-wife, then.'

'I've checked them all out. In order of appearance, they were Tabitha, Raine, Micheline, and the last one was called Giselle Rush.'

'Hey. Not Giselle Rush the actress?'

Ben shrugged. 'Perhaps, I don't know. Never heard of her.'

Jude looked at him in astonishment that a living inhabitant of planet Earth could have failed to have heard of Giselle Rush. 'Anyway, Martha could still be a girlfriend. It's feasible they don't live together, or even close.'

'Then he's managing to keep it quiet from all the obsessives online who spend their lives prying into the private affairs of the rich and famous. Not much escapes them.'

'No girlfriend, then. Daughter? Sister?'

'Never had kids. And his parents just had the one.'

Jude raised an eyebrow. 'Must be a lonely kind of guy, rattling around all alone in some big old seaside house with nothing to do except stare at the waves. I mean, even I don't love the ocean *that* much.'

Ben reflected for a moment. 'That was strange, what Hillel said.'

'Why strange?'

'From what I read, Holland's home is a place called the Whitworth Mansion, up near Lake Ontario, a few miles from Rochester. A long way from the coast.'

'So maybe Hillel got it wrong, and he lives by a lake, not the sea.'

Ben shook his head. 'I've seen pictures of the house. It's not that close to the lake. Certainly not within sight of the water, and it's surrounded by acres of woodlands. Meaning that he must have a seaside home somewhere else.'

'The guy can certainly afford it,' Jude said. 'You think that's where he's gone? It would narrow things down a little.'

Ben grunted. 'Down to any one of a million locations up and down the east coast of North America. That's assuming he's even headed there. Why would he refer to his own place as "Martha's"?'

'I don't know. Maybe she spends more time there than he does.'

'We're rambling,' Ben said. 'This isn't getting us anywhere.' He went on wearily racking his brains. Nothing was coming to him.

Jude leaned back on the bed, then suddenly sprang up again. 'Hang on a minute. I think I might've just figured this out. You said Holland was reported as heading towards Boston? Well, that tells us all we need to know, doesn't it?'

Ben was about to ask him scathingly whether he'd even seen a map of the United States Eastern Seaboard and had any notion of the scale of the place, when he saw the look on his face. 'What are you thinking?'

'All right. Here's my idea. What if Martha isn't a person?'

'Come on, Jude. I'm too tired to fuck about. What is she, an Old English Sheepdog?'

'She could be a place.'

'How could Martha be a place?'

'Not Martha. *Martha's*. You said he said he was heading for "Martha's". His exact word. Correct?'

Ben looked at him.

'Now, you know I'm a shark fan, don't you?' Jude went on. 'Diving with the great whites in New Zealand was something I've always wanted to do, since I was a kid. My favourite movie of all time is *Jaws*.'

'Now you're losing me completely. What's that got to do with—'

'Jawsfest, 2005,' Jude said. 'Robbie's stockbroker uncle was a fan too, and he took us there. It was the thirtieth anniversary celebration, this great big festival that was held at the location where part of the movie was shot.'

'And—?'

'You're slow, old man. All right, Spielberg filmed *Jaws* on

317

the island of Martha's Vineyard. Get it? *Martha's* Vineyard. It's off Cape Cod. We flew to Boston and took a bus to the ferry. It's not far away. I was only fourteen, but I remember it really well.'

Ben felt his mouth hanging open.

'Does that narrow it down enough for you?' Jude asked with a grin.

Chapter Fifty

The cold and sleet of London was a far cry from the temperate climate of Capri, but Rex O'Neill was too excited to feel the slightest chill as he hurried from the taxi to the gate of his home in Belgrave Gardens, St John's Wood. He carried his bags up the little footpath and paused at the front door to set down his luggage and rummage in his pocket for the key. He'd been smiling to himself all the way from Heathrow at the thought of seeing Megan again, and imagining her happiness at his unexpected return and the prospect of spending Christmas together.

'You're back so soon?' she'd say, flying into his arms. 'Why didn't you call? I'd have prepared something special.'

'I wanted to surprise you, darling,' he'd chuckle as he held her and ran his fingers through her hair. And then he'd reveal his next surprise: that he wouldn't be going away again to Europe, but would be staying right here in London from now on. Megan would be full of questions but knew not to probe too deeply into his work affairs. All he'd tell her was that he'd had enough of that job and had asked for a reassignment, which had been granted immediately, with permission to come straight home. He'd mention nothing of the situation he'd left behind.

He pictured the glow of delight in her eyes when he told

her the news. He'd squeeze her tight and kiss her and swear that he'd never leave her on her own again. Then, if she was feeling all right and not too tired, he'd take her out for an expensive dinner at their favourite restaurant, a great little Armenian place in Soho.

O'Neill opened the front door and stepped into the hallway, elated to be home again. He dumped his luggage, took off his coat and hung it on the hook. 'Megan! It's me!' There was no reply, but it was a large apartment and she probably hadn't heard him. 'Megan?' he called again as he wandered through to the reception rooms. 'Megan, darling? Guess what! I'm back!'

Silence in the apartment. Maybe she'd gone out, he thought as he pushed open the living room door.

She was sitting on a chair in the middle of the living room, looking up at him in horror.

'Megan?' he said, startled. His first thought was that something had happened, that she'd lost the baby, that there'd been a death in the family. 'Darling, what's wrong?' he said, stepping into the room.

'Hello, Rex,' said a voice that he'd never wanted to hear again. He wheeled round.

Penrose Lucas was standing behind the living room door. He was wearing a long tweed coat and shiny shoes. The Coonan pistol hung loosely from his hand.

O'Neill boggled at him, anger quickly gaining ground over the initial shock. 'What are you doing in my home?'

'You left Capri in such a tearing hurry,' Penrose said. 'I didn't get a chance to say goodbye. Nice little place you have here, by the way. So pleased to meet your wife at last.'

O'Neill glanced at the gun. 'I've been reassigned,' he blurted. 'It wasn't my decision.'

Penrose reached into his left coat pocket and took out a

tiny electronic device. 'You see, Rex, I trust no-one. That way I'm never disappointed when they betray me.'

'Betray you?' O'Neill burst out. 'What are you talking about?'

Penrose tutted and shook his head, then activated the electronic device. O'Neill closed his eyes and went cold as he heard the metallic playback of his own voice over the miniature speaker. It was the call he'd made to London just hours earlier, reporting his boss to the overlords at the Trimble Group. Words like 'insane' and 'psychopathic' rang out horribly loud and clear, shooting through O'Neill's brain like bullets of ice.

Megan was rooted to the chair, terrified to move and glancing from the gun to her husband and back again. Her eyes were imploring and full of tears.

Penrose switched the machine off. He paced around the room, toying with the pistol. 'I've been waiting for this moment, Rex. I've known from the start that you disapproved of my plans. The simple fact of the matter is that you were unsuited to my team all along. And if you think this foolish attempt at denunciation will have the slightest effect, you're sadly mistaken. The Trimble Group are behind me every step of the way. Nothing will change. My plans are destined to be realised, don't you see?'

Any other time, O'Neill would have let out a scornful laugh at such crazy talk. But he couldn't take his eyes off the gun. He could barely breathe. His mind was filled with the fresh memory of what Penrose had done to the prostitute. He had to do something. He didn't even care if he got shot. He had to stop this madman from harming Megan.

Penrose stopped pacing and peered at his former assistant with the look of a schoolmaster forced against his better nature to mete out punishment to a wayward pupil. 'Didn't

I tell you, Rex, that I wouldn't let anybody stand in my way? You should have listened.'

He snapped his fingers. Three more men walked into the room. Megan let out a whimper. O'Neill's blood turned a degree colder as he recognised the men. Suggs, Doyle and Prosser, three of Steve Cutter's brutes whom Penrose had adopted as his personal bodyguards, professional hardmen and bone breakers who never had a thought of their own and would do anything for another cash handout from their favourite employer.

'I can call the Trimble Group again,' O'Neill said. 'I can tell them I made a mistake. Explain that there's been some misunderstanding. We can work this out. Really, we can.'

'That doesn't matter to me,' Penrose replied. 'What matters is your betrayal. Treachery isn't something you can undo, Rex. There is no going back.'

'What are you going to do?' O'Neill quavered.

At a nod from Penrose, the three bodyguards closed in a circle around O'Neill and Megan. Doyle took hold of her arm and wrenched her roughly to her feet. She let out a scream of fear. Suggs and Prosser grabbed O'Neill.

'Leave her out of this,' O'Neill implored. 'Please. I beg you, Penrose. I'll give you everything I have.'

'Oh, I know you will,' Penrose said, then waved to his men. 'Take them into the dining room.' The bodyguards obeyed instantly without a word, and began marching their captives towards a closed door. Megan twisted and struggled in Doyle's grip. He lashed out with a muscular arm and backhanded her across the face. She sagged to the floor, moaning.

'She's pregnant!' O'Neill cried out, fighting to get free so that he could run to his wife's aid. 'For God's sake! Have pity!'

Penrose flinched at the word. 'For *God's* sake? You'd appeal to him, would you, Rex? You want to believe in him? You think he's going to send down a miracle to save you now?'

'Please, Penrose!'

Suggs kicked open the dining room door. O'Neill felt the air leave his body as he saw what lay beyond the doorway. The dining room was no longer the same room in which he and Megan had shared so many happy meals and had looked forward to sharing many more. The table was gone, and so were the chairs and the antique sideboard. The floor was covered with thick, black, shiny plastic sheeting. The walls, windows and ceiling were draped completely over with the same material, stapled firmly into place. A pair of portable tool chests sat in the corner by the door.

But what threatened to send Rex O'Neill's mind over the edge was the sight of the crude wooden frame that had been erected in the middle of the room, rising almost to the ceiling. Its top beam was fitted with four steel rings, each one of which had a length of chain passed through it. The ends of the chains dangled midway above the black floor, each attached to an iron manacle.

'No!' O'Neill screamed, and fought with all his might against the powerful grip of Suggs and Prosser. They were much too strong for him, and he could do nothing to resist as they dragged him into the room. The plastic sheeting crackled underfoot. He collapsed to his knees and they dragged him towards the wooden frame. Megan wasn't screaming any longer. She staggered behind Doyle as if in a trance, her eyes staring and her mouth opening and closing soundlessly.

Penrose entered the room last, and leaned against the doorway. At his signal, Rex O'Neill and his wife were hauled up to the wooden frame and their wrists were tightly manacled above their heads. Prosser and Doyle each grabbed the free ends of a pair of chains and heaved downwards, hoisting their victims into the air, dangling from their wrists. Megan hung limply, virtually catatonic with dread. Her husband was thrashing and kicking like a captured animal. The ends of the chains were secured to bolts in the wooden frame, holding them in place. Prosser spat on his hands and rubbed his palms together.

'You bastard! You fucker! You'll die for this!' O'Neill roared at Penrose, who was watching from the doorway, keeping his distance because he knew what was coming next.

'Shout all you like, Rex. The room is completely sound-proofed.' While O'Neill had been biting his nails in the departure lounge at Naples airport and hustling through passport control at Heathrow, Penrose and his men had winged their way over in the Learjet in plenty of time to prepare the place for his arrival.

Suggs lumbered over to the tool chests, opened them up and began mechanically unloading their contents. One was stuffed with a pair of coroner's bodybags and three sets of protective overalls. The other contained a selection of assorted hardware that clanked and rattled as Suggs reached inside. He handed a meat cleaver to Prosser and a butcher's knife to Doyle. He took out a machete for himself. It had a rubber handle. Non-slip, for when the blood really started pouring.

'Cut the child out,' Penrose said. 'I want Rex to see his baby before he dies.'

O'Neill went hysterical. Megan just dangled there, with-drawn into some altered state of consciousness.

Suggs, Prosser and Doyle paused a moment and exchanged glances. Chucking priests off bridges was one thing, but . . . 'That's a bit fucking much, innit, boss?' Doyle muttered.

'Thought you just wanted to scare 'em,' Prosser said.

'Do it!' Penrose roared at him. 'Or there'll be no money for any of you!'

The muffled screams in Belgrade Gardens would soon become far more intense. A full twenty minutes had passed by the time they eventually stopped.

Mr and Mrs Higgins next door watched television through the whole thing.

Chapter Fifty-One

With a rushed, delayed connecting midnight flight from Jerusalem and another five and a half thousand miles behind them, Ben and Jude touched down at Logan International Airport in Boston sometime after nine in the morning, Eastern Time, and hired a Jeep Patriot from Alamo car rental. They seemed to have arrived just in time for the snowy season; crews were out in force clearing the roads as they headed away from Boston and cut southwards through a picture-postcard New England blanketed in white.

In the poor weather conditions it took nearly two more hours to cover the seventy-five or so miles to Woods Hole. By the time they reached the coastal ferry port, they'd left the snow behind them and exchanged it for a blanket of freezing mist.

It was approaching midday as the long, low stretch of Martha's Vineyard coastline appeared through the thinning fog, together with the gently swaying masts of hundreds of sailing boats in the harbour that were dwarfed by the ferry gliding in amongst them to dock. Ben drove the Jeep down the ramp with the twenty or so other cars aboard, and he and Jude contemplated the island scene before them.

'Well, here we are,' Jude said. 'Now we just need to find Wesley Holland. I don't suppose he'd be listed in the local phone directory?'

'That might be just a little too easy,' Ben said.

As they drove into Oak Bluffs Jude described what a madhouse the place had been when he'd last been here, for the Jawsfest event of 2005. Then, the whole island had been heaving with tourists and movie fans. But despite the islanders' attempts to dress the town up for Christmas, it was nonetheless very obviously low season, with many places closed up for winter. They parked the Jeep in the tree-lined Circuit Avenue near the harbour, and strolled down the street past neat little stores and restaurants.

'You think we'll find him in there having breakfast?' Jude said, peering inside the door of an eatery that was still open for business.

'Nope.'

'Then what are we here for?'

'Shopping,' Ben said.

A few blocks down the street, he found what he was looking for. A bell tinkled as he opened the door of the general store and walked inside. The proprietor was a jovial, shiny-cheeked little man with round glasses and a moustache that curled upwards when he smiled. Ben asked him if he sold a good guidebook to the island.

'This one here is my best seller,' the storekeeper said, selecting a glossy pocket-sized book from a shelf. 'Opens up into a handy map. Shows you all the places to stay, eat, things to do. Bearing in mind that the Vineyard goes kinda dead over the colder months.'

'That's no problem,' Ben said. 'This will do fine.' He pointed at a stand to the side of the counter. 'I'd also like a pair of those binoculars.'

'Minolta ten by fifties,' the storekeeper said, handing them over to show him. 'Good price, too. Popular with the tourists. Don't sell too many this time of year, though.'

Ben gave the binoculars a quick once-over. 'No need for the box. I'll take them as they are.'

The storekeeper glowed behind the little round glasses. 'First time on the Vineyard for you good folks?'

Jude was about to reply, but Ben cut across him. 'Yes, it is. It's a beautiful place.'

'Sure is that,' the storekeeper said with a smile.

'In fact I was thinking of bringing my family to live here,' Ben told him. 'Tired of the city. I'd bet there's not a lot of crime out here.'

'Oh no. The Vineyard's a real peaceful place. Nothing ever happens here; in fact the only folks who don't take to Vineyard life are the ones who think it's too boring. But I've lived here all my life and I can't think of a single place on earth I'd sooner be.' The storekeeper beamed, and turned to Jude. 'And so, this must be your son,' he said.

Ben was taken aback for a moment. Before he could answer, Jude said quickly, 'We're not related.' The storekeeper raised his eyebrows. 'No? Pardon me.'

Now that Jude had his opening, he pressed on. 'Do you know if there's a man called Wesley Holland living on the island?' he asked, leaning across the counter. 'He's a billionaire. White hair. You'd know him from the TV.'

Ben would have grabbed Jude by the neck and turfed him out of the store doorway, but it was too late. He gave him a scalding look.

The storekeeper's friendly tone became instantly cooler. 'There's a lot of wealthy folks and celebrities come to live or stay on the island. They like it here because their privacy is respected; folks leave them alone and don't ask too many questions.'

The chit-chat was plainly over. Ben paid for his goods and they left the store with a nod.

'There are ways of finding things out,' he said as they walked back down Circuit Avenue towards the car. 'That's not one of them. Next time, keep your mouth shut and let me do the talking, all right?'

'What was all that crap about wanting to come and live here with your non-existent family?' Jude retorted.

Ben flipped through the guidebook as he walked, refusing to let it show that Jude's words had stung him. 'Thanks to our friend back there, we know that nothing's happened on the island lately that might not have hit the news yet. Such as no murders, no robberies.'

'And no dead billionaires found on the beach this morning. I get it.'

'So if Wesley Holland is here at all, chances are he's safely tucked up somewhere in his house by the ocean. Now we just need to locate it.'

'How big is the island?'

'Eighty-seven square miles.'

'And just how does the great detective propose to find this one house in all of that coastline?'

'The tower of light,' Ben said simply. When Jude looked puzzled, he explained, 'Remember what Hillel told us – how Wesley loves to spend time looking out at the waves and the tower of light shining across the water at night? Come on, you're an ocean kind of person. What does that sound like to you?' They'd reached the car. Ben bleeped the locks and got behind the wheel.

'A lighthouse,' Jude said as he climbed into the passenger side. 'It sounds like a lighthouse.'

Ben skimmed the guidebook onto Jude's lap. 'And according to this book, there are only five of those on the island. Wherever Holland's place is, it's got to be within easy reach of one of those five locations.' He started the engine.

'You're the guy. Where do we begin?'

'We already passed two out of the five on our way in here on the ferry, flanking the mouth of the harbour. They're called West Chop Light and East Chop Light. Let's go and check them out.'

Within a few minutes they were driving along East Chop Drive and within sight of the first lighthouse. Built in 1877, according to the guidebook, its first keeper had been a character by the name of Captain Silas Daggett. The eighty-foot whitewashed conical tower stood away from the road, behind a neat white picket fence with a gate and a sandy path that led right up to it.

They got out of the Jeep, walked around the broad base of the lighthouse and scanned the land horizon in all directions, searching for any sign of a billionaire residence with tall windows from which the great man liked to drink in the majestic ocean view. The only houses within sight were fairly unostentatious wooden buildings that nobody would have been ashamed to call home, yet wouldn't have been the abode of choice for a man of Holland's limitless wealth. Compared to the Whitworth Mansion, even a comfortable family home for lesser mortals would have seemed like slumming it.

'This is weird,' Jude muttered. 'I feel kind of like a stalker or something.' After a couple of beats he said, 'What's that place over there?' Ben gazed in the direction he was pointing, and saw a white house through the trees that, from where they were standing, looked larger than the other homes within sight and appeared to offer a view of the waterfront and the lighthouse.

Jude seemed hopeful. 'Looks promising, wouldn't you say?'

Up close, the house was obscured from the sea by thick foliage. As they turned into the gate they saw that it was a traditional white-painted wooden nineteenth-century farm-house with a broad, low veranda over the front porch. There was paint peeling off some of the window frames and the barn roof was rusting in places. Quaint rustic living, low on glamour.

'Doesn't look like it to me,' Ben said. 'Let's move on.'

'Wait. What's the harm in asking? Maybe somebody here knows him.' Jude climbed out of the car and walked up to the house. Ben stayed behind the wheel, going through his time-honoured Zippo-and-Gauloise ritual as he watched the house door open and a squat woman with pigtails come out to spend a few moments talking to Jude before shaking her head and returning inside.

'Told you,' Ben said as Jude climbed back into the car.

'At least I tried,' Jude muttered, brushing his windblown hair out of his eyes. They sped off westwards along Beach Road, skirting the harbour with the Lagoon Pond to their left, before turning north.

The second location was situated on the northernmost fork tip of the island, on the opposite side of the harbour mouth from East Chop Light. They found the lighthouse beyond another neat white fence. Nearby was a pretty wooden house with a U.S. flag hanging from a pole on the neat lawn. It had a balcony facing the sea, with the perfect view of the lighthouse.

'Possible?' Jude asked.

'A little cosy and twee,' Ben said. 'But possible. Maybe.' They parked the car and walked up to the front door together.

Ben knocked. An old man answered, and for the briefest instant Ben thought he was standing face to face with the billionaire himself. 'Mr Holland?'

'Who?' the old man asked, gurning up at Ben toothlessly. A dog started yapping from inside. An old woman appeared in the hallway behind her husband. Her legs were swollen and bandaged, and she needed to lean heavily on two crutches to stay upright. 'Who's there, Frank?' she quavered.

'We're looking for—' Jude began.

'Forget it,' Ben said. 'Let's go. I'm sorry we disturbed you, sir,' he said to the old man.

Two down, three more to go. It wasn't time to worry, not quite yet. The next point on the map was the Edgartown Light Station, a few miles to the southeast along the coastal road in the island's main town. By the time they reached it, the afternoon was already wearing on. The rising, bitterly cold wind from the ocean had dispersed the mist, and the sun was shining.

The Edgartown Light was situated within the harbour itself. As Ben could see through his binoculars, there were many beautiful and expensive-looking homes within sight; but as he scanned around him in a slow arc, taking in every house, every balcony, every window, he thought about what he knew of Holland's lifestyle and preferences, and his gut instinct told him that this was wrong.

'He wouldn't like it here,' he said, lowering the binoculars.

Jude looked at him. 'So you know him that well, all of a sudden.'

'The man's a known recluse. He's camera shy and spurns publicity. Why pick a house that didn't provide the kind of seclusion he needs?'

'Fair enough,' Jude grunted. 'Where next?'

The next spot on the itinerary was about as remote as things got in the Vineyard. The isolated Cape Poge Lighthouse stood on the neighbouring tiny island of Chappaquiddick, which a major storm in 2007 had separated from the main body of Martha's Vineyard by a narrow strait of water. Ben and Jude were lucky to catch what seemed to be one of the very few ferries just as it was leaving. The barge-like craft was able to carry only one or two cars across at a time to the islet.

'Didn't a Kennedy get shot or something here, years and years ago?' Jude asked semi-curiously, as if Kennedys getting shot was a routine occurrence throughout history.

'No, but maybe he should have,' Ben said. 'The story goes that he crashed his car off a bridge into the sea and hot-footed it away from the scene. A girl drowned in the wreck.' The moment it slipped out, he bitterly regretted his words. Jude just nodded quietly, said nothing and gazed out of the window as they rolled off the ferry and onto Chappaquiddick Island.

In the wintertime, the place seemed utterly dismal and barren. When Ben and Jude drove up the sandy track close to the lighthouse they found a forlorn, wind-battered beach where the only other living things were the screaming seabirds circling the lonely shingled tower. 'I don't see any houses at all,' Jude said. 'Let alone the kind we're looking for.'

'Me neither,' Ben said.

'Let's go. This place is depressing.'

It was a long time before they were able to catch a return ferry to Martha's Vineyard. They'd wasted a large chunk of the day, and now Ben was concerned about time slipping away from him, not to mention the prospect of exhausting their list of lighthouses and coming away empty-handed at the end of it. They had a lot of miles still to cover in order to reach the fifth and final spot on the map, inconveniently situated as far away as possible on the island, all the way from east to west at its broadest point. Ben pushed the car on fast, but it still seemed like an endless drive and his watch appeared to tick the time by at double speed as they sped westwards past the towns of Chilmark and Aquinnah. Eventually, a mad dash along the promisingly named Lighthouse Road took them to Aquinnah Circle and their destination, the Gay Head Lighthouse.

The stubby red-brick tower stood among scrubland over-looking rocky cliffs. They climbed out of the car, scrambled through the long grass to the best vantage point nearby and scanned the horizon. To the landward side, there was only empty countryside and the long road snaking off into the distance. Not a single house or farm to be seen. Bare trees quivered in the wind.

'It's not here,' Ben said.

'But this was our last chance,' Jude said. 'How can it not be here? Did we miss something?'

'We didn't miss anything. We were careful. But I was wrong about the lighthouses. We're going to have to start again.'

'Great.' Jude looked up at the sky, which had darkened as the biting wind pushed a slab of cloud over the face of the sun. The afternoon would soon be turning into evening. 'Let's get back to the car.'

Ben was silent for nearly five miles as he sped back east-wards along the coastal road that skirted the long, almost flat south side of the island. His thoughts were as black as the clouds overhead. They didn't brighten when the wind parted the cloud cover momentarily and the sun sparkled brightly across the endless miles of sea to the right.

'Maybe it's my fault,' Jude muttered. 'I might have misled us about the whole Martha thing. I mean, maybe she was a woman after all. Holland could be anywhere, really, if you think about it.' He threw a nervous glance at the zipping road, then another at the speedometer, which was hovering steady over the ninety mark. 'You could try easing off a little.'

Ben kept his foot down. 'Shut up, Jude. I'm trying to think.'

'Me too.' Jude paused, doing his best to ignore the speed-ometer. 'Thing is, though, Hillel did say "tower of light". What else could that be? Why don't we phone him and ask him what he meant by—'

Jude never finished the sentence. He was hurled forwards against his seatbelt as Ben took his foot off the gas and stamped hard on the brake pedal. The Jeep screeched to a halt in the middle of the empty road.

'What did you do that for?' Jude yelled, sprawling back in his seat.

'Look,' Ben said. He pointed out of the passenger window, towards the sea. Jude frowned, then followed the line of his finger.

'See it?'

'See what?'

'About a mile out. The sunlight caught something. There it is again.'

Jude had spotted it too, just a faint gleam in the distance before the clouds scudded back across the face of the sun. 'What is that?'

Ben grabbed the binoculars from the back seat and brought the distant object into focus. It was some kind of tall fixed structure out to sea, built on three massive yellow tripod legs, with a platform like a miniature oil rig and a latticework tower pointing up into the sky. It was hard to tell at this range, but Ben guessed the structure was about a hundred feet high.

'Let me take a look,' Jude said, grabbing the binoculars as Ben put them down to study the map. Ben traced his finger along the south side of the island near Gay Head, back towards Aquinnah. Whatever the thing was, it didn't feature on the map.

'I know what it is,' Jude said, focused on it. 'It's a coastal observatory tower. Unmanned, used for meteorological analysis. I've learned about them at Uni.'

'Tall enough to be a risk to low-flying aircraft in the dark,' Ben said.

Jude understood his line of thinking immediately. 'Which would mean it would be lit up at night, wouldn't it?'

'The tower of light shining on the water,' Ben said. He took the binoculars back from Jude and scanned the landward horizon. Trees. More trees. Grassland. And then – his heart gave a jump.

'And to think we'd have driven straight past it,' he said.

The majestic house was nestled among its own grounds close to the beach, overlooking a splendid bay and the observatory tower in the distance.

'Give them over,' Jude said, making another grab for the binoculars. He quickly saw what Ben had seen. 'That's got to be the place.' He turned excitedly to Ben. 'We found it!'

They left the Jeep and waded through long grass and rustling reeds that grew in clumps among the dunes, cutting around the side of the property to approach it from the beach. Ben trained the binoculars on the tall windows that overlooked the sea.

And behind one of them, gazing across the beach towards the whispering ocean, stood a figure of a man. He was short, with white hair and a neat white beard, wearing cords and a cardigan.

Ben was finally looking at the billionaire, Wesley Holland.

Chapter Fifty-Two

In a strange way, Wesley thought in a fleeting moment of relaxation as he contemplated the sea and stroked his beard, his being here, his being safely tucked away where nobody could ever find him or his treasure, was all thanks to Giselle.

Ah, Giselle. They'd lost contact long ago. He knew she was still appearing in movies, but he hadn't seen any of them.

Looking back, Wesley and his fourth and last wife had been completely mismatched right from the start. She'd been too young for him, too impetuous, too absorbed in a burgeoning acting career that dominated her every move and decision, and, for the three and a half years the marriage had endured, limping on, Wesley's every move and decision as well. For a man whose natural tendency was to shy away from the hubbub of the world, the constant prying of press hounds had been unbearable. Whenever Wesley opened the door, there was a camera poking into his face trying to steal a snap of the celebrity couple. He couldn't go to the bathroom or undress for bed without fretting that he was being watched through a long-distance lens. As for trying to go anywhere or eat a quiet meal in a restaurant, forget it.

Giselle had adored the attention, of course, feeding off it like a butterfly on nectar. But to Wesley the intrusion into his hallowed privacy was the death of his very soul. The last straw had been when he'd found his dear wife conducting a guided tour of the Whitworth Mansion for journalists from *Persona* magazine.

That was when, driven to distraction, Wesley had made a secret bid on a (for him) modestly-sized, yet tolerably luxurious, beach hideaway on the island of Martha's Vineyard, off Cape Cod. Through the remainder of his marriage to Giselle he'd escaped there whenever humanly possible, always on some flimsy excuse about making a business trip – Giselle had never cared that much where he was, anyway – and after the inevitable divorce had come and gone it had never once occurred to him to sell it. The deeds were held in the name of an obscure trust he'd set up decades earlier and never developed into anything, so that the real owner was quite untraceable.

Wesley so relished the serenity of his island bolt-hole that he'd always been very reticent about telling anyone about it. Not even his longtime lawyer, Bob Mooney, had any idea about the place. Coleman Nash had been in on it, and Wesley had also confided in Simeon Arundel once, after a few glasses of wine. The secret now rested with the dead.

The first thing Wesley had done on reaching the end of his terrifying journey had been to take the precious fibreglass case straight down to his vault. Built for storing artwork and other valuable items when he wasn't around (there was no crime to speak of on the island, but you could never be too careful), the vault was buried ten feet beneath the foundations of the house within walls of reinforced concrete that could (according to the architects) withstand a nuclear blast. It was unshakeably secure, fire-proof, flood-proof, humidity-proof, fully air-conditioned, and a whole host of other fancy features for which Wesley had shelled out large amounts of cash and then duly pushed to the back of his mind.

339

Only when the sword had been safely stored away on Wesley's arrival had he truly been able to relax, helped by a few tots of best Bourbon to restore his shattered nerves after the nightmare trek east. *Calm down. You're alive. Nobody knows you're here.* For a while he'd basked blissfully in the knowledge that he was safe. He had everything he needed, enough supplies and food to live comfortably for months without venturing near a town.

But now the pressure was returning, and so were the worries. Wesley was sporadically haunted by visions of death and carnage. Poor Coleman, and Hubert Clemm, and Abigail, and Kat the receptionist at the motel whose name he couldn't even remember. All these people who'd been senselessly slaughtered. And the reality was that these ruthless killers were still out there, searching for Wesley while he sat on his ass doing nothing.

Why wasn't Simeon answering his phone any more? Had something happened to him? In a moment of panicky insecurity, Wesley had taken a heavy cavalry sabre down from one of his wall displays. It had last seen action at Waterloo but the blade was still shaving sharp. The weapon was propped against a chair behind him now as he stood at the window, close to hand, just in case.

It was time to start planning his next move. He walked away from the window, picked up the sabre by its steel scabbard and carried it over to the old-fashioned Bakelite dial telephone. The mechanism whirred as Wesley carefully dialled in the prefix that would block his caller ID, followed by Bob Mooney's direct line at his offices in Rochester.

The instant the lawyer heard Wesley's voice, he exploded. 'Jesus Christ, Wesley. Why haven't you called? Where in hell are you?'

'Best you don't know. Somewhere far away.'

'What's going on? Everyone here is frantic with worry. The cops need to talk to you. In case you'd forgotten, there's a murder investigation going on at your house. You can't just up and disappear like this.'

'Am I a suspect?'

'Not that I'm aware of, but I know the way cops think and it doesn't help that you run off like a fugitive and don't tell anyone where you're going.'

'I have my reasons, Bob. You'll find out soon enough. That's not why I'm calling. There's something I need you to do for me. Can I count on you for this? It's important.'

Mooney sounded hurt. 'Hey, how long have we known each other?'

'Here's what I want. Find out who're the best personal protection team in the country. Whatever they charge, pay them double, triple, just make sure you hire them. I want the meanest, toughest sons of bitches you can dig up. I'll contact you again in twenty-four hours and you give me the number to call.'

A moment's appalled silence on the phone. 'Wesley, if you're in some kind of trouble here—'

'Don't worry about me.'

'Why do you need protection?'

'Will you do this for me or not?'

'Naturally I will. Give me your number there so I can put these people in touch with you.'

'No, Bob.'

'I'll know it anyway.'

'I withheld it.'

Bob seemed amazed that Wesley should be savvy to such modern trickery. 'Come on, Wes. You gotta give me something.'

'When it's the right time, I'll tell you where I am.'

'When will that be?'

'Once everything's in place. Then I'll fill you in as best I can. Until then, I'm keeping my mouth shut.'

Mooney let out an exasperated sigh. 'Is it serious trouble? Tell me that at least.'

'Pretty serious.'

'Does it have to do with what happened at the mansion?'

'Uh-huh. And more besides.'

'For Chrissakes, Wes, even I can't hold back the tide for ever. You've got to come forward with this. As your lawyer I have to tell you that the weirder you act, the less you're gonna look like the chief witness and more like the chief suspect. That's how the cops, and everyone else, are going to see it.'

'That can't be helped for the moment,' Wesley said. 'I trust you, Bob. Talk to you tomorrow.'

Wesley hung up the phone, picked up his sabre and walked through the airy house to the kitchen to check on how his steak was defrosting. A bottle of 1993 Bordeaux was sitting opened on the side, nothing too ostentatious, a modest little hundred-dollar table wine to go with his dinner. Thinking he'd like to replay those Bach Goldberg Variations that he'd been listening to earlier, he turned back towards the living room.

A man he'd never seen before was standing in the hallway, looking right at him.

'Wesley Holland?' the man said.

Wesley sucked in a great lungful of air and felt his knees turn to jelly. He staggered back a step. 'I'm not Holland. Who the hell are you?'

'We spoke on the phone,' the man said. 'And I never forget a voice.'

'You get away from me,' Wesley rasped. He gripped the

342

hilt of the sabre and rattled the weapon out of its steel scabbard.

'I'm not here to hurt you,' the man said, moving forward a step.

Wesley didn't believe that, not for one moment. He could see the purposeful look in the stranger's eye, and was ready to make a lunge with the blade and then run like hell for the vault. He'd lock himself in down there, even if it meant starving to death. Anything was preferable to what these people would do to him.

'Another step closer and I'll run you right through, mister. I mean it.' His hand was shaking so badly he could barely grip the sabre hilt.

'Why don't you put that down, so we can talk?' the stranger said.

'Who are you?' Wesley quavered. 'What do you want from me?'

At that moment, another figure appeared in the hallway. He was a younger man of about twenty, with a shock of fair hair. Wesley peered at him. He could have sworn the young man looked familiar.

'I'm Jude Arundel,' he said. 'You were a friend of my father's.'

Chapter Fifty-Three

A stunned silence in the hallway.

It was Wesley who broke it. 'What do you mean, I *was* a friend of Simeon's?'

'He's dead,' Jude said tightly. 'So is my mother. They were killed by the same people who are after you.'

Wesley suddenly felt unsteady on his feet. He staggered over to a chair and slumped heavily into it, dropping the sabre to the floor and sinking his face in his hands. 'Oh, no. I warned him. I told him to be careful.'

'We've come a long way to see you, Mr Holland.' Ben picked up the fallen sabre, replaced it in its scabbard and propped it against the wall. 'My name's Ben Hope. I've known Simeon and Michaela Arundel for twenty years, and I was with them when they died. I was staying at their home the night you called there.'

'How did you find me here?'

'Not too easily, you'll be pleased to know,' Ben said. 'You did a pretty decent job of covering your tracks.'

'I was lucky, that's all. They very nearly got me on the road.'

'Have you told anyone where you are?'

'You have to be kidding. Not even my lawyer knows.'

'All the same,' Ben said, 'do you keep a gun in the house? Any kind of gun'll do.'

'There's a Revolutionary War musket in the vault,' Wesley told him. 'It hasn't been fired in centuries, though.'

'Forget it.'

Wesley sighed. 'I need a drink. Let's go into the kitchen.'

Dinner was forgotten for the moment. Wesley settled onto a padded stool and emptied a third of his '93 Bordeaux into a large wineglass. Both Ben and Jude declined the offer of a drink.

'I'm so sorry for your loss, son,' Wesley said after a few gulps.

'Thanks,' Jude muttered.

Wesley turned to Ben. 'Can you tell me what happened?'

'You tell him,' Jude said to Ben. He walked over to the window and turned his back for a few moments. It was getting darker outside. The distant meteorological observatory tower was lit up, throwing a red light across the water.

'Their car was forced off the road,' Ben said. 'It was set up to look like an accident.'

'Did they suffer?' Wesley whispered.

'No,' Ben lied. 'It was very quick.' He glanced over at Jude, paused, and then went on. 'I don't think it was as quick for Fabrice Lalique. But you already knew about that.'

'I didn't know whether to believe the suicide story or not,' Wesley admitted. 'At the time, it seemed crazy to start spouting conspiracy theories.'

'In my experience,' Ben said, 'the truth is often crazier than what you read in the papers. I'm pretty certain the killers were the same people who planted the paedophile material on his computer. You have some very nasty and powerful enemies, Mr Holland.'

'You got that right,' Wesley grunted. 'These ruthless sonsofbitches can track you from your credit card and God knows what else. Who the hell are they?'

'That's what I was hoping you could tell me.'

'How should I know who they are?'

'Because of the sword.'

Wesley drained his glass, set it down and looked long and hard at Ben, then at Jude. 'You know about the sword?' he said slowly.

'We've just come from Jerusalem,' Jude told him.

The billionaire's eyes widened in amazement. 'You found Hillel?' Then a terrible thought struck him. 'He's not—?'

'He's alive and well and still enjoying his semi-retirement,' Ben said. 'He drove us to Masada and showed us where he made his discovery back in 1963. We know how much you paid him as a reward for finding it. We know just how important it is to you, and how important it was to Simeon and Fabrice. We know everything about the sword, except what really matters. What is it, where is it, and who would want it so badly they'd kill you, us, or anyone else to get it?'

Wesley hesitated. 'You have to realise, it's very hard for me to trust you. You don't understand how important this is.'

'You have no choice but to trust us,' Ben said. 'You've been pretty clever so far, not to mention lucky, but these people won't give up so easily.'

'I'm safe here,' Wesley insisted. 'And I can hold out for a long, long time.'

'You can't stay hidden for ever. You're all over the TV and internet. It's just a question of time before someone recognises you and word gets out that the mysterious billionaire is holed up on Martha's Vineyard. Then these people are going to come for you. They'll torture you until they have the sword, and then if they're feeling merciful they'll put a quick bullet in your brain.'

'Or else they'll feed you to the great whites,' Jude added, jerking his thumb in the direction of the ocean.

It seemed to have the desired effect. The billionaire gulped, then gave a reluctant nod. 'All right. The sword is here. Come with me, and I'll show it to you.'

Chapter Fifty-Four

Wesley led Ben and Jude along a bare white passage. At the end of it was a metal doorway with no handle and no visible hinges, just a shiny blank panel mounted on the wall to its right.

'I don't generally go for newfangled technology,' explained the owner of several leading electronics corporations, 'but I'm willing to admit it has its uses now and then.' He pressed his palm flat against the panel. After a very slight pause while the scanner did its work, an LED blinked, there was a click, and the door opened.

'This way,' Wesley said, showing them through. Beyond lay a downward flight of steps, immaculate and white, leading to a heavier security door equipped with a keypad and a rotary combination lock.

'It's where I store some of my knick-knacks when I'm not around,' Wesley told them. 'Seeing as the place is empty a lot of the time. Hold on while I key in the codes. They're long ones.'

As the billionaire fiddled with the vault door, Ben noticed Jude's drawn expression and felt sorry that wounds had been reopened by talking about the car accident. He touched Jude's shoulder. 'Are you okay?' he asked softly. Jude nodded. Ben patted him on the arm.

A solid metallic 'thunk' sounded from the massive innards of the vault door, and Wesley heaved it open with an effort. The vault was an octagonal room, thirty feet across, that seemed to have been cast out of solid steel. Inside, it was like a museum. *Knick-knacks*, Ben thought, looking around him at the artwork that hung behind glass on the metal walls. He was no expert, but recognised a couple of Van Goghs and a Cézanne. There was no need to ask if they were real, or if the hundred or so swords of various shapes and sizes that hung on wall racks were cheap mail-order reproductions.

'What's that?' Jude said, pointing at an object on a display stand.

'It's a Fabergé egg,' Ben said.

'How come you know so much?'

Ben just shrugged.

'Oh, that stuff's nothing compared to what you're about to see,' Wesley said, waving them across to a plinth on which lay a black oblong case, a little under four feet long. Ben and Jude stood either side of him as he produced a key from his pocket and clicked open the locks, then opened the lid.

'There it is,' Wesley breathed, his eyes glowing.

The case was lined with thick protective foam padding. Nestling inside was the sword that Ben recognised from Fabrice Lalique's drawings. They had been a close likeness of the curious sickle-shaped blade and curved hilt. The latter was bronze, age-tarnished to a dark reddish patina. The steel of the blade was dull and pitted with the centuries, here and there showing traces of its former glory.

It wasn't a large weapon, nothing like as imposing as many of the medieval battle swords in the vault, with their long triangulated blades and cruciform hilts, some of them obviously intended to be wielded with two hands, and even then with some difficulty. Nor was it any more ornate than Lalique's drawings had suggested. The metalwork of the hilt was plain and unadorned, and only the faint inscriptions on the blade hinted at any kind of special craftsmanship – to Ben's eye, at least.

One thing you didn't have to be an expert to notice was that the sword had been used in battle. The blade was notched here and there where its edge had clashed against the edge of another sword, armour plate or shield. The weapon had been a witness to the bloody reality of history.

As delicately as handling a newborn baby, Wesley reached into the case and lifted out his trophy. He held it up to show them with a look of reverence, as if choirs of angels were bursting into song inside his head.

'*This* is what everyone's after?' Jude said. 'It doesn't look like much.'

'May I?' Ben asked, reaching towards the sword. Wesley balked, but before he could snatch it away Ben had gently taken it from him and was examining it, turning it over in his hands.

'Please! Be careful with that!' Wesley gasped. 'You have no idea of its value.'

'Relax,' Ben said. 'I'm not going to chop wood with it.' He hefted the sword in his fist, feeling its balance. It was no mere ceremonial piece, that much was immediately clear. The hilt fitted perfectly in the palm and the blade just asked to be swung in a chopping motion. Ben noticed that the sickle shape of the blade gave it as many of the characteristics of a short axe as of a stabbing sword. In its day, this had been a state-of-the-art fighting implement that in the hands of a skilled soldier would have been capable of inflicting terrible injury, piercing armour and hacking off limbs. He wondered about the man who'd last used it, how long ago it had been and what had happened to him.

It was still just a sword, a lump of metal – yet one that had inspired such obsessive fascination that scholars wanted to write books about it, rich men would pay almost anything to possess it, and evil men would murder for it.

'Why?' Ben said to Wesley. 'Why this sword?'

'Simeon really didn't tell you anything at all?'

'He never had the chance,' Ben said. 'But now you're going to.'

They left the vault and returned upstairs to the kitchen, where Wesley poured the remainder of the Bordeaux into three glasses and opened another bottle. Ben had gently but firmly insisted on bringing the sword upstairs, so that he could study it more while they talked. The ancient weapon looked strangely incongruous lying on a modern kitchen table. Wesley kept glancing at it nervously, as though concerned that at any moment Ben might run outside and start slashing weeds with it – but after another glass of wine he seemed to unwind and began his story.

'If you've talked to Hillel, then you pretty much know the sword's history for the last fifty years,' Wesley said. 'Since he stumbled on it by chance that day in 1963, it's passed through the hands of various owners, none of who regarded it as anything more than a historic curio, not even Prince Al-Saud, who as a collector should have known better. He might have asked a far higher price for it. And I'd have paid it, too, I can tell you.'

'So what about before Hillel found it?' Jude asked. 'Did it just stay hidden in the ruins of Masada?'

'Given that nobody even knew where the site of Masada was for centuries, I'd say it's a fair assumption that the sword was there all that time, yes. It was well concealed in the rampart wall, for the simple reason that the men who deliberately hid it there were determined that it should not fall into the hands of their enemies after the defeat of the fortress. If what I believe – and what Simeon and Fabrice believed – is correct, then for this particular sword to be taken as a trophy by the Romans would have been regarded as a worse disaster than defeat itself. Thankfully, that didn't happen, or the sword would surely have been lost to us for ever, melted down, buried, hanging on the wall of some Roman emperor, only to be captured by the Barbarian hordes when the empire finally fell. Who knows where it could have ended up?' Wesley eyed the sword lovingly.

'Backtrack,' Ben said.

'Sorry, I'm skipping. Okay, let me lay the groundwork here. How much do you know about the history of Masada? Specifically, about the nine hundred or so men, women and children who died there?'

'I know what most people know,' Ben said. 'That after the Jewish uprising against Roman rule in 66 A.D., Jerusalem was besieged and then sacked, and pockets of refugees fled to the fortress at Masada to escape persecution. They held out as long as they could, but defeat was a foregone conclusion. The rest is history.'

Wesley nodded. 'In a nutshell. But there's more to it. The revolt that kicked off in 66 was actually the culmination of a long period of warfare, some of it open military conflict but mostly hit-and-run guerrilla raids on Roman garrisons and supply convoys, that had been going on for a hundred years. The Holy Land at that time was a revolutionary hotbed, teeming with disaffected rebel groups, cults, sects and sub-sects, all ready to do battle against each other over the smallest matter of scripture but strongly united in their desire to strike back against the tyranny of the Romans. One of the major revolutionary groups were the Nazareans, regarded by the Romans as terrorists and hunted down accordingly. The Romans had a name for such rebels – they called them the *Sicarii*, from the Latin word *sicarius*, meaning a dagger-man, a cutthroat, an assassin.' Wesley grunted. 'Same way we use terms like "insurgents" and "extremists" in the modern age to describe folks who're only trying to defend their homeland against invasion. Another nice example of history being written by the winners. But what if the Sicarii weren't cutthroats and villains, but simply brave men who opposed a cruel foreign regime, refused to acknowledge Rome as their master, and were sworn to fight to the death for the reinstatement of a rightful ruler over the kingdom of Israel?'

'I get the idea,' Ben said. 'Keep going.'

'Like I said, this is all groundwork. In around 63 A.D., James, the Nazarean leader in Jerusalem, was captured and executed by the authorities. Soon after, in the year 66, a massive renewed rebellion sparked open war, as a result of which the rebels took Jerusalem. One of their many victories against the Romans at that time was the slaughter, to a man, of the military garrison stationed at Masada, leaving the fortress empty. Naturally, Rome couldn't leave such acts unpunished. In 70 A.D. the Emperor Titus ordered a massive invasion of Jerusalem by the biggest Roman army ever seen.

'Now, the city had been sacked before, by the Egyptians a thousand years earlier. This time was much worse. The Romans surrounded the city with their siege towers and ballistas, and bombarded it relentlessly until the defences crumbled and the legions marched in. A million people died in the siege and ensuing slaughter, most of them Jews. The Romans massacred everyone they could find – men, women, children, priests, the elderly, those who tried to resist or those who begged for mercy. According to the Roman historian Josephus, the soldiers had to clamber over mounds of the dead in order to carry on the extermination. A hundred thousand more of Jerusalem's population were captured and enslaved, while anyone who tried to escape was hunted down and killed. Once Jerusalem was taken, Titus ordered its complete destruction. The army laid waste to the place, demolished Herod's Temple and levelled the city walls to their foundations.

'Meanwhile, the contingent of rebels who'd taken out the Roman garrison at Masada, commanded by a man named Eleazar ben Yair, were digging in for the retaliatory onslaught that would inevitably follow the fall of Jerusalem. Many of them were committed to the Nazarean cause, had known in advance that things were about to reach boiling point and had managed to get out of Jerusalem in time.'

Wesley interrupted his story for a sip of wine. 'And if I'm right – as I believe I am – the leaders of the Nazarean freedom fighters had brought with them to Masada an unimaginably precious icon and symbol of their struggle. An icon that nearly two thousand years of political and theological fact-fudging has left all but forgotten in the modern age. Until now.'

'Are you still laying the groundwork, or are we getting closer to the point?' Ben asked.

'I dropped a clue earlier,' Wesley said, 'when I said that the revolutionary movements in the Holy Land had existed for many years before these events took place.'

'I don't get it. How's that a clue?' Jude asked, frowning.

'Let's go back another, say, forty years, to around 30 A.D.,' Wesley said. 'To a time when the Nazareans were already a significant enough subversive force, both politically and militarily, to present a real threat to Roman rule.' He smiled. 'There was one prominent Nazarean whose name I haven't mentioned. His name was Jesus. And this was his sword.'

Chapter Fifty-Five

'That's a hell of a claim to make,' Ben said. He hadn't known quite where Holland's story was leading, but it certainly wasn't to this.

'Yes, it is,' Wesley replied earnestly, levelling a finger at him. 'And it's not one I, or Fabrice Lalique, or your father' – pointing across at Jude – 'would ever make lightly. But consider the evidence. It's well established by now that "Jesus of Nazareth" is a mistranslation of "Jesus the Nazarean" from the original Greek text of the New Testament. Nazareth may not have been the birthplace of Christ at all, for the simple reason that it might not have even existed until three hundred years afterwards. Why pretend that he wasn't strongly associated with the same rebel movements that the Romans were so desperate to stamp out, all through his lifetime and for years afterwards?'

'This is the kind of stuff nineteen-year-old theology students discuss in the pub,' Ben said. 'You think I haven't heard it before?'

'Then maybe our bright young scholars should think about it a little harder,' Wesley shot back. 'Simeon did. The evidence, both from the Bible and other contemporary historical sources, all points to the inescapable fact that Jesus was crucified as a political revolutionary. The Roman chronicler Tacitus states as much in his Annals. But Jesus was much more than just another insurrectionist,' Wesley went on emphatically. 'The gospels of both Matthew and Luke state pretty explicitly that he was of royal birth, a legitimate descendant of Solomon and David claiming rightful kingship over the nation of Israel and come to deliver his people from the tyrannical rule of a foreign invader – a liberator, wielding a liberator's sword. He was the Messiah or "anointed one", whose triumphal entry into Jerusalem was in keeping with the ancient prophecy in Zechariah 9:9 that the rightful king would ride into the city on a donkey. How else could this humble travelling holy man have managed to convince the Roman governor of Judea that his intention was to become King of the Jews, and so needed to be made an example of by putting him to death in a manner specifically reserved for enemies of the state?'

Ben kept his mouth shut. Wesley had waded into an area of biblical research that even some of the most conservative scholars had to admit was murky at best.

'This Bible stuff never stuck on me,' Jude said, 'but weren't the two other men crucified with Jesus just common criminals? Hardly enemies of the state.'

'In the original Koine Greek in which the New Testament was written,' Wesley explained, 'the men crucified alongside Jesus were described as *lestai*, which was mistranslated as "robbers". In fact, in the first century A.D. the term lestai would have signified much more than common crooks, but rather terrorists, insurrectionists, rebels. They were outlaws, like the rest of the disciples. Take Judas Iscariot, for instance. That's more than likely another mistranslation. Many scholars, your father included, believed that he was actually "Judas the Sicarius", Judas the rebel or guerrilla fighter.'

'But Jesus was a pacifist,' Jude said. 'Even I know that he advocated love, not war.'

'As a philosopher he advocated Christian values of tolerance and goodness towards one's fellow men,' Wesley said. 'The same virtues practised by, say, the Templar Knights a thousand years later, although that didn't stop them from being ferocious warriors when violence was called for. Fact is, Jesus was far from the meek, mild hippy image he's become identified with in modern times. Did your father ever tell you the story of how he stormed into the Temple and kicked over the moneychangers' tables? Hardly an act of pacifism, do you think? It must have sparked a full-scale riot.'

Jude had to concede the point. 'Okay, but Jesus and his disciples didn't go around with weapons, did they?'

'Actually, the Bible tells us that they were routinely armed, like any soldier would be. For example, they had swords with them at the Last Supper, even as they sat around eating and talking.'

'What?'

'It's right there in the Gospel of Luke,' Wesley said. '"Jesus" last words to his disciples at the supper are to urge them to arm themselves, even if they have to sell their garments to pay for weapons. The disciples respond by reminding him they already did – "Look, Lord, here are our swords" – to which Jesus replies with approval.'

'Are you serious?' Jude said.

'Sure I am. And there's more. Now, when the Last Supper is over, Jesus leads his followers to the Garden of Gethsemane, where shortly afterwards the authorities turn up to arrest him. Not just the token handful it would take to round up an unarmed pacifist, either. According to some versions of the scripture, an entire cohort of Roman soldiers was sent to capture Jesus. A cohort is one tenth of a legion. That's six hundred soldiers, accompanied by troops of the puppet Jewish regime and various officials including the High Priest and his assistant Malchus. No sooner have they appeared, but one of Jesus' disciples whips out a sword and slices off Malchus' ear.'

Jude shot Ben a look of incredulity.

'It's true,' Ben told him. 'It's there in the Bible.'

'Now, the Gospel of St John actually names the wielder of the sword as the disciple Simon Peter. Later to become known as St Peter the Apostle, of course, though he may also have been the same man as Simon the Zealot, a well-known militant nationalist of the time. There's a 1520 painting, *The Capture of Christ*, that shows him swinging a sword at a terrified Malchus.' Wesley grinned. 'I know, I tried to buy it. The painting gives a pretty good idea of what the scene must have been like. What happened next? Six hundred soldiers dispatched to make an arrest, only to be met with armed resistance? There's bound to have been fighting. Yet even despite what's clearly written in the Bible, none of this is mentioned in the conventional account of the story that's preached today.'

Ben leaned forward to cut in. 'So if I understand, your theory goes like this: when Jesus is captured, presumably along with the two other rebels who are crucified along with him, some of his men manage to escape, taking the sword with them. It remains in the hands of the rebels who continue the armed struggle against the Romans for years after the crucifixion.'

'Right,' Wesley said. 'Imagine what an incredibly important icon it would be to them. The sword of their Messiah, passed from one rebel leader to the next, perhaps in the hope that another true king would emerge one day to lead them to victory.'

'One rebellion leads to another, leaders come and go, years pass,' Ben continued. 'By the time of the major revolt of 66 A.D. and the sack of Jerusalem, the sword is in the possession of the rebel commander whose forces then take refuge at the fortress of Masada.'

Wesley nodded. 'But now, fresh from destroying Jerusalem, the Roman tenth legion turns up at Masada and surrounds the mountain with thousands of troops and siege artillery. The rebels know there's no way out, and when they see the Romans building their assault ramp, they realise they're running out of time.'

'And rather than let themselves be enslaved or slaughtered by the Romans, the rebels orchestrate their own mass suicide. But first, their commander hides the precious sword within the fortress walls to prevent it from falling into enemy hands.'

'That's it,' Wesley said.

Ben chewed the theory over for a moment or two. It was a compelling story, but there was just one small problem. 'Even if you can prove that this sword belonged to the Judean freedom fighters of Jesus' time, I don't see how you can trace it back to Jesus himself.'

Wesley considered the question, pausing to wet his lips with another sip of wine. 'I mentioned before the sword that Peter the Apostle used to slice off the ear of Malchus at the scene of Jesus' arrest. Now, that particular weapon is believed to have passed into the hands of Joseph of Arimathea, the man who gave up his own prepared tomb for Christ to be buried in.'

'I know who Joseph of Arimathea was.'

'Fine. Then you know that legend tells how Joseph later travelled to Britain, where he became the first Christian bishop there. Some accounts say that he brought with him the Holy Grail, given to him by a ghostly apparition of Jesus.

More likely, what he brought with him was St Peter's sword. We know that from there it made its way eastwards, until it finally shows up in Poznań, Poland, sometime in the tenth century. You can still see its remains on display at the Poznań Archdiocesan Museum, and I've been there to examine them. Believe me, there ain't much left but a pitted, blackened hunk of rust. That's what happens to a piece of low-grade steel after a couple of thousand years, or even just a few centuries. You should see some of the rotted old sticks in my collection, dating back to as recently as the fourteenth century.'

Wesley turned to the sword on the table and ran his fingers delicately along its smooth blade. 'Look at it. It's almost perfectly preserved, and you can't put that down purely to the arid climate of Masada.' He glanced up at Ben. 'What do you know about metallurgy?'

Ben had to admit that he didn't know a great deal at all.

'Without the development of forged steel,' Wesley said, 'we'd still be in the Bronze Age. It changed everything and made our whole history possible, but it wasn't an overnight process. The reason so many ancient weapons have simply rotted away is that most of them were made from second-rate metal. Thankfully, not all were. As far back as the sixth century B.C., master craftsmen were forging steel weapons that were as strong as those we know today. Ever heard of Wootz steel?'

Ben hadn't.

'The name originates from India, where it was being developed from about 300 B.C. onwards. It's an exceptional grade of iron ore steel, extracted from raw ore and formed using a crucible to melt and burn away impurities and to add carbon and other ingredients known only to the most skilled swordsmiths. It was a delicate process – too much carbon and you had wrought iron, too soft. Too little carbon and you ended up with cast iron, which was hard but also brittle and prone to shattering. But get the balance of the ingredients right, and you had one ass-kicking fighting sword. It wouldn't chip, snap or bend. It would withstand both the rigours of battle and the test of time. Wootz steel was so sought after that it was traded widely throughout ancient Europe, the Arab world and the Middle East, where it was known as Damascus steel. Needless to say, it was extremely valuable and expensive.'

Wesley picked up the sword. 'And here's an example of an early Damascene blade, right here. Now, I've had this thing analysed by a hundred experts. The tests show an incredibly refined internal structure, containing carbon nanotubes and nanowires and all kinds of stuff that would blow away even the most expert modern-day swordsmith. We couldn't even replicate a blade like this nowadays. It's a lost art.'

He swished the sword through the air. 'In the first century A.D. and for a very long time afterwards, a sword of this quality would have represented the ultimate technology, the equivalent of the most ultra-advanced electronics in our age. No ordinary person could aspire to owning one. It's even more beautifully made than the bronze khopesh swords found in the burial chamber of Tutankhamen. In other words, what we're looking at here was a weapon forged for a king. And not just any king, either.'

Wesley suddenly thrust the blade at Ben, the point stopping a foot from his chest. 'Again, that was all groundwork. Now here comes the best part. Take a look at the blade inscription. As you can see, it's pretty badly worn and faded, unreadable in places. Make anything out?'

Ben peered at the barely-visible markings on the blade and could just about discern the faint outlines of curved lettering engraved into the steel.

'It's Aramaic,' Wesley said. 'I paid a specialist team three hundred thousand bucks to work with a language expert and produce a computer-generated image of what the inscription would have looked like two thousand years ago. Want to know what they came up with?' He grinned at Ben with a look that said, 'Are you ready for this?'

Then he said, 'The inscription reads, "Hosanna to the Son of David".'

Chapter Fifty-Six

Ben stared at the blade. Was it possible he was really looking at the sword of Jesus Christ?

'Okay, it's not outright proof,' Wesley said, still grinning. 'But it's near as dammit, when you place the sword in its historical context.'

'Has this thing been verified?' Ben asked after a few moments' stunned silence. It was becoming harder to deny the possibility that Wesley was right.

Wesley's grin fell away. 'That's been a sticking point from the beginning,' he admitted. 'I've spent almost three years trying to persuade any number of university historians and other academics to see what's in front of them, but they won't open their goddamn eyes. The problem is that the sword is technically unprovenanced. In other words, it wasn't personally excavated by archaeologists who would've placed it on official record, dated it, certified it, and so on. As things stand, nobody will accept that it was a legitimate discovery from the excavation of Masada, and so the matter of its origin falls into question. It's frustrating, but I believe the truth will out one day. Fabrice and Simeon believed it too.'

'So this was what my dad was writing his book about?' Jude said. 'The sword of Jesus?'

Wesley nodded. 'I first met your father at a construction

site near Millau in France, where I was overseeing the restoration of a ruined medieval church. He'd turned up hoping to learn something of how it was done. Fabrice was the local minister, and the three of us kind of hooked up and hit it off as friends. At that time I was still so dizzy about the discovery of the sword, I was bursting to tell someone about it. So I confided in them. They took a little persuading, at first, but before long they were as excited as I was. That's where it began, our little fellowship. I flew them over to the Whitworth Mansion to see the sword, and sometime later we all travelled together to Israel to meet Hillel and see for themselves where he'd found it.'

Wesley gazed into space and was silent for a few moments, remembering his lost friends. 'I'm not a religious man,' he went on. 'I don't know if there's a heaven, or a hell, or if there's anyone up there watching over us. But one thing I know for sure is that I'd hate to see the churches crumble into dust along with the old traditions. I'm glad I'll be dead and gone before that day comes. That's why I was worried about the sword at first. I told Simeon and Fabrice my concerns, that going public with the idea of Christ as a freedom fighter, a kind of Che Guevara or Robin Hood figure of ancient times, might do more harm than good. Next thing the pro-atheist lobby would be using it to their advantage – "See, folks? He wasn't the son of God after all".

'But Simeon turned me around on that one. He believed it was time for the church to stand up strong against the rising tide of secularism. Talked about the responsibility of modern clergymen to move on from the old ways and bring Christ more into line with the cultural heroes of today, for a younger and more modern audience. He said the modern Christian faith was fighting a battle for its survival, and the sword of Jesus would give it the power to unite and withstand its enemies. He was so impassioned – you should have heard him talk.'

Jude gazed sadly down at the table. 'I miss him,' he murmured.

'I miss him too, son,' Wesley said. 'He was quite a man. People loved him. Because he was young and dynamic and already had a following with his TV appearances, radio and internet presence, we agreed that it would be his name on the book and he'd be the frontman for the whole show once we felt ready to go public with it. Before I knew it, he was leading the way. And I didn't mind a bit. Meanwhile, I was chipping away in the background, trying to find a university department that'd listen to me and back us up. I'd just come back from Buffalo the day the attackers came to the house.'

Ben had been listening quietly for a while, struggling with his doubts and trying to beat his jumbled thoughts into shape. 'All right,' he said to Wesley. 'Let's just say for the sake of argument that what you're telling us is true, and that no matter how wild and crazy it might sound to me, I have to accept that Simeon Arundel wouldn't have fallen for a pile of bullshit. Even if this really was the sword of Jesus Christ, it doesn't get us any closer to knowing who's behind all this.'

'Maybe it does, though,' Jude said. 'Wouldn't a lot of Christian groups be seriously against something like this? I mean, it would change everything about the way people saw Jesus, wouldn't it? Maybe some folks would be so pissed off about it that they'd do anything to keep the secret from getting out there. If they found out someone from the clergy was planning to write a book about it . . . '

'It wouldn't be the first time the church has conspired against its own, that's for sure,' Ben admitted.

'Okay,' Jude said. 'So that could be the answer. Perhaps we're dealing with some kind of crazy Christian group or fundamentalist sect or something like that. Dad often used to complain about some of the bishops, said they were a bunch of hardline old bastards who'd happily torch heretics at the stake if they could get away with it – maybe it's one of them. Or maybe there's some secret society out there, that's known about the sword all along and is determined to suppress the truth.'

Wesley looked doubtful. 'I thought about that too, but you'd have to be talking about one hell of a seriously organised and influential Christian sect. What kind of organisation has the power and contacts to cover up murders and track people from their credit cards? That's more like the kind of muscle that a government agency has, and I don't see any western government agency supporting a religious group right now, covertly or otherwise. Not in this day and age.'

'Then who?' Jude said.

'I have no idea, son. I've racked my brains and I can't figure it out. Nor can I understand how anyone could have known what we were up to. We were so damned careful to keep this quiet. Your father wouldn't even tell your mother about it, and I know how much it hurt him to keep secrets from her.'

'Your hired consultants might have leaked it to someone,' Ben said. 'That was a security risk, for a start.'

'Sure, I knew it was a potential risk. That's why I never gave any of them more information than they strictly needed, so they couldn't guess its history.'

'But you told the universities everything,' Ben said.

'What choice did I have? I was trying to persuade them, so of course I didn't hold anything back. But these guys are reputable academics. It's crazy to suggest they could be behind this. In any case, they all thought I was just some hare-brained eccentric. No, it's got to be something bigger.'

Ben reflected for a moment. 'I think you're right,' he said. 'Whoever these people are, we know that they have a lot of power and influence. The resources and connections to monitor all your landlines, for a start. That's got to be the main reason they knew so much.'

Jude frowned. 'Hold on. I don't get that. Did they tap the phones *because* they already knew about the sword, or was it by tapping phones that they found out about it in the first place?'

'I can't say,' Ben said.

'And that's another weird thing,' Wesley said. 'If the sonsof-bitches were onto us from the beginning because they were listening into phone calls, how come they never went after Hillel? For which I'm very thankful, I might add.'

'I don't know that either,' Ben said. 'I'd have to hazard a guess that the phone surveillance only began more recently, when Hillel was no longer in the picture.'

But it really was just a guess, and Ben was getting that nasty sinking feeling that they'd reached another impasse. They were floundering.

A silence fell across the table as each man wrestled with his own thoughts and nobody seemed able to come up with anything useful. Wesley poured out the last of the wine.

They'd been talking a long time. It was getting late.

'These people are still out there,' Jude said. 'And we still have no idea who they are.'

'Maybe the only thing we can do is sit tight and wait for them to make their next move,' Wesley said.

'You mean all of us, here?' Jude asked.

'Sure, if you feel like sticking around Martha's Vineyard for a while. That'd be fine with me. Or if you want to go back to England, no problem. We can protect ourselves wherever we are. All it takes is money, and money's not an issue.

I'll do what I offered to do for your father, and hire a goddamn army of bodyguards to take care of you around the clock until this thing's over. We can outlast the bastards. And if they dare show their faces, we'll bury 'em.'

Chapter Fifty-Seven

The conversation meandered on a while longer around the table, but everyone was tired and their energy was waning. Finally Jude stretched out his arms and yawned. 'I can barely keep my eyes open.'

'There are five guest bedrooms on the top floor,' Wesley told him. 'Use any one of them you want.'

'My stuff's in the car,' Jude said to Ben.

Ben was hardly listening. His mind still entirely focused on his thoughts, he vaguely dug the car keys from his pocket and slid them across the table. Jude snatched them up and went outside. They'd left the rental Jeep a little way up the empty beach road, the other side of the dunes.

'He reminds me a lot of his father,' Wesley said when Jude was gone. 'Not so much physically, but he's got Simeon's spirit. He's a good kid. I guess it's my fault that he has to suffer this. If I hadn't gotten his father mixed up in it all . . .'

Ben still found it hard to adapt to knowing whose son Jude really was. 'He's tough. He'll come through it.'

As they talked, they heard Jude come back in from the car and go hustling up the stairs.

'What'll he do now, with his folks gone?' Wesley asked, more quietly in case he was overheard.

'I'm not sure,' Ben said. 'He might finish his studies, or else he talked about joining up with Greenpeace, trying to get himself a placement on one of their ships. He'd like to do something to help the environment.'

If Wesley Holland the arch-capitalist had any problems with that, he didn't show it. 'Simeon had hoped he might follow him into the ministry one day.'

'I'd say there's not too much chance of that,' Ben said.

'Whatever he wants to do, if he needs money . . .'

'Kind of you to offer,' Ben said. He'd already decided that he'd ensure as best he could that Jude was financially secure. The tricky part might be getting him to accept help.

'Well, anyway, I'm just about done in myself,' Wesley said, stifling a yawn. 'Time to hit the sack.' He stood up and picked the sword off the table. 'I'll put this back in the vault in the morning. Keep it by me for now.'

When he was alone, Ben walked out of the front door and onto the broad terrace that separated the house's facade from the beach. He lit up a Gauloise and spent a while watching the dark waves rolling in, listening to the roar of the surf. The wind was cold, rustling through the reeds that grew among the dunes. Stars twinkled overhead and the lights of the distant marine observatory tower glowed dimly red over the ocean.

Feeling demoralised and as tired as he could remember having ever felt in his life, Ben stubbed out the cigarette, tossed the smoking butt away into the sand and then returned inside and climbed the stairs.

The top floor of the house was dark except for the light shining from a door on the left, which was open a few inches. It was the guest bedroom that Jude had picked out for himself, facing towards the sea. He was sitting on the bed, silent and still. All Ben could see of him through the gap in the door was his foot and part of his leg. He was still dressed and wearing his shoes.

'Good night,' Ben said quietly outside the doorway.

No reply. Ben tapped lightly on the door. 'See you in the morning.' When there was still no response from inside, he pushed open the door. 'Jude? Are you all right?'

Jude looked up as Ben appeared in the doorway. His face was tight and pale.

Ben stared back at him, realising that something was wrong.

And felt the blood rapidly drain out of his body into his feet.

Propped up beside the bed, next to Jude's own rucksack, was his green canvas bag. Jude had brought it in from the car.

And in Jude's hands was the small sheet of sky-blue paper, creased in the middle, that Ben had been keeping hidden in there. Michaela's letter.

Ben didn't move, or step forward to snatch it from him, or say 'Give me that'. It was too late. Jude knew.

'I thought I recognised her writing,' Jude said quietly. 'In Jerusalem. I pretended I hadn't noticed what you were reading. Wanted to take another look ever since.'

Ben didn't know what to say.

'Were you ever going to tell me?' Jude asked.

'No,' Ben replied. 'I wasn't ever going to tell you.'

'Then you should have just burned this.'

'I couldn't,' Ben said. Anger welled up inside him. Why hadn't he had the courage to destroy it? It was stupid and sentimental and selfish to have kept it and risked letting Jude find it.

'You've all lied to me,' Jude muttered. The letter was fluttering slightly in his hands.

'I know it looks bad. But they thought it was for the best.'

'For the best! To believe in a lie, for all these years?

'It's been a shock for me too,' Ben said. 'I didn't read it until we were in France. I had no idea until then. You have to believe me, Jude.'

'You and my *mum*—'

'It was a long time ago. We were young. These things happen.'

'And he knew about it all along?' Jude said, seething with anger.

'Simeon?'

'What kind of man would do that? Pretend to be the father of another man's kid?'

'The best kind,' Ben said. 'He loved you. You couldn't have asked for a better father.'

'Except he wasn't, was he?' Jude said bitterly. 'He was a liar and a fraud. So much for the good upstanding vicar, the great Christian with all his high-and-mighty fucking morals.'

Ben stepped forward. 'Jude—'

'Get the fuck away from me. You're not my father. I'll never see you that way.'

'I don't expect you to. I don't even know how to be a father.'

Jude leaped up from the bed, red-faced. He scrunched the letter into a tight ball and clenched it in his fist. 'This is bullshit!' he yelled. Grabbing his rucksack off the floor, he slung it violently over his shoulder and started pushing his way past Ben towards the door.

'Where are you going?'

'As far away from you as possible.'

'You're on an island,' Ben said. 'You can't go anywhere.'

'I'll swim home if I have to. What do you care, anyway?'

'Hey. Come on. Don't act this way. We can talk about it.'

'Fuck you, *Dad*.'

'I'm not your dad,' Ben said, trying to restrain his rising temper. 'Simeon Arundel was, is, your dad, and you should be proud to say so. The rest counts for nothing. Jude! Come back!'

But Jude wasn't listening. He stormed out onto the landing and started running down the stairs. Ben raced out after him. He stopped at the top of the stairs, gripping the banister rail. 'Oh, shit,' he groaned to himself, scarcely able to believe this was happening. It was all his fault. He should never have let Jude see the letter.

But recriminations and self-blame could wait for now. After a moment's hesitation, he plunged down the stairs after Jude. As he reached the bottom, the front door was swinging on its hinges. He flicked on a side-lamp in the entrance hall, burst outside onto the terrace and saw Jude dashing away up the beach, a rapidly disappearing running figure silhouetted against the dark sand.

Ben was about to give chase, just as he'd done back on Bodmin Moor. But then he held himself back and gave it more thought. Was it a mistake to let Jude run off like this? Or would it be an even bigger mistake to follow him and try to work things through together? Should he give him space, or rein him in?

Jude was gone now, vanished into the darkness.

Ben suddenly realised what he was dealing with. It was a parenting problem. Most parents were faced with choices and dilemmas every day bringing up their kids, and only by learning from their mistakes could they have any chance of making the right decisions. Sometimes they did, sometimes not, but after eighteen or twenty years they had at least some kind of experience to guide them through the ever-changing minefield.

Ben had none at all. He'd been thrown into the deep end with no idea of how to swim. He simply didn't know how to deal with such a situation.

But then it hit him that he knew someone who was very well equipped to deal with it. Brooke hadn't yet experienced motherhood herself, but she was wise in these things and her background in psychology was about as extensive as you could get. It was what had earned her her PhD., Ben figured, so she must be able to help him here.

Besides, he felt so alone and isolated that he'd have wanted to talk to her anyway. He knew that, deep down.

Remembering the card she'd given him with her new number on, he quickly dug out his wallet and found it. His phone was in his jeans pocket. As he dialled the number, he counted back the gap between the time zones. It'd be early morning in London. Brooke would still be in bed.

He imagined her lying there in her bedroom in Richmond, her hair spread out on the pillow. Maybe she'd be wearing those faded yellow pyjamas she liked, with a picture of Snoopy across the top and a dialogue bubble that said 'I love you'. It would be good to hear her voice, even at a moment like this.

But then he had another thought as the dial tone sounded in his ear, and it wasn't a pleasant one. What if Brooke wasn't alone? What if she had company – male company – the kind Ben didn't want to think about? How would she react to her ex calling out of the blue at this time?

Ben almost aborted the call, but then hung on in nervous anticipation. He turned back towards the house as the dial tone went on ringing. Stepped inside the hallway, trying to marshal his thoughts and figure out where to begin.

A second later, Brooke replied. 'Hello?' Her voice sounded sleepy. It sounded nice. 'Who is it? Hello?'

But Ben didn't reply. He could hear her voice coming from the receiver, but he said nothing and slowly lowered the phone to his side. With his thumb he pressed the button to end the call.

Because the hallway was suddenly filled with masked men in black. Six of them. Six automatic weapons pointed right at him.

Chapter Fifty-Eight

Wesley Holland's island refuge hadn't been safe at all. The enemy had wasted very little time in catching up with them, and now Ben was in real trouble.

The six gunmen were almost certainly a pair of three-man teams who'd approached the house by stealth from different angles and entered by different routes to converge in the middle. Ben didn't say a word. There was nothing to say, no point asking 'Who are you?' or 'What do you want?' He let the phone drop from his hand and raised his arms shoulder-high as he backed away a step.

His mind was trained to work fast in these situations, and he already had a plan. The lamp he'd turned on a moment earlier was the only light in the hallway. The sideboard on which it stood was just two steps to his right. One swift movement, and he could smash the lamp to the floor, plunging the hallway into darkness. The couple of seconds' confusion might buy him enough time to disarm one of the team and let loose four or five rounds before tumbling out of the door onto the terrace. He'd have to move fast, but if he didn't take a bullet in the process it was just about feasible.

But even some of the best plans didn't survive long in a real-life confrontation. The men immediately circled Ben as he backed away, two of them slipping around his right flank to block off his access to the lamp. The eyes in the ski masks all watched him intently, as if the men all knew exactly who he was and had been instructed to take no chances. Fingers were on triggers, safeties set to 'FIRE'. Ben was pretty certain that if he made a single abrupt move, they'd gun him down where he stood.

'Grab him and cuff him,' said one. Every team had a leader. He was it. Two men stepped closer, one from the left, one from the right, still keeping their pistols trained on him.

The team leader spoke into a tiny radio mike on his collar. 'Target acquired. Move in.' Almost instantly, Ben heard the thump of a helicopter approaching.

The man on Ben's left produced a thick plastic cable tie, the kind that police and military forces used to secure prisoners' wrists behind their backs. He pressed the muzzle of his pistol against Ben's head and took a hold of Ben's arm. His movements were slick and practised. The operation was being executed with perfect efficiency and control.

Then, suddenly, it wasn't. Ben had seen a hundred military exercises fall apart in the blink of an eye when an unplanned-for factor seemed to leap out of nowhere and blew everything to hell. Control could evaporate into chaos within a second, and it was when tensions were running at their highest that even the smallest surprise incident could set it off.

That factor was Wesley Holland. He came bursting out from the darkness at the top of the stairs, in slippers and a dressing gown. 'What the hell's going on down here?' He was clutching the ancient sword, as if he'd half expected trouble and had been keeping it by the side of the bed. He froze at the sight of the armed intruders in the hallway.

Several weapons spun around to point up the stairwell towards the billionaire, who gaped down the stairs at them for a split second and then turned to bolt back the other way.

A lot of things happened in the next few instants.

The man at Ben's left was momentarily distracted – long enough that he didn't see the elbow coming for his face. Ben cupped his left fist in the palm of his right hand and drove back hard, using the rotation of his legs, back and abdominal muscles to put every ounce of savage power he could into the strike. The point of his elbow delivered a windpipe-crushing blow to the base of the guy's throat. Even before he'd slammed against the wall, his face already turning blue, Ben had twisted the pistol out of his hand and was bringing it to bear on the others.

Meanwhile, the hallway erupted with gunfire as three of the gunmen opened fire on the escaping Wesley. One bullet splintered the banister rail next to him; one passed by his ear; the third passed through the muscle of his left calf. He cried out and fell backwards.

Holding his pistol in a rigid two-handed grip, Ben swivelled it to point at the nearest man standing and let off a double-tap to the chest. The rule in close-quarter pistol combat was to aim for centre of mass and never let the gun stay still. Before the man had crumpled to the floor, Ben's sights were already moving on, instinctively picking out the target that was the greatest threat to him.

Wesley Holland had lost his balance as his injured leg gave way under him, and now came tumbling backwards down the stairs, still clutching the sword.

The four remaining guns were turning back towards Ben. It was the quickest mover that Ben homed in on. His trigger finger flicked twice and rattled off two more rapid rounds. A scream. Blood sprayed vertically up the wall and the guy's weapon dropped out of his hands.

The thick of the gunfight lasted only a short instant, but with his heart and brain running on pure adrenaline it felt to Ben like a full minute. The exchange of shots was almost a continual deafening roar in the confined space. Empty shell cases spilled and bounced across the floor. The stink of cordite filled the air. In the chaos Ben saw the team leader's pistol muzzle line up on his head and knew he couldn't react fast enough. But before the man could shoot, Wesley Holland's tumbling body had crashed to the bottom step and hit him from behind in the legs, knocking him off-line and sending the shot wide.

A bullet from another gun seared past Ben's face and plaster exploded from the wall. He returned fire. The pistol he'd taken was a high-capacity Walther, good for at least another eight shots before he ran dry. But he'd no intention of holding his ground in a protracted stand-up gunfight against three determined assailants.

He wasn't that eager to find out if there really was a heaven up there.

He crashed the front door open with his shoulder. Threw himself out of the doorway and rolled on his back onto the dark terrace, firing wildly as he flipped up on his feet and ducked away from the doorway.

The helicopter was coming in fast, hovering fifty feet above the beach, The white-blue glare of its halogen spotlamps was blinding, forcing Ben to shield his eyes as he ran along the terrace parallel with the wall of the house; he stumbled in the glare and almost fell on his face, and it probably saved his life. A blast of automatic fire rang out from the chopper and raked the house where his head had been an instant earlier. Splinters of white wood flew. A window burst apart, raining glass everywhere.

Ben hurdled the terrace railing with high-velocity bullets zipping overhead and smacking into the wall right behind him. He landed with a grunt on soft sand, fell to his knees, scrambled up again and began to sprint hard towards the dunes at the side of the house. The chopper descended closer towards the beach, its downdraught whipping up a sandstorm.

Then Ben was among the dunes, leaping from one to another, trying to escape the glaring beam of the chopper's spotlight and find cover among the long, black shadows that it threw for a hundred yards across the beach. His heart was pounding. He wondered what was happening to Wesley, and felt bad that he couldn't go back to help the guy. Then he wondered where Jude was, and hoped he was far away by now.

The team leader and his remaining gunmen had emerged from the front of the house and were running across the beach. Voices shouted. Several more men leaped down from the landing chopper to join them. Ben halted for a second in the reedy gully between two high dunes, to check his pistol. Just four rounds left in the magazine, plus the one still in the chamber. Not enough against so many men.

And then the odds worsened. Two dark shapes came roaring in on the water, heading in a twin arc of white foam towards the beach. RIBs, rigid inflatables. Ben couldn't make out how many occupants were aboard the outboard craft, but at least six more black-clad figures disembarked as they came sliding up the wet sand. The glare of the helicopter lights picked out the gleam of their weapons.

Ben slammed the magazine back into his pistol and scrambled to the top of the dune, crackling through the reeds. If he could slither down its far side unnoticed, there was a chance he could make it to the Jeep. The key was—

Shit. Jude had the key.

Ben suddenly felt very cold. But as he crawled to the top of the dune, he saw that having the key would have done

381

him little good anyway. The Jeep was being guarded by three men.

Then he had to try to find some other way out of here. He half-slid, half-rolled down the soft sand of the dune and started desperately searching for another escape route. The voices of his pursuers were getting louder, and coming from different directions as they split up to search for him. The beams of flashlights darted through the long grass. He wouldn't have been surprised to hear the baying of dogs coming after him. The enemy had taken no chances this time. It was as if they'd stepped their game up a gear.

Ben turned and was suddenly blinded by searing white light. He covered his eyes with his arm. Nowhere to run. He was bathed in the glare, caught like a deer in a hunter's lamp with enough hardware aimed at him to blow him to pieces.

A voice yelled, 'There he is!'

Another shouted, 'Drop the weapon!'

If he hung onto the pistol for another instant, he was dead.

He tossed it away and it hit the sand with a dull thud.

And then the racing figures were closing in all around him. 'Fuck it,' he said, and put up his hands.

Chapter Fifty-Nine

There was no point in trying to resist any longer as they fastened his wrists and marched him roughly across the sand to the idling chopper.

In minutes, the whole section of beach in front of the house had come alive with activity. It looked like the aftermath of a military operation. The gunmen who'd come from the sea returned to the boats, started up their motors and churned the water white as they roared away. The team leader and the remaining members of the assault team were at the chopper, talking with the air crew as the pilot readied for takeoff. They were all still wearing their ski masks. The team leader carried a large, translucent Ziploc bag, through which Ben could make out the lustre of bronze and steel.

Wesley Holland's sword of Christ. So now the enemy had what they'd been looking for all along.

Ben could see something else, too. The sword's blade was smeared with blood. He frowned. How had that happened? As he was led closer, he was able to pick snatches of the men's conversation over the noise of the turbine.

'—about the Yank?'

The team leader shook his head and motioned to the bag in his hand, and Ben heard him say, 'He fell on it.'

Then the blood was Holland's. Ben felt sorry. The way he

saw it, the team leader had no reason to lie to one of his own people. The American must have impaled himself on the blade as he'd come tumbling down the stairs.

Poor Wesley hadn't deserved that. But then, Ben was pretty sure these people would have killed him anyway. Maybe falling on a sword was a better death than being made to kneel and having to spend your final moments waiting for a bullet in the head. The Samurai would have agreed with that one.

Thinking about it led Ben to ponder another question, one that haunted him. Now that they had the sword, why did they want him alive?

'Load him up,' the team leader commanded, waving at the chopper. Ben was shoved towards it. The helicopter was a standard U.S. Army Bell UH-1 Iroquois with the military markings removed and painted matt black. It still retained its side-mounted pair of M240 general purpose machine guns.

As Ben was pushed into the open hatch, the turbine note began to rise to a howl. The team leader and remaining assault team members clambered aboard and took their positions, watching him with hostility. Moments later, the aircraft lifted off from the beach in a whipping tornado of sand.

As they climbed into the air, Ben looked out of the window. Down below on the dark beach, the first orange-red flames were flickering in the windows of Wesley's house. They were going to burn it to the ground, erasing every trace that he'd ever been there. The case of the billionaire who'd vanished off the face of the earth would keep the media buzzing for months and go on intriguing the public for years. Ben wondered if anyone would ever find the vault underneath, and the valuable collections inside.

The chopper banked steeply and headed out to sea, flying roughly southwest. Ben craned his neck back at the dark stretch of beach and the lights of houses that speckled the island's coastline, and thought of Jude. He was down there somewhere. Somehow, he'd make it home.

Ben turned to face the team leader. 'You can take your masks off,' he said over the roar of the prop. 'I won't laugh.'

'Shut him up,' the team leader ordered one of his men, who got up and approached Ben with a fiendish grin and a roll of duct tape.

'Anyone want to tell me what this is all about?' Ben said before a length of tape was slapped over his mouth and a hood yanked roughly over his head. That effectively ended the conversation.

Impossible to tell where they might be taking him. Ben knew that the operational range of a Bell UH-1 was around three hundred miles, which meant their destination could lie anywhere within a radius half that distance; in his mind he traced a circle on the map, and it covered a whole wedge of the U.S. mainland from New York City to the south all the way up into New Hampshire in the north.

After about an hour, Ben sensed the aircraft settling down to land. As they touched down there was noise and activity all around him. The hatch opened and lights shone through the material of his hood. He was grabbed by the arms, hauled out of the chopper and marched across hard ground. Cold wind pierced him for a few moments, then stopped as he was led inside a building where voices echoed in empty space.

'This way, dickhead,' someone said gruffly close to his ear, jerking his arm. He could almost feel the presence of any number of guns pointing at him as he was marched along. Doors opened ahead and were slammed behind them, leading deeper into the building. Then he was shoved roughly down a short flight of steps. The hood was yanked off his head, and he blinked as torchlight flashed in his face. An unseen hand ripped the tape painfully from his lips while the blade of a knife passed between his tethered wrists and cut away the plastic tie.

'Sweet dreams, fucker,' said the same gruff voice, and then something hit him hard from behind and he blacked out.

Chapter Sixty

Ben awoke on a hard stone floor, shivering with cold and blind in the darkness. His head was throbbing badly. Touching his fingers to the lump on the back of his skull, he felt the crust of dried blood where his captors had clubbed him. He stood up and let his eyes adjust to the blackness, and gradually he was able to make out his surroundings. The stone cell was about eight feet square and windowless. A plain wooden bunk was mounted to one wall, a washbasin and rudimentary toilet to another.

He could tell from the airless, damp atmosphere that he was underground. His pockets had been emptied, but they'd let him keep his watch. Its faintly glowing dial read after 4 a.m., December 24th.

He settled on the bunk and rested his aching head in his hands, trying to empty his mind so that time would pass more quickly. But it was impossible to shut off the endless cascade of thoughts that kept swirling around. He kept hearing Brooke's voice, and wondering when he might ever hear it again. More than anything, he agonised over Jude, stranded on Martha's Vineyard. Jude would surely have been able to make his way back to Edgartown, on foot if need be, where he'd be able to make a credit card withdrawal. If he could scrape enough cash together for the ferry back to the mainland, maybe he could phone Robbie from there, or Robbie's uncle—

Over and over, a hundred different scenarios. One way or another, Jude was all right. *He had to be.*

The hours dragged by. Ben's headache eventually diminished, leaving him with the sick nausea of fatigue and worry. 6 a.m., 8 a.m. The cell remained dark. His mind drifted. Slowly, slowly, his eyelids began to droop, his breathing slowed and he finally felt the blessed angels of sleep coming to deliver him to a place of tranquillity . . .

And then the cell door banged open. Ben jolted upright as three men burst into the small space. 'Wakey, wakey!' said a harsh voice. He blinked, certain that he'd been asleep for just a few moments – but a glance at his watch told him it was after 11 a.m. He rose to his feet, stiff from the hard bunk. Two of the guards grabbed his arms and led him towards the dimly lit doorway as the third kept a pistol trained on his chest. They were all wearing heavy jackets and gloves.

For the first time, he was able to see where they'd taken him last night. The corridor leading from the cell was narrow, its rough walls shiny with condensation. The men shoved open a succession of doors, led him around corners and up a flight of steps. He could smell fresh air at last. The man in front opened a final door to the outside, and the morning sunlight flooded over Ben, making him blink. He stood and breathed in the sharp, cold air. He couldn't believe the surreal sight in front of him.

He was in the grounds of a magnificent mansion, formal gardens stretching away as far as the eye could see. Lawns and summerhouses and pergolas coated in fresh snow. Looking back, he realised that he'd been kept housed in some kind of bunker attached to a cluster of outbuildings and storage sheds.

The roofs and gables of the mansion itself were just about visible beyond a ring of snowy conifers up ahead. There was not a whisper of traffic noise. They were somewhere deep in the countryside.

'Move,' said the guard with the pistol at his back. Nobody spoke as they trudged through the snow towards the house and along a broad path that led through an archway and around to the front. It was a millionaire paradise to rival just about any that Ben had seen. They led him through the tall front doorway and into a hall with gleaming wooden floors. 'You guys had better wipe your feet,' he said.

'Shut up,' said the one in front, and pointed at a door across the hall. 'Get in there and wait.'

'What am I waiting for?' Ben asked, but they didn't reply as they shoved him inside the room and slammed the door shut behind him.

It was better than the cell, at any rate. He was in a large, elegant drawing room filled with tasteful period furniture, a vast Persian rug spread over the polished floor. There was a fire crackling in the hearth. Ben went over to warm his hands by it, then wandered across to gaze out of the French window at the snow-covered lawns that seemed to stretch for miles to the distant trees. He wondered what lay beyond – a road, a town?

He tried the handle of the French window. It wasn't locked. There was nobody in sight, and apparently nothing stopping him from walking right out of here. But that was what worried him.

Ben heard the door open behind him and turned to see a man walk in. He was in his sixties or early seventies, large and imposing with a strong presence that seemed to fill the room. He wore small wire-framed glasses and a dark suit that looked expensively tailored to hide his bulk. His hair was grey, thin oiled strands carefully combed across his scalp. His eyes were pale and watery, and fixed on Ben as he shut the door softly behind him.

Ben wondered who he was. The gravity of his demeanour gave the impression of an elder statesman, someone used to giving orders and making important decisions.

The man crossed the room towards him.

'Benedict Hope.' His voice was deep and resonant. His accent was that of an upper-class Englishman who'd spent a lot of time in Europe, with traces of German, or maybe Swiss. 'It's a pleasure to meet you at last. He proffered his hand. 'You can call me Mr Brown.'

Ben just looked at the hand. 'Brown,' he said. 'The colour of bullshit.'

The man didn't seem offended. 'You understand that I can't reveal my real identity.'

'I don't suppose you're going to tell me where I am, either.'

'A friend's house,' Brown replied casually, withdrawing his hand. 'It's just his holiday place. He was happy to let me use it for the occasion. I've flown in from Europe this morning specially to meet you.'

'You needn't have troubled yourself,' Ben said.

Brown crossed the rug to a large antique globe on a stand, that slid open to reveal a drinks cabinet. He lifted out a bottle, peered at it over his glasses, and nodded approvingly. 'Care for a drink? I always take a glass of pale sherry before lunch. It helps the digestion.'

'Thanks for the offer,' Ben said. 'But I don't drink with murderers, as a rule.'

'I was afraid you might be under that misconception,'

Brown said as he poured himself his sherry. He took a sip and smacked his lips with pleasure.

Ben was wondering how many blows it would take to ram the sherry bottle down the guy's throat. Maybe later. First he wanted to know the truth behind all that had happened. 'Let me get this right,' he said. 'My friends were killed in a car crash that was caused by one of your agents, a man called Vincent Napier. Your people threw the priest Fabrice Lalique off a bridge and made it look like suicide. I've been chased halfway around the world by professional gunmen trying to kill me. I saw your thugs shoot Wesley Holland and burn down his house. And you're telling me that's all a misconception.'

'What happened to Mr Holland was highly regrettable,' Brown said. 'And, I might add, purely accidental. We might have had some difficulty persuading him to keep his mouth shut under the circumstances, but rest assured we had no intention of letting him come to harm.'

He paused for another small sip of sherry, then set the glass down. 'That's enough for me. Get heartburn if I overdo it. As for the rest,' he went on, 'I'm afraid you're quite wrong. Vincent Napier wasn't working for us, at least not directly. We didn't arrange fake suicides or car accidents, and we have never purposely deployed a single one of our agents against you. In fact your presence on Martha's Vineyard came as a complete surprise.'

Ben said nothing. He was thinking how easy it would be to grab the thin, delicate sherry glass, break it and use it to slice this lying bastard's throat wide open.

'I understand you must be feeling very upset,' Brown said, eyeing him closely. 'You consider me to be the architect of some grand conspiracy scheme hell-bent on obtaining an ancient relic, killing anyone who stands in the way.' He grunted with amusement. 'I'm afraid that's a rather far-fetched notion, Mr Hope. In truth, I don't give a damn whether Holland's trinket is the genuine article or not. It's just a piece of old iron as far as I'm concerned.'

Ben narrowed his eyes and stayed silent.

'You'd like an explanation,' Brown said. 'I certainly owe you one, and I'll be as open and honest with you as my position allows me. I head an organisation that very few people have ever heard of, for the simple reason that its existence was never intended for public knowledge. This organisation goes by the name of the Trimble Group. It was founded many years ago by some very influential men whose names I'm sure you'd recognise, though you'd find no mention of it on any official record. Needless to say, there never was a Trimble either.'

'Let me take a wild guess,' Ben said. 'We're talking about a secret government agency?'

Brown made a casual gesture. 'We're all chess pieces on the same board, cogs in the same machine, and all of that. Although the Trimble Group is far more autonomous than most similar organisations. It's enough for you to know that we operate behind the scenes and are involved in many planning and decision-making processes that shape our world. Ordinarily, of course, I would never be revealing our existence to an outsider, not even one with such a distin-guished record of service to your country. I trust I'll be able to count on your discretion.'

'Do you really.'

'Yes,' Brown said with knowing emphasis. 'I do. Just as I can count on the fact that you wouldn't do anything foolish as we stand here talking. There are expert marksmen in those trees observing you at this very moment, with orders to shoot if you make any false move. Another four very well-trained guards on the other side of that door, and more personnel watching us on camera. I might add that they are not privy to our conversation. The information I'm about to reveal to you is highly classified.'

'I can't wait to hear it,' Ben said.

'Then I'll get right to the point.' Brown paced the rug as he went on. 'The Trimble Group exists to help create a new world, Mr Hope. A world of stability and peace, in which nations and the communities of citizens within them can co-exist harmoniously, comfortably, productively. A homogenised world, by necessity, discarding many of the things that have made people unhappy and created social division and disorder in the past. Class. Tradition. History. Things we no longer need. Things we have to eliminate in order to achieve our vision.' Brown made a flapping motion with his hand, as if whisking unseen obstacles out of his way.

'A new world order,' Ben said.

'That makes it sound much more sinister than it really is,' Brown said, wryly amused. 'There's nothing new about rulers of nations aspiring to create a happy world. Believe me, it'd be a lot easier to run than the old one. But it's only now, in the modern age, that we really have a chance to make it happen. Forget the old. Tear down the crumbling relics, the outdated institutions, the churches and cathedrals. They only remind us of a dark and distant past that's no longer relevant to modern life. Let's look to the future.'

'So your Trimble Group's aim is to dismantle religion,' Ben said.

'That's correct.'

'You don't think it's been tried before? Mao. Stalin. A whole procession of past dictators who wanted to impose

393

an atheist state, and all failed in the end. Religion doesn't go away. For better or worse, it's part of who we are.'

'They failed because they tried to create change by force,' Brown said. 'Open dictatorship is crude, unsophisticated, ineffective. The way you create change is to make the people *want* it, or to think they do. But you're right about one thing. There's something about the human spirit that seems irrevocably driven to revere a greater power. We can cater for that, however. We have new gods and idols for them to worship. Ones that we can control and manipulate.'

Ben remembered what Michaela had said that night in the restaurant about churches turning into McDonalds drive-throughs. 'Consumerism is the new faith, is that it?' he said. 'Your god is one that hands out glittering little toys and gadgets to the children like Santa Claus.'

'Rewards,' Brown said. 'That's the key. The children of the new world aren't interested in moral rectitude, or thought, or philosophy. It's too much hard work. Give them what they really desire, and the faithful will rally and be repaid.' He shrugged. 'Granted, in reality they may be no less enslaved to the state than the oppressed citizens of Hitler or Stalin, but they'll be willing, happy slaves, believing in a bright future.'

'And that's your Utopian vision?' Ben said.

Brown held out his hands. 'Look around you. We're already halfway there. The Christian faith is dying. Once the fading embers have been stamped out, we'll move on to the Islamics. That'll be a bigger job, admittedly, given that their faith is so much stronger. But the first steps are already in place. One by one, we'll knock down the hardline pockets in the Middle East, remove the ruling powers there and institute our own, under the banner of what we call democracy. Once we have full control, the old order will be eroded away little by little until there's nothing left.'

Brown smiled. 'We're winning this war, Mr Hope. But as you know very well, in war one can never be too careful. That's why we're always looking out for special individuals to recruit to our cause. And this is where we come to the part that involves you.'

Chapter Sixty-One

Brown clasped his hands behind his back and walked to the French window, gazing out across the snowy garden as he went on. 'Earlier this year, the Trimble Group recruited a new agent. A university professor who has made a career out of attacking and undermining Christian belief, something he's proved rather good at. He's extremely educated, intelligent, and above all, committed. His name is Penrose Lucas.'

Ben's mind flashed back to the videotaped TV programme he'd watched briefly at the vicarage the night after the crash. Professor Penrose Lucas had been Simeon's opponent in the debate on religion.

'Publicly, Professor Lucas is known as an author and militant atheist activist with a growing following,' Brown continued. 'Privately, he's been actively pursuing an agenda to discredit the Christian clergy. Every new allegation of corruption, whether financial or sexual – sexual misdemeanours strike the most scandalous note with the public, as you can imagine – serves to alienate society at large further from the church. War by attrition. Professor Lucas understood the concept very well, and even on a very limited budget he was getting impressive results.'

'And so you decided to give him a helping hand,' Ben said.

'My colleagues and I considered that Lucas could become a very valuable asset to us indeed. We offered him a generous deal, to which he readily agreed. He'd be working for us, assisted by a Trimble Group liaison officer but with more or less complete independence to go on doing what he'd been doing before, except on a more ambitious scale. He was given free rein to pick his own targets, draw on our resources to set up phone taps and surveillance, hire whatever investigators or administrative staff he might require. Virtually anything he wanted, even his own personal jet. Lucas settled into his new headquarters on Capri and got down to work. Almost immediately, he announced his intention to target one Reverend Simeon Arundel.'

Ben was beginning to understand where this was leading, and his muscles were tensing with cold rage.

'Naturally, we trusted Lucas's instinct,' Brown continued. 'We weren't unaware that he might have had some personal motive for choosing Arundel so specifically out of all the thousands of potential targets he might have picked, but we gave him a free hand nonetheless. It was clear that Arundel was the kind of go-ahead, popularist clergyman who might be capable of generating new interest in the church. He was a threat.'

Personal motive, Ben was thinking. He hadn't forgotten the way that Simeon had trounced Penrose Lucas in the TV debate. He was pretty sure Lucas hadn't forgotten the humiliation, either. It was all beginning to come together now.

'A phone tapping and surveillance operation was therefore mounted on Reverend Arundel,' Brown said, as though these things were done every day – which, Ben realised, they probably were. 'Shortly afterwards, conversations were monitored between Arundel and one Father Fabrice Lalique, proving Professor Lucas' instincts spectacularly correct.'

The sword, Ben thought.

Brown seemed to read his mind. He nodded. 'Up to that point, they had managed to keep their little project secret. The question now was what should be done about it. There was concern among the group that the alleged sword of Christ could cause something of a stir among the religious community, especially among the hardline fundamentalist movements in America where it could potentially become regarded as a powerful emblem. Whether genuine or not, this damned sword could be a major setback for us.'

Brown paused and turned away from the window, fixing his pale watery gaze on Ben. 'Now, you have to understand that the Trimble Group had given Professor Lucas a great deal of leeway to run his own operation. As I mentioned, we liaised with him via our operative – let's call him Mr Green – who fielded whatever intelligence data was gleaned from our side and passed it directly to Lucas to do with as he saw fit. When Lucas uncovered the sacred sword project, we assumed that his response would be simply to discredit it, using the same kind of smear tactics against Simeon Arundel and Fabrice Lalique that he'd been directing against other clergymen before them.'

'You mean destroying their personal and professional reputations with a pack of lies,' Ben said.

'Something like that,' Brown replied. 'As a result of which, the credibility of the project would have fallen apart. They'd have been spurned in the media, no publisher would have touched Arundel's book, nobody would have had anything to do with them. Another victory, after which Lucas would have moved on to another target.' Brown paused. 'As I say, that's what we assumed. We had no idea what Lucas was really doing, using our funds to employ professional thugs, mercenaries, to help him carry out his own personal vendetta. And to commit murder. Lalique's faked suicide, the car crash that killed the Arundels, the attacks on Wesley Holland in which several people were killed – it was Lucas, and Lucas alone, who engineered them all.'

'I see now,' Ben said. 'You're the good guys.'

'I don't appreciate the sarcasm, Mr Hope,' Brown replied. 'Though I do fully acknowledge our part in this mess. Basically, we backed the wrong horse. We should have screened our candidate more carefully, but instead we rushed in too fast. It was a mistake. But how could we have known that our star asset would turn out to be mentally deranged, possibly even psychopathic?'

'That's a neat way to disclaim responsibility for the deaths of my friends,' Ben said. 'You really expect me to believe you had no idea what was going on?'

'The Trimble Group can't be concerning itself with the minutiae of every operation,' Brown said with a note of irritation. 'Only with the larger picture. Why else would we delegate the job to someone else?'

'Sounds to me as if your "Mr Green" knew exactly what Lucas was doing.'

'Our man was tasked with assisting Lucas in whatever way necessary. As we now know, he was unhappy almost from the start with the direction Lucas was taking. In retrospect, I think he was afraid that to report his growing concerns back to us would have been seen as insubordination, or a lack of confidence in the Group's decisions. By the time he finally informed us that Lucas had gone rogue, it was too late. I regret now that we put him in such a difficult position.' Brown shook his head sadly. 'In fact I regret it very much indeed. When Lucas discovered the betrayal, he had our man murdered. Him and his wife, at their home in

London. It was . . . it was more than brutal. I can't tell you how shocked I was.'

'And after all, you're a man of such moral scruple,' Ben said.

Brown shot him a reptilian look, then went on. 'We decided at that point to put a stop to the whole operation. Lucas's assets have been frozen and he's been stripped of his power, even as we speak. He is now quite isolated in the little stronghold he's built for himself on the island of Capri. In the meantime, our surveillance teams intercepted a phone call to Wesley Holland's lawyer and traced its origin to Martha's Vineyard. Our response was to dispatch a team to put an end to this whole business. I didn't expect that we would find you there. At first I wasn't sure what we should do with you. But it then it struck me how neatly we could serve each other's purposes.'

'Meaning what?'

'You must surely have realised by now that the purpose of this meeting was to make you a proposal. I've revealed to you the truth about who murdered your friends and tried to kill you. In return, I'd like you to eliminate him for me.'

Ben laughed, despite his anger. 'I find it a little hard to believe that you people haven't got your own ways and means of making your enemies vanish.'

'That we do. But I've no interest in letting the Trimble Group become any more deeply embroiled in this situation than we already are. We're walking away.'

'I'm not a gun for hire,' Ben said. 'Some trigger-man you can just enlist.'

'Not at all. You're a man of peace, a regular saint. As is patently clear from the trail of dead bodies you leave in your wake wherever you go.'

'You created this mess. You clean it up. Now I've had enough of listening to you, and I want to leave.'

'Oh, you can leave,' Brown said. 'Nobody will stop you. Just remember this conversation never happened. And I'd advise you not to entertain any foolish heroic notions about trying to come after the Trimble Group. You wouldn't be able to find us, but we'll always be able to find you.'

'I'll bear that in mind,' Ben said. He headed towards the door.

'Not even a goodbye?'

Ben flipped his middle finger up over his shoulder. 'Here's my goodbye.'

'I didn't mean to me,' Brown said. 'I thought you might like a last word with young Jude before you go.'

Ben turned slowly round to stare at Brown. 'What did you say?'

'He's here. I'm sure he's anxious to see you, if only for a few final moments.'

Ben felt his face go numb with shock. 'You're bluffing. Jude wasn't with me on the island.'

'Then we must have picked up another Jude Arundel on the beach,' Brown said. 'A spirited young chap, isn't he? And I must say the family resemblance is obvious, once you've read the letter.'

Ben said nothing.

'He was clutching it in his hand when they found him. Don't worry, he's been very well looked after until now. Though I can't say what will happen if you persist in being difficult.'

Ben stared. 'Let me see him.'

'That's not possible, I'm afraid. But why don't you say hello?' Brown took a phone from his pocket, speed-dialled a number and said, 'Pass the boy on.' He handed Ben the phone.

'Jude? It's me. Are you all right?'

'Ben? I'm—' It was Jude's voice, but before he could say any more, the line went dead.

'Satisfied?' Brown asked.

Ben tossed away the phone. He wanted to rip the glow of triumph off the man's face. In two long strides he was on him, shooting out a hand and grabbing his tie. Brown's eyes bulged as Ben wheeled him violently away from the window, out of sight of the snipers in the trees.

Radios would be bursting into full alert. He had about two seconds before the door burst open. He slammed Brown hard against the wall, tightening his tie like a noose around his throat. 'You harm him and I'll kill you. Understand?'

The door crashed open and the guards from earlier came storming into the room, pistols drawn.

'Tell them to back off,' Ben said. 'Or else you die first.'

'Stand down! Lower your weapons!' Brown shouted. The guards hesitantly obeyed.

'That was the wise thing to do,' Ben said. 'I'd have taken your head off.' He let go of Brown's tie and stepped away in disgust. The guards hovered uncertainly in the background.

Brown slackened the knot of his tie and straightened his jacket collar. He was breathing heavily but the glow of victory hadn't left his face. 'I know you would, Major Hope,' he said. 'That's what makes you the perfect choice for us.'

Ben paced in a tight circle. His head was suddenly throbbing and his heart was beating in his throat. 'All right, Brown. What's the deal?'

'The terms are simple. You'll be provided with everything you require to take care of the Trimble Group's unfinished business. Jude will then be released and returned to you, unharmed. There will be no repercussions of any kind. That will be the end of it. The two of you walk away free men.

However, if you refuse to cooperate, you'll never see Jude again.' Brown smiled. 'We know how much he loves the water. The grieving son, driven to distraction after the tragic car crash that claimed his parents. Boats, drugs and alcohol don't mix. You understand me, I'm sure.'

Ben was silent.

'As for you, Mr Hope, you'll spend the rest of your life as a hunted criminal, pursued by every law-enforcement agency on the planet for the murder of a dozen or more government agents. Walk out of that door now, and I guarantee you'll be entering a very different world from the one you left.'

Chapter Sixty-Two

Penrose Lucas looked up in agitation from his desk as the three loud thumps shook the office door. He stopped his frenzied scribbling, laid down his pen and tore himself away from the rapidly building mountain of paper that was the manuscript-in-progress of his latest future bestseller, *Murdering for God.*

The antique clock on the sideboard read a quarter to one in the morning. He'd lost all track of time as he'd sat there writing. For the last five straight hours his pen hadn't stopped scratching, ripping the paper sometimes, the words pouring out of him so urgently that pages of it were illegible, even to him. He was breathless with hate.

Penrose suddenly realised what day it was. December 25th. He ground his teeth together at the thought of all those idiots celebrating the birth of some bearded twit two thousand years ago who'd done nothing but create a lot of harm and confusion.

Thump. Thump. The banging on the door wouldn't stop.

'*What!?*' Penrose stormed over to the door in his bare feet, his open dressing gown billowing behind him as he walked. He slid back the six bolts that secured it, turned the deadlock and opened the door a crack.

Staring in through the gap was the sombre-looking face

of Steve Cutter. Behind him stood his remaining men, Terry Grinnall in that leather coat he never seemed to take off, Dave Mills, Suggs, Doyle and Prosser.

'Ugh, it's you.' Penrose said. 'What do you want, at this time of night?'

Cutter shoved the door open without a word, making Penrose stagger back a step as it swung wide. Entering the room, he could see that Penrose was wearing only a pair of underpants under his monogrammed gown, which was getting grimy and wrinkled, russety spots of dried blood flecked across the gold *PL* on the breast. His torso looked thin and wasted, as if he hadn't been bothering to eat.

The office smelled of body odour and gun oil. Cutter spotted Penrose's gleaming Coonan .357 lying on the desk, next to the teetering pile of pages covered in furious scrawls. More loose pages lay haphazardly over the floor, along with several pens, heavily chewed, some of them snapped in half.

'How dare you barge into my office?' Penrose yelled. 'Can't you see I'm busy working on my book?'

'Came to tell you we're quitting,' Cutter said. Just looking around him at the state of the study was confirmation that the job had fallen apart. The team members who weren't dead or missing as a result of the whole fiasco had nothing to do but kick their heels in the villa's annexe quarters. The booze supply had dried up. The whores had stopped coming. So had any decent cooked meals. They didn't much fancy the local restaurants, and the nearest McDonalds was in fucking Naples.

Worst of all, they hadn't been paid for the last ten days. The six men had spent that evening grumbling their discontentment around the table in the rec room, and decided enough was enough.

Penrose's rage dwindled rapidly away. 'But you can't leave.

405

I need my Praetorian Guard around me,' he said in a small voice.

'Listen to this prick,' Grinnall sneered.

'Tough shit,' Cutter said. 'We're done, and we want paying off.'

'But—'

'We had a fucking deal with you, Lucas. Don't piss me off, all right?'

Penrose stared at him with a trembling jaw. 'Fine,' he said in an injured tone. 'If that's the way you want it. Come with me, and I will recompense you.'

Cutter followed as Penrose led the way through from the office to the adjoining bedroom. The air was stale and foul, and discarded clothing littered the floor around the rumpled king-size bed. But what drew Cutter's notice more than anything was the long, wide streak of dried blood leading from the middle of the floor towards the balcony that over-looked the cliff's edge. It looked, and smelled, as if something dead had been dragged across the bedroom and dumped over the side of the balcony. He said nothing, but his expression darkened a little more.

'In here,' Penrose said curtly, sliding open a mirrored panel to reveal the vast walk-in wardrobe behind it, its own little room all decked out in antique oak. He swept through the racks of finery that he'd ordered from top Italian designers, barely any of it ever worn. The back of the wardrobe was filled with shelving units where Penrose stored his many pairs of brand-new shoes; more compartments overhead were filled with boxes and bags. Lower down was a column of drawers for keeping jewellery and sundry items.

Cutter stood by impatiently as Penrose wrenched open one drawer, rummaged around inside, slammed it shut, tore open another. 'Here we are,' he said, taking out a glittering gold watch and holding it out to Cutter. 'Take it. It's a Rolex. Isn't it beautiful? Here, look, I have half a dozen more. All brand new. Hand them out among the men.'

Cutter grimaced and slapped the watch aside. 'I'm not talking about a bunch of sodding trinkets. Talking about money, pal. Twelve hundred a day per man. Six of us, that comes to more than seventy grand for the last fucking ten days we haven't been paid. Not to mention the boys who never came back from Cornwall, or Gant's team. You got widows and families out there to take care of. Say three-fifty, and we'll call it quits, all right?'

'But I don't have three hundred and fifty thousand,' Penrose protested. 'I've been trying over and over to access the online banking system, and it won't let me in. The Trimble assets have been frozen.' That last part was perfectly true. There was no more money, no more jet. No more backing from his sponsors, who'd now turned against their star protégé. He knew it was all over – yet his mind felt strangely detached from the situation, as if these things were all just a dream.

His words had been heard by the rest of the men, who'd filtered into the bedroom after Cutter and were standing around looking extremely displeased.

'I don't give a fucking monkey's ringpiece about your Trimble!' Cutter shouted at Penrose. In his anger he slammed a fist against the wooden partition of the walk-in wardrobe. It was solidly built, but the blow made the whole structure judder. Not enough to cause any damage.

But enough to shake loose a slip of purplish-coloured paper that drifted down in a spiral like an autumn leaf from an overhead compartment and landed at Cutter's feet.

'Hello, what's this, then?' Cutter said, scooping it quickly off the floor.

'It's nothing,' Penrose said, suddenly more alert.

'Doesn't look like nothing to me,' Cutter said, holding it up for his men to see. 'Looks a bit like a five-hundred-euro note, doesn't it, boys?' He peered up at the overhead compartment and spotted the black garbage bag that had been hastily stuffed into it, ripping the plastic to reveal the bunches of banknotes nestling inside.

'You sneaky little bugger,' Cutter said.

'You leave that alone. It's mine!' Penrose tried to stand in his way, but Cutter shoved him easily aside, reached up for the bag and hauled it down. It landed with a thump. 'About forty grand,' he said, inspecting the contents.

'All right,' Penrose said testily. 'You can have it. It's yours.'

'Too right it's ours,' Cutter said. He handed the bag to Grinnall, who stuck it under his arm. 'Now where's the rest of it?'

'Rest of what?' Penrose said, flushing.

'Don't you even fucking *think* about lying to me,' Cutter growled. 'You've got a lot more than this stashed around the place. I've fucking seen it.'

The others nodded. Cutter had already told them about the cash-stuffed holdalls he'd spotted in Penrose's office.

In fact, Penrose had over 2.3 million euros hidden in the villa, cash that he'd been siphoning off from the very start of his operation under the broad heading of expenses – the fewer questions had been asked, the more he'd clawed back for himself. The contents of the garbage bag were just what he'd had left over when the holdalls were already crammed so full he could barely zip them up.

But there was no way Penrose was going to let all that loot fall into Cutter's hands. 'I don't know what you're talking about,' he protested. 'And I object to being spoken to this way by my employee.'

408

Cutter grabbed him by the collar and shook him violently. 'I don't work for you any more, you little shit. Where's the fucking money?'

'I don't have anything more to give you!' Penrose yelled.

'Give him a slap, Steve,' Grinnall said.

Cutter slapped Penrose across the face, hard. The impact sent him crashing into the wall. He slid down to the floor, his face turning white. He touched his fingers to his burning cheek and stared at them, as if expecting to see blood. 'Traitors!' he screamed up from the floor. 'After all I've done for you! This is how you treat me?'

'We're not leaving here until we get paid off,' Cutter said.

A wild light came into Penrose's eyes. 'Money! That's all your kind care about, isn't? Good old hard cash! Well I'll tell you. There's millions! Millions, all mine, all hidden away right here in the villa. And guess what, Cutter? You'll never find a single solitary penny of it. You bloody brainless Cockney ape.'

Without taking his eyes off Penrose, Cutter stuck his arm out behind him. Terry Grinnall instantly pressed a Glock 19 into his outstretched palm. Cutter aimed the boxy black pistol at Penrose's face.

'Kill me, would you?' Penrose screeched. 'How'll you find your money then, you moron?'

Cutter pursed his lips, then lowered the pistol so that it pointed at Penrose's left kneecap.

'Go on, shoot me! Shoot me!' Penrose started laughing hysterically, then burst into tears.

'Leave it alone, Steve,' said Mills. 'I mean, look at him. He's fucked in the head. You won't get nothing out of him.'

'I want the money,' Cutter said.

Penrose was writhing on the wardrobe floor, raking his wet face with his fingertips and babbling incomprehensibly.

'What'd he say?' Doyle said.

'Think he said, "hell rip and roast you",' said Suggs.

Prosser said, 'I told you he was fucking gone.'

'Shoot the fucker,' Grinnall urged Cutter.

Cutter stared at the babbling, weeping Penrose for a second, then shook his head and stuffed the gun in his belt. 'I'm not a fucking animal, boys. Come on. Let's go and find where the bastard's hidden that money. It's got to be around here somewhere.'

Chapter Sixty-Three

In two hours, Cutter's men had torn meticulously through the rest of the villa's five bedrooms, its four bathrooms and the lounge and dining room, ripping out drawers, upturning mattresses, rifling through sideboards and bookcases, even tearing up the carpets to check for loose floorboards under which the cash-filled bags might have been hidden. They'd checked the attic space and found only dust and a stack of empty packing cases. Nothing. Now, as the small hours of the morning wore on, they were getting desperate.

'Kitchen,' Cutter said, and led the way through the rambling passages. The kitchen area could have served a medium-sized restaurant. There were dozens of possible hiding places. Cutter stormed over to the row of large cupboards on the right, while Grinnall, still clutching the money in the garbage bag, tried the ones on the left and the others crashed about the rest of the room. In moments the tiled floor was rolling with cookware, smashed plates and glasses.

'I don't think he put it in there, you twat,' Mills said to Prosser, who was bending down to gape inside the oven.

'You never know what that nutter'd do.'

'There's bugger all in here,' Grinnall said, and smashed his foot into the cupboard doors with a crunch of wood.

'This is bollocks. I'm going back upstairs and making that fucking nutjob talk.'

'He won't talk,' Cutter said.

'He will when I slice his—'

Grinnall was interrupted by a cry from Mills, who was leaning inside a deep freeze. 'Hey! I think I found something!' With a grunt of effort, he wrenched out a frost-covered black cloth holdall and dumped it on the floor. They all ran over and stood around as he unzipped it, revealing the taped stacks of banknotes inside.

'Nice one,' Cutter said, and slapped Mills on the shoulder.

'Good thing paper don't freeze,' Grinnall muttered. 'How much is there?'

Cutter crouched down next to the holdall and poked around inside. It was a big holdall. The stacks were piled four wide, four long and eight deep. The cash was all in purple five-hundred notes, twenty to a bunch. He was quick with that kind of mental arithmetic.

'One-point-two-eight mil,' he said.

'It's the fucking mother lode,' Grinnall said.

'It's not a bad start.'

'What's that come to six ways?' Suggs asked, virtually rubbing his hands together.

Cutter looked at Grinnall, then looked at Mills. The three of them all turned to look at Suggs, Prosser and Doyle.

Cutter whipped the Glock 19 out of his belt and shot Suggs twice in the chest. Mills pulled his Taurus and put a bullet in Prosser's head. Before either of the corpses had hit the floor, Grinnall had Doyle in a stranglehold and was twisting his head around. There was a crackling of cartilage, then a crunch. Doyle slipped lifelessly out of Grinnall's arms.

'Never liked them much anyway,' Grinnall muttered.

'Three ways.' Mills smiled. 'That's more like it.'

Cutter zipped up the bag and hefted its weight over his shoulder. 'We ain't done yet, boys. There's at least one more of these hidden away. He can't have spent it all.'

'Where next?' Mills said.

'Sauna room,' Grinnall suggested.

Cutter dismissed the idea. 'Nobody'd put cash in a sauna room.'

'Tool shed? Gardener's hut? Lodge house? Garage?'

'Not secure enough, any of them.'

'Swimming pool?' Mills said. The enclosed all-season pool, with its luxuriant changing rooms, had always been strictly off-limits to the hired help. Penrose was a poor swimmer, but had been seen splashing around in there once or twice.

Cutter nodded. 'Can't fucking hurt to check it out. Let's go.'

They stepped over the spreading blood of the three dead men and left the kitchen. The pool was housed in a metal-framed glass building adjacent to the main villa, most directly accessible from where they were via an outer walkway that spanned the length of the house and overhung the cliff's edge. The men passed through an arch and out into the cool night. The stars were bright, their reflection glittering like diamonds over the surface of the Tyrrhenian Sea and the rolling surf.

'I'm dying for a slash,' Mills announced as they walked.

'Can't you hold it in for a few more minutes?' Cutter said scathingly.

'Seriously, I'm fucking bursting. Catch up with you in a sec, okay?' As Cutter and Grinnall headed on towards the pool building, Mills paused to undo his flies and step up to the iron railing at the edge of the walkway. He braced his feet a little apart and sighed with relief as he urinated through the gap in the railing. His arc of piss disappeared over the

413

edge, dissipated in the breeze and splashed on the rocks far below.

He barely had time to react as a pair of hands grabbed him by the ankles and pitched him headlong over the edge of the balcony. By the time Mills opened his mouth to scream, he'd already dropped fifty feet, a dark cartwheeling figure silhouetted against the starlit surf. His brains were dashed out on a jutting piece of rock halfway down the cliff face, and it was a silent corpse that splashed down into the water and was immediately engulfed by the waves.

Chapter Sixty-Four

It hadn't been long before Penrose had recovered his wits and scrambled to his feet to run back into his office. Cutter's invasion of his personal sanctuary, and the loss of the forty-two thousand euros in the garbage bag, were quickly bringing reality home to him.

And it wasn't just money he stood to lose. He was suddenly convinced that the police must be on their way at that very moment to arrest him. Scurrying to the window, he threw it open and listened hard. He could hear nothing but the roar of the surf. No sirens, not yet. But they could come at any minute.

He hurried over to his desk and started hunting through the drawers for all the plans he kept inside. Lists of names, photographs of his victims; the discs containing the child pornography downloaded onto Lalique's computer; the artist's impression of the sword; detailed descriptions of every operation he'd painstakingly designed. All his hard work was now nothing more than evidence, enough to sink him so deep he'd never come back up.

He had to get rid of it all immediately. Grabbing the waste paper basket from under the desk, he shook out all the crumpled pages of book notes and started throwing the incriminating material into it.

Now, he had some matches somewhere, he thought feverishly, left over from the romantic candlelit dinner that had never happened, thanks to that ungrateful bitch Daria Pignatelli. He found them on the side, struck one and tossed the burning match into the waste paper basket.

He watched as the flames leapt up and the evidence began to blacken and curl. The incriminating paperwork caught light. The computer discs twisted and melted. He was safe now.

That was when it occurred to him that it was a wicker basket, and it would catch fire along with its contents. By then the flames were already spreading fast and he couldn't stamp them out with his bare feet. The office began to fill with smoke. Penrose coughed.

The pool building comprised four integral changing rooms behind wooden doors labelled SPOGLIATOIO 1 – 4. Each contained its own luxurious shower cubicle, large wardrobes for clothing and shoes, storage units for towels, robes, hairdryers and assorted items, and lockers for personal effects, offering several possible hideyholes for a bag full of money. After a couple of minutes' fruitless search of Spogliatoio 1, Cutter went next door to see how Grinnall was faring.

'Bugger all luck,' Grinnall said, standing in a heap of towels and slamming the lid of an empty storage unit.

'Where's Dave?' Cutter asked with a frown. Grinnall shook his head. Cutter sighed and headed for the entrance, pausing at the poolside to glance lovingly at the holdall and its one-point-two-eight-million cargo. Grinnall bustled angrily into Spogliatoio 3, ripping into the storage spaces and muttering to himself about what he'd like to do to that twisted little fuck Penrose Lucas.

'Dave?' Cutter called outside. 'Oy! Mills!' There was no

sign of him anywhere. Cutter strode back inside the pool building. He was about to say something to Grinnall when he stopped and did a double-take.

The holdall full of money was no longer where it had been sitting just a moment ago.

'Terry, why'd you shift the bag?'

Grinnall came out of the changing room, looking disgruntled. 'What?'

'Where's the money?'

'I don't know. Where'd you put it?'

'Right there. Don't wind me up.'

'I'm not fucking winding you up. I never touched it.'

'Then where the fuck is it?' Cutter said, frowning deeply. His immediate thought was that Dave Mills must have sneaked in and made off with it. He panicked for a second and was about to run outside after him – but then he realised that wasn't possible. His back had only been turned a moment. He looked all around him. Was he going crazy?

Then he spotted it. A dark shape at the bottom of the pool, sitting on the tiled floor of the deep end. 'Oh, fuck, no!'

Without an instant's hesitation, Cutter dived into the pool and began swimming towards the bag with powerful strokes. As he reached it, six feet underwater, he prayed the money wouldn't be ruined.

Grinnall was standing anxiously at the edge of the pool, watching and praying much the same thing, when an arm suddenly snaked out from behind him, locked tightly around his neck and hauled him backwards off his feet towards the open door of Spogliatoio 3.

Chapter Sixty-Five

Ben knew exactly who he was dealing with. Brown had provided detailed profiles on Penrose Lucas's hired guns. The big guy in the leather coat was Terry Grinnall. Thirty-six years old. Ex British Army, but he'd only followed that career long enough to learn that he could kill more people, with greater impunity and for a lot more pay, as a private soldier. Bosnia, Afghanistan, Africa, the usual trail of blood and money. Somewhere along it he'd encountered former Para, Steve Cutter.

But the trail ended here. Ben dragged Grinnall inside the changing room and slammed the door shut with his foot. He grappled the man to the floor, keeping his left arm locked around his throat and his right hand over his mouth.

Grinnall was as strong as he was heavy. He flailed out with his fists and feet and tried to smash Ben in the face with the back of his head and bite his hand. Ben squeezed harder, flattening his windpipe shut. Grinnall bucked and thrashed like a wild man.

In just a few more seconds, Cutter would be out of the pool, and Ben would have problems if he faced having to deal with them both at once. Cutter was smaller and less powerful, but he was also smarter and more dangerous. Ben had seen enough to know that as he'd watched them move through the villa.

He also knew that he'd encountered the guy once before. Just seconds. But Grinnall had only a few seconds, too.

Or maybe not. Just when Ben thought Grinnall was beginning to lose consciousness, the man suddenly gave a violent buck that broke Ben's grip on him. He twisted round and flung a vicious punch at the side of Ben's head. Ben blocked it – only just.

The next few instants were a life or death struggle for both of them. A powerful knee flew up and caught Ben in the stomach, almost knocking the wind out of him. Ben drove the heel of his hand into Grinnall's chin, slamming his head down hard with a crack against the tiled floor. Grinnall reached up with both hands clawed, going for Ben's eyes.

And Ben drew the Fairbairn-Sykes commando dagger from his leg sheath and punched its slender tip downwards through the leather coat and into Grinnall's heart. Clapped his hand over the man's mouth to stifle the terrible sucking gasp that people made when a cold steel blade penetrated deep inside their body. He stabbed the knife in again, then again, feeling the razor-sharp edges grind against bone as they parted Grinnall's ribs on their way through.

Grinnall's eyes rolled back and his body went limp. Ben clambered painfully to his feet. He plucked out the knife and wiped it quickly on the dead man's trouser leg, slipped it back into his sheath. Bundled the heavy corpse into the shower cubicle, then opened the changing room door a crack and peered cautiously out.

Straining every muscle with a groan of effort, Cutter heaved the dead-weight of the holdall out of the water and shoved

419

it up onto the edge of the pool. He hauled himself up and collapsed next to the soaking wet bag, gasping and dripping water everywhere. The money! He fumbled for the holdall's zipper and ripped it open. The stacks of notes inside were completely sodden. He moaned in despair.

'Terry!' he yelled, suddenly realising that Grinnall wasn't there.

'Terry's in the shower right now,' Ben said.

Cutter looked up and his eyes widened, then narrowed into slits. He looked like what he was, cornered and deadly. Ben kept the silenced Browning Hi-Power aimed squarely at his head as he approached. The pistol had come courtesy of the Trimble Group, along with the commando dagger and certain other mission-specific items Ben had brought with him to Capri.

'I know you,' Cutter said, watching every step.

'I know you, too,' Ben said. 'Little Denton vicarage, the night my friends died. You were making an unscheduled pick-up. And I never forget a voice.'

'Hope.'

'That's me.'

'Mills?'

'Took up high-diving,' Ben said. 'You're the last.'

Cutter gave a bitter grin. 'There you go. Don't suppose I'll ever know where the rest of that cash was, will I?'

'You weren't a bad soldier once, Steve. You went a long way. Should never have quit the regiment.'

'No future in it.'

'Not much future in killing my friends, either,' Ben said.

'You going to shoot me, then?'

'It'd make it easier for me if you went for that Glock,' Ben said, nodding towards the pistol in Cutter's belt.

'It's full of water,' Cutter said.

'You can fire a Glock underwater,' Ben said. 'You should know that.'

There was silence for a moment, just the steady tap-tap of droplets splashing down from Cutter's clothes and hair onto the wet poolside tiles and the low hum of the heaters.

'Right then,' Cutter sighed. He shrugged, as if to say, 'What the hell.' And then his hand flashed down to the butt of the Glock.

The Hi-Power spat twice. The sound echoed around the swimming pool.

Cutter's hand curled loosely around the grip of his pistol. Then he keeled over sideways and rolled into the water with a splash.

Ben left the building. He retrieved his kit bag from the shadows of the walkway where he'd left it. Another piece of equipment that had been on his requirements list, along with what was inside. He slung the webbing strap over his shoulder and went looking for Penrose Lucas.

As he re-entered the villa, he could smell smoke.

Chapter Sixty-Six

Ben found Penrose Lucas sitting alone in the semi-darkness of the wrecked dining room. He was slumped in a leather chair and seemed to be in a trance, staring fixedly into space and barely responding as Ben walked into the room and flipped on the main lights.

Ben stood a few yards away and watched him, noticing how dishevelled and dismal the man looked in his grimy dressing gown and underpants. He was a far cry from the self-confident, immaculately dressed professor Ben had seen on the videotape at the vicarage.

So here he was, face to face with Simeon's enemy.

Resting on the arm of Penrose's chair was a large, shiny handgun. Ben stepped quickly over and scooped it up. Penrose made no response. Ben jacked out the cartridge in the chamber, dumped the magazine, separated the slide from the frame and tossed the bits into the far corner of the room.

The sound of metal components clattering across the floor seemed to snap Penrose out of his trance. He turned slowly to look up at Ben. The glazed eyes focused with recognition.

'You're him,' he murmured. 'You're Hope.'

'In the flesh,' Ben said.

'Where are my men?'

'They can't help you any more,' Ben said. 'Your house is on fire. Did you know that?'

Penrose nodded slowly. 'Let it burn.' He closed his eyes for a moment, then said, 'What are you doing here?'

'I brought you a Christmas present.'

The mention of the word brought a scowl to Penrose's face. 'A what?'

Ben unslung the kit bag from his shoulder, opened it up and took out what he'd brought with him all the way from America aboard the Trimble Group jet.

Anything you require, Brown had said. When Ben had asked for the sword, the man had been quite happy to let him have it. 'As you wish,' he'd said. 'Hang it on the wall or poke the fire with it. It's the same to me.'

A keepsake, Ben had told him. Something to remember his friend by. But there was more to it.

Ben swished the sword through the air and threw it point-first at the floor at his feet. It planted itself deep into the wood with a judder. 'There you are, professor. The sword of Jesus Christ.'

Penrose's face contorted into a grimace and he leaned forward in his chair to stare at the sword. Until this moment, Ben had only had Brown's word that Penrose Lucas had been behind all this. Steve Cutter's presence in the villa was half the proof that Brown had been telling the truth. Now, as Ben saw the crazed mixture of hatred and desire in Penrose's eyes, there was no longer any doubt.

'This is what you wanted, isn't it?' Ben said softly. 'What you murdered Simeon and Michaela Arundel for.'

A smile spread over Penrose's lips. 'Those cockroaches deserved what they got.'

Ben didn't feel like wasting time talking to this man. He unholstered his pistol and clicked off the safety catch. 'I gather you're something of an atheist, Lucas.'

Penrose made no reply. He stared up at Ben, then at the gun. A nerve in his face twitched.

'Fine by me,' Ben said. 'Then you won't be wanting to say any final prayers before I kill you.'

Penrose's mouth hung open in horror. He slithered out of his chair and fell to his knees on the floor. 'No, please,' he gasped, looking up at Ben with pleading eyes and his hands clasped in supplication. 'I don't want to die.'

'Mercy is something you might have got from Simeon Arundel,' Ben said. 'I'm not like him.'

Penrose sobbed pitifully as Ben pressed the muzzle of the silencer to his forehead. Ben's finger touched the cool, smooth curve of the trigger. He visualised Simeon and Michaela in the sinking car. They'd be avenged now, and Jude would be freed, and it would all be over.

But then another image appeared in Ben's mind. That of Vincent Napier, half-submerged in the Cornish bog and about to die. And he remembered the last time an unarmed and totally defenceless man had begged him for his life. Ben had just snuffed him out with his own son watching. What he was about to do now was every bit as callous.

This is who I am, he thought. *A killer. I always was. Always will be.*

'I'm sick,' Penrose wept. 'I've done terrible things. Please give me a chance. I can change. I know I can.'

Ben hesitated. You didn't need to be a psychiatrist to see that this pathetic, wretched man was mentally ill. He needed the proper treatment, not a cold-blooded execution on the floor.

Shoot him. For Jude's sake. Ben imagined Jude trapped in

the grip of Brown's nameless, faceless associates. He thought of what they'd do to him if Penrose Lucas wasn't eliminated according to their instructions.

There was no choice. His finger tightened on the trigger.

But then he hesitated again. There had to be another way. If he didn't kill Penrose, but instead delivered him alive to the Trimble Group, perhaps they'd show clemency. They'd surely see that he was no longer a threat to anyone. They had the resources to place him in the appropriate facility, even if it meant keeping him behind bars for the rest of his life.

The smoke was thickening in the passageway outside the dining room door. Ben could hear the crackling of the fire as it spread through the villa, intensifying with every passing minute.

He'd made his decision. He lowered the gun. 'Get on your feet. We have to leave before this whole place goes up in flames.'

'You're not going to kill me?' Penrose blubbered.

Ben reached out a hand and helped him to his feet. 'Come with me. I'll see that you get the help you need.'

'Thank you,' Penrose croaked. 'Thank you.' He wiped his teary face with the sleeve of his dressing gown.

Then, before Ben could react, Penrose retreated a step and tore out the concealed .25 Beretta automatic that had been nestling against the small of his back, in the elastic waistband of his underwear. He thrust the gun out at Ben and fired.

The small-calibre bullet slammed into Ben's left shoulder. At extreme short range, the impact was enough to spin him around. There was just shock, no pain. He stayed on his feet and raised his own pistol, but his senses were jangling in disarray and he wasn't quick enough to squeeze the trigger before Penrose fired again.

The shot crashed into Ben's ribs and knocked him to the floor on his back. The pistol spun out of his grip.

Penrose howled with savage laughter. '*Now* who's going to die? Not me! Not Penrose Lucas!' His teeth bared in hatred, he advanced towards Ben.

Ben struggled to get up, but his body wasn't obeying the commands of his brain. Penrose stepped closer and leaned over him. He was just three feet away. The gun was trained on Ben's head. And he couldn't miss this time.

Ben kicked out with his legs, sliding himself across the floor. Something hard nudged against the back of his head and he realised that it was the sword blade planted into the floorboards.

'You thought you could outsmart me,' Penrose laughed. 'Now you'll rot with all the others.'

Ben's strength was ebbing fast. In desperation he grasped the bronze sword hilt with both hands and tugged with all his might. He felt the tip of the blade pluck out of the floor.

Penrose's fingertip whitened against the Beretta's trigger.

Ben swept the sword up over his head and let go.

The pistol boomed.

The shot ploughed into the floor two feet from Ben's head. A burbling scream burst from Penrose's lips and he reeled backwards. He dropped his gun and his hands went to his throat, clawing at the bronze hilt that was protruding grotesquely at an angle from the soft flesh above his breastbone. Three feet of blade stuck out of the back of his neck. Blood gushed from his throat and down his front.

Ben wobbled to his feet, fighting to remain upright. His left arm wouldn't work properly. He staggered towards Penrose. With his good hand he grasped the slippery, bloody sword hilt, wrenched it out and swung it hard, edgeways.

The sickle-shaped blade hummed through the air and slashed Penrose's throat to his spine, almost severing his head.

Penrose's knees buckled. He hit the floor in a bloody sprawl.

Ben swayed on his unsteady legs. The second bullet had broken his ribs and passed right through, but the first was still lodged in his shoulder and a lot of the blood on the floor was his own. He could feel the darkness rising, but he wasn't going to let it. Not yet. He steadied himself against the wall and headed for the door.

As he staggered out of the villa, the flames were leaping from the windows and curling up the walls. The blaze lit up the night sky.

Ben took one last look at the burning house, then turned away.

It was time for him to go and get his son.

Read on for the explosive first chapter of Scott Mariani's new novel *The Armada Legacy*, coming from Avon in 2013

Chapter One

Just after ten on a clear, cold night in late February, and the moon-glow over the Donegal Atlantic coast cast a speckled diamond glimmer across the dark sea. High above the shore-line, a solitary car was threading its way along the twisty coastal road, leaving behind the distant lights of the Castlebane Country Club and heading inland towards Rinclevan on the far side of New Lake.

The chauffeur of the black Jaguar XF was a square-shouldered former Grenadier Guard called Wally Lander. He kept his eyes on the winding road and drove in silence, studiously detached from the conversation of his passengers: his employer Sir Roger Forsyte, Forsyte's personal assistant Samantha – Sam for short – and an auburn-haired woman Wally had never seen before. Attractive – he could tell from the couple of discreet rearward glances he'd snatched at her – very attractive in fact, wearing a tight-fitting black dress that he frustratingly couldn't see enough of in the driver's mirror. He presumed she must have attended that evening's Neptune Marine Exploration press conference and was now coming along as a guest to the private party that would probably last well into the wee small hours. Maybe something to do with Sir Roger's latest caper, Wally mused. If she was alone, that meant she was almost certainly single. Definitely worth a crack at it. There was a chance he'd get to chat to her at the party, find out more about her.

Wally couldn't know it yet – none of them could know it – but that would never happen. Because Wally didn't have very long to live.

Nor would Wally ever know the mystery woman's name. It was Brooke Marcel, or *Dr* Brooke Marcel when she was in her professional capacity as a psychologist. Tonight she was just here as a guest of her friend Sam, who was sitting between Brooke and Sir Roger, all clipped efficiency with a tiny netbook resting across her knees, its screen reflected in her glasses as they ran through some NME business details together. Sir Roger had loosened the tie he'd put on for the presentation and was leaning luxuriantly back against the Jaguar's cream-coloured leather. Brooke put Sam's boss's age at around sixty, though he was in better shape than many men half his age.

As Sam started detailing the plans for the following day, Brooke tuned out and drifted back to the thoughts that preoccupied her so much of the time, with the same mixture of emotions that always came flooding back whenever Ben was on her mind.

She wished he could have been here. He loved Ireland, would have been completely in his element here on the Donegal coast. Maybe she'd been wrong in coming without him – but the fact was she'd been too plain nervous about asking him. The wrong signals, she'd worried. Moving too fast, trying to force things prematurely. Or something like that. She didn't know any more. For a gifted and highly trained psychologist, it amazed her how little she understood her own feelings.

Ben Hope. What an enigmatic, complex man he was. Even before they'd got together she'd been aware of the ghosts

432

from his past, stuff you could never ask him about and which he kept fiercely private; so closed, yet so open, so warm and tender. Sometimes she felt as if he'd been there all her life; sometimes as if she'd never known him at all.

As she gazed out of the car window at the dark, rocky landscape flashing by, Brooke wondered whether her troubled relationship with Ben would ever recover. It had started so blissfully, only to crash so senselessly on the rocks just when it was beginning to look as though it could last for ever.

The crash had come in September. The autumn months had been a forlorn, empty time, drowning herself in her work; the Christmas holiday without him almost unbearably miserable. Then, slowly, slowly, over the last couple of months had dawned the prospect of a possible reconciliation. The phone conversations between her home in London and his in France were growing longer and more frequent. Sometimes *he* even called her.

It was still fragile, though, still just a tiny candle flame that could snuff out at any time. There were moments when Brooke thought she could sense the tension between them, ready to flare up all over again. In their separate ways, they'd both been equally to blame for the split. *What a couple of hotheads we are*, she thought wryly to herself as she recalled the awful quarrel that had busted them apart. The worst thing was that, in the end, it had all been about nothing. Just a stupid, horrible misunderstanding.

'The chopper will pick us up at the house and take us over to Derry Airport first thing in the morning,' Sam was saying to her employer. 'We should easily be in London by ten-thirty, which gives us plenty of time to get things together before the meeting with Cabeza.'

Forsyte pursed his lips and gave a grunt of assent. Drifting momentarily back to the present, Brooke noticed the way he kept fingering the handle of the attaché case that was secured to his wrist by a steel cuff and a slim chain, and she wondered what was inside that must be so valuable – but her curiosity waned rapidly as she turned back towards the dark window and resumed her own private thoughts.

A flash of white light caught Brooke's eye. The road behind was no longer empty: the bright headlights of a car were coming up fast. No, she thought, twisting round to peer out of the rear window – not a car, but a van of some kind. Going somewhere in a real hurry, too.

Forsyte glanced back as the van's main-beam headlights loomed close enough to fill the inside of the Jaguar with their glare. 'Just some idiot,' he said nonchalantly. 'Pull in a little and let him past, will you, Wally?'

Wally shook his head in exasperation, then flipped on his indicator, slowed to just over thirty and steered towards the side of the narrow road to let the van by. The large vehicle noisily overtook them – a plain white Renault Master panel van, scuffed and spattered with road dirt – then cut in tightly at an angle and screeched to a halt, blocking the road.

Wally hit the brakes and the rear passengers were thrown forwards, except for Brooke who'd braced herself against the front passenger seat a fraction of a second before the emergency stop. Sam let out a little cry as her netbook went flying.

'What the hell—?' Forsyte shouted.

'Fucking arsehole!' Wally thrust the automatic gearbox into Park and left the engine running as he climbed out of the car. 'What's your game, you bloody prick?' he yelled, slamming his door shut and storming up to the stationary van.

The Renault Master's doors burst open simultaneously. Wally stopped dead in his tracks and his angry voice trailed off as two men jumped out and strode aggressively towards him. They were both wearing black balaclavas, and not because of the biting February wind. Brooke's blood turned icy when she made out the shapes of the weapons in the men's hands, a pistol and a compact submachine gun, black and brutal with long tubular silencers attached to their muzzles. She'd seen weapons like those before.

So had Wally Lander, once upon a time, but his nine years out of the army had blunted his senses and all he could do was gape.

'Oh my God!' Sam gasped. Forsyte stared in speechless horror, clutching his attaché case.

Neither of the masked men spoke a word. Instead, almost casually, they turned their weapons towards Wally and, in the next instant, white-orange fire spat from the muzzles of the silencers. From inside the heavily insulated car, the gunfire was no more than a rapid string of muffled thumps. Wally's legs folded under him, then he collapsed lifelessly at the roadside. His blood was bright in the beams of the Jaguar's headlights.

Sam screamed in panic and clung onto Forsyte. 'What do they want with us, Roger? Oh Jesus, they're going to kill us!'

Brooke hesitated, but no more than a second before she launched herself at the gap between the front seats and scrambled in behind the wheel. She wrenched the stick into Drive, stamped the heel of her Italian designer party shoe on the gas and held it all the way down. The Jaguar took off with a roar and a rasp of tyres. Clenching the wheel, Brooke had no choice but to drive grimly over Wally's dead body with a sickening *bump-bump*. The masked men hurled themselves out of the way. A jarring impact as the car slammed into the angled side of the van; a screech of buckling plastic and metal grinding on metal as she forced through the gap, the Jaguar's wheels spinning wildly and revs soaring to drown out Sam's screams and Forsyte's indistinct roar of fury. Then, suddenly, the way was clear and Brooke could see the open road stretching ahead in the car's lights. She'd made it.

But then the strobing muzzle flashes lit up the rear-view mirror and she felt the steering wheel go heavy in her hands as a flurry of gunfire blew out the back tyres. There was nothing she could do to prevent the car skidding out of control and veering across the road. Brooke caught a glimpse of a large grey rock flashing towards the front of the car – then a crunching collision and the airbag exploded in her face, dazing her.

Running footsteps. Voices. The next Brooke knew, the Jaguar's doors were opening and there was a gun at her head. She turned to face her attacker. His eyes were cold and hard in the slits of the balaclava.

'Get out, bitch,' he said.

Can't get enough of Ben Hope?

Visit www.scottmariani.com

Also available from Avon

THE SHADOW PROJECT

SCOTT MARIANI

**An international conspiracy that could change
the course of history . . .**

Ex-SAS hero Ben Hope is enjoying his new life in France,
training others in the dangerous art of kidnap and rescue
– until he is forced into providing protection for Swiss
billionaire Maximilian Steiner.

Steiner believes that a sinister neo-Nazi terrorist cell are
targeting him to seize a prized historic document, one which
could support claims that the Holocaust never happened.

Delving deeper, Ben discovers that the group are also
hell-bent on reconstructing a terrifying technology that has
lain dormant since World War II. But when a shocking
revelation about his own past throws his assignment into
chaos, he must draw on all of his powers to halt the deadly
plan. The stakes are global – and this time Ben is also fighting
to protect the people closest to him . . .

ISBN 978-0-00-731190-3

Also available from Avon

THE LOST RELIC

SCOTT MARIANI

A web of deceit – and Ben Hope is caught in the mayhem . . .

Whilst visiting a former SAS comrade in Italy, a distracted Ben nearly runs over a young boy – and unwittingly walks into his deadliest mission yet.

Ben's involvement with the boy's family runs deeper as he witnesses their brutal murder at a gallery robbery. A seemingly worthless Goya sketch was the principal target in the violent heist. Now it's up to Ben to find the truth behind the elusive painting.

Wrongly accused of murder and forced to go on the run, he must get to the heart of the conspiracy while he still has the chance . . .

A super-charged, heart-racing thriller, perfect for fans of Dan Brown, Ludlum's *Bourne* series and Sam Bourne.

ISBN 978-1-84756-197-8